$1 + 1 = 3$

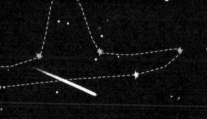

$\sqrt{\text{THE ONE}}$

THE
THEORY OF
(Not Quite)
EVERYTHING

THE
THEORY OF
(Not Quite)
EVERYTHING

KARA
GNODDE

MANTLE

First published 2023 by Mantle
an imprint of Pan Macmillan
The Smithson, 6 Briset Street, London EC1M 5NR
EU representative: Macmillan Publishers Ireland Ltd, 1st Floor,
The Liffey Trust Centre, 117–126 Sheriff Street Upper,
Dublin 1, D01 YC43
Associated companies throughout the world
www.panmacmillan.com

ISBN 978-1-5290-9634-7

1 3 5 7 9 8 6 4 2

A CIP catalogue record for this book is available from the British Library.

Typeset in Sabon LT Std by Palimpsest Book Production Ltd, Falkirk, Stirlingshire
Printed and bound by CPI Group (UK) Ltd, Croydon, CR0 4YY

Visit **www.panmacmillan.com** to read more about all our books
and to buy them. You will also find features, author interviews and
news of any author events, and you can sign up for e-newsletters
so that you're always first to hear about our new releases.

For Jamie, Tom and Freya,
with love

Rationalists, wearing square hats
Think, in square rooms.
Wallace Stevens

It is by logic that we prove, but by
intuition that we discover.
Henri Poincaré

1

RECURRING

2012
Time (t) = 0

When Mimi stands at her door, she knows that the news is not good. Her body is familiar with the rules.

'Miss Brotherton? Naomi?'

She points inside to invite the police officers in. Her words won't come.

It's a man and a woman. They brush non-existent fluff from their sleeves as they step across the threshold. They have the appearance of suicide bombers, packaged with padding and badges and belts and clips, a walkie-talkie each, many pockets. But it's terrible information – not a device – that they're about to detonate.

They take up so much space in her hallway she has to inch around them to lead the way down the passage to the kitchen, where she can ask the question she thinks she knows the answer to. Is he dead? She pushes the post on the floor with her foot as if to tidy up. She sees his name on an envelope. She pulls her jumper down to straighten herself out and smudges imagined mascara residue from beneath her eyes, attending to some abstract decorum required for these moments, just before everything falls apart.

It's impossible to prepare someone for the news of a loved one's death. But there are rules for such moments, and Mimi has seen them in action before.

She'd tell you: don't procrastinate. The person will already know something is wrong from your demeanour, from the fact that you're calling or visiting at all. We send countless signals without knowing. Their body will be preparing for an emergency.

Use plain and simple language. Start by saying the person has died. This leaves no room for doubt. Don't use euphemisms – like 'passed on,' or 'they're in a better place now.' 'Lost' is particularly unhelpful – just *imagine*.

The truth is essential.

You may need to repeat yourself.

And don't make promises that you can't keep.

Mimi's always been grateful that she was told by professionals. Dead straight.

She remembers last time – sitting on the corner of the coffee table, staring at a dry-cleaning tag that her mother had left on the rug. Her brother Art was talking. The police officers had gone.

'We need to break this down into parts,' Art had said, in a voice stunned into the rhythm of a metronome. He'd looked around, as if for a ruler with which to measure the parts of the shattered whole. 'And –' he said, his voice faltering – 'plan for our future together.'

'Yes,' said Mimi.

And, just like that, he took her hand.

* * *

2

This time, standing in her passage, she's barefoot and alone. The police follow in their boots, and she feels like a prisoner with an army walking behind her – past the mirror, where her reflection is of a different person to the one who walked this hall a minute ago, checked herself in the glass and plumped her lips.

The officers step into the kitchen, still holding their hats out in front of them.

'Can I offer you something?' she says. Tea would forestall them, but they never accept anything.

'We're all right, thank you,' says the man.

'Perhaps you'd like to sit down,' says the woman.

There's no going back now.

Mimi lowers herself onto the sofa, her arms wanting to reach for her brother. For him to be there with her while she does this, but already, she knows that will not be possible.

'Is it Art?' she says. 'My brother?'

'Miss Brotherton—'

'Is he dead?' she hears herself say. 'My brother. He's dead, right?' The room dissolves into strips that are floating away, nothing has substance, light swallows matter.

'Your brother's had an accident. He's in hospital and he—'

'*Hospital?* He's okay?' She snatches up her jacket in one movement.

'Perhaps take a moment.' The officer points back to the sofa. 'There are a few things you might wish to know.'

Art's been hit by a car.

A small car.

'Small*ish*,' corrects PC Payne. 'He's badly hurt.' The driver of the car stopped, Mimi learns, and is very shaken up. Art's unconscious – he caught the side or the wing mirror, they're not sure which, and hit his head. He leaped out in front of the car, apparently, with no warning.

3

'*N-n-no*,' she says, her old stammer appearing, on cue. 'Why would he do that?'

The driver called an ambulance and spoke to police at the scene. 'I'm so sorry, Miss Brotherton, I know this is difficult. Is there anyone you'd like us to call?'

'N-n-no. Thank you.'

'Who would you normally call?'

Nothing feels normal right now.

Despite her initial demurral, she tries her friend Rey, but Rey doesn't answer.

'And my boyfriend, I can try him too.'

She only gets his voicemail. 'I thought you were him at the door.' Her voice catches.

They offer to drive Mimi to the hospital. 'Thank you,' she says, 'thank you so much.' She pulls on her shoes and puts her coat back on. PC Payne helps with the arms.

The police vehicle, an unmarked car, has no flashing blue light. It surprises Mimi that her feet can lift to step into it, but next thing she's staring at a black headrest in front of her. She can see PC Roberts's sombre profile, his fleshy ear. She finds herself wondering if they'd be cracking jokes if she wasn't in the car, like they do on TV.

She listens to other incidents intrude. 'No further injuries, Grosvenor Park,' calls the in-car radio. 'Apparently vehicle was stolen.'

'11-19, via the hospital,' says PC Payne, then turns down the volume, though a crackle remains constant. 'You warm enough?' she asks. Kind. They do a U-turn at the dead end in the road and head off past the familiar doors of the neighbourhood – but as if transported in a spacecraft, so alien does it feel. Mimi grips the handle, and notices the door is locked.

There's a small Dell computer keyboard between the seats

and a squashed paper cup wedged into the pocket behind PC Roberts.

The sliding unnamed beast that lurks beneath their conversation, that the police have not said out loud, but Mimi feels is everywhere, is the suggestion that Art has tried to die.

I didn't mean what I said, she telegraphs, trying to reach her brother from the car. *I didn't mean it.*

Though of course, she had.

'Our stop 'n search numbers are rubbish,' says Roberts to Payne. 'It's going to be brutal in there tomorrow morning.'

She needs to get to Art's bedside. Tell him she's there. That she'll never leave.

She'd told him she was going. But now, she makes a deal.

Please, she prays, to a higher power that she doesn't believe in. *Let him be okay and I promise I won't go.*

They drive towards Art.

It's not the first deal she's made.

The deal of her life has always been: she is ordinary so that Art could be special.

'Don't bother him, he's busy,' her mother would say.

Art never understood how boring his maths could be for everyone else. 'It's not magic, you know,' said Mimi. 'It's just maths.'

'Ah, but it *is*, you see.' A light would come on in his eyes, stars lit up inside him. 'Take fractals.' He showed her the seahorse-tail patterns generated by mathematical equations. 'These are reproduced again and again into exquisitely small, *infinitely* small, identical details, all over nature. Pineapples and ice crystals, forests and river deltas, the veins in your body.' He took her wrist and turned it over to reveal the blue threads under her pale skin. 'Look how they fan out, fan out, fan out; it's all numbers. Next time you eat

Romanesco broccoli, see the pattern within the pattern within the pattern.' His hands feathered up and his fingers pleated over themselves, making brackets, balancing equations on both sides, raising things to the power of ten as he tried to explain, breathless. Mimi could not hold onto the tail of the comet. She was always left standing, her feet firmly on earth.

She'd had her brief time out there, orbiting the universe, trying to find love – a life of her own – and it hadn't worked. She'd have to stay home, reduced back to a data point in the great grand story of her genius brother and his all-important maths.

The lift doors open on the third floor of the hospital. Aluminium trolleys park along the green walls like taxis waiting in a rank.

Mimi follows PC Payne. 'Brotherton? Came in this evening?'

'Naomi Brotherton,' says Mimi. 'I'm his sister.'

'ICU. Farthing Ward. Down the passage to the seating area.'

They walk down the hospital tunnel. All the resolutions Mimi had made about her life while she was away are being swallowed behind her with every step.

'Oh my god.'

Art is flat on his back – coffin flat – his neck held rigid in a brace.

The sight stuns Mimi. Fluorescent lights intensify the daze. She feels her middle lift, as though she's watching a diorama of the scene from above.

He lies on the bed, breath shallow and even, tubes rising and falling in sync with his chest. Tubes, liquids, toxins. Electrics, needles. Beds on wheels. He wouldn't like it. The wheels make her feel queasy too – they look ready to move out at a moment's notice. Mimi stands at the foot of his bed. 'Can I touch him?' she asks a nurse.

'You *should*. We need him to hold on.'

Still feeling as if she's floating, she holds onto her brother's feet as though they are pedals. As if by some transfer of energy, she might get him going again.

The Aircel blanket falls between Art's legs, there's a cavity right up to his groin; she can make out his kneecaps. He's got even thinner in the week she's been gone. His forehead looks waxy and cool. It's slightly tipped back and makes his nose look bigger on his face, haughty somehow.

'Artie,' she says. She wills his body for a sign. But his arms lie flaccid; no hand signals, no blinks. He isn't going to flash his eyes open or tap out a hello with his index finger.

His index finger, on the arm that *she* broke. When it happened – the whole, terrible, godawful thing – her friend Rey had promised that Art would be fine.

2

PLANNING FALLACY

t = the previous year

Art's sister believed in truth and – most of the time – in telling it. Art believed in facts.

He stood in front of a full-length mirror while a tailor pinched a measuring tape from his underarm to his hip, determining the facts of his body. A muscle in Art's side twitched, a wince reflex as the man's hair, drenched in glossy pomade, came within an inch of his clean shirt.

The tailors had been there since 1689. They told you that in green and gold above their door, on their letterhead and stitched into their label. Art had been there for eleven minutes. Metaphorically speaking, it felt as if *he* had been there since 1689. The fact was – Mimi was late.

And now it had started to rain. To distract himself, Art played his favourite game. What would change, right there in the shop, if the maths question he had dedicated his life to, the famous Millennium problem, *p versus Np*, was solved? He usually relished the possibilities, even the chaos and disruption. But in the bespoke soft-carpeted interior of the tailor's, a place where invoices were still handwritten, it was hard to imagine. He supposed an equation could govern the most efficient order in which to measure a man: head to sole, neck, back, waist, wrist. He settled on that – the tailor's best route around his body. It wasn't exactly Armageddon, or Peace on Earth, but still. The tailor's breath fluttered on his neck. Being so close to another human being made Art's skin prickle. He wished he did not find it so hard.

With a pencil between his teeth, the tailor pulled on his tape with a flourish. Art imagined telling Mimi. *He brandished it about like a conductor at the Opera House*, he would say. He knew she would laugh.

He finally saw her passing the headless black academic gowns that floated in the window, ducking out of the downpour and into the porticoed entrance. Rain-splattered and flushed, she unwound her scarf from her neck, but succeeded only in throttling herself. The old-fashioned bell rang as she opened the door. On a sunny day, Mimi's hair had a copper-pan glow. Today, it looked like paint primer. It was too fine to bounce or curl and now, wet, it stuck to her face.

When she told him that she hadn't meant to be late, she was probably telling the truth.

'Sorry,' she said. 'Tubes.'

'You did not plan sufficiently well for the variables of your journey.' Art meant distance in miles, time of day, density of traffic. He acknowledged that weather in general, and Transport for London in particular, provided perennial mathematical challenges. '*And* the five minutes extra to find your keys.'

Late or not, he was glad she was there.

Mimi stuffed her scarf into her bag so that she wouldn't forget it later and pushed her hair off her face with the back of her hand. Her brother was standing with his arms out to the sides like a marionette while a man ran a tape measure down his inner thigh. His fitting had started.

'Yes, yes,' she said, in response to his admonishment.

'You succumb to the planning fallacy, Mimi,' he said, 'always thinking you need less time than you do.'

'Planning life at all embodies an inbuilt fallacy, frankly.'

'Oh, ha ha.'

These conversations were good-natured, and part of a daily ping-pong that Mimi liked. She even made them up in her head when Art wasn't around, his opinions serving as guardrails to her bouncing thoughts.

She didn't tell her brother, however, that before she'd left, she'd spent at least ten minutes on the loo reading a seven-year-old horoscope that Rey had once given her, trying to decide if it had come true. It said she had a tendency to be hard on herself, that there was conflict between her moon and her Mars, and she should consider a 'design-adjacent' career.

She had joined Art at the robe-makers at his insistence.

'Ergh,' she'd said, when he'd suggested it at breakfast. 'Do I have to?'

'I thought you might like it. Vivienne Westwood designed them.'

'I don't care if they were designed by Pythagoras himself.' She'd passed the milk.

Art laughed.

'It just makes me sad,' she said, 'going there.' At every high point of Art's academic career, even the tiny hillocks like having his gown refitted, she felt the absence of their parents more keenly.

'Sir?' said the tailor to her brother. 'Might you choose something in coral silk – the mathematics department colour? A tie, perhaps?' He reached for a box from under the glass cabinet at the till. 'Some gentlemen like cufflinks.'

'I have enough cufflinks,' said Art, sticking out his sleeve to reveal his wrist. He only ever wore their father's.

'How about some coral socks, Professor?' suggested Mimi.

After a quick figure-eight to the socks and back, the man presented a selection in orange and pink.

Colour is not an absolute thing, not a fact. It's a cocktail of surface and light, eye and brain. All those years ago, witnesses to what happened to her parents described their car as red. They'd been telling the truth – the car they'd seen was red. Mimi saw her parents' car as purple. She'd thought for a moment that the witnesses had the wrong car, the wrong people. But, as with beauty, colour depends on the beholder. Truth is the same. Mimi's purple was just someone else's red.

Just as Mimi sensed Art might be reaching his threshold of cooperation as a live sartorial dummy, the doorbell rang. She saw him flinch. He wouldn't like a spectator. 'Doctorate gown measurements?' said the customer, a young woman. 'Law?' Mimi did that horrible calculation that told her where *she* would be on the academic ladder if she hadn't left university in her very first year.

The man behind the till flipped pages of a diary back and forth in consternation, mumbling 'clash', and looking round for someone to blame.

'I'm too busy to wait,' said the young woman. 'I'll come back after my Evidence lecture.'

Art's jaw relaxed. 'The tailors appear to be as ill-qualified as you when it comes to organizing their time,' he said, as Mimi ran her finger along the grosgrain trim of a velvet slipper.

'Hmm,' she said. *Too busy to wait.* Mimi had done a half-day at the museum and, apart from getting supper, she had nothing, and no one else, to think about.

11

Evidence. That was the other word Art used for facts. 'Look at the evidence,' he'd say, ruling out suspects when they sat on the sofa watching crime dramas. 'Moira saw her at the hairdresser!' Mimi could stare at evidence all day; it did give events a certain shape. But it was the underlying truth of things that always socked her in the gut.

The evidence of the purple–red car and the truth of what happened in it, well, those two things lived in different parts of her body altogether.

The tailor disappeared behind a curtain. Art stood there, with his back to his sister, his hands dropped to his sides – clearly it was enough for him, just to know that she was there.

The air was still. The man at the till clicked his pen and poured water from a dispenser into a plastic cup; Mimi heard the loud bubble at the end as air burped back into the tank.

She was thirty. She would grow old like this.

3

VIBRATIONS

It wasn't quite true that Mimi had no one apart from her brother. She had Rey, and she adored her friend. A week after the fitting, Mimi stood alongside Rey in a high-ceilinged room at the Tate, contemplating a smudged Richter portrait. 'I'm babysitter to a thirty-six-year-old,' she said. 'And all that *occasion wear*. It was a march through life's landmarks.'

'It would send me to my grave, wearing that awful get-up,' said Rey lightly, but she turned her head and watched Mimi as she spoke, her long eyelashes prickling like antennae.

When she was ten, Mimi had spotted a new girl moving in across the road. The next day, that same girl arrived at Mimi's classroom door. Her black hair, in bunches, bolted out at the sides. High arching eyebrows framed bright, olive eyes.

Her name was *Sareyina*. A double tripwire – an 's' *and* an 'n'.

Mimi approached her as she leaned against a red-brick wall. 'S-s-sa-rey-in-n-nn,' she'd tried. Her face felt hot. 'S-s-sa-rey . . . Sa-sa . . .' Her desire for Sareyina's friendship rose through her soles. 'S-s-sorry,' she said.

13

'Just call me Rey,' said Sareyina. She smiled. 'I like your red hair. It's the colour of a sweetgum tree.'

They sat eating bagels in the Tate cafe, and Rey explained her current gig as one of the sound artists on the set of a drug-cartel drama for TV. 'I'm on my own for my bit, smacking plastic bags of flour, stomping on floorboards. I don't even get to see the unedited footage – the rushes.' She laughed. 'It's nuts. But totally fun.'

While Rey chattered away about mic interference and props, Mimi tried to remember the last time she'd had fun.

It was probably last year, when Rey had moved back to Muriel Grove following eight years in Lagos with her father. After living for Rey's regular, whirlwind visits, Mimi was delighted when Rey returned to live in the old house across the road. Rey's mum had moved out to live with her long-term boyfriend. She hadn't wanted to sell while house prices were still climbing, and the timing was good for Rey. On the first weekend of her return, she'd invited Mimi to a Halloween party. In the section of the Natural History Museum's Library and Archives where Mimi worked, Halloween celebrations involved sharing a spider cake from Sainsbury's with two female colleagues before they left to trick or treat with their grandchildren.

Rey had dressed as a pirate. Her hair was wild as a hamerkop's nest, and she wore a carpenter's belt bristling with fake knives. Mimi wore red-and-white 'Where's Wally' stripes and bobbed in time to the music, alone. It hadn't been *much* fun. Rey had tried to persuade Art to come too. 'I would like to accept, if only to show my appreciation for the invitation,' he told Mimi. 'But you and I both know I will end up standing at the snack table having run out of people prepared to talk to me, and a headache and orange fingers from too many artificially coloured rice puffs.'

'I'm breaking into the UK film industry,' Rey told everyone, while rebuffing the advances of half-drunk men who kept telling her she looked like she was in her twenties, as if that was all she could ever want to hear.

Nine months on, Rey had set up her own audio post-production business, had a van with *Sister in Sound* emblazoned on the side and a dachshund called Rizla. She charged around London like a gaming character.

'Anyway,' said Rey, 'no wonder there isn't time for men.'

Sitting on the sticky cafe stool, Mimi was ambushed by self-pity. She put her hands over her face. She didn't like how she looked when she cried.

'Oh, Mi. What is it?'

'My whole bloody life,' said Mimi through her fingers. 'All I do is look after Art and work in that hushed corner of the museum. Never mind being in a relationship.'

'Oh god, Mi. Relationships aren't all they're cracked up to be,' said Rey. '*Believe* me. But as for the rest: you need to get out more.' She'd nagged Mimi for years to shake up her life. 'You *do* know,' she said; she put a warm hand on Mimi's knee, 'it won't kill Art if you live a little. I know you feel like it will. But—' Then Rey stopped talking. She pushed out her lips the way she did when she was thinking. She shook her head. 'I'm kicking myself I didn't think of this before.'

Rey needed an assistant. Mimi needed a life.

It was almost design-adjacent. Seven years late.

They headed back to Muriel Grove. 'He's not going to like it,' said Mimi.

15

4

REFORMULATION

Art was sitting at the kitchen table in the throes of writing a difficult letter. He had missed his weekly swim this evening to finish it, and had made no progress. He stared at what he had so far.

DRAFT.

He italicized the word, then clicked Underline.

King's College London, Mathematics Department. To Gutteridge or Dorney? Should he send it at all?

He was eliminating unnecessary hyperbole when Mimi and Rey, back from the Tate, hurtled through the door. Rey was breathless with her latest idea for how to upend his life. He typed *Professor A.N. Brotherton* and snapped his computer shut. Rey was always at it: terrariums, transcendental meditation, new diets that involved curly kale, and ideas for adventurous holidays – a canal trip in France had been her most recent suggestion. Lord! This time it took the form of a new job for Mimi in a risky and unreliable industry filled with people who made unexpected hair choices and wore jeans that clung to their calves.

Mimi usually knew better and waited for Rey's enthusiasms to subside.

He enumerated his many, rational objections. Job insecurity, the relative decline of the London film industry. Mimi was due a promotion at the museum. *Et cetera.*

'That's all very well,' said Rey, staring him down. 'But she'll turn into one of their exhibits if we don't do something.'

'Do you realize how disruptive this would be?' he asked, aware his voice had gone up an octave. 'For us both?' This was a strategic error, because change was exactly what his sister wanted. *Above all else*, were her actual words. He had a wrinkling sensation behind his breastbone. Most likely related to her rejection of their current existence. And by implication, unlikely as it seemed, *him*.

He had to sit down.

'Please, Art,' said Mimi. 'Just give it some thought.'

'Assistant Foley artist' was Rey's proposal, for a lower salary than at the museum, but subject to upward revision if Rey got more work. *Foley*, googled Art. Foley artists reproduce everyday sounds that get added to movies post-production to make them sound realistic, Art read. He knew that, but his understanding of Rey's work was somewhat superficial. The last time he had thought about it at all, he and Mimi had been doing the crossword, his favourite Saturday morning ritual. Mimi was standing at the window peeling her yellow rubber gloves off after washing up from breakfast. '7 Down,' he said. '*Foley artist sound made with coconut shells*. Four letters.'

'Clop,' said Mimi without missing a beat.

'*Clop?*'

'Horse hooves. As in clip-clop. Rey showed me – you bang the shells together.' She hung the gloves over the tap to drip dry and made a trotting motion in the air with her hands. The sun was streaming in behind her and she was smiling.

'Clever!' he said. 'Though clip would also fit.'

'Huh?'

'Clip, clip, clip? Sounds like a horse to me. But you are right, because 9 Across is what you think I am, by the look on your face – four letters, *Coagulate*. Gives us the o.'

'Ha ha, *clot*. Very funny.' Mimi did a horsey prance. 'Clip-clot, clip-clot.' When she laughed, her eyes disappeared in their creases.

Now he carried on reading while Mimi and Rey looked on, leaning with their backs to the sink like two minders. Foley had some entertaining features. From footsteps to doors closing; from the rustle of skirts to eggs being beaten. It was widely used in animation too, Google told him. Art lifted his head.

Animation *relies* on mathematics. Character movements – arms, eyebrows, hair in the wind – are determined by harmonic coordinates and Laplace's equation. Every single pixel has three numbers assigned to it, each reflecting how much red, green or blue it holds. Every frame has, literally, millions of equations that need solving. Just reformulate barycentric coordinates, and *presto!* – you have the twinkles in *Finding Nemo*.

'You see?' said Rey, leaning forward.

'No,' Art replied, resisting the seduction of integral calculus and subdivision surfaces. From his observation of Rey, Foley itself seemed to involve running around sourcing unwieldy gear and hanging out in recording studios beyond the M25. 'What if I need you, Mimi, and you are halfway across London in a sound studio with headphones clamped to your ears?'

'Listen to yourself, Art,' said Rey. 'She's not your employee.'

'But you want her as yours?' It was a reasonable riposte.

'Stop snapping at each other,' said Mimi, her hands gripping the edge of the counter behind her. 'I'm taking a part-time job in London. As a sound assistant, not a flight attendant.' He noticed her use of the present progressive.

'You say that, but Rey is always off and away in that van. Sometimes for days.'

Rey sat down. 'Seriously, Art,' she said, 'I know you wouldn't like Mimi to be away. This won't involve travel. I promise.' As infuriating as Rey was, he knew her intentions were good. Just last week, she had sailed past him in her van as he walked along the road. She blew an extravagant kiss, flung out her arm and banged her palm on the roof of the vehicle. It was not behaviour he would countenance for himself. And he knew Rey might do it for anyone. But there was nobody else who would do it for him.

'What does *part-time* actually mean?' he asked. The timing was terrible. He was in the middle of a genuine crisis with his work and Mimi had chosen this exact moment to disrupt their equilibrium.

'You haven't asked me *once*, Art,' Mimi said, 'why I even want to leave the museum.'

'I know that already,' said Art. 'You complain about it all the time.'

'*Well?* What else d'you need to know?'

'And if it does not work out? What then? Rey is your only friend.' This was true. 'Working with friends is an ill-advised adventure, Naomi. Always. The museum is unlikely to take you back.' Also true: Rey was his only friend too.

'I don't want to go back!' She was shouting. The disruption had not even happened yet, and already, she was her worst self.

'*See?*'

19

'See *what*?' she said. Furious blotches bloomed up her neck.

'I do not like it,' he said. 'Not one little bit.'

'You don't have to like it,' she said. 'You have to live with it. It's time.'

Art could not bring himself to give his sister's plan his blessing. 'I trust it will not be too stressful,' he said, when she handed in her notice.

His work was stressful enough.

The draft letter sat on his laptop. Unfinished. Unsent.

5

SINGLE DIGIT

The clocks had gone back – that swiftly stolen hour – and Mimi walked the last stretch of Muriel Grove in the sudden dark. She'd had her new job for a few months now, and there was a chance her life might take off after all. Terrace lights flicked on almost as though they were lighting up for her. She felt like a plane on a runway.

Her attention was – as usual – hooked by the other women who lived in the road, in homes they didn't share with their brothers. The pregnant journalist whose husband turned up in a black cab after work each day, his suit still looking fresh. The Lycra-clad mother who leaned in her doorway and clutched her collar while a delivery driver assembled supermarket bags at her feet. All the women who had babies and partners, the lives she didn't have.

Mimi had decided to change all that.

She kept walking, her cap pulled low.

After a shower, Mimi top 'n' tailed French beans and drizzled olive oil on the baby carrots. She roasted a chicken and fat potato wedges, all of which Art loved. But in the end, she couldn't rely on bribing him with food. She'd have to say it out loud. The new job was one thing. This was weapons-grade.

'I'm lonely, Art,' she said, as he set his napkin down. She showed him the research – *Loneliness Kills*. 'You have your work. But . . .' She could hear the kitchen clock. There was no way of saying it other than straight out. He was looking at her. 'I'd like to meet a man.'

She quickly spread the *Guardian* article on the kitchen table. 'Look at the graphs,' she said. Numbers, and goals, might help. Her current age was only just younger than the inflexion point towards an irreversible decline in fertility. 'Women who have babies *live longer*.'

'I can read,' Art said, adjusting his glasses. He sounded as if he had cotton wool in his throat. He smoothed out the newspaper and examined the small print.

The data was obvious. She needed a mate.

'I don't meet men my age in my job. I find it intimidating, going to bars in the hope of meeting strangers. And it's getting harder. Not that I've really tried,' she said, making patterns in the gravy on her plate with her fork, 'but, you know . . .' She was rambling.

Art had gone white round the mouth.

'Allow me to think about this,' was all that he said.

Art took his plate to the sink and, without a word, washed it and dried it and set it aside. He straightened the cloth on the oven door. *Loneliness Kills,* said the paper. *I know I have you*, she wanted to say.

'Goodnight, Mimi,' said Art. Tucking *The Guardian* under his arm, he went up to bed.

Mimi stood in the centre of the room.

She hardly slept.

In the morning, she put his porridge on early, laced it with honey and prayed that he hadn't clammed up for good.

He appeared bang on time in his favourite shirt.

'Good porridge,' he said and opened the page of *The Guardian* again.

'The first step,' he said, as though a decision had already been made, 'for successfully finding a partner, is to decide how long it is that you have for the search.'

Mimi just nodded. Her insides loosened.

'The thing about this, Mimi, is that trial and error is no good. I will support you. *If* you agree to follow my plan.'

'Which is?' She took a step back, to look at her brother. Was he *really* okay?

Art turned his placemat, just a fraction, so it was exactly aligned with the table's edge. He rearranged the salt and pepper cellars, as if they were soldiers bracing for battle. She had seen this behaviour before. 'First,' said Art, 'you have to set yourself a time limit.'

He had taken control.

'Time limit?' said Mimi.

'For the length of your search. How long it should take.'

'Well, not that long, ideally, but if you're about to launch into one of your extended mathematical explanations, it's not going to get any shorter.' She hoped teasing him might ease the pull in her chest. Art likened the sensation of being teased to taking an effervescent Alka-Seltzer. It fizzed his insides, he said.

'I give myself two years.' She tapped the graph. 'Eighteen months would be better.'

'Sensible,' said Art. 'A man would have more time.'

'Quite.' She offered him toast.

'The theory is this,' Art began once the toast had popped. 'After a month or two of dating, you add up how many men you have met. You use those numbers to calculate how many men you *ought* to meet over your full eighteen months, assuming you keep going at a steady pace.'

23

'Where's this going, Prof?'

'A well-known hypothesis,' said her brother, 'suggests that when you have reached thirty-seven percent of the total men you might meet—'

'Thirty-seven percent?'

'It seems random, I know. But strangely, it works. It is actually called The Secretary Problem, discovered in a study of how best to interview secretaries.' Art was warming to his theme and had stopped military moves with the breakfast utensils. 'Bosses hiring secretaries would identify the thirty-seven percent mark among interviewees. And then hire the very next candidate that was better than the ones who had gone before.'

'And that works for falling in love – *how?*'

'The same. After thirty-seven percent, you settle on the very next man who is better than the ones who have gone before. That is the moment you can stop wondering if there is someone better out there. In all likelihood, there is not.'

Mimi laughed nervously. 'That's ridiculous. What happens if you fall in love – or find a brilliant secretary – *before* the magical thirty-seven percent?'

'You let them go – and keep searching. The model is strict on that point. There will be a better one around the corner. The numbers guarantee it.'

The toast was cold. 'Love doesn't work like that, Art.'

'How do *you* know?'

It was a fair question. She blew out, as if to expel the hollow inside her. 'Everyone knows that. You can't decide to fall in love. It happens to you, not by you. It's not like choosing a secretary.'

'Do you want my help or not? I can only give the help I am qualified to give.' He looked sad for a moment, as if he knew it was pointless to imagine the distinction for himself.

24

'They say it is hard to tell if you have definitely met "the one". From fictional accounts, no one is ever sure.'

'I should've known you'd come at this from an unexpected angle,' she said. 'So . . . Okay. I agree. When I get to thirty-seven percent, I'll pay attention. You can help me work out when that is.'

'Excellent,' said Art.

'*Meantime,*' she said, gingerly again, 'I need your help up front.'

'As a go-between?'

'Er – no, darling brother. I need to generate a stream of good prospects. Of the right age – unlike those fresh-faced sound techies. I want to go online. Dating websites are all built on algorithms. You're the perfect person to choose the best one.'

It might not be possible to know love when you see it, or for Art ever to imagine what it might feel like – romantic love, anyway. But the love she felt for her brother as his face lit up, when he realized how useful he'd be; he looked suffused with pleasure. His smile folded in that way of his when he was overcome. 'I see,' he said. She loved him so much she wondered why life with him wasn't enough.

It wasn't, though, and she felt a deep stab inside at exactly what she was getting him to sign up to. Did he realize? Did he know?

What would happen to them both if it worked?

6

MATRIX

The next night after supper, tasked with finding a superior algorithm, and with Mimi across the road at Rey's, Art settled down in his tracksuit and slippers, the door to his study shut.

Art's post-doc, Ernest, had already taught him how to surf online incognito. Art had thought he might deploy the anonymous dark screen for his investigations into *p versus Np*, the maths problem he was working on.

(He still had not finished his letter.)

Ernest had blinked especially long at Art's request and scratched his elbows, but with typical delicacy, he did not pry. Ernest seemed to have divining powers when it came to what Art needed. Not that Art believed in any such powers.

Now, in white writing on a black background, he read that free dating sites might harbour bots posing as people. The thought of Mimi being stalked by a bot made his feet sweat. Expect disturbing feelings, he read. Mercifully, Art was immune to the way enervating emotions skewed rational thought, so he could be of real service to Mimi here. It would be his job to protect his sister from disturbing feelings. And bots.

26

Art stood up. He breathed out slowly to calm his parasympathetic nervous system, which he sensed was overactive.

By the time he finally found the perfect website, he thought his vertebrae might fuse. It was called Matrix, with an elegant algorithm and an intrinsic mathematical logic that made it beautiful.

Art stared at the empty data fields that required filling in. Skin, Hair, Eyes. Personality.

In most respects, Mimi was ordinary. She might not like to hear it, of course, but that itself was a standard sensitivity. He tried to imagine where she might fit on a bell curve of ordinariness. Certainly, his own data point would not sit in the swollen hump of 'normal'.

If you had a superpower, what would it be? asked Matrix. Good grief. *Do you wear glasses?* Mimi had needed new reading glasses just last week. 'Where is your old pair?' he had asked her.

'I sat on them,' she said. His sister had a tell when she lied – she touched the left side of her face, an involuntary tic. He would not encourage her to put *that* online.

Mimi's eyes were blue, but not bright blue, and she always said they looked sad. Importantly, they were wide apart, a universally accepted sign of attractiveness.

She also had even features – something Art prized. As a boy, fitting his foot into the crook of his arm, he had discovered heel to toe matched elbow to wrist. But his feet, he found to his immense irritation, were different lengths.

Art had anaesthetized the needs of his own body in the service of his higher calling, but he was not insensitive to the impulse to fall in love and couple up. From an evolutionary point of view, he understood his sister's imperative.

Yes, Mimi was ordinary. And the more ordinary you were,

he had just learned, the more likely men were to believe they had a chance. The more inclined to press 'Like' on any photograph of his sister's face, made of pixels. The very idea made Art's throat close.

He had promised to help her find love.

But they needed to take it one step at a time.

He signed into her Matrix account on his own PC. She did not need to know. It was a simple precaution, just in case. And then he waited for her to come home.

'He spent the evening reading Matrix's small print,' Mimi told Rey the next day. They had the studio in Holborn to themselves for a change and were working amid feeble Christmas tinsel, recording footsteps for a TV series Rey called 'countryside noir'.

'But he's agreed, right?' said Rey from behind the projector.

'I hope so.' Mimi pulled on a pair of steel-capped boots. 'He's dragging me off to that blooming Maths Awards thing again this year. I'm only going to keep him happy.'

'Just keep him involved. Have you chosen a photo? Let's dress you up!'

'I am *not* dressing up, Rey. God. Between you and Art, I feel like a pet being groomed for Crufts.' She laughed. The blue light was blinking.

'Ready?' said Rey.

Mimi stepped into the pit.

'Rolling,' called Rey from the back, and the screen sprang to life.

Mimi watched the actor on the screen in front of her while she marched on the spot in a square metre bed of gravel. She matched her gait to his from the movement of his shoulders, swung her arms in time with his as he strode up a country road towards an isolated shack.

It was going to be hard to sound interesting online.

The actor reached the shack. He had a gun.

She imagined herself with a gun. She imagined herself without a gun. With an axe.

Her heart was thumping. The film kept rolling, silent. He smashed the door. Mimi knew what was coming; she'd seen the rushes. A plain room; light leaking in through a dirty window. Bodies lay on the floor, eyes open. Two children quivered, terrified, under a table, holding hands. A boy and a girl.

'Stop,' said Rey and froze the image on screen. She came down to the pit. 'Hey, where are you, girl?'

'Sorry,' said Mimi.

'Just find your centre. *Then*, watch his arms. Tune your rhythm to his, but first, find your own – hey, are you okay?'

Mimi stayed in the pit. Her arms hung at her sides.

'Mimi?'

'D'you think we could take a short break? I'm trying to think what the hell I'm going to say about myself online. I'm so nervous about this whole thing, how Art's going to handle it. And then – this film. Those two kids, clinging to each other, you know.' Her voice faltered and she stepped out of the path of the projector light. 'It makes me think of me and Art.'

'Oh, Mi,' said Rey and blinked on the lights. 'Oh honey. I'm sorry, I guess you just never know when something's going to hit you. It didn't even occur to me.'

'Why should it? We weren't kids, and it's not as though our parents were murdered by a woodland killer. But them holding onto each other like that? It's sort of how it's always felt.'

'I can see how. All of it.' Rey's face got this awful pinched expression whenever Mimi spoke of her parents' deaths, as though it physically hurt her, too. 'And I guess, taking control of your life, as you are now, feels scary. I really get it.' Rey turned off the projector, which continued to whirr as it cooled down. 'Come, let's go get a coffee and discuss how we're going to describe you online. Boudicca or Jessica Chastain?'

'That's just it,' said Mimi as she pulled off the heavy boots and stood in her socks. 'Never mind what colour my bloody hair is,' she said. 'First, I need an upgrade on the words pinging round in my head. Those same old six words: sister of a mathematical genius. Orphan.'

Art heard Mimi return from work. He still had the Matrix website open on his computer, and from the little icon he had set up to flash when she was online, he could see that she had come inside and logged straight on. He gave her half an hour and, when he could stand it no longer, he went downstairs. A diamond of light was thrown into the kitchen by weak afternoon sun, and a pair of crows grubbed in the lawn. Mimi was at her laptop, gripping the scar on her lip with her teeth – she had been gnawing at it ever since they had agreed on his plan and now it was starting to chafe. He leaned in behind her.

'So, what d'you think?' she asked. 'Will it work?'

He paused before answering. 'No. You skipped all the difficult questions.'

Mimi minimized Matrix's personality assessment question-naire and spun round. 'Like what?'

'Like – Are your parents alive? Did they die of an inher-itable disease?' Her pupils contracted so fast he could see a radial of amber in her blue eyes, but she did not speak. 'Have you ever had a learning difficulty?' he said. 'Are you afraid of the dark?'

She did not take her eyes off him. 'I'm not afraid of the dark.'

'*I* know that. But I bet that you also passed over that question.' Perhaps Matrix, with its unusually personal questionnaire and specialized psychological algorithm, was too intrusive.

'And a stammer is *not* a learning difficulty,' she said, closing her laptop. 'Anyway, how did you know?' The crows took off, making a racket as they cleared the fence. 'Art?'

'Seventy-three percent of people dissemble when they respond to questionnaires. You do not fit the profile of the remaining twenty-seven. You were trying to hide the questions you do not want to answer. The ones about our parents. About your old stutter. So, you avoided a couple of extras that you thought other people might also avoid. About cheating at games. Or fears that normal people might have – like the dark.'

What Mimi was afraid of included a particular universe of things. Not the dark. Or spiders, another question she had omitted. Art watched the sun shrink behind the houses. The viburnum needed cutting back, it was killing the grass.

Mimi's life was a clock ticking steadily away, apparently. 'Getting older frightens me,' she said. But searching for love seemed to frighten her more.

Art understood. People you love can abandon you, Mimi knew too well. And there were other reasons to be frightened of love, and what it could make you do. Consider his parents.

They had not had to search for their love. Christine was the administrator of a large medical practice in Johannesburg when Walter strolled in one afternoon. He was already a professor, a good decade older than her, and allergic to something that had brushed against his arm on a walk in the veld. 'Contact dermatitis, I could've diagnosed it myself,' Christine told her children as their family sat on an oilskin ground cloth on the beach for Art's birthday, eating jam sandwiches with the crusts cut off. 'But I kept him in the waiting room. I liked his hair with its random upward sweep, like Beethoven. I liked his wide-apart, Highveld-sky eyes.'

Walter had overheard a female patient complaining about delays to see the doctor. He had watched the tops of Christine's eyelashes as she followed her finger down the list of patients, humming 'Morning has Broken'. 'But her appointments were a shambles,' their father told them with a smile.

'When he delivered a new colour-coded super-spreadsheet a week later, he wedged open a space in my heart,' said his mother, her palm on her chest.

'Mum kn-n-new she would marry him,' translated six-year-old Mimi, tucking herself into their father's side.

Art could picture the spreadsheet; less so the wedge-shaped gap in their mother's heart. He turned a triangle sandwich in his hand.

Their father rubbed jam off Mimi's chin. Their mother absently clipped and unclipped the lid of the Tupperware. 'Dad took me for a walk in the Wilds, a sprawling rocky outcrop on the outskirts of the City,' she said.

'I told her to wear comfortable shoes,' said their father.

When his parents had reached the famous sundial at the Wilds' topmost point, Walter told Christine that the air was so thin you could understand why it took a minute longer to boil an egg up there. He looked over the Ridge, pointing to where they had found Australopithecus, a fossil that dated back 2.3 million years. 'You probably think *I'm* a bit of a fossil, hey?' he had said to their mother, and laughed.

'The thirteen years between us melted to nothing. I knew that I'd never be bored.' Their mother pushed Walter's composer hair off his forehead. 'On the way down the stone path,' she continued, 'he held my hand.' Art remembered every word. 'He wore long socks, shorts and rubber-soled, practical sandals. He had strong muscled legs. I didn't let go.'

Whether or not his parents had fallen in love that day had never occurred to Art before. What *had* occurred to him was that the curiosity his father displayed in the medical schedule and the angles on the sundial was an inherited pulse that beat in his own bloodstream. He too wondered how our relative sense of time could accommodate 2.3 million years. Maths was everywhere, and all the time.

It was their father, in the end, who could not let their mother go. He loved her so much he had died for her. Even though he did not have to. Even though she was already going to die.

Even though they needed him.

Was that the kind of love that frightened Mimi? Or was it what she longed for?

7

P VERSUS NP

Art was chasing an elusive idea when Mimi poked her head round his study door.

'I need your old Yellow Pages,' she said. She looked past Art, not at him.

'You had another response?' he asked. 'On Matrix?' Two weeks on, he seemed more invested in seeing if Matrix worked than his sister, who did not refresh her page nearly as often as he did. She had an above-average viewing rate but had not yet 'liked' anyone back.

'Um, no.' She touched the side of her face.

'Why are you lying?'

'Because he had sad eyes.'

'Your eyes are also sad. You told me yourself.'

Mimi looked at him with her supposedly sad eyes. 'Give me the phone book, Art. Please.'

'What for?'

'Body thumping to the floor. Episode 3.'

Mimi's Foley work had been quite an adjustment, right down to her new lexicon – 'omnidirectional microphone', 'background walla' and *work drinks* – but chopping frozen cabbages to mimic a decapitation already seemed as old as analogue.

Art withheld the book on his lap. He felt like a child reluctant to share his favourite toy. 'Rey lost the last one. You are helping her, but that does not mean she can help herself to our things. They do not make these any more.'

'I'm *working* for her, Art, not helping her.' She stuck out her hand.

He handed it over, but only after writing BROTHERTON across the top with a permanent marker. If he could label individual teabags at work, he would. He considered property ownership a Venn diagram that should have no intersections.

'I need to keep going,' he said. Waving his arm, he went back to marshalling the contents of his brain into a serviceable form, equations and diagrams spilling onto the page with an urgency that ate him up.

Art had been working on the *p versus Np* problem all his adult life. His obsession was now the subject of a million-dollar prize from the Clay Institute, although no true mathematician was motivated by money, in his opinion. When he had first encountered the problem, aged seven, it was uncontaminated by such public attention.

If *p* equalled *Np*, Walter had told him, then there was a universal solution. *For everything.* His father understood how maths could change the world – nothing would ever be the same. Art wrote it up in his notebook and had nurtured the private ambition to be the person to solve it ever since.

The work of Art's life became not only to find out whether this 'universal answer' existed. He believed that it was his calling to protect the answer too. Art felt a kinship with Robert Oppenheimer realizing the potential of the atom bomb. The contemporary world was simply defenceless to the wrong person solving dangerous problems.

Wrong, wrong, gonged in his head. If p equalled Np, every single password and encryption in the world would be rendered useless. It would advance the cure for cancer, universal education would be possible, trains could be on time, neural networks optimized, plane wings designed to reduce fuel consumption – all manner of things that the world thought it wanted. But the risks! Bank accounts, military units, nuclear power stations, hospitals, pacemakers, airlines, electricity grids, social media – even those ridiculous apps like Angry Birds that people stayed glued to while crossing the road. Chaos was inevitable.

Nothing would be safe from the tendrils of an Np algorithm's devastating power.

Art concentrated so hard the lines and numbers distorted into graphics that danced on the paper. The pain in his fingers from gripping his pen seemed to belong to someone else. And that was the problem. Whether it was for the million-dollar prize, the prestige, or some deeper malintent, Art was convinced that someone out there was after his work.

Ernest, whom he trusted unreservedly, knew of his concerns, but Art had not yet shared his worries with the rest of the department at King's. He had not sent his letter. Instead, he decided, if he worked a little harder, concentrated to the point where his brain became an almost separate entity, articulating things through his body as though he was just a vehicle – he had achieved this state before, a soaring, enlightened, almost conscious-free euphoria, a place of omniscient clarity – *then*, he would get there first.

It was a race against time.

He bent closer in.

* * *

When he came downstairs later, his head feeling like a scoured pot, Mimi and Rey were sitting at the kitchen table, each with a glass of wine. And no sign of his supper. The phone book was splayed on the floor, its spine fractured.

'My phone book!'

Mimi scuttled round his feet and scrabbled in the kitchen drawer for masking tape. 'I threw it too hard.'

'I'm sorry,' said Rey. 'I needed wine. I left the shoot in a bit of haste.'

'A liaison on set gone wrong,' Mimi informed him. It would not be the first ill-judged romantic escapade of Rey's, whose faith in human nature did not always guide her down the ideal path. 'One of their techies.'

'Not a techie,' said Rey, 'a scheduling assistant. With a cute ass.'

'And a fiancée.'

Childish repartee, thought Art. Rey topped up her glass with more deep yellow wine, the kind that had a ridiculously high alcohol content.

'Did you tell Rey about your Matrix responses?' Art forced himself to ask when he saw that Mimi's laptop was down from the shelf. He sensed his enthusiasm starting to wane now the project was translating into actual men. Faces he imagined turning up at the door. Faces who had pressed 'Like'.

His sister was looking at him as though she already knew how he felt. He was transparent as a sheet of glass.

'Open her laptop, big brother, let's see who's available,' said Rey, rubbing her hands together.

Mimi's home page popped up. Along with 'Charles, Tort Lawyer, CV attached' and Reagan, who sounded like a neo-con.

'Eew,' said Mimi.

'At some point you have to press "Like",' said Rey. 'Go on a date.'

'You know this is not a team sport, right?' asked Mimi out of the side of her mouth, as she pulled off a strip of masking tape with her teeth to repair the phone book. Then she tore pieces of salad into a bowl.

'Are you going to wash that?' asked Art. Mimi rolled her eyes.

'You sound like a married couple,' said Rey.

8

VECTOR

A few weeks later, Art had gone downstairs with his jacket on, but Mimi took another minute to clip up her hair and change into her green cardigan – the neckline worked better with her V-neck floral dress. She didn't imagine the Mathematics Awards would be a hotbed of prospects, and the last thing she needed in her life was another man obsessed with numbers. But the awards were an annual ritual that she endured to please Art, and she felt each year, with ever-diminishing conviction, that she was also going for her father. In which case, she wanted Walter Brotherton's daughter to look pretty. She was dressing for him.

Mimi was already tiring of the ticker tape of uninspiring profiles popping up on Matrix. Based on the volume of the last five weeks, Art had worked out that in eighteen months she would probably find thirty-one men that she'd actually be prepared to meet. Thirty-one sounded like a lot. So far, she'd only met two. Neither outing had lasted long. One rugby jock, whose prize possession seemed to be his deviated septum, and one man with soft hands who she kept having to ask to speak up. But she would hit the thirty-seven percent that Art was so focused on pretty soon – after 11.4 men.

And then? The next point six of a man? She imagined a small homunculus sitting on a bar stool, legs unable to reach the ground. 'I'm your dream man,' he would squeak.

At least it would give her something to think about this evening while Art's colleagues droned on and the wine got warm. She and Art ascended the carpeted stairs to the Regus Room on the first floor, where Ernest met them with their name badges. 'This event is something of a networking opportunity,' Art's post-doc told her, his label announcing 'ERNEST' in all caps. He laughed. 'I know what you're thinking. An introvert mathematician looks at his shoes. An extrovert mathematician looks at yours.'

'Ha ha,' she said. 'Totally unfair characterization.' She pointed to her brother, who was talking to the carpet next to a colleague. Ernest himself was chatty, and a loyal acolyte to Art. Physically, he was small and shambolic, but he seemed comfortable around people, and put them at their ease.

Ernest found seats near the front. Before joining them, Mimi slipped off to the loo while a technician tested the microphone. The only Ladies' was underground and there was a queue. Mimi had a quick pee, but then got distracted by the plumbing sounds in the bowels of the old building and how she might record them, and by the time she returned the ceremony had started, and she was trapped at the back. Art turned and admonished her with a shake of his head. '*Sorry*,' she mouthed. Impassive, her brother turned his attention back to proceedings.

'As we all know,' said the MC, while Mimi nipped to the drinks table for a glass of white wine to see her through, 'mathematics is fifty percent formulas, fifty percent proofs and fifty percent imagination.' The room chuckled, reassured that the familiar old joke had been trotted out. 'Each year,

40

the Mathematics Association has the imagination to bring us together . . .'

The awards recognized outstanding achievements by British mathematicians and ranged from the acknowledgement of lifelong achievement to highlighting recent papers of distinction. Services to the Mathematics Community, Best Paper, Numerical Analysis – the words washed over her; she would have liked to sit down, she had that dozy feeling that made your head feel as though it was bobbling slightly on your neck. She closed her eyes, just briefly.

When she opened them, she spotted a man standing across the grand panelled room, looking as though he too was out of place. He had an open face and high forehead and an air of such insouciance that he wore the dreary proceedings lightly, as though amused by a life larger than the one in the room. And then she caught his eye, and he was staring back. She might have looked away, but she smiled instead.

As the winner of the Randolph Teaching Medal was clapped onto the stage, she watched as the man made his way round the back of the seated audience, a fresh glass of Sauvignon Blanc in his hand.

'It's a little less warm than the one you're holding,' he said as he gave it to her. He wasn't wearing a jacket and had rolled up his sleeves.

'Thanks,' she whispered, struck by his startling blue eyes. Then she looked towards Art, sensing him squinting back at her over his shoulder in irritation.

She felt a flutter of panic. 'I'd chat, but I guess we're s-s-supposed to be quiet.'

The man smiled back and, ignoring both her instruction to be quiet and the untimely appearance of her stutter, introduced himself. 'So, Naomi,' he said, looking at her handwritten name badge. He tapped his own label. 'Frank.' His smile was warm, and it calmed her. Just then they announced the award in her father's name. Walter Brotherton.

Any mention of her father's career made Mimi feel sad. She'd once overheard her mother tell Aunty Pam: 'Walter's world shrank when we left Johannesburg. He'd been such an *enthusiast*.' That was the word Christine used. Mimi had never forgotten it; it was the father she knew was there but only glimpsed periodically. 'We got to England, and it was as if the fog rolled in and blurred his thinking,' said her mother. 'London felt cramped. It throttled him, you know? His physical response to the weather – those hunched shoulders of his – was like a manifestation of his diminished mathematical virtuosity. And then, his depression,' her mother had said, as Mimi sidled off and pretended not to have heard.

'The Walter Brotherton Award for distinguished writing in the field of chaos theory, for a mathematician over the age of fifty,' said the MC. 'It's a young man's game,' her father had complained, and bequeathed a prize himself.

Her collar prickled on her neck, but Frank seemed oblivious that the Brotherton name meant anything to her, and suddenly, as if she could let those terrible words go like balloons into the air – *cramped*, *throttled*, *depressed* – she felt strangely elated and free.

She could hear Art's deliberate clapping in the front row from where she stood. She was grateful that he was sitting down, confined, unable to come over to chaperone her, which he was quite capable of doing. And grateful that her badge, no doubt in an attempt to seem inclusive and relaxed, said simply, *Naomi*. No connection to either Art or the unknown mathematician whose name was engraved on the odd-looking contraption on stage.

'What are you doing here,' asked Frank. 'Collecting an award?'

'Umm, you know,' she said, her hand vaguely sketching some design of her own in the air, 'family. S-s-support.' She tried to smile as she stammered, praying he somehow wasn't noticing. He didn't flinch. 'My family,' she said, 'it's – well, here I am.' She didn't seem able to form a coherent sentence. She landed on *am* with relief and felt she wouldn't mind never speaking again. Frank looked perplexed, but she just pointed at the wiry woman with cropped grey hair walking back to her chair, dangling the award beside her.

Mimi turned slightly towards Frank, closer in. She could smell aftershave, just. Her wrist touched his arm. He was warm.

'I'm here for the wine,' he said, his face creasing as he smiled.

She swallowed.

'Actually, I work for the Mathematics Association,' he said. 'We run these events.' Frank then ran through an amusing commentary on the proceedings, without ever giving her the feeling he was laughing *at* anyone. Mathematicians paraded to and from the podium – no doubt in some kind of esoteric order only they were privy to.

'You're not an actual mathematician, then?' she asked.

'Oh no, I am,' said Frank. 'Every *inch* a mathematician. Can't you tell?' His smile was slightly crooked and dug a deep dimple in his left cheek. 'I'm responsible for these dazzling badges,' he said, patting his name. 'An effort by the association to improve their non-hierarchical sociability co-efficient.'

'Ah-ha,' she said, laughing, picking at the peeled edge of her own badge.

'I'm not sure name badges are such a good idea for a group of people who don't need another excuse not to look you in the eye. I argued for a sixty-four-point font you can

43

see from twenty feet, with no luck. Hence – ' he smiled – 'I was forced to come over to read yours.' The final applause died down, the MC thanked everyone for coming, the Mathematics Association for providing Burlington House, the prizewinners and the judges. Mimi felt disappointed that their relative privacy at the back was about to be breached. The crowd started to disperse in a sort of Brownian motion around the drinks and towards the loos before the MC had finished explaining the best way to queue for their coats.

Frank made her laugh. She didn't want her brother to come over and spoil things. She could see him in the corner, talking to Ernest. They both turned towards her and Art did that little thinking thing with his eyes, narrowing the corners.

'Well, maker of Specsavers name tags,' she said, 'it's been good to meet you.'

'Is that your exit?' asked Frank. 'I was starting to have fun.'

'I, er.' She could feel Art's attention like a laser. These occasions tended to bring out the worst in her brother. Perhaps it was the line-up of revered mathematicians painted in oils on the walls that unsettled him. Her own mind's eye portrait of her father had started to blur from overuse – like the worn corduroy of his yellow chair.

Daddy, don't leave me.

'You okay?' asked Frank.

He leaned into her with the kindest eyes and she had this overwhelming sensation of wanting to put her head on his chest, just under his collarbone. She could close her eyes, and rest, and the world would melt away.

'Naomi?'

Art was stalking across the room towards them. 'Unfortunately,' she said quickly, 'I have to dash . . . Frank.' Saying his name out loud electrified her body. She smiled, and he smiled back.

44

'That's a shame,' he said. 'Naomi. Naomi . . .?'

'Um,' she said. A portrait of John Wallis hung behind him. 'Wallis.'

'Naomi *Wallis*,' he said. He looked directly into her eyes as though stamping her with this new name. 'I'm glad I came.' Frank took the tip of her little finger and gave it the lightest squeeze. 'I don't suppose you'd give me your number?'

She swallowed. 'Do you have a pen?'

'I'll remember it,' said Frank.

All those sevens, all those s's. Breathe, she thought, breathe. Think of the song. The chorus line of 'Yellow Submarine'. As she silently played the old tune in her head, the numbers skipped out in time to the syllables, just as they were supposed to. Before she knew it, she had told him her number, even the sevens – the mercurial stammering gods giving her a reprieve. Frank rattled it back to her. She wished he was writing it down. Then, as if sensing that she didn't want to share him, he left first, with a casual wave. She watched him go. His back was wide and relaxed. He ambled as if he'd never hurried anywhere in his life.

'Who was that?' asked Art from behind her.

9

MATHEMATICIAN

What an idiot. Now, almost a week later, Mimi was still chastising herself. Frank. Nice name, she thought. Again. Nice eyes, she thought, for – what? – the seven zillionth time.

Lying about her surname. Not writing down her number. 'You great twit,' lamented Rey when she heard. 'Good men are like shooting stars.'

When he hadn't called that evening, or the next day, Mimi knew he was gone. He didn't even know her real name. That had been a mistake. But she also knew why she'd done it. The release had been immediate. To be Naomi Wallis. Not Art's sister. Not Walter Brotherton's daughter. Not Mimi Brotherton, the stammering sibling of a genius. She'd felt the joy of something heavy slipping from her shoulders.

And now it was Thursday, a whole week.

Just then, as Mimi reached for an *Evening Standard*, her phone gave a familiar ping.

She'd have to re-ignite her faith in Matrix, having let a real live man slip away.

She usually waited until she got home before she checked her 'likes'. That way, she saw all the candidates in the same context. She didn't want to let a gem escape just because she'd seen him in the sooty light of the Northern Line or while standing outside Boots in a bad mood from trying to match concealer to her chafed lip line.

But the air had a snap of early spring. Narcissi brightened the shade under the trees. Perhaps still encouraged by her brief encounter at the awards, she decided to have a quick peek.

She had one new like.

Her heart sank.

The man staring from her small screen was altogether too hairy, with a cagey beard and shoulders too small for the size of his head.

She sent him to oblivion.

Did this algorithm work at all?

Her phone pinged again. This time with a WhatsApp, from a number she didn't know.

Is this you? it said, and she felt immediately queasy, as though it might be the man she had just dismissed to the ether.

She touched the little round picture in the corner.

Clear eyed, rough shaven, wide shouldered.

Frank.

Frank, the mathematician.

He wore a plain grey T-shirt in the picture, and a sombrero slung at his back. Frank!

In his photograph, his eyes were a workaday Wednesday blue. Despite the sombrero – which very briefly made her wonder if he was self-consciously goofy or just an 'annoying hat' kind of guy – it looked like a picture taken in London, backed by a plain city sky.

And she remembered his touch. She imagined his hand taking hers. It would be warm – he'd hold her hand as if he meant it. Her heart was beating but she wasn't breathing.

This face, she would 'like'. She did like.

She clicked her phone off and stepped onto the crocus-lined path. Home was minutes away. She pulled her bag closer in and ran. How had he found her? Had he really remembered her number? Why had he waited so long? A mathematician in a sombrero! What if he changed his mind? Met someone else in the time it took her to think straight? She tore down the road.

'I'm home!' she called to her brother upstairs as the front door slammed behind her. She leaped onto the sofa and jammed her password into her phone.

Why hadn't she replied right there on the green?

'Mimi.' Art walked into the kitchen. 'Is everything all right?'

She waved her arm above her but didn't look up.

Frank? she typed. She already loved that name. **Is it you?**

She stared at her cursor blinking on the screen.

It's Naomi here, she wrote.

Hi Naomi, he said.

Call me Mimi, if you like.

Art had watched from his study as Mimi ran down their road. Heading towards the house, flapping and urgent, her legs moving independent of her arms, she half fumbled in her bag as she ran. Was she frightened? There was something about her demeanour that was disconcerting. By the time she reached home, her face was lit as though from a strange internal sunshine.

He went downstairs to check on her and found her plunged onto the sofa, stabbing her phone with a finger as though her life depended on it.

'What is the matter?' he asked as he walked into the room. 'Mimi?'

. . .

48

'Mimi! Is everything all right?'

She waved him away.

Mimi put down her phone, then picked it up again. There was no hiding her excitement, her hands were shaking as she stared at the screen, held it to her chest and then put it back in her bag.

'He phoned! Well, I mean, he messaged!'

'And who is *he*?' said Art, trying to keep his voice neutral. 'I thought you knew not to give online strangers your telephone number.'

'I didn't – well, it's not that. This is not an online guy. I met him. I just—'

'Where? *When* did you meet him?'

She hesitated for a tiny, just discernible moment, but it seemed infinite. Staring at his sister's shining face, Art felt the full weight of her hesitation.

'His name is Frank,' she said. 'Frank.' She said it twice, even though he had heard her the first time. 'I met him at the awards ceremony. He's a mathematician.'

A mathematician. Art's heart jolted, and an uncomfortable sensation squeezed his organs. He walked towards the sink to get a glass of water.

'Art?'

'That must be a good thing, if he is a mathematician.' Even saying the word *mathematician* seemed inexplicably difficult just then.

He opened the window to get some fresh air.

'Art – please don't just stand there.' He realized Mimi was trying to talk to him. 'Please say something.'

'I did – I said it must be a good thing.'

'That was about five minutes ago. And also – you said it as though he might *not* be a mathematician. You said: *if* he is a mathematician, as though it was a question.'

'I did not mean to give that impression, Mimi, I apologize.'

'Please can we start this conversation again? Come and sit down. Leave that.' He was holding an empty glass. 'Put it down, Artie.'

He sat on the sofa while she filled his glass with water and put it on the table in front of him.

'His name is Frank,' she said. Why the constant repeating of the man's name? 'I met him at the awards,' she continued, 'we chatted for a bit and then he left before you came over. You may even remember.'

Art did remember. The casual-looking fellow who slipped away before he could see him properly, the one with whom Mimi had chatted incessantly during the presentations. Rude. He wanted to ask how she knew he was a mathematician, and what kind he was, but he did not want to say the word out loud.

'He's really nice, Art, I liked him. And it feels good that I've already met him in person, that I don't have to go through the hell of wondering if he's anything like his postage-stamp photograph online. I've seen him. He's real.' And there it was again. That shine.

So, this is how it will feel, he thought. To share her.

Before Art's fifth birthday, his mother's belly had swelled, and he was told about the baby inside. His mother had always been there. She poached two eggs for breakfast. She agreed which puzzle pieces went where, edges first. She read him a story each night. She knitted his jumpers, with rockets on the front.

Art's genetically wired scheduling instincts told him that with the arrival of another person, things were going to change. He found her doing the crossword, chewing the back of her pen. 'Two children are *double* one child,' he informed

50

his mother. 'Two children mean *half* the time.' This did not suit Art. At. All. He imagined waking alone, only one egg, half of a story, half of a kiss.

'Oh, Artie,' said his mother.

He suggested an alternative plan for the baby inside. An alternative mother, ideally.

'Come,' said Christine. He watched as she whisked eggs and sifted flour mixed with six tablespoons of cocoa, to make a chocolate cake in the shape of a clock. 'My time is limited,' his mother said a bit later, as she knocked the chocolate rounds from their tin and onto a wire tray. She smoothed white icing with a hot wet knife until it shone. She cut segments of liquorice into clock calibrations. Then she cut the clock-cake in two. 'You're right,' she told him, handing him half the cake on a dinner plate. 'You will have to share my time. But my *love*, I promise you, is infinite.'

Art understood infinity. His mother's tin of cocoa powder had a figure of a nun on the front. The nun on the tin held a tin of cocoa, also with a picture of a nun holding a tin on the front. And so on, and so on.

He clutched his plate as she took him outside. 'Do you hear the wind?' said his mother. The wind was shushing through the jacaranda trees at the bottom of the garden. 'Can you see the sunlight?' They stepped off the polished veranda, out of the shade and into the sun; the slasto was hot under his bare feet. 'The feeling you have of wanting me, of not wanting to share me? That feeling is love. I have it for you too. It's like the wind and the sun, it just keeps coming. It's infinite. There's no end to the wind, no end to the sun. No end to my love. No knife in the world can cut it in half.'

10

SINUOSITY

Frank suggested to Mimi that they meet for an early drink at a bar near the river, the kind of place with massive windows, industrial bar stools and art deco posters. Wednesday evening suited her because Art went swimming; she'd need to be back by 8.30, before he got home. He'd turned to stone when she told him about Frank. She'd have to keep him involved, as Rey said. Or *not*.

Either way, it felt a good idea to have a time limit on a first date.

Wearing a navy top she'd chosen for its soft neckline, and her mother's sage coat, which she knew looked good with her hair, Mimi went early. She chose a place at the bar where the light was soft, and she could sit on the side that didn't show the old scar above her mouth. It had been so long since she'd been in this situation – her previous two dates had been waiting when she got there – she didn't know whether to order a drink before Frank arrived, or which way to sit. She angled her legs to make sure her inner calf faced the entrance. She ate a peanut from the small bowl that had been put in front of her and then felt mortified. Was peanut-breath a thing?

She looked at her watch; she'd come way too early. She pulled out her phone to look busy.

'Hey,' said Frank at her side. She looked up, and he smiled. 'I'm sorry, I thought I was early,' he said, 'but you are too.'

'It must be a sign,' she said. *A sign, Mimi?* Of what? *Earliness?* She felt herself blush.

'I quite agree,' he said, slinging his jacket and book bag over the chair. 'A good sign. Punctuality's not usually my strong suit.' He brushed her knee and bubbles rose to the surface of her skin. He pushed his sleeves up his arm and pulled the bar stool in behind him without taking his eyes off her. 'What are you having?' He took a peanut and gestured for the barman. 'I never know whether to order when I'm waiting for someone. On the one hand it seems rude, but on the other you always feel so damn awkward just sitting there. That's why I came early, by the way – I thought *I'd* better be that awkward person. You beat me to it.'

Frank told her that the Southbank was a good spot for him to meet on a Wednesday because he worked at the local library, helping them with their cataloguing system. 'Hence the book bag,' he said. 'You can take a look later at what they've given me, if you like.'

Mimi forced herself to concentrate on the fact that he helped at the library, rather than *later*. 'I thought you were with the Mathematics Association?'

'I am, but I grew up on library books. My mother was a librarian. She made me promise that for the rest of my life I'd give an afternoon a week to a public library, no matter where I lived. I used to play a game with her: What if I end up living on a boat? In a tent? On an island with cannibals? It was like Dr Seuss's *Sam I Am*.' Mimi laughed. 'None of which seemed that unlikely to my mother, I might add. I

53

never thought I'd live in London, but here I am.' He put out his hands. 'And you? You always lived here?'

Mimi wanted to avoid her family history; she hadn't yet cleared up her surname. But she didn't want to lie – *again*. 'I was born in South Africa, but I'm a London girl.' She moved on swiftly, to the museum – she knew all about cataloguing – but was doing something altogether different now. She loved talking about Foley, and her stories made Frank laugh.

'Leather gloves, for bird flight? Really?' he said. Apparently delighted, he strummed his hands on his thighs, like wings.

'Mm-hmm,' she said and nodded. It felt as if he was drumming on her heart.

'So, how did it happen, you working in film? Is that what you always wanted? Am I going to have to watch a heap of weird genre movies I've never heard of to impress you?'

'God, no,' she said, smiling. His questions were rapid fire, but he seemed genuinely to want to hear her answers. Just sit right there and never move, she thought. 'I once thought I'd be a biologist, but I'm happy doing this.' She hadn't said that out loud before, and she realized she meant it. 'It was more a meandering river than a straight-line kind of thing.'

'We've all had meanders in life that don't go anywhere – our oxbow lakes,' said Frank, and took a sip of his beer.

'That's one way of saying it.' She'd almost finished her wine.

'Do you *know*,' he said, leaning forwards, animated, 'if you measure the path of a river straight from its source to its mouth at the sea, as the crow flies, and compare it to the length of the *actual* river, meandering round rocks and hills, its oxbow lakes and stuff – I just *love* this,' he said, and started moving his glass and the bowl of peanuts on the bar to demonstrate mountains and water. Then he paused. 'Stop

54

me,' he said. 'Are you bored rigid – I mean, *maths*? I kind of assumed because you were—'

'Not at *all*. Carry on.' More territory to steer clear of. But she did want Frank to keep talking.

He was looking at her, as though he wanted to ask her a question. An unspoken something hovered, just briefly, between them. But then he carried on. 'Well,' he said, 'the ratio of the crow-flies length to the actual, wandering river – its sinuosity – is almost the same for all really old rivers. And, guess what? That ratio is pi. Or at least, the average approaches pi. Isn't that just unbelievable? Think of all the different terrains, all over the world.' Somehow it didn't feel as if he was trying to *make her see*, which is what she was used to, more that he was wanting to share. 'The mountains, the plains –' he was leaning forwards, his elbow on the bar – 'isn't it incredible? I mean, the tension between order and chaos in nature . . .' This man. Mimi could hardly speak.

'It *really* is,' she said. She ordered another glass of wine.

At 8.15 she looked at her watch. '*Shit!*' she said, 'I need to go.'

'*Go?*' said Frank. He looked around, as if her reason might have suddenly walked into the room.

'I'm sorry, I—' She should've had an excuse ready. 'I, er, I'm sorry, I just have a . . .'

'It's okay,' said Frank and touched her arm. 'But only because you said *shit*, and you look disappointed.'

She laughed.

'Can we do this again?' he asked.

'Yes. Please,' said Mimi. She didn't want to leave in a hurry, but Art would be back soon, and she hadn't told him she was going out.

'Are you okay getting home?' asked Frank, and when she

nodded, he gestured to the barman. He stood up to take her to the door, and pointed to her coat, which she'd slung over the back of a neighbouring chair. 'Yours?'

'Thank you,' she said and gathered it up. 'Thank you. That really was—' And then Frank kissed her on the mouth. Right there, at the bar. She closed her eyes. When she opened them, he was watching her face, and she smiled. '. . . fun,' she said. 'Thanks.'

'Yes, it really was,' said Frank.

'Just stay here, don't come out,' she said.

'Okay, Naomi. See you soon.' He was grinning. 'I look forward to it.'

She turned to wave as she walked out the door and saw him watching her. She was far too warm to wear her coat, although the night was cool. There was the lightest rain and it felt as if she was fizzing inside and out. She walked slowly around the corner, trying not to betray any sense of urgency, but as soon as she was out of sight, she picked up her step. She'd have to take a taxi; she needed to get home.

To her immediate relief, a yellow light came into view. Mimi collapsed into the seat and flung her arms out either side of her. *Next time*, she thought, in the dim light of the cab. She put her head back and closed her eyes. Next time I'm telling him my real name.

Next time, I'm telling him everything about me.

Art felt mentally revived after his swim. His muscles were tired, but pleasantly so. He had swum his lengths, caught up with his notebook at the pool cafe and decided on some new software to help with his security concerns. Whether someone was circling because of the Millennium Prize, or something more sinister, he hoped to discover. He felt calm.

But when he arrived home, he was surprised to find Mimi

standing in the hall, with her favourite coat in her hand. There had been drinks at the studio, a birthday. 'I've just got home,' she said.

He could see that. He was not blind.

But he also saw her touch the side of her face, her tell.

11

THIRTEEN PERCENT

What about owls? Frank texted Mimi first thing the next morning.

What about owls?

I saw an owl on my way home last night. Their flight is so silent, wrote Frank. **They've got fringes on their feathers to soften the sound. How cool? Howl cool ;)**

Ha. Ha. She couldn't believe he was thinking about sound first thing in the morning. *Don't write that.* **I had a really nice time last night.**

Me too. I read that the average chance of a second date is 13 percent. How am I looking?

Like a mathematician.

Ha! So? I'd like to see you again.

I'd like that too.

She heard Art's bathroom door open.

He'd be wanting his breakfast.

GTG, she wrote quickly. **Later . . .**

Mimi couldn't think of something flirty or witty now that Art was in her head. She shot downstairs, where she heated Art's porridge in the microwave rather than the stove and hoped that he wouldn't notice.

* * *

Art added extra boiling water to his porridge, which was a little sticky. He had come downstairs to the radio on loud. Mimi had used the nice napkins for breakfast. 'You are very cheerful this morning,' he said, stirring the oats. He pointed at her laptop, which was open on the table. 'I see you have had rather a lot of likes overnight – is that why?' He knew that she had not responded to Matrix for days.

'Um, sorry, what?' she said.

He did not tell her that *he* had logged on last night on her behalf. He had even 'liked' someone.

Graham, a radiologist from Newbury, had replied straight back.

Hi M
I'm Graham, I live an hour outside London. I like your picture, and your work sounds interesting. Id never heard of foley.

It was to the point. And although he had missed an apostrophe, he had made an effort to look up her line of work.

Did his sister want to spend her time with a radiologist? Moot point – she needed someone *in* London. It was never only an hour.

He had googled 'Newbury'. Then, 'Radiologists'. Then, 'Radiologists in Newbury'.

Reviews on Yelp could not tell him anything, but Salarygenius suggested a radiologist might earn $178,000. That was when he realized that he was looking at salaries in Newbury, Ohio.

What was he *doing*?! Mimi was not about to go on a fresh blind date with a radiologist from Newbury, whom she had not even chosen herself. Goodness, this thing was distracting. He pressed Delete.

Sorry Graham. Goodbye.

Now his sister was staring out the window with a benign smile, watching a squirrel damage the walnut tree. Art got up and opened the window. 'Shoo!' he said. 'He will ringbark it, you know.'

'Sweet,' she said. 'Have you eaten your porridge?'

'Mimi?' said Art. 'Are you all right?'

'Sorry, yes I'm fine. What did you say?' She opened the fridge door and stared into the light.

'Well, apart from being worried about the walnut, I asked if you acknowledged any of your likes.'

'Oh, um, no, I've had quite a bit of Foley to think about.'

'You started off quite methodical and disciplined. I expect the algorithm can detect apathy. You do not want to attract people for whom apathy is an attractive quality.'

She snapped round. 'I do not want to attract people for whom *discipline* is high on their list of romantic attributes. God, Art.'

'This is not something to do with that fellow from the awards, is it?' Something made him say it. 'The one who left without introducing himself and talked through the ceremony? Has he made further contact? Since his message?'

'Um, no,' said Mimi. 'Well, yes, actually.'

'Is it yes or is it no?'

'It is yes, and I am thinking about it, and I don't want to talk about it right now.'

The man had probably already let her down.

'Very well,' said Art, not able to judge his sister accurately this morning. 'Just do not forget Matrix. It will be tracking your behaviour.' He suddenly realized that for the last twenty-four hours it had tracked *his* behaviour, thinking it was Mimi's. He must guard against confusing the algorithm.

Graham had been a mistake.

* * *

60

On her way to work on the bus, Mimi received another text from Frank.

Have you ever been starhopping? he asked.

Sounds like one of those retro toys – the big orange rubber ball with handles?

Ha! That's a space hopper. It's not that. You keen?

When? *Please don't say Friday.* Art is home early on Friday. He doesn't have swimming on Friday.

Friday?

. . .

Mimi?

What time does starhopping happen?

Night-time. Late.

In the studio, Rey was checking the cue sheet for the day that told them exactly what sounds they had to record, the exact timing for each and what equipment they were going to use. 'Art's already gone stubbornly negative on the idea of Frank,' Mimi told her. 'He won't use his name.' She filled a tin basin with water. 'I guess he'll come around, but Friday nights we always stay in and watch *Countdow*n.'

'Can you pretend you're going out with someone from Matrix?'

'He'll ask me to show him the guy online. I want to go starhopping with Frank. Whatever it is.' She lugged the basin back towards the mikes.

Rey tacked the cue sheet to the board. 'Seems that you'd like to go *anywhere* with Frank,' she said. 'I'm not doing anything on Friday. I'll watch *Countdown* with him. Tell him you have to work late, that we need someone with a bit of imagination – like that camping scene – there are some tricky moments with the Gore-Tex jacket and the backpack, and lots of different surfaces they're walking on. Plus all the tent flaps, and sleeping bags – you're good at that layered stuff.'

61

'Really? Really?!' Mimi leaped round to hug her friend, but Rey stopped her.

'Really, Mi,' she said, 'but after that you have to tell Art if you see Frank. That's my price. Or this won't end well. And, you know, full disclosure afterwards – and I mean *details*, sister.'

Rey didn't know, though, all that Mimi hadn't yet told Frank.

12

INFINITY

On Friday night, Art and Rey sat down to watch *Countdown* with supper trays on their laps. 'Excellent lasagne. Thank you,' he said to Rey.

'No worries. Cath makes a mean bechamel sauce.' Cath had worked for Rey's mum and still came in once a week to clean. 'I'm Heineken with a vacuum,' she'd say, battering untended corners with the machine. She called Rey 'My Heart' and occasionally left pre-cooked dishes for her to pop into the oven. She kept her phone, her car keys and a pen in her bra, which interfered with her contours somewhat.

Art had seen Cath just last week. She ran a small crafts business and, as a surprise for Rey from him and Mimi, she was knitting a Christmas jumper for Rey's dachshund, Rizla. Art had insisted on going round when Rey was out, to measure the dog. Rizla had proved surprisingly uncooperative while he and Cath tried to ascertain his back and chest size with a wooden ruler.

'I've got the general idea,' Cath had said, cackling, as Rizla squirmed out of her arms, again. But Art wanted to be certain the gift would fit.

'We used a piece of string in the end,' he told Mimi over

supper. 'And I chose the snowflake pattern from the photographs in Cath's plastic folder. It is something of a heresy compared to the complexity of a real snowflake, but still, the tension in Cath's knitting looks impressively even. I expect Rey will be pleased.'

Right now, Rey was balancing her wine on the arm of the sofa. Endless ads for gambling and cars assaulted them. Art got up to get napkins.

As he handed one to Rey, he was about to thank her again for coming round. But he checked himself. Strictly speaking, it was he and Mimi who were doing Rey and her business the favour.

Rey patted the cushion beside her, and Art settled back onto the sofa, as the blue tiles of *Countdown*'s numbers game followed onscreen.

'Where's your pen and paper?' asked Rey.

'I do the calculations in my head.'

'Of course you do,' she said.

Mimi and Frank were juddering along in a carriage on the Northern Line, heading for a park that had a particularly black sky. Frank had shown her his dark sky calendar. 'We won't be able to see a thing. It's ideal,' he said, smiling at her. 'Have you got your fingerless mittens?'

'And my hat, and layers, like you said.'

Frank had a backpack full of equipment.

They sat in silence as the Tube whistled through tunnels that were so deep they made your ears pop. She stared up at the Underground map above her – Stockwell, Clapham, Balham, Tooting, Colliers Wood – but her mind was zig-zagging.

She'd taken forever to shave her legs, shower and get dressed. Art had quizzed her through the door – *What are you doing?* She'd had to look as if she was going back to work, and a pile of clothes lay on her bed.

'At least go insurance level,' Rey encouraged her. Mimi hadn't slept with a man for years. 'Legs, armpits, underwear.'

Now Frank, dressed like a camper in a dorky fleece and puffer jacket which she found endearing, was going backwards up the escalator on the way out of the Underground so that he could face her. They cruised past ads for the latest theatre and movies on the station walls. 'I would be nervous to suggest a film to you,' Frank said. 'Would it even be relaxing? Or do you ruin it for everyone else by wincing at badly synced chewing sounds?'

'Oh, I love going to the cinema,' she said, as though she went all the time, 'but this is much more exciting. I don't even know what starhopping is. I had to resist looking it up.'

'Ah – a woman who like surprises, Naomi. I'll remember that.'

Her tummy flip-flopped. Frank took her hand briefly as he stepped backwards off the escalator. As they walked away from the station, arms swinging at their sides, they passed busy kebab shops and phone repair kiosks, closed flower shops and hairdressers, accompanied by reflections of her and Frank in the windows. That this ordinary walking alongside another human being felt so thrilling to her was surely visible to everyone else.

They stepped off the pavement to cross the road, and Frank reached for her again. She had to stop herself from exploring his hand with her fingers, like a blind person finding her way.

Mimi would happily have walked right through to the other side of the park, but when they reached an open patch next to a glade, Frank stopped. 'Here,' he said. 'This is perfect. It's quiet.' They weren't the only people there; two other huddles were visible as moving silhouettes in a glow of red torches. Frank laid out a blanket on the ground, then placed another more padded one on top of it.

'Is your backpack bottomless?' she asked.

'No, but it contains almost bottomless hot chocolate.' He pulled out a flask. 'And rum.'

'Oh, my god.' She felt like yelping. 'I *love* starhopping!'

She was suddenly desperate to know if this was Frank's routine. Did he bring all his dates starhopping, with hot chocolate? Was this his dead-cert second date?

'We're going galaxy hunting,' said Frank. He opened his star map and it lifted away from him in the light breeze. He flattened it on the blanket with his knuckly, long-fingered hands. His hands were mesmerizing. It had been so long since she'd had anyone's hands on her body, what if she froze up? It was all very well flirting. What if years of in-activity had rendered her sexually inert? She didn't know what it would feel like to have someone look at her, her whole body. Touch her.

'Hey, have you already skipped off to a galaxy somewhere?'

'Sorry,' she said, 'just, you know, this is lovely.' Frank smiled. He shone his red torch on the map and showed her: they were looking for the Sombrero Galaxy. 'What's with you and sombreros?' she asked.

'They're kinda crazy wonderful. My dad gave me one once, along with a poem that encapsulates my world view. Mad, I know.' Before she could ask the name of the poem, he showed her the first star they needed to find before hopping along a series towards their destination. 'See? Spica. One hop along from the Big Dipper,' he said. 'Come, lie on your back.'

'And so he said to all the girls he took starhopping,' she said, laughing, but also, wanting to know. If Frank could tell, he didn't show it – he just laughed. They lay on their backs, each holding a pair of binoculars. Frank had given

66

her the lighter pair. They followed Spica along to the Crow, which looked more like the sail of a small ship. She lost her way for a moment and put her binoculars down. 'My arms are getting tired. Sorry!'

Frank took her hand and pointed it at the sky. 'I'll hold you up.' He traced a line with her arm, suspending her wrist in the air. 'This is where we're going.' She could hear herself breathe. People murmured and laughed softly in the other groups. London hummed around them, the odd siren breaking the underlying thrum. She could sense the cold air falling around her, dewing the ground; the wind threaded an easy path through the trees, still bare of leaves.

Back with the binoculars they found the bright chain they needed, then Stargate – a triangle of stars enclosing a pair. 'Okay, now concentrate, it's not crystal clear,' said Frank, 'but I see it, it's there.' Just beyond a tiny arrow of stars was a blurred disc of stardust – the Sombrero.

'I see it! I see it! Oh, my god!' And she did. Like a smudge of smoke, a signal to her from the sky. 'Oh, Frank, it's beautiful, it's incredible. I see it!' She had to stop herself from kissing him right there.

'Now try and see if you can find it with your naked eye,' he said. 'It doesn't look quite like the UFO you see in pictures – I'll show you some photographs of it later.' She was so happy there'd *be* a later she couldn't speak. 'And think,' said Frank, 'the photons you're seeing have been travelling for sixty-five million years and now you're the only person who's just seen those particular ones. One moment in sixty-five million years.' Her heart was lodged in her throat.

He rolled onto his side. 'Can I kiss you?' he said.

His kiss was so tender, her whole body melted into it. She'd forgotten how wonderful it felt. To be kissed. She was sure it had *never* felt this wonderful. She kissed him back.

She wanted to lie there, with her back getting cold, the ground getting hard, the night sky lowering down like a giant black cape, made of feathers and star-spangles and the night sounds of the park.

They shared the hot chocolate and rum straight from his flask, not bothering to use cups. It was rich and hot and burned her tongue and he kissed her again and she could taste the sweetness in his mouth. They lay down once more and Frank wrapped himself around her and showed her more stars.

'Do you know why the sky is black?'

She shook her head in the dark.

'It's maths,' said Frank. 'Beyond the stars that we can see, are stars too far away for their light to have reached us yet. I got into the night sky trying to get my head around really large numbers, trying to put infinity into perspective.'

At the mention of infinity and maths, Mimi felt as if the enchantment had broken. She thought immediately of Art, and before she could stop herself, she looked at her watch. She saw Frank notice. 'Hopefully we'll have more time to discuss infinity,' he said.

She tried to will the magic back, but it was seeping away. After a while lying there, Frank kissed her forehead and peeled himself off the blanket. He quietly packed their things into his bottomless bag and said, 'Come, it's getting cold. Let's get you home.'

Waiting for the bus, Frank was quiet. Too quiet.

'You said Camberwell? I'm not too far, so let's get there and see where we are, okay?' he said, climbing on with his hand – just – at her back. London rolled by with the occasional ping for the doors. Strangers getting on and off the bus did not make much impression on their shared silence.

As her stop approached, she turned to him. 'I'm here, I'll jump off – you stay on.'

'All right,' he said. She couldn't tell if he was disappointed or not.

'I had a wonderful time tonight,' she said. 'I can't remember the last time I had such a magical evening. Thank you.' She leaned in before the bus slowed, and she kissed him chastely on the cheek and hoped that it was enough, before she collected herself and got off, and the bus sped away.

Before she took a step, she texted him.

*** That was,* in every sense, *** heavenly, *** thank you, she wrote, sprinkling her text with asterisks. It was corny, but it felt like she needed the stardust.

She kept checking all the way home, but Frank hadn't seen her message. Or hadn't replied.

13

RESISTANCE

When Mimi walked in the door, Art was waiting up.

'You lied to me,' he said. Art had noticed that she hadn't taken her Foley bag with her. It was a fact. 'And not for the first time.'

She didn't have much to offer other than the truth. His name, as she'd told Art before, was Frank. He was nice. She liked him. A lot. She'd only had a few sips of rum, but was unable to stop herself from saying exactly what she felt. That Frank wasn't weird or controlling or scary or irritating, or immature. He didn't stick his tongue too far down her throat – she didn't tell Art that – or any of the other things that she and her girlfriends complained about, back when she had girlfriends other than Rey. She liked him. It was simple.

Art took it reasonably well. 'There was no need to lie.'

'I'm sorry,' she said, although she actually blamed Art for the fact that she might already have messed things up. She could imagine Frank's head leaning on the bus window as it drove away.

Her brother nodded. 'Well. This does take you closer to thirty-seven percent. As long as you keep that in mind,' he said.

'Of course,' she said. 'Promise.'

'That is all that I ask,' he replied, and she felt so relieved, she didn't pay enough attention to what she'd just said.

Her phone pinged.

You home okay? asked Frank.

Art stared at her. 'Are you going to answer that?'

'Um,' she said, and moved towards the kettle, where she typed quickly. **Yes, just making tea.**

Rey's upturned wine glass was on the draining board. Art just stood there.

'You want tea?' she asked him.

Art said no thank you, but in a voice that made her worry about what he did want instead. 'See you in the morning,' he said.

As soon as Art was gone, she whipped out her phone. She held it in front of her for a good two minutes, as though advice might spring forth from Siri, the new voice app. **Frank,** she wrote eventually, **I'm sorry I got nervous tonight. Even without the stars I loved it all.** She took a deep breath. **I just haven't done this for a while.**

It wasn't you, she added. She looked at the message and pressed Send before she could change her mind.

Thank you for that, he replied, straight away. **I understand.**

It's late now, he wrote. **Let's chat tomorrow, F x**

Mimi resolved that, at least for a while, she'd make plans with Frank for when her brother was busy.

Assuming there were plans with Frank.

Her text, at least, had been honest.

But it was still Naomi Wallis who'd sent Frank that message. It was Naomi Wallis who'd gone starhopping. Frank has kissed Naomi Wallis.

And it was Naomi Wallis who went upstairs and texted

Frank again, **Goodnight x**. It had been so romantic. She cradled her tea and imagined Frank's hands, and where she would like them to go.

Naomi Wallis didn't have a brother who, if she listened closely enough, she could hear in his room across the passage. He had just snapped his spectacle case shut.

14

PROPORTIONALITY

Mimi's first encounter with what might have been romantic love had been with the chemist's son, Matthew.

She was seventeen and her mother's cancer had metastasized. One evening, as the light sank into the cul-de-sac end of Muriel Grove, Matthew parked his scooter at a jaunty angle to drop off the small white paper packet with Christine's details under the NHS logo. He handed it to Mimi. 'I hope your mum is feeling better,' he said, and then his words ran on into would she like to see a movie sometime, maybe even *Something About Mary*, which everyone was talking about? Almost as if he had asked her by mistake.

Mimi was equally taken unawares when she heard herself saying yes, laughing out loud during the movie, finding his hand in hers, his fingers rubbing the inside of her knee, her jeans tingling and his tongue in her mouth, filled with popcorn.

It was easy to confuse a steady supply of lip gloss and tortoiseshell hair clips from a kind boy who waited for her words – with love. Matthew fumbled with the condom the first time, and rubbed her cold feet warm with his soles. She had more sex during that year than she'd have for a decade.

Together, they rented movies from Blockbuster and

73

badgered Art about the Y2K meltdown. Art was obsessed with a maths problem called *p versus Np*, which had the power to elicit a meltdown all over the world, apparently. Y2K posed a similar threat. 'I'll be stocking sliced bread and loo roll,' said Matthew, ever practical.

I heart M, Mimi wrote on her schoolbag with Tippex.

While Mimi's father cared for their mother, Art focused on mathematics, *p versus Np* specifically. And the International Mathematics Competition for Universities was coming up in Blagoevgrad. But he had a new obsession too, with their parents' belongings, that Mimi completely failed to understand. Thinking at all about her mother, who was very ill, burned her inside.

She remained preoccupied with nail polish colour, which songs her girlfriends liked, *was* Ricky Martin actually cool, or not; and what to wear when she said she was staying at Rey's, but was actually going clubbing with Matthew or these same friends, whom she still felt she hardly knew at all, with their football-team-supporting fathers and brothers who smoked, and mothers who balanced takeaway cappuccinos on their dashboards.

On the day their lives changed, Mimi had fallen out with Art because he'd been driving her mad with this idea that her parents were hatching a plan. They'd carted off at least two carloads of stuff to the charity shop. From felt hats, formal jackets and long dresses, to bridge club tablecloth and scorecards, old recipe books and unused Magimix attachments – it was a lifetime of possessions.

'My Scalextric cars and first abacus! How *could* they?' he said. No doubt Art thought his abacus would one day be a fixture in the Museum of Art Brotherton – the Man who Saved Humanity.

Mimi told him it was perfectly normal to reassess your life when one of you was dying and your youngest child had just taken A-levels. She hadn't meant to sound heartless, but these *facts*, as Art just so loved to say, were unarguable.

Now he wasn't talking to her.

A rerun of *Walking with Dinosaurs* was on television when the police arrived. Art was criticizing the unconvincing visual effects. Hector, the old dog, was sprawled on the floor, fast asleep. Mimi answered the door. A policeman and woman stood there and asked if they were at the right house – the home of Mr Walter and Mrs Christine Brotherton. They looked at their notepads to make sure they had the right names, and Mimi had felt in that moment the absence of her parents like a cold wind, that somehow, they were already reduced to names on the page. That the police hadn't asked *for* their parents, she thought afterwards, was the telling thing. Mimi led them in. Hector was sitting up, leaning towards the strangers. Art looked at Mimi, his eyes as wide as plates. Everything in his face said I *warned you, I warned you*, as the police told them, as they sat, with their knees touching, one on the sofa, one on the chair, the police still standing, that their parents were dead.

They were quick and professional. 'I am afraid we have some very bad news for you.'

Mimi knew that already; her heart was pounding so hard she felt it might leap out onto the coffee table. 'Your parents are dead.'

The world swallowed her up. The horror, the loss, the shock. And, like a yawning pair of jaws that would clamp its bones around the rest of her life, guilt.

The sadness was all too much for Matthew. Mimi persuaded herself that she was relieved when he dissolved into the background after sending a condolence card from the chemist, with a glittered lily on the front, that said 'Thinking of you at this difficult time'. It left silver on Mimi's fingertips, reminded her of her mother at Christmas, and made her cry.

15

EPSILON

Frank appeared to accept Mimi's excuse of second-date jitters. And to avoid unsettling her brother, Mimi found herself engineering a daytime third date.

I haven't figured out yet how competitive you are, texted Frank.

Huh?

I've shown you my favourite galaxy, he said. **You told me it was hard to beat . . . so now it's your turn.**

Yikes! Competitive dating?

Why not?

After a while, she replied. **Okay. I've got a short day on Thursday, finish at 12.**

12. okaaay. Can be. Where are we going?

Wait and see. She paused. **Aka, I have no idea.**

It wasn't possible to show Frank something bigger than infinite space. Instead, she decided, she'd show him something very small.

Meet me at the Black Sheep coffee shop on Eastcheap. 1pm, she wrote.

The benefit of working with cool people on production teams was that she now had a (tiny) Rolodex of cool places she'd actually been to. What she liked about Frank was that he wasn't particularly cool, so she didn't have to pretend to be either. Rey always told her the antennae of her 'cooldar' had snapped off in her pram. But the Black Sheep was 'sick', with its floorboards and *leavetheherd* hashtag. The coffee foam was patterned with leaves, not hearts – no one could accuse her of not thinking this through – and it would make both their hearts race, it was so strong. As if hers wouldn't be galloping already. And it was right near the smallest thing she knew in London that qualified as an attraction.

'Nice,' said Frank when they walked in. The baristas called to each other in what sounded like improvised rap, about coffee and orders. Mimi had a cappuccino, and Frank a double espresso, which was great except that it was over rather quickly and next thing they were standing in the road again.

'So, I thought,' she said, suddenly nervous that her whole date idea was very lame, and *very* short, 'that you'd taken me to see infinity . . . so I'm taking you to see something tiny. It's not very far. In fact, I've made an error. It's actually too close. I was quite excited about this but now I've realized it's also going to be the shortest date ever. Which I guess is appropriate given the theme . . .' She was babbling.

'You do seem to like to end them rather abruptly.' She looked at her shoes and didn't answer, but Frank laughed. 'C'mon then – you have my full attention, for – er – the next few nanoseconds.' He wasn't cool, but he was so very lovely.

They stood on the corner of Eastcheap and Philpot, about twenty steps from the coffee shop. 'Okay,' she said. 'Close your eyes.' She shuffled him around to face the wall. 'Now look up.'

Frank opened his eyes.

Two little painted stone mice tussling over a piece of cheese

78

were carved into the lintel of the outside of the building. 'See,' she said, 'aren't they funny?'

'I've walked past here a million times and never seen them.' Frank looked delighted. 'What are they?'

'It's actually a sad story,' she said. 'They're there to commemorate two builders who fell to their deaths when arguing about whether one had pinched the cheese from the other's lunchbox. Turned out to be mice.'

'Aw. Sad. But brilliant.' He pulled her towards him, and she felt inordinately pleased, as if she'd won a story-writing competition at primary school. It was the middle of the day, in the City, but when he kissed her, he didn't seem to care. They leaned against the wall. Her hand was pressed flat against the cold stone. He kissed her eyebrow. 'God,' he said. She could feel the plaster and she held on by the tips of her fingertips as the rest of her floated away. He kissed her neck, then clapped his hands and said, 'Okay! That was sweet. Amazing! And yes, very short. So, now what?'

'Well,' she said, aware that she was smiling and smiling.

She hadn't been sure about this next part. 'There's a very tiny place, called the Yellow Door. They serve lunch – but it's halfway across London.'

'We have the whole afternoon,' he said, and they were off, walking down the road towards the Tube, talking as they crossed the road, him wondering aloud how many other tiny things there were like that all over London, raising their voices above the traffic because they couldn't stop talking, not then. Did she know how extraordinary the mathematics was that helped build the Gherkin? And did he like the red steel tower for the Olympics? Did it happen to her that she always put her USB stick in upside down? And what about pancakes? He made *awesome* pancakes and if they weren't careful they'd get run over and then the little yellow door appeared. They spent a blissful afternoon sharing food and stories and a cocktail and a bottle of wine and her licking the mayonnaise from the chicken goujons off the ends of her fingers and goujon was such a funny word if you said it over and over again – goujon, goujon – and him holding her sticky hand and not minding, and choosing the same pudding and dividing it in half. And occasionally steering the conversation away from the things she couldn't talk about – Naomi *Brotherton* things – but batting that worry away. 'Come,' said Frank eventually, though she could have stayed there for the rest of her life. They divided the bill. It was darkening outside.

'You win,' he said. 'That was ace.'

'Starhopping was pretty cool.'

'This was gem-hopping and I've never done *that* before. We've done infinity to epsilon.' She loved that idea, but she was still irked by the idea of being on a list of girls that Frank had taken starhopping. They didn't discuss where they were going next. Frank took her hand, and they caught the Tube back to Stockwell and chatted all the way and he asked her if she'd come to his flat, which was on the raised ground floor of a modernist block across the green. She nodded and felt terrified and elated all at the same time.

She needn't have worried.

Frank's flat was simple, had stacks of books everywhere, a plant in the corner, packets of biscuits on the counter, and some actual food in his fridge. His sombrero hung off the bookshelf. One upturned coffee cup had been washed and left next to the sink.

'I've got two things to tell you,' he said, and leaped onto the sofa, leaving her standing in the middle of the room. 'First, I tidied my flat. It's unlikely ever to be this tidy again. Just saying. And second, I want you to know that I loved going starhopping with you. I've always done it as a solitary thinking-time thing. On my own. I've never shared it. I just wanted you to know that. I don't know how many people you've shown the mice and cheese to – you can tell me when you're ready. Of mice and men.' He laughed and then put out his arms and she almost jumped into them. A voice in her head asked her if she felt ready, but it retreated as she stared into Frank's quite extraordinary eyes; they seemed navy blue right now. He smelled of their day, and full of wine – but no doubt, so did she. Frank started to undress her right there on the sofa, slowly, as it got dark outside. 'People can see straight in here,' he said, and they held hands, half-kissed, half-stumbled to his bedroom, where he very gently showed her what it was like to have someone look at you as if they can't get enough, glazed with desire, but taking care too.

After a while, with Frank asleep next to her, Mimi slipped out of bed and padded round his flat. In the guest loo, she found his sombrero poem, by Wallace Stevens, framed and hanging on the wall.

> Rationalists, wearing square hats,
> Think, in square rooms.
> Looking at the floor,
> Looking at the ceiling.
> They confine themselves
> To right angled triangles.
> If they tried rhomboids,
> Cones, waving lines, ellipses –
> As, for example, the ellipse of the half-moon –
> Rationalists would wear sombreros.
>
> Wallace Stevens

81

Later, she lay on his bed and stared at the patterns the lampshade made on the ceiling – a far cry from the night sky. No half-moon ellipses, but as wonderful as anything she'd ever seen – lying there on her back in Frank's flat. She asked him what the poem meant.

'Rationalists should wear sombreros,' he said. 'Everyone, especially us mathematicians, should think outside the box. Never limit ourselves to straitjacket thinking.'

'Hmm,' she said. Us mathematicians, Frank had said. Frank still didn't know there was another mathematician in her life.

'So, tell me Naomi,' he said, circling her belly button with his index finger, 'do *you* have a favourite hat?'

It wasn't a favourite exactly, she said, but she'd kept it.

It seemed like a good moment to tell Frank. Everything.

Chemotherapy had made her mother tired, Mimi said, so she sat on the sofa while they both unwrapped Christmas decorations; fat jewels from their tissue cocoons. The baubles left glittery films on the tips of her mother's fingers. Mimi remembered shiny fingerprints, like silver reindeer footprints across the sky. 'Just like the stars we watched in the park.'

She was lying on her side, facing Frank, leaning on her elbow with a sheet over her middle.

Her mother's breath had seemed too feeble to sustain her tiny frame. 'I wanted her to stand up, you know? Be strong?' Frank nodded. But each bauble quivered at the end of her mother's bony hand. 'You could've snapped her wrist.' Mimi pulled the sheet up over her shoulder, feeling cold. Frank tucked her hair behind her ear.

'Further back,' Christine had instructed her. 'It needs more red on that side.'

'Mum, I'm an adult. I know how to decorate a tree.' She

82

felt so cross but she couldn't say why. She rubbed the glass of a giant red ball.

'Oh!' So thin, it had popped like a bubble.

'What was that?' said Christine.

'N-n-nothing,' said Mimi, 'just s-s-spiked by the pine needles, that's all.'

'Oh, Naomi, you've *broken* it.'

'S-s-sorry,' Mimi muttered, annoyed.

Her mother leaned her head back on the sofa. She had silver imprints on her forehead from the glitter – she was shiny, starry, bony. Fragile.

Mimi's windpipe felt as if it was filling up. 'Mum,' she said, 'I need money to get Art a Christmas present, today. And we need lemons.'

Her mother couldn't take her. 'I hope you wrapped that glass in newspaper,' she said instead.

Mimi looked at the shattered shards of bright glass she'd tipped into the bin.

'Get on that bike of yours and get him something from the High Street.' Christine peeled a tenner from her purse, and then, as if suddenly remembering it was for her son and not Mimi, she took out another ten and hooked it into the slanty side pocket of Mimi's jeans. At some level Mimi knew that she looked for moments of favouritism and found them where they probably didn't exist. It was as if she needed something else to be angry with her mother for. Something other than dying.

Nevertheless, her bike? Was her mother living in a parallel universe? Mimi hadn't touched her bike in years. It was *tiny*, the saddle was like cheese. 'I'll walk,' she said.

She closed the front door behind her and shoved her hands into her jacket. It was so cold your ears could snap off like tea-cup handles.

In the charity shop window, a bust wearing a hat caught Mimi's eye. It was parked behind an Andrew and Fergie memorabilia cake tin and standing on a pile of board games. There had to be something in there that her brother would like. It would have to be cheap. Because Mimi was staring at what *she* liked, what *she* wanted, *needed* actually, she told herself. Although she wouldn't ever really wear it because it prickled her – see? – she was already in the shop trying it on, convincing herself that the very thing in the world that would fill the funny hole in her life that was taking shape in her tummy round about then that she neither liked nor understood – worrying about her mother and feeling angry with her all at the same time – was the sunny-coloured hand-knitted beanie from the bust's marble head. It was already on hers.

She was paying for it before she could stop herself.

Mimi rang Rey's doorbell to borrow a few lemons. 'Cute hat,' said Rey. 'Come on in. How's your mum?'

Mimi kept the hat on inside. She was trying to get used to the feeling – it felt as if her hair was on fire. 'Mohair,' said Rey as Mimi gave her head a scratch. 'It does that.' The word meant nothing. She'd take it off the minute she got home. She rattled the small packet carrying her brother's present.

He already had a key ring, but he'd use this someday.

Mimi looked round Frank's room, as if waking up. The prints on the walls, the books on a stool. She'd said 'brother'. Had she also said Art's name? Frank was looking at her. 'Go on,' he said. He had a knack of allowing her to go round the landmines she'd made for herself. He was holding her hand.

'You've got yellow hairs on your shoulders,' Christine said when Mimi returned, the hat stuffed in her pocket.

'I tried on a fluffy hat in the charity shop.' Mimi held up the lemons to divert her attention.

'Was it mohair?' asked Christine.

It seemed to Mimi that buried in the question of mohair was something else – unpredictable and a little jagged. 'I don't know.'

'You know he's allergic. It's goat hair.'

'Art's allergic, Mum. *Art*,' she said, angry, realizing she could never show her mother the damn hat now. 'And I was trying it on for *me*.'

'Well, yes,' said Christine. Softly, as if making an effort, for a moment, to figure out her daughter. 'Yes. Better go and get it off your clothes,' she said, and turned towards where Walter was reading. Mimi stomped up the stairs to her room, feeling hollow.

'What's up with her?' she heard her father ask.

'I've no idea,' her mother answered. 'She's just so bloody tricky.'

'It's not easy for her, Christine,' said her dad. Mimi slammed her door.

Her brother was surprisingly pleased with his Rubik's cube key ring. The squares were small and fiddly to turn – it kept him occupied on Christmas Day while she did the bumper crossword with her dad.

'He's a mathematician too,' she *almost* said, about Art. *And so was my dad.*

She'd intended to tell Frank her full story, right there, really she had. But then – what was Frank going to think when she told him she'd lied? And had kept on lying? Would he pull his hand away? As she got closer to the moment of no going back, she panicked. It would spoil their day. Their incredible day. And so, she retreated from the truth. She stuck to a story of a beanie that itched. 'It reminds me of my mum,' was all that she said.

Frank pulled her towards him and stroked her hair. 'That was difficult,' he said. 'I could tell.' She tucked her head under his chin and felt safe. She could hear his heart. He kissed her temple and rubbed his hand down her arm.

At seven she got out of bed and pulled on her clothes. 'I've got to go,' she whispered. 'My housemate is tricky,' she said, 'and I've got the keys.' She had told Art his supper might be late.

'Stay,' said Frank.

'I can't,' said Mimi.

16

SPIN

The days got longer; it was already spring. Weak slats of sun filtered through Frank's blinds as Mimi got dressed, her skin goosebumped from leaving the warmth of his afternoon sheets. 'Don't leave this time,' said Frank, nudging the spaghetti strap of her dress down her arm with his thumb as she reached for her sandals. He kissed the knuckle on her collarbone and pulled her backwards onto the bed. It was all she could do not to wrap herself around him again.

'Stay. Tomorrow's Sunday.' Frank pushed up the slippery fabric and cupped his palm between her legs. Sweet Jesus.

She rolled over him. His hands slid down her back, lifted the elastic off each cheek of her bum as he took in her two moons of flesh and pushed her down towards him. 'Maybe just a while longer,' she said.

'Now I do have to go,' she said a bit later.

'I really don't know why.'

She ducked his kiss.

'What are you doing tomorrow?'

'I—' Not much, was the answer. She'd made a chicken pie for lunch. Art would be waiting for her now.

'I thought we'd go cycling,' said Frank.

Mimi hesitated. 'I don't really cycle. I'm rubbish. I grow extra limbs and my knees knock the handles.'

He laughed. 'You can't grow up in London and not know how to cycle.'

'It's a long story.'

'Growing up in London?

'Why I don't cycle.'

'How long can a story about cycling be? Though I'd like to hear more about the growing up part. About Naomi Wallis as a young girl.' She leaned over and fiddled with the strap on her sandal, struggling to get the prong of the buckle through the hole. 'Sometimes it feels as if I don't know who you actually are,' said Frank. 'Like you're holding out on me.'

'I have to hold out on you occasionally, or I'd never get out of this bed.' She tried to laugh.

'Okay. Whatever. C'mon! Live a little. Cycling – it'll be fun. Just Battersea Park.'

She couldn't come up with a reason why not quite quickly enough.

'I'll meet you there round eleven,' he said, taking her silence for agreement and bouncing off the bed. He was immediately cheered, like a puppy who sensed he was going for a walk. 'What's funny?' he asked when she smiled.

'You're so easy to please,' she said. Now her shoe felt too tight.

'It's true – you please me very easily. And,' he said, 'when you lean over like that, it pleases me enormously: I can see your tits.'

Back in her bedroom, her dress unzipped at the back, Mimi picked up her phone to text Frank.

'Mimi?' Art's voice rang like a hard bell as he came upstairs.

88

'Mimi?' He walked in without knocking. 'What are you doing?' he asked.

'Nothing. I was about to shower. Out.' She shooed him with her hand.

'No need to snap. You were not about to shower. Who were you texting?' Art reached for her phone.

'Art!' She swung her hand behind her back more aggressively than she intended. 'Frank. Okay?'

'You have *just* seen him. Why do you need to communicate with him ten minutes later?'

'It's none—' She took a step towards her brother to edge him out the door. She felt a violence under her diaphragm that made her reach for the door handle and hold it tight. 'Look,' she said, softening her voice, 'let me shower, okay?'

'All right,' he said, but he paused before he turned, as though she looked different. 'Since you missed it, I have recorded *The Weakest Link* semi-final to watch after dinner.'

Mimi sat down heavily on her bed, her phone still in her hand.

Realized I don't have a bike, she messaged Frank. **Might have to take a rain check.** It was true. Her childhood bicycle leaned against the back of the shed with its perishing plastic tassels, leaves collecting against its tyres – useless. She would just stay at home, with Art. Again.

Sorry, she wrote.

You don't need a bike dummy. Meet at bike station corner Battersea Park. F.

And before she could answer – **Wear trainers,** he wrote.

Art stacked the dishwasher as though the dirty crockery needed disciplining into its slots. He upended the colander into the front rack and pushed the bottom tray in so hard the plates smacked against the backboard.

'Those cycle paths can be treacherous with frost,' he said.

'It will have warmed up by eleven.'

'You seem determined to go,' said her brother.

'It's cycling in the park, for god's sake, not swimming the Channel.' She opened the newspaper lying on the kitchen table: 'Families in Benefits Trap', she read. She stuffed it into the bin and took a deep breath.

'Would you like to come?'

'No thank you.'

'The three of us could go,' she said. 'You'll like him.'

'It is not appropriate for me to meet every man you see more than once, Mimi. You are the one looking for love.'

'Art.'

'As it happens, I am too busy.'

Thank God, she thought.

'And anyway,' said Art, 'I do not have a bike. For that matter, neither do you.'

'It's those hire bikes,' she said. 'Look, I *am* going cycling. But Art . . .' He looked at her, and his face was that of a young boy, his fear transparent.

Rey, who had quickly understood just how hurt Art was when the two of them had conspired to lie to him, had warned her. *Keep him close*. Saliva clagged in Mimi's mouth. 'You know I'll never leave you, right?'

She wasn't sure why she'd said this out loud, but Art's face – the relief on it, all his lines softened – his shoulders relaxed. 'I promise,' she said.

'Wear a helmet,' said Art, and hardly spoke for the rest of the evening.

I'd like to hear it, Frank texted later that night. The long story. About cycling, growing up in London.

Your whole long story, he added.

Doesn't show me in a very good light.

Might be time I found out what that means. X

His sister seemed stuck on man number three. It was that, more than her chequered history on a saddle, that disturbed Art.

Nevertheless, Mimi on a bike was not a good idea.

In 1989, the Kingsbridge Community Hall had been raising money for swings. Beatrice, a stout girl from Art's class, arrived at their door with a jar of coloured jellybeans. How many were there? One pound per guess. Their father said they could each have a go – a bike was the prize.

'I grew up near a park. I know how important swings are,' grunted Walter, not usually given to justifying his actions.

'I do not go on swings,' said Art.

'They're not *for* you,' said his sister.

The jellybean jar had a screw-lid top and was fat enough that you needed to hold it with both hands. Art inspected its underside. He enjoyed the effects of refraction on the coloured sweets.

Beatrice leaned on the door frame. She was keeping the beans. 'Mr Chesterton said I could,' she said, tugging her shirt down on each side. 'He donated the bike. A girl's or a boy's, depending.'

'Two hundred and eighty-eight,' guessed Mimi. Beatrice held her paper up against the door frame to fill in Mimi's name.

Art shook his head at Mimi's ill-judged guess and turned the jar. 'There is an equation for this, you know.'

'Oh, hurry up!' said Mimi.

'Rats,' said Beatrice, 'my biro's conked out.'

'I'll get another from the kitchen.'

Art followed Mimi inside.

'You did not account for the unfilled voids left by the jellybeans' irregular shape,' he told his sister. 'Please tell Beatrice – my number is two hundred and sixteen.'

'Two hundred and s-s-sixteen?'

'Yes,' said Art, and poured himself some milk from the fridge.

'Keep the biro!' he heard Mimi call as Beatrice left.

When Donald Chesterton arrived at their door with a new bike for Mimi, he pressed the buzzer so hard Hector barked as though it was an emergency. 'Well done, clever girl!' he said, beaming. 'Almost bang on.' The upright handles framed his flushed cheeks while Hector licked his shoes. Mimi looked pale and left Christine holding the handlebars. Mr Chesterton handed over a copy of the local paper to Art and said goodbye.

'Not possible,' said Art.

'What's not possible?' asked Christine.

Mimi wrenched the bike from Christine's hands and rang the bell. She pushed it along the passage and its plastic handle left a mark on the wall. Its tyres were still clean. She rang the bell again.

'Not inside,' said Christine.

'Not possible,' said Art.

'I'm going to ride my n-n-new, my n-n-new bike,' said Mimi, and she steered her shiny new bike back down the passage and out the front door.

Mimi did not have a helmet on, and his mother did not tell her to be careful in the road.

Art stepped outside. 'Mimi!' he called, wanting to warn her. 'Wear a helmet! You are on a *road*.' With one foot on a pedal, Mimi looked round.

'It's a dead end, Dodo.' She flicked her plait down her back.

'Half of the people who die on bikes are not wearing helmets!'

She sped off.

'Eighty-eight percent of accidents happen near home,' whispered Art to himself, closing the door on his heedless sister.

Mimi knew how to ride, of course she did, but fluid bubbled in Art's tummy. He went to her bedroom upstairs to watch – the bike spun her along the road, the tassels flapping over her small hands. She was going too fast.

She turned around at the cul-de-sac.

'Congratulations to Mimi Brotherton,' the local paper said, 'Winner of "Guess the Jellybeans" and a lovely new bike! 2 shy of 218, the actual number.' Art rolled it up and put it in the wastepaper basket. He did not care that Mimi had won the bike, but wished she had asked, instead of just stealing his number.

He had started downstairs when he heard the bell ring, the commotion outside. His mother left the door open onto the street as she ran out. Art followed. He watched his mother run towards his sister, who lay at a funny angle next to her bike. She was already coming round as he got closer, but he could see that her face would be scarred; her lip looked like red jelly. But as he stood there, he felt most sorry that Mimi did not get to see just how fast their mother ran, as she raced towards her daughter lying in the road.

When their parents cleared the shed before they died, they moved the child's bike that Mimi had won – the one that had broken her ankle, that had torn her knee, that had split her mouth – against the back wall, where it stayed. Spokes rusting, hibiscus decals peeling off the crossbar.

In the morning, Mimi walked towards the park alongside the Thames. The river had a pewter sheen under a clear pale day, the odd swell from the boats. She was grateful for the sun on her back. Frank was waiting for her at the bike station, his hand above his eyes like a visor as she walked towards him.

She registered how tall he was, how straight his shoulders. He smiled when he was sure it was her, his eyes transforming his otherwise ordinary face. Today they matched the river, lit with a layer of sky.

When he kissed her hello, he was already faintly sweaty.

'You came.'

'Of course,' she said.

He had the bike codes ready. He punched in their numbers, heaved the bikes out of the stand, adjusted the heights and then rubbed the overnight dew off her seat with the bottom of his shirt. 'These bikes are fantastic,' he said, 'though it makes me laugh, thinking about the trucks that have to scoot around all night restocking the popular places, like parents tidying the toys once the children have gone to bed. They're less eco-friendly than we think.'

Mimi knew about these trucks. Working out the night-time routes was a *p versus Np* problem. Art called the trucks 'dedicated repositioning vehicles.'

'You're so right – especially when we add in the petrol my ambulance might need,' she said.

Frank held her bike steady as she climbed on.

'Ready?'

'To humiliate myself? Yes.'

'Follow me.'

They wheeled around, following paths, Frank pointing things out and her, unsteady, trying to see. After a while, they stopped for a drink at a cafe, leaving the bikes parked up against a wall close by. She fanned her cheeks as they walked to a table. 'You're flushed,' he whispered.

She fingered the initials on his wallet.

'F. T. T. Frank Taylor. What's the middle T for?'

'Timothy. My dad. *Father* Timothy.'

'Hmm. My father was practically an atheist,' she said. 'Though he used to say that maths proved the existence of God.' Not the wisest line of conversation. It was getting harder and harder.

'*God made numbers, all else is the work of man* and all that?' Frank smiled. 'Dad left the Church when he married my mother. She was an American divorcee.'

'You're Catholic?'

'No, he just couldn't reconcile divorce and God. Left the Church for love.'

'Big decision.'

'Worth it. He adored my mother.' He looked at her and smiled again. He'd been smiling all morning – every time he'd turned around to see her frantically pedalling – as though everything was amusing.

'What's so funny?'

'Where do I start? I'd never contacted a woman I've only met for five minutes at a mathematics awards ceremony before – one who didn't really have to be there, by the sounds of it. And it's as though I went to the supermarket for the first time to find a full trolley parked at the till with my shopping list already packed. What are the probabilities?'

It felt surprisingly good to be compared to a shopping trolley.

'Seriously, though. Why aren't you shacked up with some lucky guy? And why,' he said, and suddenly he really wasn't smiling any more, 'why, when it comes to going home, to yours, or staying the night, do you freeze over? Why is it that sometimes we're having a perfectly good time and you suddenly look at your watch and it's as though you've been electrocuted?'

She took a sip of her drink, and bit on her straw.

'Are you sure you're not married?' he asked, his tone light. But she could tell, he was really asking. He looked right into her eyes, as if to see if she was lying.

'I'd know if I was married.' Her voice squeaked over the razor in her throat.

'It would make sense. Mimi.' He paused. 'Naomi.'

'What makes you call me Naomi right now?'

Frank took a moment to answer. He looked at his lap, as if deciding something first. 'Well, for starters, you have zero online footprint, Mimi Wallis, or Naomi Wallis. It's . . . unusual.'

She drew a line with her finger through the condensation on her glass.

'Your surname's not Wallis, is it?' A light gust dislodged blossom petals from the tree behind Frank. Improbable pink flakes settled on the ground.

Mimi shook her head.

It was time.

'It happened to be the name of the mathematician whose portrait was behind your head when I met you.'

'Is this the story? The long story?'

'That was about cycling. And this,' said Mimi, touching the scar on her face. 'But yes, it's the long story too.'

'I've got all day.' He gently rubbed her scar, the thin misshapen line above her lip, as though it was something precious. Then he took her hand.

Mimi squeezed down the feeling that she was about to cry.

'Tell me,' said Frank. 'It'll be okay. In fact, I promise you – it'll be better than okay.'

She took back her hand and dug her nails deep into her thigh.

'My surname is Brotherton,' she said. 'Let me tell you about my parents. And my brother.' Part of her was amazed that the sky didn't fall in. 'You may have heard of him. And them.' She sighed. 'And I might need something stronger than homemade lemonade.'

Frank was kinder than she'd ever dared hope he would be. 'You don't seem that shocked,' she said, as she kept saying sorry, for lying, for not trusting him more. As free as the initial lie made her feel, discharging it felt tenfold good. To be honest with Frank, to have shared her past, to be totally herself, and – despite her fears – all consequence free.

17

INTERSECTION

After supper that night, Art re-organized the canned goods by expiry date.

Mimi wiped round the sink. 'He thought I was married, you know – that I was hiding a husband,' she said.

It annoyed Art that when Mimi said *he*, she was automatically referring to Frank, as though he was exclusively entitled to a universal pronoun.

'That is ridiculous.'

'Not really.' Mimi pulled the rubbish out of the kitchen bin. 'Take this outside, will you, and this for the bottle bank?' She knotted the top of the bags. 'Your lack of curiosity about him surprises me. After all your help with that website.'

'It is not that I am incurious,' said Art, one hand on the doorknob. The recycling bag was heavy. Rey had been round – he had decided to forgive her for propping up Mimi's lies – and there were three wine bottles in there. Three! 'I admit to a desire to see what he is like, if he measures up to the variables we have put in place on Matrix. After all, that should still be your benchmark. Certainly, it would be interesting to run haphazard meeting data alongside those of the algorithm and compare the two. Do you know, that in breeding programmes for the white colobus monkey – I was reading an article just the other day, Belfast Zoo, I think it was, about their stud programme – they employ very similar—'

'Art!'

'Yes, all right. Anyway, this is rather heavy.'

When he walked back inside, she was still standing there. 'I've made a decision,' she said, in an uncommonly definite way. 'We're going to have supper – you and me, Frank and Rey.'

Art bit the inside of his cheek.

'It's time. And he really wants to meet you.'

'Very well.' There was something about her that brooked no argument. 'I am prepared to do that,' he said. 'But do not book somewhere you have read about in that free newspaper you pick up on the Tube. Somewhere with spicy food unrelated to its advertised nationality, loud music and a wooden floor – I could do without the sonic assault and I need to hear what he has to say.'

'You're not interviewing him, right? You're getting to know him.'

'Not mutually exclusive.'

'I'll book somewhere that has carpet,' she said.

'That would be perfect.'

'I was joking, you goose. Nowhere fun has carpets.'

'Does it have to be fun?'

Art had always struggled with the men in her life. There was no reason Frank would be any different. Even Matthew, the unthreatening son of the chemist, had unsettled her brother.

And it hadn't helped that Art had eventually found out about Jason Findlay.

Mimi's A-level results were good. But instead of the university she'd imagined, in a new city far away from her parents

– who'd been as uniquely embarrassing to her as any other teenager's – surrounded by brilliant people who weren't her brother, where she'd wear glasses and read something clever-sounding, like biomedical science, or zoology, or even cleverer, biochemistry, which had the small hurdle of having actual chemistry in it, Mimi stayed in London to be near Art. Because their parents were dead.

Queen Mary University. Biology. It started off okay. She felt oddly in control, if a little detached. As if life was *fine*.

The course was broad, covering genetics to large African mammals, neuroscience to fungi. She took copious notes, wrote her headings in capitals. But as soon as the students scraped back their chairs, the reality of what had happened opened up a chasm inside her. As everyone else drifted off down the hall, clutching their bags, she'd be left, standing, under large metal windows, looking at the sky. She was flotsam, her grief so much bigger than her, like a sea; she could drown in a four-walled classroom. Even her stutter retreated in shock. Losing her parents? For being able to say *suitcase* and *sorry*? It wasn't a trade she'd ever have made. She wandered around campus, accepting invitations to clubs or parties and hardly registering the difference, not minding or even noticing whose company she kept.

'Those boys are the same crowd who traded ecstasy at school,' Art warned her one day when a boy walked her home. 'Stay away.'

Mimi wasn't crazy about Jason Findlay. She just didn't give a damn. Nevertheless, a small pulse of alarm had gone off – that she shouldn't ignore her brother. Art's lifetime of warnings: – her parents, the bike. She touched her lip.

Jason Findlay and his friends were the kind of boys who'd teased her about her stutter at school. But that night they showered her with attention. With all their leering masculine heat, they'd seemed lusty and appealing, and why not? She knocked back her drinks, her hands on her hips, thumbs forward, aware how her hair wisped at her neck, how it worked when she dropped her chin and looked at them all through her lashes, thrilled at how eloquent she'd suddenly become. The pill was so small, so yellow, so cute, imprinted with a bunny.

The unfamiliar combination of Bacardi Breezer and navy liquid eyeliner emboldened her, even as her brother's admonitions rang in her ears. She snatched the bunny pill out of Jason's hand and looked him in the eye. She kept his gaze as she opened her mouth and put it on her tongue. Then she danced up close. In the loo with the other girls, she saw her eyes sparkle, her lips deeply red. She chugged a litre of water before going back to the music, the dancing, and Jason.

It wasn't long before she found herself holding his hand as he led her through a door that was helpfully marked EXIT – that seemed funny at the time – and standing in an unlit car park behind the club with her back pressed into the passenger door handle of a Toyota Corolla, her knickers stretched between her knees and Jason's penis grating at her insides like hot stone while he slobbered into her neck and grunted. Semen dribbled down her thighs as they walked back into the club, Jason two steps in front of her, smoking. She watched the tip of Jason's cigarette glow and subside, the smoke twist and then pirouette away. Chaos in Nature, her father had called it. Back inside, Jason pushed up against her, then passed out on a leatherette bench with his mouth open. The last thing she remembered was the scrape of the concrete on her knees and her stomach lurching, and a girl she could hardly remember grabbing the back of her dress.

Art came to collect her from A&E – folded her spaghetti

legs into the car, so he told her, and cleaned her vomit-strewn dress. He watched her for days. But he didn't know half of it. The Jason Findlay half. He didn't say, *I told you so*.

Mimi was confused and relieved when Jason never spoke to her again.

At first, she told only Rey. 'I could murder that prick,' Rey said.

'He didn't force me,' said Mimi.

'No,' said Rey carefully, 'But he's not an idiot.' She squinted at Mimi's face as if she was checking for marks. 'I take that back,' said her friend. 'He absolutely *is* – a grade A idiot.'

Mimi was grateful to Rey, but her response hadn't made Mimi feel good. *Am I the idiot?* she wondered. She was more grateful that she hadn't got pregnant, and tried not to think about it much. Not *that* much. But months later, after a night of too much wine, when Art had been nagging her about something else, she'd barked at him. And out it came.

She hadn't chosen their parents' deaths, she shouted at her brother, who went pale at her outburst. It was like sex with Jason Findlay. She hadn't wanted that either, but so what?! It got her nowhere. *Nowhere!* Nothing mattered any more.

She watched how he struggled, when he asked her: *Did he hurt you?*

'What are you going to do if I say yes?' she'd said, spitefully, and she could see that she'd wounded him. Killed a light in his eye.

She avoided Jason on campus, if she could. Her stomach did a rollerdip, a mixture of inexplicable longing and shame, whenever she saw him, or when the cloying spice and lavender of Drakkar Noir drifted off another man, another boy.

Soon enough she avoided campus itself. She sat in classes,

the lecturer's voice providing nothing more than a meditative hum from which she sank into reveries she couldn't recall. One day, she looked at her notebook and she'd written nothing there.

As if responding in tandem, Art too fell apart. Mimi would come home and find him staring at the table, unable to work.

She was struggling with her parents' deaths, she explained to Student Advisory, as though she could reduce what she felt into a box that you ticked on a form. Personal issues. Check. *Grief.*

It suited her brother, at least.

In time, when the months had spooled too far along, she wrote to Queen Mary: permanent withdrawal.

The lights of the bridge twinkled ahead, but Mimi was nervous. 'Go easy on him,' she said to Frank, on the way to their dinner with Art. 'He's very protective. Be yourself, you know, but don't talk too much, let him talk. Though he doesn't actually talk that much.'

'Whoa, girl!' Frank said, and took her hand. 'Stop worrying. He will like me, you'll see. I'll make him like me. It's going to be fine.'

18

GAME THEORY

Art would have preferred to stay local, but Mimi had chosen a little Italian across the river, presumably so that everyone was on neutral territory. He and Rey had met up to walk there together. He pressed the pedestrian button to cross the road. 'Relax, Art,' said Rey, 'it's going to be fun.' The street-lights on the Embankment had just come on.

He listened to Rey's chatter, not wanting to think about his trying day. He'd come across colleagues discussing a TED talk about hacking and security and his stomach had gurgled. It may have been the liquorice-smelling teabag that one of the mathematicians was plinking in and out her mug, but he suspected it was more that he had not yet made headway with his own security concerns. If anything, things were worse.

After work, he returned to his long-neglected letter. He would have preferred to stay at home and finish it. It was in his pocket now.

DRAFT
Department of Mathematics
King's College London
The Strand
WC2 London

Dear Professor Gutteridge
I am concerned that my work on complexity
theory, specifically p versus Np, has been the subject
of uninvited attention. I have not thus far shared my
efforts – for obvious reasons. The significant
consequences of someone proving the p versus Np
question are undeniable, and would be ~~devastating~~
less than benign in the wrong hands. Security
remains ~~PARAMOUNT~~ paramount.

He had struggled for the right words. *Escalation*, he tried,
Surge? *Increase*? He had clicked on Thesaurus and decided
on *Spike.*

There has been another spike in online traffic in
signifiers that pertain to my work. This may suggest a
security breach – a leak, or hack. Theft?
The recent approaches from Number 10 and MI5
suggest further speculation. Given the security
considerations involved; military, financial, health and
*data, etc., I trust that this matter will remain **highly***
confidential.

He was not a fan of bold font, but in this instance, it achieved
the appropriate tone.

I await your speedy response.
Sincerely
Professor A. N. Brotherton

He and Rey had crossed the road. 'Apologies, Rey, what was that?' he asked.

'I said that it's going to be fun. Come, there they are.'

Frank practically pumped blood the wrong way back through his ventricles with his handshake. 'Hello!' he said. He was a whole head taller than Art. Disconcerting. 'At last!'

Art had thought about this moment and the need to balance veracity with politeness. 'Frank.' He nodded, and tried to smile.

The proprietor made a fuss as if they were all lifelong friends. You never did know with Rey; she was friends with everybody.

Frank looked healthy and clean enough, though his clothes were mystifyingly irregular – everything seemed to hang at an angle. Even his hips, as he walked towards their table, seemed articulated like a puppet's.

But he was chatty, had a good line in maths jokes that Art had not heard before and was also a fan of *The Big Bang Theory* on TV. He agreed that the characters were a little linear and neurotic and spent too much time reading comics. He was attentive to Mimi, but not so much that it got on Art's nerves. Initially, anyway.

Mimi did look happy, he had to admit. She drummed the table lightly at one point, not out of impatience, but as though she had energy to spare.

'I don't know, it all looks delicious,' she said, hugging the enormous menu to her chest. Rey too, seemed to have developed an instant, Velcro-like attachment to Frank. He hoped

106

that she, at least, could maintain her objectivity. It was abundantly clear that Mimi had none.

'I'll order for you,' said Frank. 'It'll be a surprise.' Mimi looked so delighted it hurt, and Art could not think of anything bad to say about it.

'Everyone okay with loads of garlic?' said Frank.

'Art doesn't like it,' said Mimi.

'Do not mind me,' said Art, hoping that she did not blurt out that it made him gassy.

'We'll get two pastas, one with, one without. Easy,' said Frank. Art wondered how easy he found actual mathematics. If he was a true mathematician. He was reluctant to bring up mathematics, but had to broach the subject some time.

'Do you deal with students in your work, Frank?'

Frank was in the middle of ordering a pasta that Art had never tried. He ordered it in an Italian accent; Mimi laughed, and the waiter shouted across the room – 'Rigate for the signore!' Art had to admit to the whole evening being more pleasant than he had anticipated.

'Sorry, Art, what was that? Students?' said Frank.

'Mimi said you used to work at Warwick but are now with the Mathematical Association?'

'Students – sadly not,' said Frank. 'I'd love to. The association's main job is to help standardize best practices for teaching mathematics, but we also organize events like the awards.' He smiled at Mimi. 'I help with grant applications. Though I still do my own research – game theory mainly. And a lot of my time is spent understanding the undercurrents of our world. And, you know, helping people see maths' value in the everyday.'

Art had to suppress a spasm of irritation that Frank called it 'our world'. It did not seem to Art that they occupied much intersecting territory, *at all*. He had a sip of his fizzy water. Italian sparkling water was too carbonated – it tasted as if it had a pH of 3. 'Game theory?' he asked. 'The behavioural economics end or computer science?'

'Both, really.'

'Thank god we've got menus to read to keep us entertained,' said Rey, smiling at Mimi.

'Game theory predicts how humans will behave, en masse,' explained Frank. 'It's economics really. Like – how many people sign up for gym memberships on New Year's Day.'

'Naomi, for one,' said Art. 'People are naive about their own willpower.'

Mimi laughed.

'Exactly,' said Frank. 'You could call me naive, but I'm just optimistic by nature.' Frank passed the basket of grissini round the table, having snapped off half a stick for himself, and put the other half back in the basket. He offered it to Art.

'No thank you,' said Art.

'Most optimistic thing I ever did was taking your number at those awards,' said Frank to his sister. Art thought he noticed Frank reach under the table for her knee. The pasta arrived. The shells looked like the toes of a human baby, but captured the sauce in their little whorls rather well.

'It's so great that you're both mathematicians,' said Rey. 'I mean, what were the chances?'

'Quite high,' said Art, 'given Mimi grew up around maths.'

'A turn of phrase, Art,' said Rey.

Frank looked round. He held up his glass and clinked it with Art's.

'It's great to meet you. *Saluti!*' said Frank. Art sipped his sparkling water and could not quite say why his mouth dried so that he could not speak. Was it the bubbles, he wondered, the pH, or something else? Trying, and – against his nature as it was – failing, to invoke the spirit of optimism that Frank had referred to, about how all of this was going to turn out.

19

SIMULTANEOUS EQUATIONS

'Well?' Mimi asked Art, the second they walked through the door. Frank had kissed his sister and whispered something in her ear, before leaving them both to head home. Now, she did not even wait for Art to divest himself of his jacket before launching into an inquisition. 'What d'you think?'

'He seems nice.'

She hung up her jacket and did not react when it fell straight to the floor. She followed him into the kitchen, like a pamphleteer hounding a passer-by. He washed his hands. 'Could you *be* more non-committal?'

'Mimi, it takes time to get to know a person.'

'I get that, but first impressions?' She suddenly sounded young. 'Did you like him at all?'

'He was extremely friendly, and made an admirable effort tonight considering the different constituencies he was having to address. You, me, Rey. It cannot have been easy.' He turned off the tap. 'Rey certainly seemed taken with him.'

'Yes,' said his sister, 'she did, at least.' Art looked around for a tea towel, his hands were dripping water onto the floor.

'Art, it's important to me. Did you like him?' asked Mimi, again. He felt there was some work to do, to bridge the gap

110

between how much he liked and trusted Frank, and how much his sister wanted him to.

Obviously, Frank was not the ultimate answer to Mimi's quest for love, he was just an interregnum. Many men were still sending her likes on Matrix. But Art had the sense to prevaricate right then. He dried his hands and looked at his sister. 'I liked him, Mimi. Yes,' he said. 'More than I expected to.'

That, at least, was the truth.

Four nights later, with Art out at a Fellows' gathering at the university, Mimi stood in Frank's flat wearing clumpy boots and jeans, straight from work. Frank had just returned from a Maths Education seminar in Glasgow. He was on the sofa, twirling her *Sister in Sound* cap round his finger; Mimi hadn't seen him since the dinner. He'd texted: **Loved that, your brother and Rey are GREAT. Rey's hilarious.**

'Well?' she said. 'Was he what you expected?'

'I guess so,' said Frank. 'I'd seen photos. I thought he'd be the kind of intimidating mathematician that made me give up full-time academia – and he was.' Frank smiled. 'And I mean that as a compliment.' He leaned back with his arms behind his head, his feet on the coffee table; it was a pose she was getting used to. 'Maths is so pure, you know, so perfect. A proof is a proof is a proof, it's an absolute thing. Your brother sees things that way. It's rather beautiful – he's very logical.'

'Yes, a kind of annoying black-and-white clarity.'

Frank took a biscuit out of the top of its sleeve and offered her one. 'Maybe I should have been a scientist,' he said, casting crumbs from the sofa onto the floor with the flat of his hand. 'Science is so different to maths. Scientists have to experiment, come to conclusions according to what actually happens in the world. I love the clarity of maths, but the

111

real world is pretty messy.' He trailed his fingers against the nap of the velour sofa. Mimi sensed he was somewhere she couldn't reach him. 'Yup, real life is messy,' he said, and smoothed the raked pattern he'd made.

'Like your sombrero poem says.'

'Exactly! Oh, thank god I'm not a scientist.' He flung out his arms. 'I wouldn't have met you.'

'Would you really like to be a scientist?' she asked later, as they walked across the green in the softening evening light. 'You do love physics and stuff.'

'I think I'd miss those moments with maths, when you're in the flow, when everything just *fits*. Nothing like it,' he said. He grabbed the rail of a roundabout as they walked past and spun on it halfway before hopping off again. They were on their way to have a drink at a new bar in Brixton, but Frank sat on the swings, and tipped his body back. The light was purpling behind him, the last birds twittered their way into the night. The swing swung.

Frank dug his heels in to stop. 'Any chance you've heard of the Halting Problem?' he asked. 'Turing's Halting Problem?'

Turing, the code-breaker. 'Yes, but I don't understand it,' she said. 'Why?'

'I was trying to come up with a good explanation for it, for a teaching module. It's tricky stuff. Can I try my explanation out on you?'

'Go for it,' she said. He was so enthusiastic. He hopped off the swing to join her on the edge of the roundabout. He *should* be a teacher, she thought.

'Okay.' He tapped his foot on the ground. Then stilled. Their knees were almost touching. It felt as if the world quietened around him. 'Imagine giving a person – or a computer – an instruction.'

'Okay,' said Mimi. She pulled the hairband off her wrist and played with it while he spoke.

'There are certain instructions you could give a computer, that make it impossible to predict when it might stop. Or halt. Hence the Halting Problem.'

'Okaaay.'

'So,' he said, taking the band from her hand. 'Imagine you give a computer a very specific instruction. One that has a finite life. Yes?'

'Like what?'

He twanged the elastic.

'A really simple instruction will do. Like: tell your computer,' he said, looking intently into her face in the dusk, 'tell your computer to print the words: "Mimi is beautiful".'

He said it without blinking, which was more than she could manage from a foot away, the bar of the roundabout pressing into her back. She blinked and swallowed.

'Your computer prints out the words: "Mimi is beautiful". It's followed your instruction, and now its job is done, right? Its only job. So, it halts. It stops.'

'Frank,' said Mimi, smiling, trying to concentrate on the halting bit rather than the Mimi is beautiful bit, and failing.

'But,' said Frank, planting the heels of his hands on his knees, his fingers struck out like stars. 'Say you give a different, *two*-part kind of instruction.' The roundabout moved a bit as he pushed the ground with his foot. He leaned towards her.

'One,' he said, and took a breath. 'One. Print: "I'm falling in love".' She swallowed. 'Two,' he said. '"Go back to One". *That* programme will run in a loop forever. Printing "I'm falling in love" to infinity.'

'It'll never stop,' she said, in a whisper.

'Never.'

113

'Frank—' She didn't know what to say.

'What's harder,' he said, interrupting her – and saving her, because really, she had no words right now – '*very* hard, in fact, is this: Is there a programme that will never stop? But we can't prove it. The only way we can ever know if it will halt is if and when it actually *does*. It runs to infinity. Unless it doesn't.'

Mimi felt as though the world itself had stopped spinning. It was getting dark quickly. Frank was sitting in front of her, and she could feel the cold metal of the roundabout through her jeans. Say something, she thought. She moved towards him.

She climbed into his lap, put her mouth on his.

'I understand what you're saying,' she said, after she'd kissed him. But she couldn't say it. The *falling in love*. 'I know exactly what you mean.'

The truth was, it frightened her. Surely, he knew how she felt.

20

GAME THEORY

Art sat with Frank alongside the Thames at a trestle table with its benches attached. The river swelled against the concrete sides as a barge went by. It was not that hot, but Mimi looked as if she had summer in her veins.

As she climbed over the awkward benches, Frank put his hand out to steady her. It was a small thing, but Art felt that he was watching them from the periphery of a bubble that included just the two of them.

'What a day,' said Mimi. The clouds were high and racing. Early lime leaves marbled the treeline and a saxophone player belted something swinging outside a bright new Southbank cafe.

'I've got a surprise,' said Frank.

Art put down his tea. He hated surprises.

Frank waved a set of tickets, like a magician – 'Ta da! For your birthday, Art.'

'Oh, you.' His sister seemed to swoon. 'Cricket. Art's favourite thing.'

Art had not expected Mimi to fall in love so quickly, which – if television was anything to go by – was happening in front of his eyes.

* * *

Art's cricket cushion sat on the kitchen table with his wide-brimmed Kookaburra hat, along with his small cooler-box with sunblock in the front pouch, his score book, pens, pencils and rubber, his binoculars and the day's *Guardian*.

'I do not want to be late,' said Art.

'Just behave, Art, please. Frank bought the tickets for your birthday. It's a treat.'

'Exactly. We owe it to him to make the most of his generosity.'

But it felt like a mistake from the moment Frank arrived.

'What is *that*?' said Art, looking aghast at Frank's enormous picnic basket, and his embroidered sombrero.

'Lunch.' Frank beamed. Mimi felt a ripple underneath her ribs.

'I can see by Mimi's face she does not want me to say anything, Frank, but you cannot take that thing.'

'Why not?' said Frank. 'Apparently there are picnic spots around the ground. That's why we're going so early, right, to guarantee a place?' He looked at his watch as if to confirm that they were indeed setting off at 9 a.m. for an 11 o'clock game that was around the corner.

'That is Lord's,' said Art. 'Not the Oval.'

'You eat on your lap,' said Mimi. 'The seating is tight.' She looked at Frank's kit – a wicker basket with chunky leather handles that stuck out at the sides like ears. It was rather large.

'Fine,' said Frank. 'We'll leave it behind.' He put the basket down a little too hard. It crunched in a way that triggered a shuffle through the Foley index in her brain – crunch, chomp – crackers, celery.

'Good idea,' said Art. Mimi stood in the middle of the kitchen, her left hand on Frank's basket, the other wanting to slap her brother flat across his face.

116

'Don't ruin this, Art,' she said under her breath, as Art hoisted his specially adapted shoulder-strap cooler-box onto his back.

'And that *hat*,' said Art.

Her brother took especially long fussing over the blinds – lowering them so that the kitchen wouldn't be too hot when they returned – and then declared that they must not waste time. They left the house to catch the bus at the end of the road with Frank less chatty than usual.

They got off near Vauxhall and made their way to the ground. 'Relax,' said Frank, rubbing her between her shoulder blades, 'this is supposed to be fun.'

'It's amazing,' she said.

They spent a lot of the day standing up and down again between overs, letting men slopping buckets of beer go past, belly to belly, standing on their toes, joking about balancing their drinks on the rim of Frank's sombrero. Frank delighted in the concept of swing, when the seam of the ball weighs in to change its trajectory. Mimi would never have sought another mathematician in her life, but here he was, and she felt herself leaning into his conversation about critical speeds and equations, and spin. The visitors' captain raced to a century before lunch.

'He's a cumbersome player,' said Frank when they returned to their seats after wandering around.

'He is not known for technical beauty,' said Art. 'But if you had to build an algorithm to predict his centuries, you would have to include big-match temperament.'

'Have you tried?' asked Frank.

Here we go, thought Mimi, wishing for a wicket to interrupt the inevitable monologue.

'There are so many variables,' said Art. Cricket and statistics were already intertwined. The weather, the captaincy;

117

even groundsmen were key. 'Of course, if p equalled Np, it would be possible to predict even the most complicated results. However.' He paused, his face tweaked with concern. 'Inappropriate constituencies would profit; there has already been considerable trouble with illegal betting.'

When Mimi had run into Ernest a month ago at Art's office, he'd mentioned Art was getting touchy about security again. Was Frank ready for a dive into Art's paranoia about his research?

Apparently. They spent the afternoon referring to Art's scorebook, talking about trajectories, rotation of the ball, the empirical value of a spin bowler versus fast. Mimi foresaw the rest of the Test – a bottle of wine for her at home, the men comparing notebooks and tiny numbers.

'I'd like to buy a scorebook at tea,' said Frank, reading her mind.

'I can lend you a pencil,' said Art.

I can lend you a pencil.

Like the captain and his big-match temperament, an algorithm for Art and his relationships would have to include how he handled his personal possessions. Lending a pencil – the correlation with his heart was touchingly high.

I can lend you a pencil felt like a beginning – a small seed of something separate from Mimi. It almost seemed too much to ask, but maybe, just maybe, it was possible that Frank might become a friend for Art.

A warning launched itself like a cuckoo clock in her brain, on the hour: don't ask for too much.

21

ENVY FREE

She didn't have to wait long for Frank and Art to make plans without her.

In August, as the excitement of the London Olympics was coming to an end, Art extended an invitation to Frank, to come and watch the third Test with him, at home. Art had just finished drying the dishes and Mimi saw how he pulled at each end of the dishcloth in front of him as he spoke, like a small child tugging at his uniform on stage. 'The afternoon sun casts a glare onto the television set through the sliding doors,' said Art, 'just after the tea break. But—'

'Come to mine,' suggested Frank.

'All right,' said Art. The dishcloth relaxed in his fist.

'Am I invited?' said Mimi.

The day of the match, Mimi dropped Art off at Frank's, before going to run errands. 'Hello, Frank,' said Art as he walked in, taking in his surroundings.

Frank's apartment was compact, light and airy. A bamboo tree stood in one corner; a high, wide window overlooked the green across the road. The kitchen had a hatch through to the TV and sofa. 'Did you lay the parquet floor yourself?'

asked Art. 'It looks as if it was done with the block. Parquet laid transversely has that optical effect. Very useful for such a narrow room.'

Mimi had given him strict instructions. 'Compliment Frank,' she said. 'Your opinion's important to him.'

'It is a pity that these panel-built post-war urban developments are doomed,' Art said, feeling pleased with his pertinent observations on Frank's abode. 'Where is the loo?'

'First door on the left,' said Frank.

Frank was not tidy. The new loo roll was perched on an empty cartridge that he hadn't bothered to discard, bank statements lay on top of his book collection. Books in the lavatory were a cultural contagion that Art had never understood; surely it was a place to think, not read. Art did read Frank's bank statements, though. Apart from some rather large payments to an R. Silver which gave Art pause – noteworthy for both their amount and memorable name, which conjured an image of a person dipped in precious metal – Frank appeared to keep life simple. Art felt bad snooping, but it was important background research. Next to the loo was an old hockey stick and ball. He banished the image of Frank twiddling a hockey ball in here. Behind the door a framed poem by Wallace Stevens hung crooked on the wall. He had heard Frank refer to it.

Frank did seem to have rather an *ir*rational fondness for sombreros. After considerably longer than he would normally spend in a guest toilet, Art reappeared and commented on the poem. 'You always quote "Rationalists *should* wear sombreros", Frank,' said Art. 'But the actual poem says *would,* not *should.*'

'It should be *should.*'

'You cannot go round changing a famous poem.'

'I don't really "go round", Art, but anyway – mathematicians need sombreros!' Frank waltzed over to his sombrero, which hung on the bookshelf. 'Here!' he said, and whistled it over to Art. Surprised, Art caught it with one hand.

It was almost as if Frank was his friend too.

They settled in to watch the cricket. 'Your field came up this week at work,' said Frank after a while, quite casually.

'Field?' said Art, half turning towards Frank, but keeping his eye on the field on TV.

'*p versus Np.*'

Art stiffened.

'Someone's looking into the overlap between game theory economic decisions and envy-free cake cutting, an *Np* problem, right?'

'Right,' said Art, 'so really a game theory mathematician?' He felt his shoulders relax again. Art understood that hundreds of mathematicians were working on the *Np* problem, but he always imagined himself to be the only one taking it seriously. It was his way of coping with the crippling tension of dedicating his life to something while knowing that someone might beat him to it.

'Actually,' said Frank, 'I would love you to take a look at the proposal. You would understand if this guy's theory has legs. I need some insight into *Np*. There's someone else at the association who'd be fine, but it'd be good for me to take it to decision stage myself.'

'Are you allowed to share other people's grant proposals?' asked Art. 'With external mathematicians?'

'Well, I know I can trust you,' said Frank. 'I wouldn't do it otherwise. I guess I also thought it might be interesting for you.'

'It would not be appropriate,' said Art. 'I am surprised the association does not keep you on red alert about such conflicts; I would have expected part of their remit to be

121

making sure mathematicians' intellectual property is scrupulously guarded.' He sensed his voice tighten; internally, his organs almost rearranged themselves. He felt *very* strongly about this. 'If you would permit me an observation, Frank, I would recommend that you be a bit more careful.'

'How so?' said Frank, shifting a little further away from Art, but also facing more towards him. A confusing pair of moves.

'Having clear boundaries about the world of mathematics, for a start,' said Art. 'You are too slapdash. As a more general example, beyond mathematics – I noticed when I went to the loo, that you even leave your bank statements lying around. It is not advisable.'

'If you think so,' said Frank. He returned to his original position and seemed to take the constructive criticism in the right spirit. A wicket had fallen. 'Okay!' Frank clapped his hands. 'So, who's this now, this new batsman?'

Mimi balanced a carrot cake on her knee with one hand, and let herself into Frank's with her new key in the other.

'Hello, you two,' she said as she walked in, holding the cake aloft. Art turned and smiled.

'Speaking of envy-free cake cutting . . .' said Frank, giving her a kiss. 'Thanks!' He put the cake in the kitchen and bounced back onto the sofa next to Art.

'What's envy-free cake cutting?' she asked, watching the two of them, feeling as if her insides were lined with warm honey. 'Sounds good.'

'It's a theory about how to divide a cake between two or more people so that no one envies anyone else's piece,' said Frank, over his shoulder. 'The number of ways to divvy up the cake is infinite.'

She unwrapped the carrot cake with its cream cheese icing. 'Surely for two people you just cut a cake in half?'

'Actually, no.' Frank turned so that he was fully facing her. His T-shirt rode up. He held his hands in the shape of a cake.

'If you cut your half yourself, you may not cut a perfect half. But if one person cuts, and the other chooses –' he sliced the imaginary cake with the side of his palm – 'it feels fair.'

She loved how he loved it when maths was that simple. When he explained to her with things like cake and icing. She wanted to reach through the hatch and just grab, all of him.

Art was facing the TV. She took a swipe of cream cheese off the carrot cake and slowly licked her tongue down her finger for Frank.

He came round to the kitchen, rested his chin on her shoulder and held her from behind. Her body fitted into the hollow of his body as if they were carved from a single tree.

22

VENN DIAGRAM

Six weeks later, weary from lectures, Art pushed the front gate open. Even from the front door, he could hear that the radio was on, and he was glad Mimi was home. He wanted to tell her how he had helped Frank with the paper on game theory that Frank had posted on ArXiv. But also that, when he had browsed the usual maths community message boards earlier that day, the online babble about a possible proof for *p versus Np* had rattled him. He needed to talk to his sister. A headache threatened.

On second thoughts, he did not want Mimi telling Frank. There was still a lot they did not know about him. And she might tell Art he was being ridiculous, paranoid even, when really, she had no idea. He was genuinely glad to see how happy Mimi's work with Rey made her, but she struggled to finish the crossword with him before getting distracted, let alone relate to his thirty-year dedication to an intransigent maths problem that no one understood.

He was still the right side of forty. But he already had longitudinal ridges in his nails, he saw, holding his key. He needed to solve this thing soon.

Aged seven, and bored at the back of the after-school extension class, Art had sat up when the maths teacher mentioned a set of complicated, important problems for which *no solutions existed*. He had felt an unfamiliar and not altogether unpleasant sensation run down his spine. What if someone did find solutions to those problems, he wondered? His calves dangled against the stainless-steel legs of the plywood chair. Chalk dust clambered in the air around the blackboard and the Highveld sun threw an angled shadow off the Science Block. Heat rose from the tar. The world quivered with mathematic potential.

Art needed to speak to his father. 'What are the super-complicated maths problems she was talking about, Dad?' he asked that evening, as soon his father came in from his walk on the *koppie*.

Walter wiped sweat off his forehead. 'Nondeterministic polynomials,' he said. *p versus Np*. Solving it would change the world.

Walter placed two kitchen chairs outside, a couple of feet apart on the grass. 'Imagine maths problems are like high-jump bars,' he said. He tied kitchen string between the chairs at seat level. 'Your average school kid can clear this basic height, right?' Art watched as his father waved his hand under the string. 'This jump, this space here – is the set of easy problems called *P*. Let's call them 'easy *Peasy*.'

It was obvious if a person *had* made it over the easy-peasy bar. The bar was still there.

'Now, *Np* is a different level altogether. A high jump so high, or a maths problem so hard, that even most high jumpers can't do it.' Walter tied another piece of string from the top of one chair's upright to the other. It was as high as Art's neck. 'Now imagine. Just occasionally, a high jumper goes over. If he clears it, it's obvious to everyone – the bar is still in place, right?' His dad smiled. 'Problem is, he isn't sure *how*.' Art could imagine his dad sailing over a really lofty bar, his strong calves powering him far above the impossible rail.

'So, there seems to be a way over, a *solution* for this very complicated maths problem, this very high bar, and you can easily check that the guy's gone over, right? But there isn't a fool-proof *technique* yet.' Walter touched the taut string of Np. 'An algorithm is another word for technique. Like a recipe, for Mum's cakes – which we wouldn't want made by trial and error, would we, Sport?' He ruffled Art's hair.

Art shook his head and repaired his parting.

'Now, what if someone could work out a fool-proof technique for how to jump a very high bar, or solve a set of very difficult maths problems?' his dad asked. 'Can you see that the technique would work for *all* the levels *below* the bar too?' p and Np would collapse into the same group: jumpable, *and* easy to check. p *would equal Np*.

Art *could* see. 'If you have a technique to jump the high bar, you can jump everything underneath it?'

'You've got it!' His father high-fived him, his large palm stinging Art's hand.

As Art opened the front door at Muriel Grove, he remembered the frisson of that day. And something else his maths teacher had said: that the world's security codes and passwords were only safe because *no one knew the answer*. That if p *versus Np* was ever solved, all security systems in the world would be vulnerable, overnight.

'Is that true, Dad?' he had asked.

Holding a kitchen chair in each arm, his father had looked across the garden, elevated on the ridge. A flock of sacred ibis flew in a V shape away from the gold mines to roost near the zoo. 'It is, Sport. It is. God forbid the wrong person ever figures it out.'

'Mimi?' Art called. The radio was loud. He hung up his coat. 'Mimi?'

'It's only me,' said Rey. A jumble of Foley equipment clogged up the surfaces in the kitchen – a large plastic container and boots on the table, a pyramid of waterproof fabric heaped next to the sink.

'Where is Mimi?'

'She popped out with Frank.'

'I see,' he said. 'Please move the Wellington boots.' He recognized that he was displacing his irritation at the news that Mimi was out, *again*, towards the boots. And the too-loud music, which he snuffed out with a twist of the dial.

Rey squinted at him and put the boots on the floor.

'You okay?' she said.

'I am fine.'

Rey flopped onto the kitchen chair. 'Let's discuss Mimi's birthday,' she said. 'What are you doing?' The issue had already caused him considerable anxiety. Art had never not shared Mimi's birthday with her, not since the day she was born. Frank had suggested a weekend away – just him and Mimi. Mercifully, they had decided not to go, but it put Art on notice. Things were changing faster than he liked.

'It falls on a Monday,' he told Rey. 'I will be at the university.'

'I mean her present, you *olodo*. D'you need any help?'

As it happened, after all his worry, he was particularly pleased with his idea this year. 'Actually, I do not, but thank you, Rey.'

Mimi had noticed a pretty string of beads – amber ceramic, marbled with orange, an exotic amalgam of colours on a

127

fine leather cord. She'd paused at the store window on the way home from dinner. 'I memorized the name of the shop. I am going tomorrow to set them aside.'

Rey looked odd. 'Last week?' she asked. 'After supper at the bistro?' Her hand drifted up to her neck.

'Yes?' said Art.

'You were with Frank,' Rey checked. 'Gail's Gifts? Near the bicycle shop?'

'Yes,' said Art. '*What?*'

'Oh, Sweetie,' said Rey. She sounded so – what? Disappointed? At first, he thought she was going to say Mimi would not like them, and he knew she was wrong. Then, before Rey actually said it, he realized her expression meant something else entirely.

'Frank's bought them already. He's bought her those beads.'

The very next day, in his lunch hour, Art went to Liberty, Mimi's favourite store. He found a scarf for her birthday. It was a tessellated pattern in blue, green and cream. Pretty enough.

And if she wore it with those beads, it would cover them right up.

Art's mood had blackened, and Mimi wasn't sure why.

A few weeks after her birthday, Frank said he had something to give them both. **All good**, he texted. **It's something I've been meaning to do for a while. See you at 7.**

Had Frank remembered Art hated surprises? Frank told Mimi she worried too much. Let happiness unfold, he urged her. While pouring happiness into her life.

'Hi!' said Frank, transforming the ordinary front door of their ordinary house. 'I have something for you guys. Art's here, right?' He tapped his bag and came inside.

Art came downstairs and frowned at Frank. 'You are late,' he said.

128

'Late?' said Frank.

'Late.' Frank had said seven. It was 7.09. 'You do know, Frank, that if you only allocate the exact amount of time to get somewhere you will be late fifty percent of the time?' said her brother. 'That's how bell curves work. I assume you know that. You seem to know everything else.' Mimi ran cold.

'Sorry,' she said to Frank. 'He's—'

'Do not speak about me in the third person, Naomi, I am right here,' said Art, as if chiselling his words from a stone.

'I—' Mimi tried. But it was pointless. Her words flapped in the air.

Art said he was busy. Too busy for this. He did not need supper. He went back upstairs.

'What the hell?' Frank looked at the stairs, to where Art had gone.

Mimi stared at the floor. 'I'm sorry,' she said.

'Come,' said Frank, 'Forget it. I'll open some wine.' Whatever he'd brought remained in his bag.

They ate supper on their laps, watching the news on TV, but all Mimi could think of was Art being rude, on a loop. Afterwards, Frank stood, wine in one hand, remote control in the other, and channel-surfed with no particular enthusiasm. He fiddled absently with a pellet of cartilage, his old earring scar – a signal Mimi recognized. He turned down the volume and walked over to help tidy up.

'When I'm done, we could watch the *Bake-Off* final on catch-up,' she said. 'Someone uses a hair-dryer on a cake.'

'Probably not a cake you'd want to eat,' said Frank, sounding distracted. 'But, speaking of food,' he said. 'I've been thinking.' He supported one arm on the counter and leaned in close as she rinsed the sink. 'It might be time for your brother to cook for himself.'

She didn't look up. 'I know,' she said, with no idea how to change anything. She started drying the plates, but Frank gently took the towel from her hand. They could hear Art above them, his tread on the floor of his bedroom, the drag of the heavy drawer at the bottom of his wardrobe where he kept his jumpers.

'You two can't live together forever, is what I'm saying.'

She knew what he was saying.

She looked around the kitchen that had hardly changed since her mother had stood in her exact spot. Mimi had added a pot of basil to the windowsill, and a Nespresso machine next to the kettle. Hector's bed was gone from the corner – that had felt like a last wrenching goodbye to the chapter of their lives that included their parents. Not much else was different. Leaving this house would be like a mollusc losing its shell, never mind leaving Art. 'I need to finish up here,' she said.

'You need to think about yourself.'

Mimi looked at this man, in her kitchen, in her life. Holding her tea towel.

'And – about us,' said Frank.

'I know.'

'Do you?' he said. 'Then why not try?'

Mimi turned the taps back on, then off again. She picked up another dishcloth and wiped the blue-rimmed plates. More often than not she'd forget to put the dried plates away and her brother would sigh when he saw them in the morning, but tonight she stacked them on their shelf and closed the cupboard door.

Frank had been so understanding. Of her hesitancy, of her ducking and diving before he met Art, about her name, before he knew. She still hadn't even told him she loved him. That felt like a gate – if she swung it open it would swing shut

130

behind her and close her off from the promises she'd made to her brother.

But there was a new impatience in his voice. 'Mimi?'

She turned to face him, and her hands were shaking. 'Are we really having this conversation?'

'Yes, we are.' He handed her more wine. 'Look, I'd love to come home to you every day. But I know it would be too soon, you probably don't feel ready. It doesn't have to be that. I really don't want to push you, but it feels as if something needs to change.'

She nodded and used the back of her wrist to stop the tears. She felt joy and anxiety lurching in opposite directions. 'I get that we need to discuss it, at least.'

'Why don't you start by leaving him to cook his own supper when we go out, instead of doing it for him before you go?' he suggested. 'He's not incapable.' She knew he didn't mean to sound hard.

Mimi felt sick. But she nodded.

'We'll make a night of it,' said Frank, softening. 'I'll make it worth it. I promise.' He kissed her on the shoulder.

Spaghetti. Art's favourite. How hard could it be?

23

FACTS

A week later, the newsagent handed Mimi Art's *Mathematics Magazine*. 'You're cheerful today,' he said.

'Boyfriend's taking me out tonight,' Mimi said with a smile that belied her nerves. Tonight, she and Frank were talking about her moving out.

'The one I've seen you with? Tallish bloke?' He put his hands up on either side of his head. 'Jug ears?'

'I suppose that's him.' Frank's ears did stick out, a bit.

There were plenty of people around, so she took the shortcut home across Camberwell Green, past the Magistrates' Court. *Jug ears?*

'Hey!' called Rey from outside her house. She crossed the road. 'I was coming to say cheers, I'm off to Wales tomorrow. The shoot's a full week.' She pointed at the Tesco bag Mimi was carrying. 'I thought tonight was the night? Art sorting out his own dinner?'

'I bottled, just a bit,' said Mimi, unlocking her front door. She'd been going to the supermarket anyway, she said.

Art didn't seem to be home.

'You're disabling him, you know,' said Rey, as she followed Mimi into the kitchen.

Mimi had just bought the ingredients. She wasn't going to cook them as she usually did. He'd have to get out the pans, put salt into the water, all that.

Rey put the box of spaghetti away. 'He needs to darken the door of Tesco himself. Imagine if something happened to you.'

Mimi washed her hands. 'Small steps.'

'You're only scared because you know where this actually ends – and him living alone terrifies you both,' said Rey. 'But if you did move in with Frank, or wherever, remember, I'm across the road. So is old Mr Raikes next door. I'm just saying. We love Art.'

'I love you for being so bossy,' Mimi said over her shoulder, but then her spine prickled.

She turned fully round. There, standing at the kitchen door, was Art.

'*Art*. We, er . . .'

His face looked strangely blank and flat, as though he'd been smacked and hadn't yet come round. A towel hung over his wrist. 'I am going swimming,' he said, and turned.

'Art!' called Mimi, but they heard the front door close.

'Did he hear us?' asked Rey.

'What d'you *think*?' said Mimi.

She raced down the hall.

Art upped his brisk pace.

'*Art! Art!*' He could hear her.

Eventually, it would become evident that he was ignoring her on purpose, and he knew that would serve neither of them well. He stopped in the road and turned around.

Mimi reached him and stood in front of him, arms akimbo, folded over herself, catching her breath. 'Art,' she said, puffing.

He just looked at her.

133

'Wait, please wait.' Her face was flushed and suddenly she looked like a little girl, her eyes watering in the wind. She was pulling on her lip.

'I *am* waiting, Mimi.'

'Please can we talk about this? I'm not going to make any decisions about my life without talking to you first.' Her words ran into one another. 'Surely you know that?'

'You have made it perfectly clear that you are going to pursue your current path and see where it takes you, heedless of any other facts, so I am not sure what there is to discuss.' He found he could not say Frank's name.

'What other facts?'

'The fact that we do not know a great deal about him, or his background. The fact that you have not met his family. Most of all, the fact that you have not given the model a chance. We agreed on a plan and it seems that you have not had the patience to follow it through.'

'Model? What?'

'Do not be obtuse, Naomi. We agreed. You would follow the thirty-seven percent plan, based on your Matrix likes. You have simply let them pile up, for *months*. How are you ever going to know if the model works? If it works to find love?'

'Art. *S-stop*. Just s-s-stop.' She looked as if someone had stuck a tube down her throat.

He needed to tread gently, he could see that the truth might be upsetting. If Frank was not the right man for her, she had invested a lot of time in him, and it was time that, as she herself had acknowledged, she did not have to waste.

'What do you mean, *I am letting them pile up*?'

'I *mean* that there have been some perfectly excellent candidates that you have ignored. Most recently, a fellow

134

called Gordon, a property developer who works in London. He has a full head of hair.' He should not have mentioned the hair. Frank was losing a little of his.

'Gordon?!'

'You saw him?'

'And you know all this, how?' she asked. Her mouth had gone into a flat line that was a little alarming. '*Art*? I deleted Matrix ages ago. Months.'

There was nothing for it. He could not lie. 'I had it on my computer.'

'You have got to be kidding.' His sister went still. 'Listen,' she said, through clenched teeth. 'You can look at my matches all day. I don't care what Matrix says. I'm with Frank. *Have you got that?!*'

'But Mimi—'

'No, Art. Do you not understand that Matrix was there to help *me*? I'm not a human experiment, only there to prove or disprove that it works. For crying out loud! What are you thinking?'

'I am thinking of you, Mimi. It is all I ever do.'

'Art—'

'I am thinking of finding you the person who is *perfect* for you. Not just suitable or good-enough. *Ideal*. If you cannot see that, then I do not know what to say. It seems that yet again in our life we are at serious cross-purposes with one another, where you are not able to listen to me. That never ends well. Nevertheless, I am going swimming. We can discuss whether or not to terminate our commitment to Matrix on my return.' He turned on his heel and walked away. He had sounded perfectly reasonable and was relieved that he had managed to retain his composure.

But as strode off, he felt as if a rope was attached to them

135

both, one at each end. It pulled from his middle. He wished that the pavement would swallow him up and cover him over with concrete, the pain was so great.

Art looked small as he walked away. This time, she let him go.

24

SQUARES

In the changing room at the pool, still unsettled from the upsetting encounter with Mimi, Art opened his personal red locker. He needed this swim – he planned to do laps, to count each stroke in a soothing, distracting rhythm.

As he changed, his thoughts kept going back to the afternoon, like a tongue seeking out a sore tooth. Mimi had simply not exhausted the possibilities that there were better men out there than Frank. Art pulled on his Speedos.

In addition to Frank, worries about his research were jamming his brain. A good swim would help.

But when he got to the pool, there was a man in the only lane that was roped off, a single blue cap rising and sinking with each freestyle stroke, back and forth along the far lane. Art looked around. After triaging his disappointment, he chose to float on his back with his head resting on a foam noodle, his feet paddling gently. He could feel the waves made by the swimmer, the reverberations back from the tiles on the wall.

Mimi turned the lamps on to chase away the grey corners of winter already creeping into the house, and lighten her gloom. It was dark, felt too late for tea and too early for wine. She had a swig of orange juice straight from the carton in the fridge, and felt the frisson of a minor rebellion. She lit the wood burner, then settled down with props at her feet to take her mind off her brother.

Her recorder was charged and her microphone's windshield was off. She pressed record, then marched a bunch of keys across the kitchen table in a deliberate walking rhythm, to imitate chainmail, clanking. When she'd captured the sound well enough, she filed *Walking in chainmail* next to *Body crumples into side of car*, and dropped the keys into her bag of props. She spat on her thumb and rubbed at a spot on the table, hoping Art wouldn't notice where the keys had marked the wood.

It was a good thing that Art had gone swimming. He'd need to clear his head – before boiling his own spaghetti.

She wasn't going to be able to leave him to do that, she realized, not after this afternoon. But she couldn't cancel on Frank. She felt queasy and trapped. He was picking her up at eight. If she got going now, she could do Art's supper and still be ready on time.

With a deep sigh, Mimi picked up her cap from the sofa. Sometimes it was all about deciding which hat you wanted to wear, she thought, putting it on. It was black and had *Sister in Sound* embossed on the front in bumblebee yellow – a bit alarming with her red oxide hair and pale skin, but she liked it all the same. The cap made her feel part of the game. What exact game, she couldn't really say, but you know, the game out there.

The game that had love in it. Life.

Sooner than she expected, she heard the front door open.

She transferred the cooked spaghetti into a bowl. 'Art? Hiya!' she said, trying to sound cheery.

Art, the man who had strong opinions on shoelace length and the correct way to de-pill a jumper, looked completely bedraggled. He trailed a towel behind him.

'Hey – you're wet!' She turned off the tap and went to him, but he recoiled. His eyes were darting around. 'Are you okay?' He was shivering, and his chin trembled in that way that always made her want to hold him tight, just when she knew he'd least want to be held.

'I am going to have a shower.'

'You didn't shower at the pool?' She could smell chemicals. Art *never* came home without showering first. She tried to be rational, while her insides broke into a spongy, guilty mess. 'Art, it'll stain the wooden floor, you'll hate that. Use the – why are you *so* wet? What can I do?' Her hands kept reaching out to him involuntarily.

He just stood there.

'What's happened?'

'I am going to shower.' He almost tripped over his towel.

'Art!'

But he was gone, dragging his sodden towel up the carpeted stairs. Mimi followed. He dropped his belongings in a soaking heap outside the bathroom. She could hear the water running. Steam fogged the fanlight.

'Art?' She banged on the door.

The bathroom door didn't lock – but Mimi knew better than to open it. She sat outside and waited. As long as she could hear him moving around, she didn't need to worry.

She rubbed her temples. Of all the things to overhear. And of all the nights. But something else must have happened, for *this*.

Taking a deep breath that didn't do much to release the pulling in her chest, she took out her phone and left a message when Frank didn't pick up. 'It's me,' she said. 'I'm so sorry.

I'm going to have to bail on tonight. It's Art.' He was going to be so hurt. She was screwing this up. 'I'm sorry.' God, she felt rubbish. 'I'll call you tomorrow.'

So, that was it. Their plan. Frank's plan. Their evening. Gone.

What's going on? Frank texted back straight away.

She had no idea.

In his room, Art pulled on his tracksuit pants, always a bad sign, and curled into bed, facing the wall. Mimi sat at his side and only when she could hear his breath fall soft and slow, did she put her hand on his back. His scapula rose sharply against her hand. He was thinner than usual.

Her phone buzzed in her pocket. **Mimi?** asked Frank.

An absolute mess, she wrote. **I haven't seen him like this for a long time. I'll explain tomorrow.** She turned it off and climbed onto the single bed. Last night she'd lain spooned with Frank upstairs, naked and warm. Tracing the scooped hollow of a different neck. 'Hey Beautiful,' he'd said. He made her feel as if she was. Now she felt cold, as if she was hanging onto the edge of a raft.

Who'd she been kidding?

It was never going to work.

She could never leave Art. And Frank would head for the hills when he realized.

She imagined *not* having her brother in her way. Her thoughts took a very dark, murderous turn, in a way that alarmed her. She didn't mean them, of course. But she was angry. Angry with him for taking up all the space in their lives. Angry for needing so much from her. *Of* her. She was hollowed out. She inched away from him and sat on the edge of the mattress – it wasn't right to hug him while wishing him dead. She fetched her duvet from her room and, clenching the corner of her pillow in her teeth, lugged it back to Art. She lay fully clothed on the carpet, with her arm slung up onto his mattress, her hand wedged under her brother's back, so he'd know she was right there if he stirred.

Mimi woke with a bloom of fire in her hip and her hair pasted onto her cheek, feeling frayed, assailed by guilt for her murderous thoughts of the night before.

All okay? texted Frank.

Yes. I'm so sorry about last night. I could strangle my brother. She was very worried about Art, but she wasn't sure how much to tell Frank right now.

Meaning???

Can we chat about it later? I've had a rough night. I feel so shitty for letting you down. Letting us down, she typed, and tears plopped onto her phone. **I wanted to** – she started, but then deleted it and wrote: **I'll make it up to you. I promise,** she added, wanting to pull Frank in close.

No worries.

Mimi sent him an X.

Time we worked something out though.

Mimi read that over and over.

Time we worked something out.

xxx, she wrote and put her phone on the table, screen facing down.

Art slept until noon.

She heard him pad across the passage upstairs. The bathroom door didn't smack the towel rail when it opened, and it closed again with a controlled click.

Then he came downstairs, hair combed to the side, wearing his checked flannel shirt with his buttons done up to the top.

It made her furious, how neat he was, as though his incontinent emotion of the night before could be tidied away with well-pressed clothes.

141

'Breakfast?' she asked, keeping her voice even. 'Bacon? Eggs?' He nodded. He wanted the works. 'Orange juice? Granola?' She spooned it out for him, sprinkled on the linseed that kept him regular. She cooked his eggs.

'So. Are you feeling better?'

His eyes were clear. Amazing what seventeen hours of sleep could do.

'It will not be possible to go to the pool again.'

'*The pool*? Why?'

'The middle red line of a Rubik's cube.'

'I'm not in the mood, Art. Did something happen at the pool?'

He ate his poached egg, neatly pruning away the white and liberating the yolk, the only part he liked.

'What's going on, Art?'

'I told you. Three red squares.' He gave her that look, as if he might have some clever puzzle for her to work out.

'Art. I'm tired. I haven't s-slept. I'm s-s-sick of . . .' She could feel tears coming.

Art picked at his bacon, trimmed the fat off in a neat strip and set it to the side of his plate. He reached for the pepper mill. It was stainless steel and the size of her arm, a Christmas present from Rey. He turned the silver screw at the top, twice. Two quarter-turns. To tighten the grinder, make the granules finer. Then he turned the mill once, sifted fine pepper onto his lean bacon and returned it to its place on his left-hand side. He adjusted it slightly, she knew, so the salt and pepper were equidistant from the tray. Mimi watched, her teeth on edge, her fists clenched at her sides. 'Art?'

'Three red squares,' he said in an almost nursery rhyme sing-song voice.

'You're not five, Art.' She was crying and he didn't notice.

142

What had gone wrong? What had gone wrong was her whole damn life.

He focused on a peppercorn, a big one that had somehow escaped the teeth of the grinder and landed on his egg. She wished he would just put the fucking thing in his mouth. But she stood there and watched, as he neatly excised the single peppercorn from the edge of the yolk.

Mimi picked up the pepper mill. It was comforting to hold. The top, like the head of a chess queen, or the top of a baseball bat, sat perfectly in the palm of her hand. It was stupidly heavy – 'a ridiculous thing', she'd said to Rey with a laugh when she'd opened it on Christmas Day.

'I had a thought,' said Art. 'About Frank.' His laugh had an odd, tinny ring.

'And what's your *thought*, Art?' At least he was talking. She rolled the pepper mill round in her hand. She smacked it into her palm, and it stung, and the pain felt good.

'He would make a good lifeguard. He has the jaw.'

'What?'

'Lifeguards, they are frauds really. They dress up like superheroes and all they do is stand around.'

'*Lifeguards?!*' She twiddled the screw of the mill in irritation.

'All their authority vested in a little whistle.'

'What on earth has that got to do with Frank?'

'Frank.' Art put his head to one side as though really considering the question. Mimi wanted to whack him. 'Frank is a bit – predatory, really, if you think about it.'

She felt dizzy as Art slid the peppercorn to the very edge of his plate with a single tine on his fork.

'I think it is his eyes, and the way that he walks. His hips are sort of slightly disconnected; they roll.' He looked at his sister.

She knew exactly what he meant because she found it so sexy. Frank's walk. Jesus. 'They roll?'

'Yes. He is altogether too casual, and altogether too selfish. And now that I have recovered my composure—' said Art.

'*Yes?*'

'We need to talk about him, Mimi. I am afraid that we do.'

Art went back to his breakfast after this announcement.

'No! You cannot do this! No! You are *not* going to do this to me. I can't take it any more!' Was she shouting? 'I'm leaving! This house. *You!*' she screamed. She could see his soft white forehead, his neatly combed hair. He stared up at her, his mouth a dark red hole. She lifted the pepper grinder high above her head. 'I'm leaving here and I'm going to live with Frank!'

It all happened in an instant. She flung her arm down, just as she heard the front door open. Before she knew it, the round steel head flew off the pepper grinder's base and spun through the air. She saw Art's face, just before his arm lifted to his eyes and she heard a crack, a sickening sound.

Mimi dropped the pepper grinder.

'Mimi? Mimi! Art! Jesus fucking Christ!' said Rey as she walked into the room.

Art held his wrist, which was at a peculiar angle. He made a keening noise, wheezing and groaning. Then Art, who wouldn't speak when you most wanted him to, wouldn't shut up. He shouted about a lifeguard's shorts. Red shorts, red locker. Three red squares. Saying he was sorry, over and over. He would tell her, he cried, he did not mean to upset her.

'Lucky I turned up when I did,' Rey said. Art's wrist was swelling at the side like a ping-pong ball. Rey fetched ice for Art and then Mimi watched as she tidied the mess. The

144

toppled chair, the smear of egg, the bacon off the floor, the broken plate – Rey scraped it all into the bin. Then she gave Art tea. He'd gone deathly pale.

Rey kept looking at Mimi in the same way you'd look at a dog that was trapped in a corner.

She'd hurt her brother. In all their years, through all her rage and frustration at his weirdness, at her parents, at her life, at her *non*-life, she had never, ever, hurt him before. He was still saying sorry.

She couldn't say it. The word was too small.

Rey was there, wiping his face.

'Stop saying sorry, Art, you're the one who's hurt. Let's focus on clearing all this up, how does that sound? Shhh. Just stay still.' Rey lifted his swollen wrist, gently, as though it was a broken bird, and wrapped it in a clean cloth; it was discolouring fast. She was firm but tender and did not ask him to explain. He tried. He tried to tell her what had happened at the pool. The confusion he felt. The shame. That he had to run away. But it came out all wrong; his sentences would not form. Rey smoothed his hair and held a tissue to his nose. Telling him everything would soon be okay.

Mimi curled up on the sofa in a ball.

'Sweetie, why *now*?' asked Rey, searching her face. 'It was all going so well.' Mimi stared at Rey and at her brother, with his shocked, blotchy face.

Then Rey was on the phone. It sounded as if she was talking to a doctor. 'I'll bring him to see you myself.'

Mimi stood in her bedroom, in her vest and knickers. 'Come,' said Rey, holding her jeans open. Mimi lifted one leg, then the other, feeling as if she was sleepwalking into her clothes. 'This jumper?' Rey held a stripey top. Mimi wasn't sure what for. Rey zipped the make-up bag that lay on Mimi's unmade bed. Where was her duvet? A suitcase blocked the door. Was Art going somewhere? He needed her. 'Where's Art?' she asked Rey, a sense of panic rising. 'Art!'

'Shhh,' said her friend, 'Don't worry, Mi, Art's okay. First, we're going to see the doctor. Then, you need a break. I'm taking you with me to Wales. I'm going to be busy and maybe you can help me, but also just take some time out, walk on the beach for a week. It's peaceful and no one will bother you there. Art will be fine.'

25

DIVIDED IN TWO

After filling up the fridge for Art with supplies from her own kitchen, and arranging for Cath to pop in over the next few days to prepare Art's food, Rey drove Mimi over the Severn Bridge, towards the coast. Their bed and breakfast was near an ancient castle – the film Rey was working on was a gritty Welsh drama being shot amidst ivy-clad ruins. 'Please don't tell Frank what happened,' Mimi said, 'if he asks. Not yet. I need to figure out what actually did happen myself.'

'And *why*,' said Rey, sliding a quick look at Mimi before checking her rear-view mirror and changing lanes.

Mimi made a call to Frank when they stopped at a village store. 'I'm on my way to Wales with Rey,' she said. 'She needs me on a shoot at a castle—'

'Oh. OK. I guess that sounds exciting—'

'It's a bit unexpected and I probably won't do that much but, you know. Anyway, I'm sorry, last night, and now this. It – I didn't – It was a rush,' she said, her words falling like hurdles under clumsy feet.

'No problem,' said Frank, though he sounded a bit flat. 'I'm up to my eyeballs for the association anyway. Crazy week.'

147

She wasn't sure how much more to say. 'It's all a bit of a mess. I had a huge argument with Art last night. He, well, he ended up very upset and – that's partly why I've come away with Rey. A day or two. Rey says a week.' A week felt like infinity. 'But Frank – I know there's stuff to sort out.'

'Hang on.' Frank was quiet for a moment. She heard a shuffle and she imagined that he'd been standing in his kitchen eating a sandwich when she'd phoned. She could picture him wiping his mouth and moving to the sofa. 'I'm listening,' he said. 'Tell me.'

Mimi pulled at her collar. 'I can't really. I'm standing on the side of the road and Rey's in the car. Just give me a day or two – okay? I'll call when I'm settled.'

'Are *you* all right?' he asked. 'Or do I need to be worried? About you?'

It felt as though there were bits of herself dangling from her body, strings of her mind that weren't governable just then. 'I'm fine,' she said, 'apart from, I wish you were with me. Really, I'm fine.'

'Okay then, you,' he said. She could hear him relax. He believed her.

The B&B, a small cottage, was near the sea, though not very near the castle, it turned out. Mimi smelled salt and brine as soon as she got out of the car. 'It's more remote than I realized,' said Rey, winging her bag from the car over her shoulder. 'Oh well. The quiet will be good for you.' They were greeted by Phyllis, who stayed in an adjacent room and had already heated a heavy-bottomed griddle pan for Welsh tea cakes. She dolloped butter on top and showered them with caster sugar. Phyllis's life stacked up around them – choir pamphlets under the armchair, a tower of LPs, stained knitted tea cosies, church flower rotas taped to the wall.

The cottage wasn't well heated, but there were extra

blankets over the backs of the armchairs, the local cream was thick and autumn bulbs had naturalized on the lawn. Neither sea nor village were too far away.

Rey brought Mimi tea in bed, then left for the morning, suggesting that Mimi turn off her phone. 'I don't generally want to disconnect you from the world, but you need to think. Take a few days with no incoming. Send Frank a message – tell him the signal's lousy and you'll be in touch in a couple of days.'

After a day's rest, Mimi walked the coastal path, which tacked close to the edge of the cliff. She'd shouted at Art that she was moving out, leaving him, but as she stood there, watching the sun struggle and the wind knock caps into the surface of the water, she did not know if she ever could.

Stay here, in the now, Rey said.

She wanted to give Frank her future nows. Art had taken his fair share already.

Down on the rocks below, the ocean's undertow had contoured the twisted geological layers. Families were like rocks, she thought, pounded and pulled into shape by the greatest force around.

She saw a path to the side and from there to the beach. It would be a long climb back, but the one thing she had was time. She descended towards the sea.

If she pretended, her father could be walking in front of her, his feet finding the best path between the stones and tufts of grass, feeling better for the fresh air and getting out of London. Her mother would be behind her, picking things up along the way, pieces of stone with layers of pink, shells dropped by birds, flowers to name. And behind Christine, Art. A family of four walking down to the sea.

What would her parents have said about the incident at

home? She could still see Art's face, the split second as the top of the peppermill hurtled towards him. Lifting his arm to protect himself.

But sick as she felt about Art, the revolting squirm inside her at the thought of losing Frank was worse. **Signal here totally rubbish**, she'd messaged him. **I'll call in a day or two x.**

You know where to find me ;) X, he'd replied.

The path met the shore. Mimi took off her shoes, stuffed her socks into them and placed them on a rock. She stepped onto the sand. Rey was right. The peace of the cottage, the wide coastal sky, the wind ribboning round her ankles on this hard, flat beach, would help make space in her head. She examined it all.

She'd work out which bits she should blame herself for. And how to be free.

26

RETURN

Days later, Mimi woke in the morning with a sliver of Welsh moon still suspended in the frame of her window. She'd made her decision.

A short lease, close to home, but her own.

She squinted at her phone – the reception at the cottage really *was* awful. It hadn't even been necessary to turn the phone off; it had been as much use as a paperweight. She and Rey had two more days here, but she'd call Art today. And Frank. Rey had been right: the silence was bliss. But this morning she knew she'd been silent too long. She'd kept thinking, *I'll find a spot and call today* – but the mornings had slipped by. She'd walk, make lunch, read, sit with Phyllis's LPs spread on the floor while she played them on the turntable, lost in thought. She'd fall asleep, and then somehow the afternoon too, would be gone.

Today. She must call today.

After lunch, she walked along the coastal path in the opposite direction, checking her bars. She was in Wales, not the Tora Bora. How far should a girl have to go for a signal? When – finally – there were three bars on her phone, she considered settling immediately on a bench to savour her messages from Frank, but it was covered in a shawl of moss; the damp would go straight through her jeans. As Mimi walked, she scrolled the headlines of Frank's messages – they were blander and less intimate than she'd hoped they might be. Rey had sent a message too. She'd be late that evening, and there'd be work for Mimi in the morning if she wanted it.

But there was one, recent, single-line message from her brother.

Mimi, you are going to have to trust me. Art.

She stopped. **What??** she typed. She tried to call, but her signal had disappeared. *Trust him about what?*

Her guts turned.

She walked, checked her phone, and picked up her pace. He'd not sent another message all week. Yes, she'd harboured herself in a remote wave-cut bite of the Welsh coastline with no signal, but Art had avoided her too.

It hadn't been a good idea, leaving him on his own. She'd been so wrapped up in her decision, in her life, she hadn't been thinking of him, on his own, nursing his wound and his version of what had happened. She kept moving, with a drumming behind her sternum. Her trainer rolled on a loose stone, which flew from her shoe and over the cliff.

A distant phone mast became a steel ladder to her brother, manifest in the sky. 'Please leave a message,' said an automated voice. She stamped the red button.

It was just after three. Art would do his marking, and then he'd walk home. He wouldn't be swimming.

What? she texted him. **??? Answer! I don't understand.**

At the top of the hill, her lungs bagged in her chest as she punched in his number. 'Please leave a message.' The air tasted like iron.

'Art. I'm in a remote square foot of signal, miles from anywhere. *Please*. Pick up.'

152

Finally, she called Frank.

'It sounds like you're in a washing machine, not a castle,' said Frank. He sounded just like he should. Whole. Hers. Frank. She turned her back to the wind.

'I'm on a hill . . . above the sea.' God, she'd missed him.

'Everything okay?' he asked. She pictured him frowning, the crease of his eyes.

She cupped her left hand over her ear and tucked her phone into her neck. 'I'm fine. I've just missed you so much, stuck up here.' She could sense him listening, attentive, almost feel his thumb trace a line round her shoulder, checking that she was okay. 'I'm worried about my brother.' The wind whipped her words. 'I got a weird text.'

'Weird like how?'

She would have liked to tell Frank the whole story. 'You haven't seen him, by any chance, have you?' she asked.

'Why?' asked Frank. 'What did it actually say?'

'Oh, you know Art,' she said, 'he can be strange.' She tried to laugh but instead almost choked. 'I guess I just haven't spoken to him all week. He's not used to that.'

Frank was quiet for a moment. 'We can chat about it when you get back,' she thought he said.

She pulled her hair away from her mouth. 'I walked miles to get to this damn spot and now I can hardly hear you.' She banked her body against the rush of noise. 'This is hopeless. I'm shouting.'

'Does the B&B have a landline?'

'Look.' She decided as she said it: 'I'm coming back, tonight.' Art didn't like a change of plan, but his text worried her. And anyway, it was time.

'Are you done with your work?' asked Frank. She would have preferred him to sound more excited.

What was she *doing* here? 'I'll call you on my way.'

153

'Travel safe,' he said.

'I'm sorry,' she said, not sure which unformed confession had tried to wrench free.

Mimi checked her watch. She couldn't stand around for the next hour and wait for Art to call or text her back. Her chances of getting back tonight would vanish with the dark. Already, the feeble light was soaking away.

I'm coming home, she texted her brother. **Tonight. OMW.**

She ran back to the cottage, texting Rey her plans, listening to the hup-hup and whistle of a shepherd's call, suddenly not sure that she wanted to leave.

What the?! wrote Rey. **Give me ten.**

I know I know. Getting a train. Chat later.

The cottage fire had smouldered down to baked logs in the grate. Mimi unhooked her knickers from where they'd been drying on the radiator and left a scrawled note for Rey, with a mass of x kisses, *Thank you!* and *Sorry!* Taking one last look backwards and hoping that Phyllis might see her wave, she walked down the hill.

A taxi was dropping someone off in the village when she got there; the driver nodded to her and she climbed in. The headlights swung round hedges, and soft tongue syllables ran out of Radio Cymru like water over stones. The landscape blurred by.

Mimi tried to focus on everything she'd decided, rather than Art's message. Moving out was a big step. It would feel as if she was leaving her parents, in a way. Art would say it was a waste of money. Well, it was her money. Mimi balled her scarf into a pillow. As nervous as she was to tell Art, she was excited to tell Frank. He'd be so pleased, she told herself, quietening the voice that said anything else.

And the one that said, trust me.

The taxi turned right at the red station sign.

'Just in time, you'll be,' said her driver. 'Last London train.'

27

EMPTY SET

Mimi turned into 19 Muriel Grove, and the gate whined. The house was dark.

A flyer was stuck in the letterbox slot. She unlocked the door and pushed it open into the quiet. The cold felt wrong; the heating was on low, and the wood burner hadn't been used. The whole place had an empty feeling, a stillness that sank to the floor. The post lay next to the radiator, still scattered from the day's delivery.

'Art?' she called into the dim. She turned on the lights but kept her jacket on. 'Art?'

She looked round the kitchen.

Art's mug, glass and bowl from breakfast were upturned on a folded tea towel next to the sink. She realized just how much she'd been looking forward to seeing him, how disappointed she was not to find him home and see his earnest face. Check he was okay. That *they* were okay. A new, sensibly sized pepper grinder stood in the corner. She opened the bin. In the bottom of a fresh recycling bag, she saw the foil peeled from a new pot of yoghurt and an empty carton of orange juice – smooth, no bits.

Art hadn't actually asked her to come back, she reminded

herself. But here she was. Again. She felt she'd been beckoned, and he wasn't even home.

'Art?' she said as she pushed her shoes off and ventured upstairs with her bag, flicking lights on as she went. Art's room had the look of a space where time had stood still. His Rubik's cube key ring was attached to the lock on his cupboard door. But it had been like that since the nineties. It wasn't cause for concern.

Next to his bed was a photograph of a mathematician called Mahalanobis. It had been there for a while, too. She picked it up, and underneath was one of the childhood notebooks that Art guarded and cherished. It fell open on a diagram he'd drawn of his mother's crocheted blanket.

Mimi replaced the notebook and photograph and wandered through the rest of the house. Art's study was locked.

Locked?

'Art?' She knocked on the door. Art always locked the main drawer of his desk, paranoid as he was about his precious theorems. But his actual study door? She imagined him lying on the floor – and banged on the wood with her fist. 'Art!'

She could use her body to bash right through. She gripped the frame and peered through the keyhole instead. She could feel her lashes on the brass plate, but there was no report of light back to her eye.

She blinked and stood.

Up in her bedroom, she tried unpacking, but all she could manage was upturning her clothes, out onto her bed.

The last time she'd slept in this bedroom, she'd been so aware of her brother's room below.

She'd tiptoed across the floorboards, with Frank's gaze following her in the half light. 'What are you looking at?' she'd asked him, hoping for a compliment. She scootched

156

up under his arm. She remembered the warmth of his body against hers.

Frank had kissed her hair. 'I'm thinking . . . I'm *hoping* . . . that I'm not an oxbow lake,' he'd said.

She'd pulled away. 'What do you mean?'

'I feel that I constantly need to draw you back in. That if I didn't, there are forces that would take you away.'

'I don't know what you mean.'

'It's okay,' said Frank. 'I understand. It's hard for you, I know.'

'I—'

'Mimi.' Frank pushed his lips to hers as though he was stamping her with a seal.

Later, he'd whispered, 'Just so you know, I'm your valley. I won't stop pulling.'

She stood at the top of the stairs, looking down. Uncomplicated, straightforward Frank. Catapulted into her heart. It was possible that Frank knew by now that she'd skirted around the truth about her trip to Wales. The sooner she sorted things out with her brother, the sooner she could get back to him. Tell him everything. *The sooner she could leave this house.*

Mimi's hand took the rail – she couldn't move her feet onto the next step. What she would have liked – really, really liked – would be to keep life simple.

But instead, she'd come home.

28

THE BUTTERFLY EFFECT

Mimi's phone pinged on the kitchen counter. She'd missed a call from Frank. **Call me it's urgent**, said a text.

Frank didn't think anything was urgent, ever.

But there was no reply when she dialled his number.

All okay? she asked. **Where are you? Any idea where Art is?**

Nothing.

For want of a better alternative, she opened a bottle of wine. She shouldn't have started a whole bottle for herself, but she hadn't had much all week and, anyway, that's why screw-tops were invented. She poured a generous glass and kept trying Art and Frank. Rey too.

Perhaps Mr Raikes knew something.

'I thought you were in Wales, dear?' he said, when he heard it was her on the phone.

'I was.' She twirled the landline cord round her finger, her unease coiling inside her. 'Rey's still there – you've got Rizla?'

'Right next to me,' said Mr Raikes. Rizla barked on cue. 'Cards soon? I'm dealing, I believe.'

'Maybe in the next day or two? With biscuits.' *Shortbread*, she wrote on her hand.

She threw logs into the burner with a couple of firelighters and retrieved the wine from the fridge. There was nothing to do except wait.

Curled up on the sofa, Mimi poked her fingers absently through the holes in the crochet blanket, the same one drawn in Art's old notebook. It would be a terrible invasion of privacy to leaf through his precious book. On the other hand . . . She nipped back upstairs.

It was an exercise book covered with brown paper. The Scotch tape that held the paper down had long since lost its stickiness.

Back under her blanket again, Mimi had a sip of wine and smelled the paper – the blue lines, red margins. Memories of her mother rose off the page. 'No one else covers their exercise books, Mum,' Mimi, aged eight, had said.

'We do. Pass me the scissors,' said her mother, as she origamied another book into its brown paper shell.

Failing to convince herself that she wasn't trespassing, Mimi read the first line in Art's journal. Just two words: *Np hard*, in a young boy's scrawl.

She turned the page to find pencil drawings of the patterned crocheted blanket that was wrapped around her now, beneath which Art had written, *To make sure no two squares of the same colour are adjacent, a blanket needs four colours. Like a map.*

Mimi pulled the blanket tighter and tucked her feet up underneath her.

'You can see straight away that no two countries next to one another on a map are the same colour,' Art had explained to her once, 'but try *colouring* the map.'

Mimi remembered sitting on the floor, looking up at the sofa as new sections of the blanket materialized through the dip

159

and twist of her mother's crochet hook. Art was reading in the corner. The ball of wool sat in the hollow of Christine's lap, the string lurching upwards with each pull of her hand.

'Chain, three treble.' Her mother's face had been a prism of concentration. 'One, two . . . three.'

Mimi tried to show her the birthday cards she'd drawn for her dad. 'Mum?' she said.

Her mother stared at her wool. 'Chain. Three loops, one, two . . .'

'Mum?'

'Two. Three . . . *What*?'

'Mum! Look. Please.'

'I can't – oh damn. What *is* it?' Christine lifted her head and yanked at the blue wool. A coil of stitches unravelled as she pulled. 'Now I've lost my place.'

'Sorry,' said Mimi. She held up the birthday cards. One of her dad, his grey thatch standing straight up, the other of Hector the dog in her dad's yellow chair. 'Which d'you prefer?'

'He never looks at the picture,' Art piped up. 'You are wasting your time.'

'Don't be mean,' said their mother.

'He goes straight to the writing,' said Art. 'She should use her time properly. Do something constructive.'

'Well, you're sweet to worry about that but let her do it if she wants to, it won't hurt anyone. Come, Art, darling, I need your clever brain.' She put four balls of wool on the floor and Art slid over on his knees to look. Mimi watched as he laid them at their mother's feet. Cherry, Mustard, Ocean, Mole.

Mimi's throat tightened. *Won't hurt anyone*?

'When I sew these hexagons together, no pieces the same colour can touch each other,' said Christine, in her soft-for-Art voice.

'You only need four colours in total for every edge to be different,' said Art, looking happy.

'Mum!'

'What? Oh, yes. Either's fine. *Lovely*,' Christine said, as she bowed her head over Art without even looking up.

Christine didn't see Mimi take the knitting scissors and chop through a skein of red thread, as though it was a stringy vegetable. Chop! Two dismembered halves, with veins. It felt good. Snip slicey blades, so sharp. She got carried away. The last thing to go was the corner of her mother's cushion. The piping on the edge had a satisfying density as the scissors clipped right through it.

Christine *had* seen that.

Mimi remembers the way her mother bit into her lip, as if containing her anger in her mouth, not letting angry words fly out. Mimi was smacked on her thigh and sent to her room.

The thing she nursed upstairs was not the slapped streak of red on her leg, but *Let Mimi do it if she wants to.*

Art gave his father store-bought cards – they weren't the same. Mimi held a cushion in front of her mouth. *Either's fine*, her mother had said, but she hadn't even looked.

Mimi had torn up those cards. She didn't give them to her dad. What if she had? What if he'd kept them, sitting on his shelf? So that ten years later, on the day that he walked out the door, they'd caught his eye somehow and detained him. His beloved butterfly effect. Ten seconds might have been all that was needed.

Mimi was halfway through the bottle of wine when the doorbell rang.

Frank? At *last*. That was her main feeling about Frank, she realized. At last. At last.

161

The bell rang again, more insistent this time. She was glad he felt impatient.

Whether she was leaving this house or not, she must get him a key. No matter what Art said. She shook Art's voice from her head. Honestly – describing Frank as *predatory*. She checked herself in the mirror. There was a pretty enough flush to her face from the wine. It heightened the scar above her mouth, but she was used to that. She fiddled with her bra, pressed her lips together, and wished she'd brushed her teeth.

It wasn't Frank at the door. Standing there were two police officers. A man and a woman. The woman was holding a notebook and they were both wearing hats.

Mimi's heart contracted in readiness. Blood descended to the bottom of her legs as though she wanted to run but was standing in wet cement.

This pair were young for the job. The policewoman picked at a phantom bit of fluff above her badge. She adjusted her vest. There was a universe between Mimi and them, between the world as it was now and the world her insides were hurtling towards. Could they stay still in this synapse of time, before they said anything?

It was the man who asked: 'Miss Brotherton?'

Mimi pointed a hand to direct them inside. She knew the rules.

On the side of the road in Brixton, a newsagent stood under a streetlight, blood staining the knees of his trousers. He smeared his temple with blood as he wiped it with the back of his hand. People started to cluster. An ambulance wheeled in, buoyed by sirens and lights. The sky seemed large from down there, an infinite black dome.

'Thirty-seven-year-old male. RTC. Head injury. Seizure.'

'Do something! That's his second one. His second seizure.'

'Sir, please stand back. Sir. We're doing what we can.'

Jackets leaned over him. Bin men, in blazers. Firemen? No. He bounced between voices. A blue light in orbit.

Blood, sticky and warm, leaked from his ear.

'He's time critical. Get the stretcher. Diazepam?'

'Any other witnesses?'

'Driver only. And a bystander, called ambulance. Stand back, please!'

'He ran straight out!'

'He's seizing again. Uncontrolled hypoxia – radio in. Did he somersault? Elevate?'

'Negative, according to driver. Looks like maybe his hip hit the wing mirror? This bandaged arm – that won't have helped. It's his head—'

'Take the pelvis. Ready. Set. Slide.' He was lifting. He was leaving his feet, falling back to the road.

Jackhammering motion filled blood in his head like a plughole backed up in a gurgling bath. Streaks of pain, needles, pierced the orbs of his eyes, impaled his sockets, punctured his skull. Circles and circles slid into each other. White lines drawn on black.

p equals Np, for a whisker, a moment. The whole world exploded, like a star.

29

REPETITION

t = 0

The police are still at the hospital when Art's doctor, Dr Sipos, comes to talk to her. When Mimi asks if her brother is going to be okay, he is blunt. 'Right now, we don't know.'

'They said he ran into a car.' She tries to elide the disconnectedness from her voice, her strange sense of not actually being there. 'What part of him was hit, where's he hurt?'

Dr Sipos looks along the length of Art's body.

'To start, he sustained a blow to his hip,' he says. He knits his hands into a cat's cradle and holds it to the left side of his own pelvis, to indicate where the car had hit Art. 'He came in with a cast on his wrist – presumably you know about that.'

She doesn't reply.

'Unfortunately, he fell to that side,' says Dr Sipos.

'Did it make his arm worse?'

'His arm's fine. But it was in the way – he couldn't break his fall because of the injury. How did it happen?'

But Mimi just looks at her brother.

'It's why his head hit the road. The real trauma was falling *away* from the car.'

He's going to die, she thinks. *And I've killed him.*

'His leg has a spiral fracture, very unpleasant but not life threatening.' Dr Sipos turns his hand as though twisting a doorknob. Mimi hopes they're running out of physical injuries for him to convey with hand gestures. 'And we ruled out internal bleeding elsewhere. But the brain. It's his brain that we need –' he pauses – 'to protect.' Dr Sipos touches his head.

'Because he's a mathematician?'

'I didn't know that. No.' Dr Sipos looks at Art as though he may no longer be a mathematician.

'Oh.' Mimi shifts from one foot to another, to try and arrest the image of Art's life's work draining away down those tubes. Dr Sipos is explaining the trauma, and Art's brain injury. SBI, he says. S for severe.

'He's not in a natural coma,' says Dr Sipos in a tone that suggests this should somehow be reassuring. 'An induced coma is best right now.'

Barbiturates keep Art in his coma to protect his brain, and the catheter in his skull can both monitor the pressure and drain cerebrospinal fluid. For Art to survive at all, they need the swelling to come down. Only then can they assess the extent of the damage.

She hears *damage*.

'Of course, there may be none.'

'I understand,' says Mimi. What she sees is blood above Art's ear where they've shaved his sandy hair to insert the ICP. If you could ignore the bandages and medical paraphernalia, he looks strangely beautiful – his hair short on the side, his stubble – the planes of his face stark and sculptural.

'How long?' she asks, 'till we know?' What happens if Art is bad, but alive? Alive *without his maths*. It's like imagining the world ironed flat into a 2D sheet.

'For this, we need patience. It depends on many things. What is important now is that we give him a stable night.' She realizes he is parcelling information to her in the smallest bites. Each is indigestible, but he is doing his best to make it easier for her. Later she'll remember the doctor's hand on Art's hip, his fingers gently touching Art's head, where Art's maths is supposed to be.

Dr Sipos explains to her that patients in induced comas often report intermittent awareness of their surroundings. 'Like old television static. Occasionally you get a clear picture with sound, then suddenly, it's gone.'

She nods. *Gone* has a ring of permanence to it. 'So, talk to him,' says the doctor. She imagines Art's consciousness, broken into inaccessible shards of signal.

'Miss Brotherton?' PC Payne interrupts from behind. 'Before I go – was your brother on any medication that you know of?'

Mimi isn't finished with Dr Sipos, but the question yanks her out of her cotton-wool fug. 'What makes you ask that?'

'It's a standard question.'

'Huh.' She ducks the question and asks who the driver was, but they aren't at liberty to say. She asks if they've been breathalysed. Dr Sipos touches her shoulder; he needs to go.

The police tell her that all correct procedures were followed, and that the ambulance picked her brother up near Olive Morris Park. 'Do you know what he was doing there?'

She shakes her head. It's near Frank's house, so she knows the area. 'It's not his normal route home.' The route that Art didn't vary. Not ever.

No phones, says a sign.

* * *

'Oh, thank you.' She accepts a warm drink, not registering who has given it to her. It tastes like tea with hot water from a coffee machine. But it's cold in here, and the hot drink is soothing.

The police have gone, telling her that they may need to come back and talk to her at some stage. Her nod is non-committal. She doesn't know if they mean this evening or next year. All she wants to do is lie down next to her brother and keep him warm. He looks so cold.

'Artie? Do you even know I'm here?'

But there are only the monitors, communicating nothing except that her brother is still alive.

Mimi can smell hospital, chemicals, blood. Already, he doesn't smell like Art. She holds his hand.

She remembers reaching for her mother's hand at her hospital bedside, the way it lay alongside her body, like the upside-down bowl of a wooden spoon. Mimi was supposed to be the one giving comfort, but as she'd rubbed, she'd tried to absorb some too. Had she been sapping her mother of energy while drawing reassurance? Was comfort what Art called a zero-sum game?

Art didn't like holding hands, but he'd taken Mimi's when they arrived at the hospital that first time. She remembers the large *shwoop*ing doors, the assault of the smell, the squeak of the floor, lost families, inscrutable faces, the framed Madonna, hands clasped in prayer. Art not letting go until they reached their mother's ward.

Avoiding the tubes and tape, she squeezes this same hand now.

As she does, just discernible alongside the protective impulse that floods her, she feels an involuntary throb of resentment. What has he done?

167

All her plans. Her decision. She grips his hand harder. Then cautions herself – *Let go a little*.

Find Frank – he will help. She stumbles on Frank's name like a runner needing to stop for rest, but her mind keeps moving. All the things that life with Frank means. She wants those things. She lets go of Art's hand.

'I love you,' she says into his blood-encrusted ear.

Art's eyelids are lilac, bruised. Nurse Kanda, who radiates vitality you can almost touch, taped them down earlier with butterfly tape. They'd started flickering, apparently, opening without seeing. Mimi sees them strain against the transparent strip. What activity there is in his brain beats under his lids like Morse code. She imagines him tapping out *p . . . Np . . . p* and she prays that he still knows what those letters mean.

Sad eyes, she remembers Art saying to her. Now *these* are sad eyes. She touches the tape, quietens his lids.

'I love you,' she repeats, and walks out the ward.

Art is hovering, occupying a synapse of space where words float in, words he recognizes. Comforting, they go by like a vapour trail, dissolving before he quite gets hold of them.

'I love you.' It is Mimi. *Mimi – stay*. His hand hurts. She brushes his forehead.

I love you too. He knows she cannot hear him.

She never did.

She heard him talk, but not the extra beat of his heart. Not the blood rush when things were going wrong, the knock under the bone in his chest. He tiptoed close in, close to her life, as close as he could get.

He loved her so.

30

DISEQUILIBRIUM

Mimi has hardly stepped out of Art's ward when Nurse Kanda taps her elbow. 'Ms Brotherton, there's a telephone call for you.'

'For me?'

The nurse points down the passage to the station monitoring the entrance to all of the ICU wards. 'You won't be able to talk for long,' she says, 'it's our internal line.' Mimi follows, feeling detached. She doesn't want to talk to anyone. A nurse passes her the phone; the twisted cord slung over the desk.

It's Frank.

'Oh, thank *god*. I'm at the hospital, it's Art—'

'I know. I know. I'm so sorry. So sorry.' Frank's voice punctures her detachment, her feeling of not being there.

She looks around. 'How did you know I was here? In ICU? Your text—'

'*Listen*,' he says. 'Is someone there with you?' It's frightening to hear her fear reflected back at her by Frank.

'No, I've been trying to reach you. It's not good. Please, just come.'

'I'm already here. Stay right where you are – I'm coming up.' She hears the phone click.

Under the grim hospital light, Frank walks down the passage towards her. As soon as she sees him, a pressure gives way, a sob spilling from her mouth. 'Oh Frank.' He looks shaken too, as if his edges are blurred. It's just a few short steps and his arms are out and folding her into his chest. But even in those, what, ten steps, something is off.

'Oh god, Mimi.' His voice is raw. Mimi feels a gag rising in her throat, but she doesn't know what she needs to say to right the axis that feels strangely skewed. Frank is leaning on her.

'I'm so sorry. I tried to get hold of you,' he says. 'But the police . . .' He holds her tight. 'I'm so glad you're back,' he says. He is clinging to her.

'Frank.' She fastens her hand to the crook of his arm and steps back to look at him. 'They said he—' Then she sees what it is. There is blood on Frank's shirt.

'Frank! Are you okay? Were you with him?'

Frank blinks.

'Have you been here already?'

Frank snaps back into his body like an articulated toy with elastic joints. Rigid. 'They haven't told you?' he says. Even as it is happening, Mimi is aware that she will remember this moment. How large his eyes are, how grey. How afraid. She understands what people mean when they say, *the whites of his eyes*. They take up his whole face. 'They haven't told you.'

Frank's not making sense. Something about his car.

'What? *What?*'

'The car, Mimi. It was my car.'

'Your c-c—?' Her mind overshoots her ability to get the words out.

'I was on my way home, going past those shops – you know, the grocer, Bhati's, the newsagent on the corner – the radio was on, he – I – he came straight out into the side of my car. I swerved but not enough. Not in time. I – he hit the – fell on the . . .' Mimi sees his words rather than hears them, as if typeset in her mind. *It was my car. He came straight – I swerved*.

Frank is still talking. To her. At her. 'They're talking about dangerous driving. They've taken my car. I wasn't, I – I just needed to see you. It happened so fast.'

A sound comes out of her that she does not know. A tuba, or a horn. Brass.

Someone's at her side. 'Miss Brotherton.'

'F-F-Fraa-ank?' His name chops out of her mouth.

Someone grabs her arm and she's taken to a chair.

'I'll be okay,' Mimi insists, feeling that she will never be okay again. Frank is standing in front of her. 'I'm fine,' she says again and flaps her hand at the nurse, or the orderly, or whoever it is, and they say something about tea and they leave her and Frank, and she thinks, like a crazy person, *Ha! Here I am again*, sliding off the edge of the earth. *Frank's car?*

'I don't understand,' she says. 'They said – he ran out. In front of *your* car?'

Frank shakes his head, but doesn't say no. 'Nobody understands,' he says. 'Nobody saw. Christ knows – *I* don't know. One second I was going along and then, out of nowhere, there he was.' He bats his hands in front of him, as if transported to the moment of the accident. 'I can only think he was surprised to see me, wasn't concentrating, tried to flag me down. I didn't see him till he was right in front of me.'

'What was he *doing*?'

'I don't know. When I saw his face, he—' Frank's whole

171

body shudders. He takes Mimi's hands and pulls her towards him.

'Frank.'

Neither of them has the right words for this.

'Has Art been taking his meds?' he asks.

'Of *course*.' She wriggles away. Art would be livid to know she'd blabbed to Frank about his anxiety medication.

'I'm sorry. I'm just saying—'

She'd explained to Frank that they kept Art calm, kept the edge off the paranoia he sometimes felt about his work, the obsession. He'd been good for so long, it wasn't a fact she should have shared.

'Maybe he hasn't been looking after himself? Working too hard? He seemed unsettled, especially when you were away.'

'I need a moment,' she says. *I'm going to throw up*. She walks back down the passage feeling as if she could topple over, her legs liquid.

The loos smell of too much human, covered by too many chemicals. In one of the cubicles, she lifts the toilet lid as though she is still a functioning person. She bends over the base, clamping the cold porcelain between her knees, but can only dry-heave. She's still dressed from her trip home from Wales. There's a tea stain down her front, she has 'shortbread' written on her hand. Her mouth tastes acid, sour.

She's completely alone.

The cubicle door smacks the frame as she leaves.

She stands in front of the stainless-steel basins and squirts sanitation foam onto her hands. She splashes her face with cold water and it dribbles down her front. She can't dry her face on the hand-dryer – it's angled too close to the wall. She collects a wad of toilet paper instead and pats her face – patting herself back together.

172

Her phone buzzes. It's Rey.

Sorry missed yr calls, you back okay? So exciting the production company here has a link to Foley legend John Roesch, you know guy who did ET's jelly-wobble sounds!! Hoping for intro day after tmrw! Woohoo!

As much as she needs Rey, she cannot reply that Art is in a coma. There's nothing her friend can do right now. She'll tell her in the morning. She turns her phone off and puts it away.

The passage echoes with the smack of her canvas shoes on the linoleum. The light in here is artificial, it suggests no time at all.

Frank is standing in the middle of the waiting room, watching down the corridor for her to return. He looks lost.

'You okay?' he asks as she comes towards him.

'Well no. But I'm better than he is, I guess.'

'Can I see him?' Without slowing down, she nods, touches Frank's elbow, and walks into the ward.

'Artie.' His sister's voice. 'What *happened*?' Her voice trembles – he feels it cling to the inside of his ribs.

This mess is not all her fault. She never meant to bring a cuckoo into their lives. But she did not think, either. She never did. Acted first, thought next.

Everything whirls, faster and faster, like gears click-clacking down a chain, through his nerves – catching the spokes of a wheel in a rhythmic light drum, a three-sixty turn.

Dum. Dum. Dum.

The fragile beat of his struggling heart.

Then another voice.

'Hello buddy.'

Buddy? His fingers singe at Frank's touch. 'What were you thinking?'

173

Mimi! He has called her name a thousand times.

'It's okay.' His sister. Warm pressure on his ankle. 'I'm here.'

How can he keep her? He feels a pull, an elemental surge. A liquid metal whorl to the portal of before. A silvery trail. A silver woman. Silver. Silver.

A trigger is refired. Art runs the numbers in his mind. *Np* hard – the numbers are too large; they blow into the sky.

Eventually, Art's monitor calms down. Mimi is holding his ankle.

Frank is looking at her.

His eyes were what she first liked about him. Dancing, diamond blue. Frank, whose eyes have never been sad. Their blue always took the colour of the world around him, the palette of the sea, the steel of a storm. The blue of his T-shirts played under his lashes.

Today they are dull. A flat grey uniform blue. Office carpet, she thinks. Hospital waiting room.

Is there such a colour as car crash blue?

Frank's gaze returns to Art's injured arm. 'What actually happened here?' he asks, touching the caked bandage.

'I'll explain,' she says. In her mind, Art's face flashes in horror. His arm rises up. His head flings onto the pavement, his arm strapped impotently to his side. 'But later, and not in here.' She smooths Art's blanket before they leave the ward.

Art never changes his routine, she says, when they're out. 'He either comes home or goes to the pool.' Without looking at Frank, she sits, with her hands tucked underneath her bottom, palms flat on the bench. It pulls on her tendons; the pain in her fingers is something to focus on. 'Did the two of you have a plan?' she asks. 'Why was he there, near your house?'

Frank shakes his head. 'No,' he says, 'no plan. Out of the blue – there he was. He just stepped straight out into my car. He wasn't running or anything. But he didn't look surprised.'

'To be *hit*?'

'It was as if he knew I'd be there. He seemed completely focused on me. He was staring at me, and his face kind of changed.'

'Well, it would, wouldn't it? If you'd been hit by a car. Are you meaning to put this on Art?'

'It's just—' Frank looks at his shoes. She does too. They are such ordinary, brown, leather lace-ups. In contrast to the trim of blood, their ordinariness is a jolt. She can't imagine him pulling them on, or tying the laces, this morning.

'You've been wearing those all day.'

'My shoes? What? I'm in the same clothes. Why?' He has blood on the inside of his sleeve; even on the hem of his jeans, there is blood.

'You've even got blood on your shoes.'

'I know. Christ, Mimi, I know,' he chokes out. He rubs his hands hard down the seam of his jeans, as though there is blood on them too. It seems it is taking all he has not to cry.

'This is a lot to take in,' she says.

'I know, believe me, I know.' He looks round the room. 'I'm not finding the right words. Would it work if I drew it for you, where it was, what I remember seeing?'

Mimi nods. She slides closer towards him. 'Use Google Maps,' she says, looking round to make sure no one is going to yell at them for using a phone.

On Mimi's app, Frank zooms into the corner. He enlarges on a hedge. 'Art must have been here.' Through blurring pixels, they can see the children's playground with its roundabout, a Stop sign and white-painted markings on the road. 'I was driving this way.' His fingers touch the screen as though trying to coax a different outcome from the satellite map.

She touches the spot where she imagines Art's body, lying on the road, his bandaged arm useless at his side. 'Is there blood on the street?'

'I don't think a lot,' says Frank. 'Mimi—'

'Don't say it. I know.' Her eyes fill.

'I need to,' says Frank. 'If I say I had nothing to do with it, what am I saying? Was Art trying to get himself killed? I want to say—'

'That it's not your fault.'

Frank nods.

'I know.' But she doesn't really know what she means. She puts her hand on his thigh. 'We all feel guilty,' she says, as though this is a sort of universal feeling, like an umbrella, or a tarpaulin. Not a knife.

'Thank you,' he says, and now he does cry, and she holds him, and his shoulders are heavy on her frame, and she lets him lean on her anyway, even though it is difficult to breathe.

31

OMISSIONS

In the dark of the cab on the way home, Frank asks Mimi to tell him what happened to her brother's arm. She'd rather throw herself out of the taxi, arms wide open, take a lungful of fresh air and dive onto the tarmac, a Foley thud of shoes and weighted cloth on a hard surface, than tell him the full truth – what Art said about Frank, and how she'd hurt him. But, with the trundle of the road underneath the taxi's diesel engine, she manages a version that almost sounds like something that might happen in an ordinary family. Art had a meltdown that she still doesn't fully understand, partly triggered by him overhearing her and Rey – she thinks. They had an argument – as she'd said – but the top of the pepper grinder flew off by accident. It was awful, she says. She doesn't mention screaming at Art that she was leaving. 'I'm sorry I didn't tell you everything at the time. But it felt terrible. Rey suggested I take some time to think.' They stop at the end of Muriel Grove. 'I didn't work at all in the end,' she says in a last bid to clear her conscience as Frank reaches for the handle.

He lets go of the door. 'You spent the days on your own?'

She nods. It's not the first time she's had to confess to a lie.

Frank takes a breath. 'It sounds like a shitstorm.' She looks at the floor, at the gaps between the ribbing in the rubber mat, like omissions. Frank opens the door. 'Let's get you inside,' he says, although he sounds shaken. 'We've bigger things to worry about.'

Mimi stops him. She's just realized that Frank had suggested earlier that he'd *seen* Art while she was in Wales.

'What?' says Frank. 'There's more?' He leans in towards her. She shakes her head.

She's too tired. 'Nothing more.'

Inside, Frank wraps himself around her, great tentacles of muscle that hold her so tight it squeezes her chest. She opens her eyes against his jumper, it's completely dark and she sees only a galaxy of cobwebs and pinprick stars.

She smells layers of the day. Petrol, police stations, hospital.

'It'll be okay. Somehow. Though I know it doesn't feel like it right now,' Frank says, and she can hear that he means it, but he's also persuading himself. She keeps her eyes closed, her face buried, and doesn't answer.

'Come,' says Frank after a while. 'Let's take you upstairs.'

'I think I need a bit of time.'

'Time?' There's a frill in his voice, just contained. He's tired too. 'You need *sleep*.'

'It might be better if you – if I –' she can't quite imagine how it will feel to lie with him tonight – 'if you go home?'

Frank rubs his ear. He looks at her for a long time before he talks.

'Mimi, this is going to be incredibly hard. The police will prod us both about what happened, people will ask uncomfortable questions and think things that they don't say but that will show on their faces. Awful things. There are only three people who know that I would never want to hurt Art.

You, me and, hopefully, Art, who isn't here. We need each other right now. *I* need you,' he says. 'And you've been away. It would be madness to try and cope with this each on our own.' He goes still.

Her tongue feels thick in her mouth. 'I'm sorry,' she says, 'of course you can – *should* – stay.'

Frank pulls down his jumper where it's ridden up his back.

'I'm sorry,' she says again.

'Yeah. I'm sorry too. This is hell. I get that. Look, I've got to go back to the police station in the morning,' he says. Then he stops. The mention of the police station is like a sudden wipe on a dirty window, a reminder of where things stand.

'Urgh. Maybe you're right,' says Frank, his hand pushing his forehead. 'I'll go home. I need fresh clothes and that way I won't wake you. I can come back afterwards to take you to the hospital, before going to work, if you like. *Work*, Jesus. How am I going to work?'

He holds her once more before he leaves. She lets him go, but in the small ticking hours without him lying next to her, before she falls into a cave of pre-dawn unconsciousness, she knows that she made a mistake.

32

HEURISTICS

There's a lifesaving beat of breath when the world is still and she doesn't yet have her bearings, when her mind is still chasing her dreams. Then it catches her like a blanket being ripped off, and she remembers.

Frank's car hit Art.

She rolls over.

Hey, says a text from Frank. **Did you sleep?**

Some. She remembers an eyelash of moon in the window in the middle of the night. The same moon over Frank. Over Art, in the hospital.

She burrows back down with her duvet right over her head, but she's wide awake.

She reaches out an arm and turns on the lights, checks the time on her phone. 6.25. She'd brought Art's old notebook upstairs last night – it's on her bedside table. Still lying on her side, she opens it now, straightens a folded corner and fingers her brother's pencil marks. They have renewed poignancy.

The notebook is like a magic wardrobe to Art's inner world. She wishes she'd listened more closely. Or he'd slowed down a little when he'd tried to explain.

There won't be any answers in here, but it's still dark outside and she doesn't want to move, or face reality – so, she turns the page.

When people solve Np problems in real life, they are often doing so by mistake, Art's written. *They are using heuristics.* He's mentioned heuristics before, referring to the police. He called it a bad rule of thumb, or a faulty *heuristic*, to assume that because police wear a uniform, they know what they're doing.

Heuristics are useful 'best guesses'. But hard for people like me to employ in daily life, his notes say. *They require an intuition that is contrary to my mathematical view of the world.*

And then, scrawled in his adult hand, in ink that looks almost fresh – *Heuristics: human shortcuts to impossible problems: love?*

Since when did her brother ever think about love?

She carries on.

The Best Route Home, says Art's journal. Art always took the best route home. It was the same, every day. It took him nowhere near Frank.

She's about to close the book when she realizes: it's full from the back too.

Mimi sits up.

Columns and columns of minute writing are delineated in pencil. It's an odd list for Art. Dates and emotions. There's an entry every few days, sometimes a week or two apart, and the occasional day is ringed.

Stable. Excitable. Emotional. Withdrawn. The list looks like words Mimi used with her mother. *We need him to be emotionally articulate*, Christine said. Diligent student that Art was, he'd written a meticulous record of his feelings. She flicks through the entries, feels sore to her ribs at how hard he tried. The book's first half is his maths – the minutes of his mind; this is a journal of his heart.

Anxiety, Anger, Restless, he writes. *Contrary, Jealous, Worry and Joy.* It's carefully transcribed. His attention and care are heart-breaking to see. She imagines him trying to decide on each word. *Weepy and Selfish. Simmering rage.*

Weeks and weeks. Months. *Years* of recording.

Back thirteen years.

He's recorded his every emotion, since their parents died.

Her mobile rings. It's 6.50 a.m.

It's Rey. Mimi needs to be vertical for this. She pushes her covers off and stands at the window, holding the curtain in one hand, looking at her phone, ringing.

'Rey,' she says.

'Oh, Mi. I've spoken to Frank. Oh, angel.'

It's hard not to cry. 'He's—' But she doesn't know how he is. She coughs as she tries to talk and breathe. Rey's struggling too, and keeps saying *Oh Mi. Oh Mi, no.* Mimi takes the phone downstairs, where she's greeted by the sour smell of wine. Rey says she's coming home.

'There's no point,' says Mimi. 'Stay there.'

'Don't be mad. Who's looking after you?'

'Frank, when he's here,' says Mimi. 'And Art's post-doc, Ernest.' She still hasn't told Ernest what's happened. 'Art's faculty. Ginny, his assistant.' She tries to sound cheery, as though a great spirit-lifting infantry has swung into action on her behalf.

She looks around the empty kitchen where this imaginary army might be stationed.

'Listen, Sweetie,' says Rey, 'I'm not hanging around here. I'll stay today, which feels like a nightmare. But I'll be home tomorrow.'

When Mimi puts down the phone, she grabs the edge of the kitchen table, folds her head onto her arms and cries. She is crying for Art, yes. She is crying for Frank. But really, she is crying for herself.

33

THE HALTING PROBLEM

'Good morning,' says Mimi, as she enters Art's ward. She hopes a smile to the nurses will elicit good news about her brother, as if by sheer force of friendliness, she might alter the course of his condition. In fact, he is worse, paler, his face more shadowed and sunken.

She signs for the release of Art's belongings – the backpack he had with him yesterday, and his clothes in a clear plastic bag.

Sitting next to his bed, Mimi opens the backpack. As she might expect, there's a maths book inside, an old one her father loved – *Chaos Squared* by Jack Freeman. It gives her a jolt because it was her father's favourite book, but she supposes it's unremarkable that Art's carrying it around. It's still got the strawberry sticker she stuck on the dust jacket as a young girl. Of more interest is a foil emergency blanket, a flask of tea and Art's mobile phone, zipped into the front pouch along with the key to his study.

Art had enjoyed making her work out his password when he'd got this phone. He'd given her a crossword clue – *'Take pie back.'* Pie, inevitably, was mathematical pi. Mimi loved the satisfying clarity of finding an answer Art wanted her to find.

3141 she'd typed, smiling. **Incorrect password**, said his phone. 'Take pie *back*,' her brother had told her. 'Standard crossword practice.'

'Don't be irritating.'

'Backwards,' said Art. '1413.'

Mimi wants to know his movements yesterday – did he ignore her texts or not receive them? Before she does that, she flicks through his wallet, which reveals nothing. But then, there, behind the front pouch of his bag, in the discreet compartment where she knows Art keeps his passport when he's travelling, is a letter. Addressed to her.

No. No. No. Oh dear god, *please no*.

It might be an ordinary letter, on an ordinary day. But the envelope is Art's favourite stationery, Basildon Bond, 200 gsm.

Dr Sipos is walking towards her, and gestures to Art's bedside. Mimi stuffs the letter back into her pocket and walks over to him with her hands shaking. 'The first forty-eight hours it is critical,' says Dr Sipos. 'I know his condition looks grave, his body is coming out of initial shock. And the next twenty-four hours, they are *particularly* important. Keep talking to him.'

Dr Sipos's voice and soft, irregular English are calming, but they are background now. She can't concentrate. And anyway, before she can pull herself together, he's gone, rounds calling.

She goes to the Quiet Room, a windowless space where families come to sit in silence and stare at the walls. It is furnished with plain chairs and a corner table. Alongside a framed watercolour of geraniums in a window-box are posters for a bereavement service and the Patient Advice and Liaison Office.

The envelope from Art is sealed, with NAOMI BROTHERTON on the front, in capitals.

She slits it open. Inside is a letter written in black roller-ball – Art's pen of choice – in his distinctive, spidery hand. His writing deteriorates; by the end his words mash up against one another and it's hard to read.

It's difficult to read anyway. In every way.

Mimi

I am in my office and you are in Wales – 207 miles away, an almost straight line due east from here.

You will not get this letter. But if you did, I can imagine you rearranging your face as though you were looking at a bank statement, knowing it is not to be read with people around. Your face is easy to read. From me that is saying something. You would put it into the back pocket of your jeans and find somewhere private.

I assume you are in jeans right now. You always are.

Mimi. First, I forgive you. That is the easy part. My arm will heal.

Much harder is this: you cannot leave to go and live with Frank. Not because I cannot cope without you. I would miss you, but I would manage. Rather, because he is the wrong man for you.

I know how much you like him. But you know I am right about the big things in our life. It was difficult for me to believe too, at first.

I know that I cannot come to you with the idea that Frank is in our life for the wrong reasons without convincing concrete facts. I intend to use the next few days to remedy that. My proof and your future are both at stake.

I have kept even Rey out of this. The only person I can rely on implicitly is Ernest – I know you would

186

trust him too. When I see you, I will know more. But, like the Halting Problem, I will only know once I know.

Of the various scenarios available, this made the most sense. I explored them all.

Art

P.S. *Perhaps it is better you are not here. You would think I was off my medication, or want to inform the police – I am NOT involving them.*

She scans the letter again and again.

The wrong man for you . . . in our life for the wrong reasons. Those words especially. *Who is he, really?* Art had said. For nearly a week, she's dismissed his words.

But also – *my proof* – she can't have missed Art finding his proof, surely? She's always understood that the moment *p* was proved to equal *Np*, or not, would be the equivalent of discovering the Bomb.

Perhaps it's the proof that's sent Art over the edge. Or not quite over the edge, according to his unconvincing P.S.

His letter offers nothing about what happened the night at the pool. No *convincing concrete facts* at all.

Art despises the police, so the reference to them shouldn't totally surprise her. But why he thought the police might be involved at all, *before* this accident even happened, is confusing. Accidents like this are their actual job, for heaven's sake.

Back at Art's bedside, she touches his frayed, soiled cast. She left for Wales five days ago – five missing days that she needs to understand.

First, I forgive you.

For breaking his wrist? For saying she was leaving? She can't forgive herself for either right now.

The monitors beep, ventilators exhale in long breaths, other families come and go. The nurses give them well-worn smiles that seem to be reserved for people whose expectations have had to realign themselves with their new futures. Art's chest rises and falls.

'How will they cope?' Mimi remembers overhearing someone ask Aunty Pam when her parents died.

'One foot in front of the other,' was their aunt's reply. And so it is now.

'I gather you've been looking for me.'

Mimi swings round.

Ernest stands at the entrance of the seating area, pale as the wall. He has a wheelie bag trailing behind him like a forgotten limb. 'I didn't know. I should have been here. I – I was supposed to be back.'

They don't know each other well enough to hug. Ernest is in his usual ill-fitting shirt and two-sizes-too-big trousers. His shoulders writhe around as though trying to shrug off his jacket. His hair looks less like he's neglected to brush it than like he's forgotten it's there at all.

'I didn't know, until, when – I went via the university from the station,' rambles Ernest. 'How *is* he?' He looks past Mimi to where Art lies, but closes his eyes in an extra-long blink, like he'd rather not see what is there.

'We don't know,' says Mimi. 'Stable.'

'And we don't know what happened?' says Ernest. 'I mean, how sure are we that this wasn't, *you know* . . .' He is breathless. 'He has *not* been in a good way.'

'What do you mean?'

'You've been away, right?' Ernest looks to Mimi, then Art, and back again, like a pendulum. 'In the last few weeks,' he says, still out of puff as he explains, 'there's been a lot of

188

noise about *p versus Np*. People seem to think there's a breakthrough in the collective thinking. Maybe they realize how close Art is. Or maybe his work has leaked. Or someone else might be about to solve it.' He rubs his hair round his head. 'Which would destroy him.' Ernest doesn't appear to use 'destroy' lightly. It feels as if he's pushing the words out as fast as he can in an attempt to reverse events.

'Why didn't he tell me?'

'It came to a head last week,' says Ernest. 'It's why I panicked when I first saw his arm. I was worried that he'd done something really stupid. Drastic – you know, hurt himself. On purpose. I was so relieved when he told me he'd just fallen over, that it was a crack. But now – *this*.'

'I had no idea,' says Mimi. In that same week, she'd told Art she was leaving, *and* injured him. She rubs the trim of her jumper between her fingers. 'I wasn't there to help him.'

'That's not true.' Ernest touches her hand. The hand that held the pepper grinder. That held Frank. 'You're cold,' he says.

'I've let him down so badly. I hurt him. I—' she says, pulling on her lip. Ernest is quiet. 'It explains so much.' She pictures Art dragging his wet towel behind him, hauling a carcass of worries, alone.

'What did the driver say?' asks Ernest.

Mimi looks at Art's trusted post-doc. Art's letter is in her pocket; it feels as if it's written in ink on her face. 'You haven't heard,' she says. And then, just over Ernest's shoulder, she sees Frank, coming down the corridor with a paper bag in his hand. He lifts it to her in hello, then talks to the nurse at the ICU desk, pointing at Mimi. What a mess. 'It was Frank's car,' she says.

'*He* hit Art?' says Ernest, whipping round. '*Frank?*' Ernest looks as though he's been tasered.

'His *car*,' she says quickly. 'They say Art stepped straight out in front of it.'

Frank walks towards them, defenceless. The everydayness of the paper bag in his hand seems to mark him somehow, as though he hasn't fully understood the seriousness of what he's done.

He touches her back and kisses the top of her head, but he's looking at Ernest – they've met briefly a couple of times at King's. Ernest's face is cast in disbelief – he's blinking more rapidly than usual, moving from foot to foot.

'Ernest,' Frank says.

Ernest's tone is flat. 'Frank.'

'How is he?' Frank asks.

'Mimi?' presses Ernest. Unfinished conversation runs in a current between them. 'If I could see him, just briefly?'

Mimi nods, and indicates to the duty nurse that Ernest is with her.

Frank hands her the paper bag. There's coffee which has spilled a bit in the bottom, but there's an almond croissant too, her favourite. She tries to smile. 'I was worried you wouldn't eat,' says Frank.

'I don't think I can.'

She watches Ernest walk towards Art, hoping that his restless energy won't disturb her brother. But he slows right down, with the reverence of someone approaching a shrine. She watches him whisper in Art's ear. She sees him tuck Art's arm in at his side. He straightens the blanket and puts his hand on Art's shoulder. His head is bobbing as though he is talking. He might know what to say.

'Mimi?' says Frank.

Ernest looks reluctant to leave. Then, through the blanket, he holds Art's foot, his palm to Art's sole.

* * *

190

Art skims the edges of waves, skateboarding the rim of his consciousness. Endless numbers tumble about.

'Can you hear me? Art?'

Ernest.

'I've got your back. I'll find out more about Frank. I'm not sure I believe what I've heard about last night.'

Art's insides squeeze.

'I've got her,' says Ernest. Art feels the rhythm of his voice, the perfect amplitude of his words. The words dissolve. He senses pressure on his foot, its warmth is welcome, a flat pad on his sole. 'She'll be okay,' says Ernest.

Trust feels like this, thinks Art, letting go.

In his experience, getting people to trust you was hard, even when you knew you were right.

All those years ago, when Art discovered that his parents had sent their old stuff to the charity shop, his sister had not trusted him enough. He had been shocked by the treasures they had deposited there.

'What is going on?' he quizzed his parents at breakfast the next day. But they stared, their expressions a uniform blank. 'Your things? *My* old things? I found them all – at the *charity* shop. The loft, the shed – what are you doing? Why all the change?'

Walter lowered his eyes to the paper, to the football pages, which he never read.

'You have cancelled *Good Housekeeping*. Got a refund on your weekend away. Tell me, Mum. Or I will speak to Mimi.'

'I wouldn't do that,' said Christine. 'She doesn't have the same sense of order you do. We're taking stock. That's all.' She reached out, her thin hand hovering, but he turned and walked away.

He went to find Mimi in her room. She was wearing headphones, lying on her rug with her legs in the air, staring at her freshly painted toenails, her schoolbooks splayed on the floor around her.

'Why do you think they are doing this?' He put the charity shop's business card on her tummy.

'Huh? What are you talking about?' She snapped her headphones back on, turned her ankle, and appraised her toes in the light.

'Mimi.' Art hissed into her headphones. He flapped the card in front of her face.

'What? It's just the charity shop. Why the fuss?'

'Mum and Dad are getting rid of their things.'

'So?'

'Something is up.'

'Oh, scoot. Get a life. I'm having a break from my uni applications.' Mimi went back to her music and left him looking at the flimsy paper card.

He did not give up.

Days later, he was back. Mimi had strung pink gauze over the lamp in her room, so the walls were the colour of a seashell's inner cavity. It made him feel ill. He felt for the door frame. He had sleuthed through the bins, the phone records, eavesdropped, he told her. They were packing up their life. '*Our* life,' he said. 'I went to the station. To tell the police.'

She stopped and turned down the corner of the page of her book. 'You went *where*?'

'Something is not right. You know Dad. He has been so much better over the last year, but he gets some pretty odd ideas. And Dad may appear cheerful, but Mum is really ill again.'

Finally, she sat up. 'What? How—'

'The police would not listen.'

'What did you say?'

'That they ought to come round. Stop our parents from doing something stupid.'

'No, about Mum? Being ill again?'

He could not answer her. He did not know how.

'Art!'

'I heard her say, "No drugs this time" on the phone to Aunty Pam in New York.'

Her mouth dropped open as though her jaw had broken. He wished he had not told her. '*No*,' she said. He heard her voice wobble, saw her face fold. 'Art—'

'The police told me to go home. Go to bed, take my meds.'

'What made them say that?'

Art shifted his gaze. Dust motes criss-crossed the room in the afternoon light. Life might be turning upside down, but the laws of physics were stubborn like that, they kept playing on.

'Art?'

'I told them I am on medication. That I would not cope with major change.' Her face suggested it was a mistake to reveal that particular detail. 'They would not take me seriously otherwise.'

'So, you told them you're mentally unstable and can't cope. Terrific.' She sort of laughed. Though it seemed she might cry; he could not quite tell. 'That should do it. Bet they come rushing over.'

'It is not funny, Mimi.' She was not always rational. It was sometimes hard to know what she thought.

Later he heard her footfall on the stairs, voices swelling up and down from below: Mimi, their mother. When she returned to her room, Mimi closed the door. He heard her lean against it before shuffling to her bed, where she must have lain down to cry.

Mimi had not trusted him when it had mattered most. And he had been right.

Ernest emerges from the ward, shock pasted on his face. 'I've got to go,' he says. 'But are you staying here all day? How do I get hold of you?'

'It's difficult,' says Mimi. 'You're not supposed to use mobiles in here.'

'I'll find you,' he says. 'We need to talk.' And the person she's been told is the only one she can trust exits the corridor in a fluster of too much material for his body.

Frank watches Ernest scurry out. 'What did he mean? What were you talking to him about when I arrived? Was it about me?'

'He just wants to know about Art.'

'He's kind of intense.'

She leans into Frank's jumper and for a moment she feels like a small girl pressing her forehead into her father's knee because she's fallen over. But her mind is on Art's letter – what it says about Frank – and on Art's missing days.

34

PROOF

t = minus five days

Familiar as life was at King's, Art felt unmoored with Mimi away in Wales. He squished soap from the dispenser in the toilet. It was sticky and pink and – his bête noire – *communal*. Wales might as well be on the moon. He ran the hot water over his fingers, careful to avoid his bandage.

Heading back into his office, Art walked past his assistant Ginny, who had no doubt secreted another Werther's toffee into her cheek in the time it had taken him to urinate. The imbalance between her calorie intake and her tiny frame was a source of mystery to him. 'No messages,' she said.

He closed his door.

Art supposed he was fortunate that his office was high enough to have a view of the buildings across the river, low enough to see the trees, and that Ginny, whom he shared with Professor Dorney, sat right outside his door. But it faced west and was gloomy in the mornings. He sat down, briefly tapping the photograph of his family to give him resolve.

As if the altercation with Mimi was not unsettling enough, chat rooms in the last few weeks had lit up with details of another possible proof for *p versus Np*. Some of the details were inexplicably similar to his own work.

Searching for an uninvited presence lurking on his computer, like the traces of a light-footed thief, Art sat hunched for hours, his feet planted square on the floor, his muscles firing off painful reminders of his inactivity. Months ago, he had installed extra malware detectors: Lavasoft, Trustport, Bullguard. Now, he checked for software changes and foreign addresses on Virus Bulletin. They covered China, Russia, Korea. All the while he should have been working on the proof itself. What a colossal waste of time. His armpits felt damp.

Wireshark showed the active connections his computer made with the Internet. It was fiddly, time-consuming work, cross-checking 32-bit-number IP addresses. Days had gone by and each time he found nothing. His wrist ached.

Although he felt more alienated from Mimi than he ever had before, he had promised Rey he would not call his sister in Wales. The GP who had sorted out his arm talked to Rey, and concurred with her instincts that a short time apart for him and Mimi was required. And – he insisted, with Rey standing there – *no* contact.

Perhaps just a text?

He picked up his phone.

Sweat prickled down his back, a glandular response to adrenalin, he guessed. He laid his phone next to his computer and cradled his hands in his lap.

He put his head round the door. 'Has Mimi not called?'

'You said she's away?' Ginny bobbed up and down.

'In Wales,' he said. Art looked at the squares on the Downton Abbey calendar behind Ginny's desk, the days crossed with Xs. Mimi would be home in five days. 'It is rather remote.'

'Not my thing,' said Ginny, before licking an envelope and

rubbing it down with her lacquered nail. 'By the way, Ernest said he'd come past before he leaves.'

Art went back to his work. Apart from his sister, Ernest was the person he would most like to see.

Art started as his window rattled. The wind had picked up and a plane tree leaf stuck to the glass like a hand trying to get in. His arm hurt. He cursed his sister and avoided his phone, pushing it away to the corner of his desk. Fine, he would give Mimi time to recover from her outburst – but another *five days*?

The afternoon wore on. The sun swung low in the belly of the clouds, lighting the river from clay to rippled rose gold. And then, it was black. 'You cannot sit here in the dark like this,' said Ginny, and switched on the light.

Then Ernest put his head round the door. 'Art?' He never knocked, but Art had got used to that. 'Crikey! What happened to your wrist?'

'An accident. At home.'

Ernest blinked his slow blink. 'How did you—?' Art replied that he'd rather not discuss it – it was just a wrist – but Ernest continued to fuss. 'You weren't alone, were you? Was Mimi there?' Ernest reached out to touch Art's injured arm, then drew himself back. His eyes flickered down the bandage. His face looked odd.

'Mimi was there. It is all sorted now.' He directed Ernest's attention to the numbers on the screen. Ernest took another glance at his wrist instead, looking overly troubled for such an inconsequential injury.

'The ulna is cracked, that is *all*,' said Art, hanging his arm out of sight.

Ernest pushed his glasses back up his nose and seemed to let it go. He smelled nice, like baked goods, and clean. It was always surprising for someone so rumpled.

197

'More important,' said Art, 'I am worried that someone is spying on my work.'

'*Still?*' Ernest bent closer in. He peered at the army of digits stomping along.

'As you know, I always track traffic on *p versus Np* – key words, equation phrases – to monitor what other mathematicians might be doing. Naturally, I never post my own.'

'Naturally,' said Ernest.

'You know I am trying a Mahalanobis approach to *Np* problems? Well, recently, the traffic has spiked in statistically significant correlations around the same salient equations that dominate my work. I would have thought they are unique to me. Effectively, my fingerprints.'

'You've conducted your own plagiarism detection.'

'Exactly,' said Art. He had known Ernest would understand.

'It's possible,' said Ernest. His forehead folded in a square-root sign between his eyebrows. 'Have you told the university? The department?'

'I drafted a letter a while back. But I don't know how secure even the Maths Department is. Did I tell you that Downing Street tried to get us to sign a disclosure agreement – to release any proof to Number 10 first? As if that place weren't a leaky colander.'

'Too right,' said Ernest. He was going away next week but offered to help Art on his return.

'I may know more this weekend,' said Art, feeling more settled than he had all day.

'Okey-dokey. Call me, or I'll see you when I'm back.' Ernest blinked and gave the door a little rap with his knuckles, his way of saying goodbye. Art was starting – he realized – to see Ernest as a friend. He did not want him to go.

* * *

198

Art pulled his cardigan on carefully over his bandage and walked out of his office to get another cup of tea, with a much brisker step than before. His focus was a hard button of concentration as he went through the possibilities of how to tackle the problem. Beyond the walls of the university, fringes from a student protest clanged lampposts as they passed.

In the cubby department kitchen, Art was briefly challenged by the prospect of making tea with one hand. He held the door of the fridge open with his foot to replace the milk.

Tea in hand, he walked back to his office. The last lectures of the day had finished. Colleagues strode the corridors, chatting, their heels clapping on the tiled floor.

If he had not looked up at a loud wail outside, he might have bumped straight into Frank. Frank looked unusually smart in a shirt and tie and was walking down the corridor, towards Art, with a somewhat familiar woman, his arms swinging at his sides. Art recovered his balance just in time to step out of Frank's eyeline.

Art was not sure if Frank knew what had happened between him and Mimi, and he did not relish the prospect of questions concerning his arm. Indeed, he did not want to be detained at all. He slipped the hand of his bandaged arm into his pocket, hoping the dressing was not obvious under the sleeve of his cardigan, and walked towards Frank. The finger curled round the handle of his mug was getting hot and sore. He needed to cut short this unwelcome interruption.

'Frank,' he said. 'Hello.'

'Art,' said Frank, without introducing the woman at his side.

Art felt required to speak. 'That is a fine tie you are wearing. Red.'

Frank looked down at his tie, as if he was surprised to find it there. 'It's a jute pattern. I call it my Mahalanobis tie,' he said. Then he winked.

Why was Frank mentioning Mahalanobis? Art's proof's fingerprint?! And who ever heard of such a thing, as naming your tie? There was a moment when no one said anything. 'I'm being rude,' said Frank. 'Er, Rachel, Art Brotherton. Professor Art Brotherton – Rachel.' Frank seemed in a hurry to move on.

But Art thought he recognized the woman. 'Rachel? I believe we may have met?'

The woman looked quickly at Frank, as though for approval. 'Rachel Silver,' she said.

That was it.

'Good to see you,' she said.

'You *know* each other?' Frank's eyes darted between them.

'We met briefly,' said Art. 'The American exchange, I recall?' But he felt off-kilter. Frank's red tie made him think of the evening at the pool. Of the lifeguard with his square red shorts. But something else was wrong. His discomfort was knotted around Frank's odd behaviour, and his mention of Mahalanobis. But also, that name. *Silver*. Rachel Silver. *R. Silver.*

His mind went back to the day in Frank's flat, when he had, admittedly without Frank's permission, sneaked a look at Frank's bank statements in the loo. He had scrolled down the length of the debits and credits, all pedestrian stuff, *except*, Art remembered, very clearly, that name. R. Silver. Who could forget it? The amounts were substantial. *Thousands* of pounds.

Rachel Silver. Now, here she stood.

And, Frank had winked. Art had always found winking confusing.

'Quite a hullaballoo, huh?' asked Frank, pointing outside. 'Damn right, too.'

There was a roar in Art's ears. But it was not the clatter of helicopter blades juddering over angry chants of students protesting about tuition fees. It was not the procession of media crews, or police batonning them off the road.

'Art? You okay, buddy? I wouldn't worry too much about it.' Frank waved his arm in the direction of the protests outside. 'It'll blow over. Always does. How're you getting home?'

'Exactly the same way that I always get home.'

The fan of lines at the edge of Frank's eyes squeezed. 'I'm sure it'll be fine—'

'There is not much you are not sure about, is there, Frank?' said Art.

'Huh?'

'Tell me something.' Art put the hot mug to his stomach as a small sound escaped.

'Mate?'

Mate? I do not think so. Frank had not even mentioned Mimi, not *once*. 'Never mind. Excuse me,' said Art. He could not read Frank's face.

Back in his office, alone, there was not enough air in the room. He got up and lifted the iron latch on the window. He paced the room, then stood and watched the protesters, spotting students and colleagues he recognized.

His head jerked up. The unwelcome guest in his system could be someone he *knew*.

He did not choose for Frank's name to be the first that he thought of, but the mind is a powerful autonomous machine. He tried to separate the *idea* of Frank from the physical sensations he was having. Those very same sensations he experienced when he worked out a maths problem, his body suffused with a chemical flood that told him he had, at last, found an answer.

The moment required the application of cold logic, to identify three things. Means. Motive. Opportunity. He had watched enough television to know that.

He would have liked to run it by Ernest, but Ernest was gone.

35

REFLECTION

Art ignored Frank's many calls the next day, Saturday. But at four o'clock, he heard the doorbell ring at home.

There at his front door stood Frank, pushing his hand through his hair. It was spitting icy needles of rain. Art invited him in.

Frank brushed his wet shoulders. 'I noticed your arm yesterday,' he said, 'and wanted to check – I tried to call, but you didn't pick up – are you okay?' Art did not offer to take Frank's jacket, in the hope he was not staying long, but Frank hung it up himself. 'Thought maybe we could have a drink?'

Honestly. It was mid-afternoon.

Art poured Frank a beer, while Frank went *on* about his arm. Possibly for the first time in his life Art understood, at a visceral level, what Mimi meant when she told him how off-putting it was when people did not look you in the eye. Frank talked *at* his arm, and it was strangely insulting, as though Frank would like to take Art's arm home with him and babysit it until Mimi got back.

'I've been worried about you,' Frank said. 'Is there anything I can do?'

'Supposing I said yes,' said Art. 'What *would* you *do*?'

Frank's face crinkled, and he put his glass down on the table, a little hard, thought Art. Was that what they called a micro-aggression? He had read the term in the newspaper. Art backed up against the oven and the burner knobs dug into his backside.

'Look,' said Art. And next thing, he'd blurted it out – Rachel Silver, *who was she*?

Frank took a sip of beer. 'Rachel?' His fingers curled tighter round his glass. 'She was here for a conference.' He scratched his ear. 'And collecting papers.'

Then Art asked Frank about Mahalanobis and, admittedly, Frank *did* look lost.

'What's up, Art?' he said. 'Honestly, I'm a little confused.'

'Why are you in our life, Frank? What do you want from us? From me?'

'What?' Frank's mouth sort of gaped. 'I don't want *anything* from you. What could I possibly want?'

To be quite so dismissed – to have it said out loud that he had absolutely nothing to offer. *Well.* And it was patently untrue. Had Frank not sought his advice for maths conferences? Had Art not helped him write the abstract for his submission to ArXiv, with its overlap between game theory and agency? He had taught Frank about cricket! Art knew he was yammering on at Frank. He managed to avoid directly mentioning p *versus* Np, but he was talking too fast. Still. Most important of all, he had – and he was sure that Frank knew this – *he* had been the one who had persuaded Mimi to come to that wretched awards night. He had practically dragged her there. Without Art, Frank would have nothing.

Frank's beer spilled on the floor as he put it down. He smeared it with his foot before tearing paper towel off the stand to wipe it up.

'We need Mimi here for this,' said Frank, holding the dirty clod of paper. He pressed the pedal bin open with his foot and threw it away. 'I think I should go.' The lid smacked down. Frank scooped up his bag, breathing out noisily through his nose. 'Art, I –' he looked so distressed that Art thought perhaps he was going to confess to something – 'I'm not going to tell Mimi about this conversation.' He shook his head. 'Not yet. I don't want to say something I'll regret.'

'I *will* tell Mimi. As soon as I can.'

'I'll let myself out,' said Frank and he walked down the passage, his shadow flung back; bent at the knees where the floor joined the wall.

He grabbed his coat. Then, with a slam of the door, Frank left.

Certainty shuddered through Art's body.

He spun round. Had he been alert enough while Frank had been there, all these months? In their house, with who knows what intentions? He scouted the house, touching everything once: the newspaper lying on the kitchen table, his post at the phone, his books on the shelf, as though to check that they were in fact, untouched.

His thoughts circled back to all the previous times that Frank had been there. He recalled Frank ascending the stairs, up to his sister's bedroom, straight past Art's own. The photograph of Mahalanobis was *right by his bed*. His lungs felt like glue.

Upstairs. Back downstairs. He checked the sliding door. The garden was secure. It would be easy to leap over the neighbour's fence, jimmy the door to the bins.

He pulled on his tracksuit pants and went to bed early, but not before he had tried every window, locked the pressbolt on the sash above the kitchen sink and turned the security key above the front door. He closed the bathroom fan light that overlooked the road and wished he had bought that super-secure Jackloc restrictor. When he retired to his room, the Mahalanobis photograph set off a fresh volley of anxiety. He riffled through his notebook, then his wardrobe, and opened and closed his bedside drawer. He even looked under his pillow – he did not know what for. By the time he slid into his sheets, the house and everything in it had been lifted, turned over, examined. Every exit hermetically sealed.

Lying in bed, his breathing exercises did little to quell a cascade of unpleasant sensations – he did not feel good.

Art lay on his back and thought about Mimi in Wales. How would he tell her Frank was not who he seemed? About Rachel Silver? Perhaps, while she was away, he ought to spy on Frank. He had encountered all sorts of novel spyware devices in his investigation into how someone might be spying on *him*. There was that shop on Black Prince Road . . .

He stared at the ceiling, at the strange shape of the shadow from the smoke alarm stuck up there. He bent the gooseneck of his Anglepoise lamp so that the shadow morphed from UFO to new moon, to a lonely hunchback squatting on a rock.

He missed his sister. Pain flamed in his chest. He missed his parents.

The biggest loss in Art's childhood had been that, somewhere in the transition from South Africa to London, he had lost his father. His father had still been there, alive, but his mathematical intellect, undermined by depression, had been like a flashlight with the batteries removed. Walter taught at the university, but his research was pedestrian – Art actually heard the word being used. It stuck to his father like a stain. Art's father had always been such a vigorous man; the word *pedestrian* seemed to confine his imagination to black and white, like zebra crossings in the city that limited his life.

Responding to what appeared to be a once-in-a-lifetime opportunity at a London university, Walter and Christine had packed up their eight-and-a-half-year-old son who combed his own hair in a firm side parting, and three-year-old daughter with her bright strawberry wisps, endless babble and unstable run – to build a new life for their family.

The evening they left Johannesburg for the last time, jasmine was in flower at the gates; its scent in the air as the family took leave of their home. Thousands of flying ants rose out the ground in a dusky cloud. Mimi, already in her pyjamas for the flight, had knelt on the grass and picked at their wings.

'Walter!' said his mother. 'Hold onto her, *please*. Now she's grubby, and we haven't even left home.' But Walter just laughed and brushed off Mimi's knees. His mother stuffed the last bag into the boot of their maroon BMW. Their father loved that car. Despite the cost and impracticality, he planned to ship it to England once they were settled.

As they finally drove out the gates, his father clasped his mother's hand on the armrest between the front seats. She squeezed it in return, then adjusted the mirror so she could see her children. 'Art, stay in your place. Please. The child locks aren't on.' The child locks were on *zero* percent of the time.

'Stain place Artie.' His sister giggled and smacked her knee. 'We goin' on a *plane*!'

The Brothertons landed in London in the black early morning. His father stared out the window of the plane. *Look*, he was saying. *Look*. At their new home of lights and dark and airport tarmac. His smile did not reach his eyes. Rivulets of water slid across the glass.

They climbed into an odd-looking car with an amber light on top. 'A London cab!' said his mother. 'Art, face forwards.' Sunrise watercoloured the sky as they arrived in Muriel

Grove. Muriel was such an English name, their parents said. 'Even our address will make us feel English.'

But the house was unlike any house Art had ever seen. It was attached to another matching one on the side, and every pair in the road looked the same. 'Terrace housing,' said his dad, 'it's an English thing.' The houses were like butterflies, each house symmetrical to its opposite wing, attached down the centre.

Art was familiar with the concept of symmetry. It implied a reassuring consistency. But here, in the house where they would live, with the neighbours separated by only a thin wall, going about their business in rooms that were a perfect reflection of their own? Another family living their inverse life in their inverse house?

His mother had been staring at her new home from the window of the taxi. Now, she turned towards Art. 'You've gone pale, Artie. What's wrong?' Art could not think of a single example in the animal kingdom that lived in symmetrical housing. Christine's gaze sprang between her one-wing house and her son.

The taxi driver helped his father lug suitcases through the low wooden gate and down the path to the red front door. The paving was uneven, and tufts of scraggly grass grew in its fissures. A terracotta pot with a cracked lip squatted at the door, filled with sand and a cigarette stub. Everything was covered with moss. Art's head buzzed.

Bees! Symmetrical hexagon hives. No wasted space in between neatly interlocking geometry. It maximized the honey for the hive. Art imagined London as if from above. Rows and rows of densely packed houses, optimizing space. Perhaps it could work.

'Bees have symmetrical hives,' he told his mother.

'Quite right,' she said. 'And now that I think of it, there's

208

bivalves too.' Pulling him close, she rubbed his arm, which he disliked. 'You know – mussels and tellins, cockles and clams?' Her voice sounded tinny as they walked through bare rooms. 'This house is a bit of an empty shell itself right now. But we will fill it up, you'll see.' She knelt down so her eyes were level with her son's. 'And I promise we'll take you to the sea, soon. I'll find you an English bivalve. Think of this as your bivalve house. I know it feels strange. But before we know it, it'll be home.'

Art looked at his father. He was standing at the sliding door, which Mimi was trying to open. Mimi made a new stuttering sound. 'S-s-stuck!' she was saying. His father held her hand, and they watched the rain.

Art's inventory of unanswered questions surrounding his parents' deaths kept him awake deep into the night, as it had on countless nights before. Had his father *really* given up?

Art had known then that something was wrong.

Something was wrong again now. Floating in the water that evening at the pool, trying to organize his discombobulated thoughts, Art had been aware that his initial reservations about Frank were curdling into a deep-seated antipathy. He had climbed out of the water, unaware that he was being watched.

He accepted that the incident with the lifeguard was not actually Frank's *fault*. That it was rooted in something deeper about Art himself, something he would have to address. It was ironic that Mimi's quest for love was forcing him to confront some uncomfortable truths of his own.

Perhaps knowing yourself was the most important thing of all. He had spent so much time trying to prove the rules that underpinned the world, the universe even, he had failed to know himself. Technically, knowing yourself required a turning in towards one's own consciousness that Art was not sure he was capable of. He was not a human Möbius strip, after all.

Art thought about the lifeguard's red shorts, his flat stomach, pale tendons pulling hard either side of a dark beetle line from his belly button, down.

Perhaps he ought to look for someone in his life?

He quickly redacted the idea, the whole conversation, from his mind. There was nothing wrong with being a virgin. How he *hated* that word. Still, it was not the end of the world. Immanuel Kant and Isaac Newton were virgins when they died. As he had many times before, he went over the roll call of famous names that he ached to be considered alongside, and finally, after an unsettling day and night wandering the landscape of the things that tormented him most, lonely in life but less in his dreams, Art slept.

36

PLANNING

And so, Art made plans. Just a few days after being clobbered with a pepper grinder, Art Brotherton broke the habit of a lifetime.

He did not walk the best route home.

Breaking habits was difficult for Art. Even so, he did not do his marking. He did not have his cup of tea.

Up in the Nash lecture theatre of King's College, Art underscored the last line on the whiteboard and turned to face the class. 'I believe it is ten to three,' he said, conferring with the wristwatch he was wearing on the wrong arm.

'Professor Brotherton,' said a girl at the front.

Art did not welcome a delay to the end of the lecture. But faculty–student interactions were high on the KPIs of the Belongingness programme. 'Yes?' he said, in what he hoped was a tone that did not invite too prolonged an encounter. His timing was tight. 'Leslie?' Art had learned the names of the students who regularly asked questions, identifying them by their singular characteristics – in this case a fringe chopped into the shape of a protractor.

'Your shoelace's undone. D'you need help, with your injured arm and all?'

The class laughed kindly and, in his relief at not being detained, Art allowed a smile. 'Thank you, I will manage,' he said. 'Assignments by Friday.' The undergraduates spilled out; his lecture, he hoped, had made at least some impression on their brains.

Back in his office, through the Crittall windows, Art could see the river sludge along the Embankment. Clouds hung like the inside of a tent, as if the air was thick and low.

The weather would be worse in Wales.

Art checked Google Earth for the cottage where Mimi was staying. He could make out the slate cliffs of the Welsh coastline and a puzzle of farms – and wished he could see Mimi too. Her words echoed in his mind. *I'm leaving. This house. You.* It sheared his insides. *I'm going.* He could not track her FindMyPhone and Rey had said satellite signal was poor.

But Frank, he could find. He knew where Frank worked, where he lived.

Mimi was far; she did not have to know.

Art derived comfort from life being but a series of mathematical outcomes. That at the root of every question, no matter how domestic, was a mathematical answer. Whether Mimi unpacked the groceries or made dinner first presented a potential scheduling inversion, easily solved; he still believed the dating algorithm, given a proper chance, might yet work to find her a suitable match. She had hardly given it a chance.

But he had to acknowledge – he was about to embark on something most *un*mathematical. He was going to have to watch and wait. He did not know for how long.

He touched the frame that held the photograph of his family, his talisman. He had been right about his parents. He had told Mimi and she had not believed him. Today, though, he experienced an unfamiliar sensation as he looked at his mother's face. A soft glove of gratitude held his anxiety.

Gratitude that she was not around to witness the mess they were in. As hard as he had tried to do everything she had asked in her letter, he had probably failed.

The very *idea* of failure almost felled him.

He swayed, then steadied himself with his good hand on the edge of his desk. His urge to speak to his sister rose like a rash. From deep in his belly to under his collar, he felt hot. He pulled out his phone to send her a text, but just stared at the blinking marker.

He had promised to leave her alone, and he would.

Instead, he pulled a single sheet of paper from its sheath and clipped the lid off his favourite pen. *Mimi*, he wrote, bent over his desk. Just writing that down, just her name, lanced his panic. He kept going, as if he was talking to her. *I am in my office*, he wrote. Without even realizing, he lowered himself into his chair, his bandaged left arm falling into his lap, and wrote. He pictured Mimi reading his words, even though she never would. No need to alarm her. He saw her as clearly as if she was in the room, as if she had just popped in to ask him for Sellotape. When the black ink was dry, he folded the page. Communicating *something* to his sister subdued the snaking sensation under his breastbone. NAOMI BROTHERTON, he wrote on the front of an envelope, in firm, square capitals, then put the letter into his bag.

In her absence, he would start to set things right.

He crossed the Embankment and looked into the canopy of a plane tree on the corner. He closed his eyes – the traffic was loud. By the time he reached the bridge, the wind had strengthened, scuffing the water with painted white peaks. He felt the force stiffen his face. With his right wrist supporting his aching left arm across his chest, Art walked forwards, straight into the squall.

37

SENSITIVITY

t = 0

Art's missing days are a mystery. Mimi has spent the afternoon massaging the dry creases of his feet that look like contour lines, talking to him, trying to decipher his thoughts and the meaning of his letter from the code of his breath. She's worried that he's leaking intelligence as he lies there, his cortex marinating in barbiturates and blood. She pictures a long silent stream of zeroes, his maths leaving his body, one breath at a time.

Now she walks out the hospital doors to head home, with Art's letter in her pocket. And without calling Frank. Cars and people whizz around, unperturbed. The world feels like toy town.

Muriel Grove is quiet. Rey's house is still locked up. A new fall of leaves patterns the pavement; the dark has forced everyone inside.

Mimi has a job to do that she's dreading. She knocks on Mr Raikes's door and lets herself in with the key he has given her. 'Mr Raikes? Hello?' She picks up his post. *Undercover Boss* is on TV. The house smells of baked potato and burned toast. 'It's Naomi.'

'Oh, Rizla – cards!' she hears him say.

Mimi pulls up a chair and lifts the dachshund onto her lap. 'Ooooph! Hey, heavy boy.'

'I overfeed him,' says Mr Raikes. He smooths the table in front of him for cards.

Mimi puts her hand on his. 'I'm afraid I can't play today.' As she tells him about Art, it is hard not to cry. His eyes widen, he brushes imaginary crumbs off his chest, a swallow travels down his soft goitred neck. 'Oh my,' he keeps repeating. 'Oh my.'

She doesn't tell Mr Raikes that it was Frank. Frank's *car*. He is holding his Union Jack playing cards when she leaves, opening and closing the pack as though they might still play.

Biscuits, she'd meant to bring biscuits.

She should've left the lights on at home. She stands at the door searching for her keys, when Ernest steps out from behind the rubbish bins.

'Ernest! You gave me a fright.'

'I need to talk to you.'

'Fine, but that's what front doors are for.'

Ernest sidles into the house, where he sizes up the kitchen like a loss adjustor might. Still tingling with adrenalin, Mimi lights the burner. Ernest walks over to the windowsill and turns on the radio, then across to the TV and turns that on too.

'Habit,' says Ernest when she asks what he's doing. 'Are you aware of the sensitive nature of Art's work?' He fiddles with the remote. 'Everyone, Mimi, wants this stuff.'

Mimi looks around for the stuff.

'Art's proof,' he explains.

'He's always saying that.'

They're very careful about who might overhear their

215

conversations, Ernest tells her. 'Hence the radio?' She has to smile.

'Seems silly, I know.' He shakes his head as though denying it. They can only just hear each other over Jo Whiley on Radio 2 and Greek politicians arguing on TV.

'Can I turn it down *a little*?' His face is so pinched, she daren't make fun of him. Then he suggests they check Art's phone.

'I meant to do it earlier,' she says, getting Art's backpack. That held his letter. 'But look, you need to get home. What was it you wanted to tell me?'

'Oh,' says Ernest, as though it's hardly worth mentioning, 'the thing is, Mimi, I think I'd better stay.'

'Stay?'

'Something's not right,' he says, and his eyes are soft, yielding. 'Art doesn't want me to leave you alone. I think I should stay till he wakes up. And then . . .'

No one has yet articulated the spectrum of life-changing losses that Art might face when he surfaces. But they lurk, ready to snap into every conversation. Ernest puts his hand on her shoulder, and it is only just enough to steady her.

Ernest can't stay, but she's glad he's there now. His hand is on the small of her back, the lightest pressure on her jumper. He guides her to the sofa and then heads outside to have a cigarette. She's holding Art's phone.

She punches in the code, knowing that Art would not welcome this intrusion. Too bad. He hadn't opened any of the messages she sent during her journey home from Wales. But: I'm coming home. Tonight. OMW. He saw that.

She looks at the calls *to* Art's phone. There are many, obvious ones from her, and a couple from Ernest. But then, suddenly, just a few days before the accident, there are seven calls from Frank. None for the rest of her time away, and

216

then seven. In one day. After that – none. And Art hadn't picked up. Only Frank's calls look out of the ordinary, and Art had ignored them all.

Mimi dials Art's number from their landline, just to hear his voice. His phone buzzes in her hand. 'Please leave a message,' she hears her brother say. '*Art.*' Love and resentment strain to fit into the single syllable of his name. It feels like the click of a leash.

Ernest wanders in from having his cigarette. There's discordant music on the radio. On television, David Attenborough examines something small between his fingers and talks about the Sumatran rhino. Ernest lifts the cordless phone. He inspects the base station. David Attenborough talks about the rhino's hairy back, the twinkle in its eye. Finding true love is no easy task for a rhino. There's a fine line between attraction and antagonism, he says.

Ernest fingers the underside of the kitchen shelves.

'*Ernest!*' He stops fiddling with a start.

She sees her own phone light up on the table. It's Frank. Before she answers, Ernest says he's going home to get his things, and Mimi doesn't stop him.

'I've been trying you,' Frank says. 'Has your phone been off?'

Just then, Ernest calls, 'Bye!'

'Who's that?'

With her phone hooked under her chin, she opens the fridge for some wine. 'Oh, Ernest.' She tries to sound casual, as though everything's perfectly normal. 'He's invited himself to stay.'

'To stay? You hardly know him.' Frank is understandably nonplussed. '*I* should be looking after you.' Mimi sees Attenborough hold a white, translucent Croatian olm in a bottle on the television; its sightless eyes pressed up against the glass. Trapped. 'He can't stay. *Obviously*,' says Frank.

Nothing feels obvious.

She twists the wine's screw-top, but catches the metal spiral below the cap. 'Shit!'

'You okay?' asks Frank. Mimi stares at the red shine on her fingers, the black-red dots on the floor.

'It's just a cut. Bloody wine tops,' she says, and sucks her finger.

'Ooh, *ouch*.'

She tastes copper on her tongue. 'So cheaply made.'

It isn't a lot of blood, but Mimi holds it under the cold tap longer than she needs to and watches the streaky patterns run into the sink. She yanks paper towel off the roll and wraps her finger. Red blooms through the layers.

'You okay?' Frank asks again as she fixes her finger, a disembodied voice on speaker-phone. He's quiet for a moment. Then – 'Please,' he says. 'Let me help, Naomi.' She's not used to hearing Frank sound anxious. 'Don't shut me out. This is so shitty, for us both.'

She rewraps her finger, then looks at the floor. Her feet are far away, as though her head is stretching from her body, her thoughts dissociating. *I know how much you like him*, Art said in his letter.

'Mimi? Let me – I don't know – call people, let them know what's happened. I'll come round, make supper, run you a bath. I'd *like* to look after you. Ernest can't do that.' She just holds her finger and shakes her faraway head. Tears fall onto the tips of her shoes.

'I can't, Frank.'

'You can't what?'

What can't she do? 'Talk to you right now.'

'I see,' he says. His words are clipped.

She picks up the phone. 'You're right, though, I'll let everyone know. I'll text people a standard line, something non-committal.' Talking seems pointless. 'I'm sorry,' she says. She feels a sob rise up through her throat. She needs him so much. *The wrong man for you.* 'I'm sorry, I can't think.'

'You don't believe me,' he says, slowly.

'Believe you?'

'He came *straight* out towards me. I can't believe I have to persuade you.'

'It's not that. God, Frank, no. But I—'

'I don't know how you imagine it was anything else.' His voice runs between anger and injury, a shaky, seismic line. 'Call me,' he says, his words blistering with hurt, 'when you're ready.'

Mimi clicks off the phone, holding the bloodied pulp of paper round her finger, her back to the wall.

The doorbell saves her from her tangle of thoughts. Through the fish-eye in the door, she catches a drift of Ernest's candy-floss hair. A bag humped over his shoulder makes him look more like a hermit crab than ever.

'That was quick,' says Mimi, feeling flat.

'Yup, well. Is Frank coming?' Ernest ducks his head this way and that, as though Frank might be hiding in a hallway corner, then exclaims when he sees the wet, red mess around her finger. He puts his bag down at the foot of the stairs, takes ice out of the freezer and wraps her wound in a fresh tea towel, then gives it a squeeze. 'I know what you're thinking, I hardly know you, you're perfectly capable. Et cetera.' He holds her finger pointing up. 'Either way, I promised Art. There. Better?' He's very gentle. All she can do is nod. 'Hey, are you okay?'

'Not really.' She's using the fridge as ballast.

Ernest steers her into a chair, as if all her bones are broken.

'What a nightmare. Art in hospital, Frank done for dangerous driving.'

'He hasn't been accused of anything. The police said – it was an accident.'

A small sound escapes Ernest, like a little balloon of pity that pops out by mistake. 'You're right, he hasn't been charged.' But he doesn't look at her. 'Look, there's a lot to talk about. Perhaps better over food?'

'I don't think I can eat.'

Ernest seems programmed to keep moving. He pulls out two plates and slides them into the bottom oven to warm. 'We should make sure there's nothing else from Art, check out his study.'

Oddly, she can imagine getting used to Ernest; it's calming to watch him potter about. He has a mesmerizing tenderness, the way he goes about setting things right, wiping down a small smear of blood off the kitchen counter, tidying the long flag of paper towel back around its stand. It's futile to resist his insistence on staying.

'I'll meet you up there.' As she climbs the stairs, Ernest orders takeaway butter chicken and naan for supper.

She puts her head into the spare room to check it's okay. Laundry hangs over a drying rail, and a basket spills over with sound magazines.

This used to be her room. She knew every chimney pot on the roofs across the road, including where the pigeons preferred to mate. She could see the neighbour's satellite dish that leans towards the road as though it's listening in on passers-by. She should have stayed in here. Opposite Art, across the carpeted hall. In her single bed.

Her vintage iron hospital bed.

In September, just before her birthday, she'd moved into their parents' bedroom on the top floor because of Frank.

Art had agreed, but he'd stood outside on the landing and watched with his mouth set. She'd bought a new mattress and cried when the old one got carted away, her parents' saggy imprints with it. She still feels like a visitor up there, the small girl that pattered down the passage in the middle of the night. 'Can't s-s-sleep,' she'd say to her dad, who was often awake with a small reading light trained on obscure, tiny print. He would shepherd her back, his hand on her shoulder, his lion hair wild.

Even now, years later, she can imagine the sound of his tread, the creak from his weight on the third stair.

Ernest appears, his head cocked to one side. 'How're you getting on?'

38

TIPPING POINT

Mimi and Ernest head to Art's study. With a short beat of trepidation, she turns the key to the study door.

When she switches on the standing lamp, light pools on the carpet, catches the desk – which looks as it should. His locked computer, his cup of Pentel 0.7 mm mechanical pencils with gel cushions that prevent callouses. His plain paper. Mathematicians don't use lines, he always says. She picks up the glass dodecahedron paperweight – the heft of it is gratifying. 'Why d'you think he locked the door?' she asks.

'So, this is where he works,' says Ernest, without answering her, looking round as though in a trance.

Mimi pulls on the brass swan-neck handle of her father's old desk and slides the drawer open. Paper clips, stapler. Post-It notes. Tidy.

Ernest leans across her and closes the curtains. 'Does Frank stay over often?'

'Not that often. Why?'

Ernest scans the bookshelves, where their father's old books rest alongside Art's. 'I mentioned to you at the hospital, that this all started when Art noticed a spike in conversations online that seemed to refer to his work. It can happen, you know, like Alfred Russel Wallace arriving at the same conclusions as Darwin, from deep in the forests of Borneo? The cumulative knowledge gets to a tipping point. And then – well, it's a race to the tape.' Ernest *woomphs* down into the armchair.

She sits too. 'Art speaks of his proof,' she says, without mentioning the letter, 'as though he's done it?'

'He hasn't.' Ernest's smile is wry. 'He just thinks of it as *his*. That it belongs to him. But Art believes someone is actively after his work. I encouraged him to report it.'

'That would completely upend him. Still, it doesn't explain what he was doing near Frank's house,' she says.

Ernest rubs the side of his face. 'This sucks,' he says. 'Look, Mimi, this isn't easy to say.' But then – as though someone has fired a starting gun, he canters off about Art's maths. Frank. Frank *and* Art's maths.

'I don't understand.'

Ernest shakes his head. He explains that when Art bumped into Frank at King's, Frank mentioned a mathematician called Mahalanobis, and it set off an alarm for Art. Mimi's seen the photograph of the man with small round glasses and a resting smile next to Art's bed. 'It's distinctive stuff. The chances of another mathematician legitimately looking into Mahalanobis's model as a springboard for solving *p versus Np*? At the same time as Art? It's vanishingly small.'

'But Frank's never even *suggested* he's looking at *p versus Np*!'

Ernest knots and reknots his fingers. 'I know it's hard to hear,' he says. He may have invited himself to stay, but right now it looks as if this is the last place on earth he wants to be. 'Mimi,' he says, 'um, Art *also* thinks Frank is with another woman. Someone called Silver. Rachel Silver.'

'I'm sorry? What d'you mean *with*?'

223

'Art saw her at King's.'

'There's *hundreds* of women at the university.' She's almost yelling at poor Ernest; she can't help it. 'This all feels like some sort of joke.' But nothing feels funny. 'I'm phoning Frank.'

'You can't speak to Frank, Mimi. No.' Ernest is calm but there's metal in his voice. 'Not yet.'

'I'm listening,' says Mimi. She sits on her hands.

Art had called Ernest to say that he didn't know what he was looking for, but he was convinced something was up with Frank. Then, just before the accident, Art found a book – Ernest doesn't know *what* book. Or what it meant. 'Art called me, ostensibly about something else, but I asked if he'd made any progress with his security concerns. He said this book raised yet more questions.'

An unnamed book. Terrific. 'So *now* what?'

'Well, this is Art. He'll have had a plan.'

'Always the planner. Well, his plan clearly failed, Ernest. I assume we agree on that? Landing up in a coma is a pretty big cock-up, all by itself.' She feels the rumble of something coming towards her that she cannot control, a familiar rage against her brother and the way he has always, *always*, fucked up her life.

'Art can be stubborn and not see things, and naive.' Despite the criticism of her brother, Ernest's voice is tender. 'But he's deliberate, and careful. Logical. He doesn't leap to conclusions. We have to listen to our heads here. Not our hearts.'

Her heart feels like chopped liver.

Ernest reminds her that Art puts evidence before *everything*. Even when he shouldn't. 'I understand that better than you might realize,' he says. His words are like bricks of truth that solidify on her chest. Mimi picks up the dodecahedron on Art's desk. She tosses the heavy glass from one hand to the other; catching it hard in her palm, displacing the pain that she feels inside. Coloured light prisms all over the room. She'd like to send it flying through the window, hear the glass smash, force the drama outside her own body.

Be patient, Ernest tells her. The next few days might be critical.

'A different critical to the one he's in now?' She immediately regrets her sarcasm.

'We cannot let Frank know that he's under a spotlight. If you speak to him, you blow any chance we have of finding the unvarnished truth.'

'*We*? I'm not the one with these wild ideas, Ernest. Frank needs to be told, and soon.'

Ernest reiterates how dangerous it is. 'Art's maths,' he says. 'The risk almost can't be exaggerated. We have to pick this up where Art left off.'

'We don't even know where that is. The whole thing's crazy.' She imagines her brother parcelling up his various facts, like little bombs in her life.

Ernest rubs the chair, as if trying to glean something from the leather. 'I believe in Art,' he says simply.

Mimi tests herself to see how much she believes in Frank. She does, she does. But the answer feels as elastic as the bottom of a trampoline.

Mimi tries to take it all in. 'You're shivering,' says Ernest. He takes the soft quilt from the back of Art's armchair and folds it over her legs. His eyes have flecks of charcoal on grey slate that could never look unkind. 'I just wonder,' he says, 'if Frank knew that Art was onto him? We never know what people will do when they're cornered.'

Ernest's language is an affront. 'This isn't a game, Ernest, it's my life.' But Art has cornered *her*. Somehow, from a

225

coma, from his hospital bed, he's contrived to control her. Again. She can't confront Frank. Not about this book thing. Or Mahalanobis. Or this other woman. She's stuck.

She needs Rey.

'Don't forget, it's Art's life too,' says Ernest. 'In more ways than one. But I know, it's a shock.'

'Shock.' She hears herself repeat the word back. She pictures the fizzing spark at the end of a finger that flares through your body and then leaves you buzzing.

The shock of her parents had been a different kind – like a great grey boulder that rolled down the middle of the street, ran you down, and pulverized you flat into the surface of the earth till your bones were ground powder. What a tragedy, people said. The tragedy, she sometimes thinks, is that you *don't* die from the shock.

She's living proof.

She'd wrapped herself up in this same quilt for days, picking at the cornflower stitches, tying loose threads round her thumbs until the tips went scarlet. She remembers being permanently cold then too – she'd nested down in the quilt like a hibernating mammal. It was Rey who'd finally coaxed her downstairs. 'You have to come out,' Rey told her. 'Art won't survive on his own.'

Ernest looks at the gap between his knees. 'I feel so responsible,' he says.

She doesn't know who's responsible for anything right now, but she's pretty certain it's not Ernest.

'I didn't listen,' says Ernest. 'I asked him if he'd told you – his mood, it felt dangerous, you know? Standing there, grimly asserting that he knew he was right.'

Mimi closes her eyes and nods. Behind her lids stalks an image of Art, arms at his sides, clenching the material on his trousers – restraining himself from yelling: that she had not listened and now they were dead.

226

You know I am right about the big things in our life, he said in his letter.

'When he told me his concerns about Frank,' Ernest continues, oblivious of the guilt entwining itself round her gut, 'he was pacing the room in exact steps, tapping his wrist. I expect you know the drill. He asked if I supported him. I said yes. And I did. I still do.'

'You might have tried to *stop* him.'

'I had no idea he'd end up in hospital. It ought to have been harmless. The fact that it wasn't, well – Art kept saying he couldn't believe it was happening, again. That people don't ever listen to him. I don't know what he meant by that.'

'I do,' says Mimi. It's been the soundtrack of Art's life, and hers. She feels goblins gathering in velvet wings on the side of the stage. 'He could have been killed.' She tries to shove aside visions of Art's useless arm, unable to prevent his fall. Of damage, to his brain. 'The thing is, Ernest – Frank doesn't drive like an idiot, never talks on his phone while he—'

Emotion dislodges like rubble. She holds her knees.

'Come here,' says Ernest, as pieces of her roll away in chunks.

'I can't.' She is really crying now. Embarrassing, gulping tears.

'I know.' Ernest puts his arms clumsily around her. He cannot possibly know.

I should be looking after you, she can hear Frank say. But she is aware of a terrible feeling, like a moth-eaten black shawl inching over her body, of needing to shrug Frank away, of looking out of his arms and over his shoulder and wondering who he is and why he is there.

'It'll be okay,' says Ernest, as Mimi's tears stutter. 'In the end, we will make this okay.' He wipes her snotty face with a tissue from his pocket.

'Can you think of a single scenario in which this whole mess resolves into anything remotely okay? We don't even know if he's going to survive,' she says, 'or what he'll be able to do if he does.' Cold climbs through the crack in the curtain.

'It's a lot to take in,' says Ernest, looking at his watch. 'Phew, it's past nine. Supper will be here soon.' Silence settles between them.

'I hope he's right about this,' says Ernest after a while.

'Oh god,' says Mimi. 'I pray he's wrong.'

39

LOGIC

Mimi walks into her bathroom and sheds her clothes, trying to piece together what she's heard from Ernest. What is Art thinking now, trapped in that cold, brightly lit ward, with only machines tuned into his brain? At least for the moment he's safe.

She squeezes toothpaste from the tube. Her mouth feels sore, the toothbrush bristles hard. Blood runs from her gums and strings into the basin. If she's stressed, her gums bleed. Does that mean that whenever her gums bleed, she's stressed? Logic folds over itself, trapping her mind on an Escher-like staircase. And then, as if tapping into an unexpected revealing bleep on Art's heart monitor, Mimi sees the logic in Ernest's advice.

If Art is wrong, if Frank *hasn't* got hidden motives and is in their lives because he loves her, she would destroy things by questioning him.

If, however, the whole thing's a chimera and Frank is guilty of some as yet unidentified underhand behaviour, including another woman, it will reveal itself in time. Either way, she will know for sure. There's simplicity in waiting. She almost senses Art take a lower, slower breath in his hospital bed across town, for knowing that she's come to this place.

In the mirror, the face that she's had for the last few months has gone. 'Your eyelids were drawn with a quill,' Frank once said of her upsloping eyes. But the new muscles that happiness awakened in her face, that made her look pretty – those eyelids, that smile – that whole face, has disappeared. Back in its place is her old face. Her forehead as blank as a chopping board. It was a face that no one loved. It had sad eyes. She can hide many things from Frank if she absolutely has to, but her sad eyes are back for everyone to see.

40

CHAOS

Ernest is gone when Mimi wakes. He's cleared all signs of last night's curry, the kitchen smells of lemon, and the dishwasher is humming. *I hope your finger is better, see you later,* says a note on the table.

Franks texts her. **Can we talk? X** She doesn't reply straight away.

Instead, on her way to the hospital, she calls Rey. 'This whole thing's a clusterfuck,' she says. She hears her friend swing out of bed – wooden floor, bare feet. She tries to summarize, but it's too long a story to catch up now.

'For what it's worth, I do think you need to talk to Frank. This is not some game. But just wait, okay? Don't do anything stupid till we've spoken properly.'

'Can I do something stupid after we've spoken properly?' Mimi coughs out a laugh.

'Oh hon. This'll all clear up. God knows how, but it will. And I promise, we'll go and do something really stupid together then, okay?'

Mimi feels like a child again, the one whose mother promised her an ice cream, when really, she was dying of cancer.

Before Mimi leaves for the hospital, she texts Frank. **I'm sorry about last night. Yes please. x**

But she doesn't call.

Hospital sounds scream into the sockets of Art's ears. Wave after wave breaches his eardrums, into the pockets of curling small bones. They ripple out, amplified. His eyes are stuck closed. He cannot use his hands to deafen the noise.

'Give him a shot of adrenalin. He's reacting, hold him down.'

He is rammed into something, a door or a wall. His skull hits the pavement. Mimi's voice slices through the crunch in his head. He reaches out to keep her. He does not want to lose her.

There is milk in his ears, behind his eyes, it is stars, then – silence. The universe, cloudy and streaking, is wisping away. He is lifting.

'Jesus! The monitor!'

'His ICP, quick! Fuck! The tube's leaking, *again*!'

'How long do you think? *Dammit*.'

Art watches, as if from above, a doctor climbing onto his bed. A nurse steadies his arm. The doctor places a knee either side of Art's head to stabilize his skull. He tries to secure the leaking ICP bolt.

'Iodine, now. Just fucking squirt it on.'

'We need a consultant.'

Art waits for the pain. The drainage bag wheezes, collapsing, to empty. The pressure scale falls, again and again. Eventually, zero.

He feels hot breath. His skin scrapes like grass in the wind. The metal bolt judders the probe in his brain, sucks on his ventricles; his face glitters with pain.

The burst of pressure in his skull abates. He rocks softly in jelly, his edges dissolving.

232

'Get out a crash call.'

'I've done it already.'

'What are you holding – the tracheo kit?'

'It's too late for that. Call Sipos, just tell him . . .' The voices are fading. Art is still floating.

Heels clip away. Plastic knocks against tile, a rhythmic tap.

Like a knuckle on wood.

41

NON-VERBAL REASONING

Mimi steers into the hospital car park, guided by a grim internal homing device, rather than the arrows that this morning look like a non-verbal reasoning problem. Her wipers squeak the half-rain away. The yellow boom lifts. She remembers this car park in hot July sun, tar melting, dashboard black and baking after the first round of visits to her mum.

'Dad will take you for an ice cream,' her mother had said, as they'd left her lying in her hospital room, her face turned to the window.

Mimi's car lights flash amber in the dark morning as she locks her Kia and walks away.

She needs to call Frank.

It's hard to believe it's only been a day and a half. The critical forty-eight hours. That's what Dr Sipos said. They're on – what? She calculates the time. Hour 37. She climbs the concrete steps from the car park, a tall wall banks up next to her. It's badly lit, and the rail is wet. She's out of breath and a hospital weariness seeps into her feet. Hour 37. Of forty-eight. That's, what? Eleven hours left. *Left?*

She takes the stairs two at a time.

* * *

Art is gone.

His bed is stripped and the nurse at the central station is new.

Mimi's body is ready. Her heart beats harder, pushing extra blood into her muscles. She assesses the nurse – an automatic part of her brain is checking: is this a person who knows what to do?

Does she know the Rules?

How to tell a person what they don't want to hear? Mimi's joints are dissolving.

'S-s-sorry,' she says. 'Where's my brother?' A shaft of cold descends through her middle. She gives the nurse a moment to recalibrate her face. 'Art Brotherton?' Mimi points to the empty space in the circle. Her mouth is dry.

The nurse sighs. 'HDU, I think, don't know. High Dependency Unit. You'll have to ask his doctor.'

'But the doctor's not here,' says Mimi, holding the edge of the desk.

She looks up to see the father of a patient – a twenty-four-year-old motorcyclist – watching her. They had acknowledged each other yesterday. His hand lies on top of the unresponsive hand of his man-child. He probably knows where Art is, but she can't ask him. His son's traumatic brain injury was three months ago. He notices her looking at the cover of the book he's reading to his boy – a whitewashed dome against Aegean blue sky.

'He loved his holidays in Greece.'

'It's a good idea,' Mimi says as the ventilator breaths oxygenate the boy's bloodied brain. GCS of 2, Mimi's heard. Measured out of fifteen, your Glasgow Coma Scale, or GCS, is the measure of your brain activity. Two is low. Very low.

'This is useless,' she snaps at the nurse, and spins round to leave the ward. She needs to find Art.

Art is moving. Gliding. Wheels on smooth floors. Each sound is distinct, rollers on floor, suction of air as doors open and close, the breath of the person above him – warm, rolling, alive.

They are going down.

It is quieter down here. Sounds muffled. But he senses a whirring, a beast of machinery just out of reach. He turns to the noise, to the source of the hum, but his body cannot follow. He twists; there is pressure in his ear.

'He's tachycardic, we need to be quick.'

'Wait for him to settle.'

'The ICP monitor would tell us, if we could get him plugged in.'

'Not happening, mate.'

'Then how the hell do we know?'

'We can't really. It's guesswork.'

He is manoeuvred round a corner, headfirst.

'What's the story here, anyway?

'ICP sensor wasn't attached properly, but we sorted it. In time.'

'How'd that happen?'

'Maybe not put in correctly, or it got caught on something when someone came near him? Don't know.'

Bars of light run across Art's lids.

'Miss Brotherton,' says the senior sister as Mimi passes the main ICU desk on her way downstairs. 'Your brother's gone for an fMRI. His ICP monitor needed changing.'

ICP. MRI. HDU, GCS. Bloody acronyms. Medicine seems to be populated by humans who speak another language entirely. 'Remind me – ICP?'

236

'Intracranial pressure. Says here the catheter was faulty. He may have been leaking cerebrospinal fluid, so they needed a scan. You'll have to ask—'

'His doctor. I *know*.'

'It can seem that you're not getting any information,' says the sister. She puts her hand flat on the counter, as if in lieu of taking Mimi's own. 'They don't try to keep you uninformed on purpose. And it's not because there's bad news. It just takes a while for the picture to become clear. Everyone reacts differently to a TBI.'

'He's an *S*BI,' interrupts Mimi. 'S-s-severe. Not a T, not a traumatic.' The biker man-boy is a T.

'They're just labels,' says the sister. 'Depending on where the brain's injured, how quickly he was helped and what shape he was in in the first place.'

'His brain was in perfect shape,' Mimi says. 'It's a *perfect* brain.'

'I'll let the Neurological Unit know you're coming.'

Mimi thanks the sister and walks towards the lifts, past the hand sanitizer, past the flyers for dementia coffee mornings, discharge medications and avoiding pressure ulcers, to go and find her brother.

Mimi can tell there are expensive machines purring behind the doors of the Neurological Unit – it's quiet and plushy. There's wooden skirting and travel photographs on the wall.

The fMRI Art is going to have is 'a very sensitive tool', the attractive neurologist tells her. She talks quickly, as if she's used to explaining things in the fastest possible way, achieving an alchemical cocktail of maximum understanding *and* maximum confusion. She has good fingernails.

Mimi imagines her clipping a scan up onto a board, like they do in *Grey's Anatomy*. A fingernail tapping a picture

237

of Art's brain, pointing at a white mass. The damage. 'Thinking is a very active process,' says the doctor, at speed. 'It's metabolically expensive, so it needs a lot of blood, and what we are needing to monitor is whether – Arthur, right? – whether Arthur's brain is getting enough blood. We're trying to give it the minimum on the one hand, in order to reduce the swelling, but enough to keep it active and cognitively responsive. The bangs he will hear in the scanner – *if* he can hear, that is – are radiofrequency magnetic pulses; the speed they ping back to us tells us how much oxygenated haemoglobin is in there.'

She leans past Mimi to sign a form for a nurse. The nurse nods reverentially and pads off. They pad down here. Upstairs, they scuttle and race. The doctor's still talking. 'He might hear, of course. Hearing is the last neurological function to perish.' She looks over Mimi's head while Mimi rocks back on her heels, lashed by the doctor's cool assessment. 'Are we ready?'

'What's it like?' asks Mimi. She sees a machine through an open door. She hears a grinding, clunking sound. She thinks of milking machines near the cottage in Wales. Of threshers in autumn. Aeroplanes, the Tube. The squeak of rope on the swings that Art hated.

'Will he be frightened?' she asks.

Art's head is clamped; he feels heat, and pressure on the sides of his skull. A shadow descends over his face, a cage over his half-fluttered eyes, lined light. Straps over his ankles.

'What's going on here, gentlemen?' Female. Not Mimi. 'What's taking so long?'

'His heart was galloping, Doc, we needed to wait.'

'Let's start. If he's going to make it, he'll make it through this.'

238

Whirring. Sliding. He is made of slabbed granite. A juddering thud and a clank jars his teeth. *Mimi. I did not mean for this to happen.* He focuses on the middle of his brain. It hurts, like bruised bone. Kang! A hard spoon on metal, inside his skull. A long winding drill. He finds a still centre, somewhere to go – to stop his heart from pushing through his throat.

He names the feeling, just as she taught him. *I am frightened.* She is holding his hand. *Go to your safe place.* He hears her, beyond.

Numbers. His numbers. *Where are his numbers!?*

He searches – a matrix. His heartbeat, his brain speed. His pressure. His pulse. His blood levels, his O2, his toxic high, his functional low. A Rubik's cube tumbles. The squares remain stubbornly mixed. Mimi gave him a Rubik's cube once. The colours. Try and focus on that. The click and the slide of the planes as they twist in his hands.

That is better. Yellow square, blue square, green, orange, red. His heart races again. Not red square. *No.*

Swimming in the pool was Art's favourite time.

That night, he had closed his eyes and felt himself rise up, float above the morass. His distress about Mimi and Frank. The rumour, the speculation about *p versus Np* – weeds tangled in the bottom of the pond of other mathematicians. It was important to stay above it all, to skim the surface with the lightest touch. He would think about Mimi later. He would try not to think about Frank.

When Art was done swimming, he had clambered out, and runnels of water mapped his body, collected at his feet on the white tiles of the men's changing room.

'So, hello, sexy. Enjoying yourself there, were you?'

He hardly had time to turn round. The lifeguard was right

239

there, in front of him, their bodies almost touching. Art stepped back and hit the locker. The lifeguard's flat stomach was level with Art's, his chest was bare, he was wearing red shorts. Tight and square, they rode up his thighs, his crotch bulged.

Art had seen him before. His eye-catching haircut shaved off to one side. His eyes close together; he looked like a fox. Intimidating, but also – not wholly unattractive.

'Were you waiting for me? I've been watching you . . . lying in that warm water, legs all splayed out. Must've felt good.'

Art shook his head.

'C'mon, say something – I've seen you here before, don't pretend we haven't eyed each other across the tiles.' *Lock on a detail*, thought Art. *And say nothing*. He felt his breath shorten, his heart beat harder. Most disconcerting was that another part of him, a part that he did not seem able to suppress at this minute, was electrified in a way that was unfamiliar and fizzing. *His* groin stirred. The lifeguard stepped closer. He took Art's shoulder in his hand and turned Art around. Art did not stop him.

The man's stomach flattened into Art's spine, his hips graunched into Art from behind. He pressed his face right next to Art's, his forehead on the locker. Art felt the scrub of stubble on his cheek.

'Nooo,' groaned Art, mortified by his own desire. The lifeguard spun him round.

'Hey – why not?' The lifeguard released him immediately, but Art still felt that his back was pinned to the metal, a key dug into his skin like a tiny tin spade. 'Were you just teasing me out there?'

Art looked down.

He could smell sweat and soap, edged with chemicals.

240

He stared: the red shorts. Stare only at that. Do not look up.

The lifeguard trailed his index finger from the base of Art's throat to his navel.

The lifeguard's voice was raspy and Art did not trust himself to say a word. 'Look at me, Gorgeous.' It was a fierce, urgent whisper. His mouth was up close to Art's face. Hips in red shorts, square red shorts, pushed up against him, burning.

'We don't have to make a sound.'

Then a door slammed wide against the tiled far wall. 'What's going on here? *Tony?*'

'Nothing,' said the lifeguard, jumping round to his boss.

'Get the fuck out.'

Tony, in his red shorts, picked up Art's wet towel, handed it over and winked. He didn't look back as he left.

'Mate,' said the manager to Art. 'What was happening there? Are you okay?'

'Sorry,' stuttered Art. 'Sorry.'

'You sure you're all right?'

'I am fine.'

'Look, best you go home. I'll make sure things are sorted next time you're back.'

When Art *did* go back, Tony was gone.

Red squares, the Rubik's cube – interlocked shapes – they tumble and turn.

But his numbers are rolling in waves. He cannot pin them down.

Colour is all very well. Art wants his *numbers*, his maths. He knows that they cannot show everything. He will not stay alive by controlling his numbers alone, but they predict outcomes. They are his survival heuristic.

42

SCALES

Mimi is told to wait – they don't know how long it will take.

Sitting in the cafe downstairs, staring at the detritus of unfinished coffee and toast, she is unexpectedly buttonholed by a Detective Constable Collins. The detective is enormous, his seams shiny with strain. His hand makes his radio look like a Dinky car.

As he sits, he explains that, because Frank and Art know one another, the incident is automatically treated as suspicious. He declines Mimi's offer of coffee and drills her with questions ranging from her whereabouts on the night of the accident to Art's life insurance. Mimi feels the fuse of her patience run down to the wire. She doesn't have anything to do with her brother being run over and if they don't know that – 'I didn't have time to help wallop him with the side of Frank's car, if that's what you're thinking.'

Frank's car. Frank's name bubbles out as though it is normal, but it isn't – it's changed. Could it really be a Frank she doesn't know? The idea stabs her as though someone's skewered her vital organs.

Collins flips his notes closed as deftly as a croupier. His

neck is so thick, he nods from the waist up. 'One more thing,' he says as he squeezes out from behind the table. 'Does the name Rachel Silver mean anything to you?'

'Who is she?' Mimi asks, hoping the detective cannot hear her heart.

'Oh, a long shot. Don't think about it. We're just looking into all contacts, you know, as we do. And sorry, very last question.' His radio hisses.

'Yes?'

'Where did you and Frank Taylor meet? I gather he's also a mathematician.'

She'd never before questioned how she met Frank. Now, she struggles to say it. His presence at the awards ceremony, how he sauntered straight over to meet her. She's aware that she can actually smell the polystyrene of her takeaway cup, a chemical trace in her coffee that makes her feel sick. 'Over a glass of wine,' she says bluntly, unsure why they care, or why she's evading the question. 'Modern love.'

She needs to go back up to Art. But first, she has questions for Frank.

Perhaps it will be enough to hear his voice, to check whether the man that is morphing in her mind resembles the one down the line. 'Please leave a message,' says Frank's automated recording. She's partly relieved, but unarticulated questions bounce around her head like a children's mobile. Swinging among them all is a silver woman, dancing.

'I'm your valley,' Frank had said. *I'm falling in love to infinity.*

Art is back in the ward.

He's like a slab of marble. Lifeless apart from the almost indiscernible rising of his chest, his sculpted face unchanging.

When she squeezes his hand, it's like a rubber glove filled with wax.

'Miss Brotherton?'

She turns to see Dr Sipos. He holds a green file in which she hopes are Art's results. But he shakes his head. It will be another day. The images were clear enough to establish which centres in Art's brain are receiving sufficient blood supply and which might be compromised, but the interpretation takes a while.

'This morning was a setback,' says Dr Sipos. 'We're doing what we can. When we get the results we'll be in a better position to know your brother's prognosis. I'm sorry.' He seems to assess how much Mimi can take in. 'It helps if he's a fighter. Encourage him when you talk to him. Even the most endangered patients can be surprisingly aware beneath the coma. I don't promise he can hear, but – remind him of life.'

'Art,' she tries to talk calmly, but her voice is shaking. 'It's me, I'm here.' The sigh of his ventilator is almost inaudible. Shadows bruise his eye sockets, his mouth is lightly parted and now that they've taken his mask off, she can see his tongue drying between his lips like a stuffed reptile. She closes his mouth, making sure she doesn't accidentally detach his nasogastric tube.

She puts her head down on his tummy, just briefly. She hears his intestines, sluiced by thin liquid plugged into his veins. 'I need you,' she says, blinking. 'Please, Art, come back.'

43

THE BROTHER PROBLEM

The nurses clear the ward. Mimi wants to go to Art's office – to gather in the sense of him there. His work, his life, his maths. She also wants to poke around.

She drops her car at home and takes the Tube. At Temple station, a third message from Frank: **How is he? Trying to reach you. x**

Sorry – difficult day. I'm at King's. Will call in a bit. M x

She walks up to the historic facade of the university's Department of Mathematics, passing students in their parkas, smoking outside. She spots Ginny, Art's assistant, heading through a pair of double doors.

'Mimi!' Ginny's hair is sprayed into shape like a piece of thrown ceramic. 'How's Art?' she asks, clutching the brooch on her lapel. 'And *you*? Such a terrible shock.'

Ginny swipes her security pass over the blinking eye on the wall and the lift opens, while Mimi fills her in.

Untwisting her lanyard, Ginny opens Art's office. A scarf hangs on the hook. His calculators are perfectly in place, in a row. Files, all labelled. He's probably set traps to detect any disturbance. She wonders if Frank's been in here.

On Art's desk, a white slab of papers looks like a tombstone.

Mimi scans the bookshelves. For all she knows, the book Ernest mentioned could be in here, but she has no idea what to look for.

Maths is everywhere. String theory, game theory, meta data, big data. Turing machines. Chaos theory. Dynamics of complexity. The Theory of Plafales (falafel, Mimi always says in her head when she sees that name among Art's things). The Halting Problem. The *p versus Np* Problem. A lot of problems.

'Maths is Life,' Art always says. His books agree: *The Mathematical Universe and the Nature of Reality, The Beginning of Infinity. Certainty of Uncertainty. Order from Chaos.* The titles mean nothing to her.

But they mean everything to Art.

She feels as if she's occupying the grid of an ice tray – it's so cold and rigid in here. Her real problems feel muddled and spongy, mercurial, impossible to grasp. The twitching palpitation at the side of Art's head when he came downstairs to find Frank making porridge for breakfast, or when Frank said, 'Hey, Beautiful.' Art's cheeks now – oyster-coloured and concave. An unknown book, a phantom woman, a vulnerable, dangerous proof. Frank shapeshifts in her mind. She can't settle on a version of him that feels like the truth.

Mimi looks round.

The purple-haired troll that Mimi gave Art when she was eleven is on his desk, stuck down with Blu-Tack. And Art's photograph of Mimi and their parents is still there. Standing outside the Royal Albert Hall, Christine looks grey, Mimi anxious, and Walter, distracted and drawn. Of *all* the photographs available – they look neither healthy nor happy. Art took it a few months before the end; you can tell Christine is sick. Art hated the evening because there'd been a curtain-raiser with too much percussion and boisterous brass, which challenged his labyrinthitis.

Mimi was somewhat surprised when she'd first seen the picture on his desk. 'You might've found a photo where we all look a little more cheerful,' she'd said.

'I do not have it there to remind me of you, Mimi.'

'Well, the folks, at least. They look awful.'

'Yes, I know. That is why I have it.'

'That's horrible. I don't understand.'

'I have it here to remind me. When I am right, I know I am right. I was right then, about them. I should have listened to myself.'

'Art—'

'I have to pay attention to my inner voice.'

'Well, we all know where that gets us.'

'It should not upset you. I do not need a picture to make me think about you, or Mum and Dad. I think about them every day. *You* are right in front of me most of the time. Why would I need a picture of that? It was one of the most important lessons I have ever learned. I cannot put up a poster saying, "You are always right." People would think I am odd.'

'God,' said Mimi. '*Imagine.*'

Never mind the N*p* Problem or the Halting Problem. She has the Brother Problem. Does the sum of her brother's needs exceed what she is able to give him? Is that the heart of it? That she cannot divide herself equally? Is Art unequal to the challenge of letting her go?

Or, is it as Art suspects? That what Frank seems, what he says – just doesn't add up? A mathematical version of too good to be true?

Bloody hell, Art. She pushes a lever-arch file from the shelf in frustration. *Thwapp!* Not a phone-book body thump. A messier sound.

'Are you looking for something in particular?' asks Ginny, almost falling into the door jamb as she opens the door.

Mimi can't admit to hoping to find a book whose title she doesn't know, or something on a woman named Silver. 'No one else has been here?'

'Not that I know of. And I haven't moved a thing. Haven't even cleared out the rubbish bin. I told the caretaker to leave it all until Art gets back.' Ginny licks her finger and lifts a single square of white memo paper from the desk. She scribbles down her number. 'You only have to whistle. Night or day.'

Mimi double checks the rubbish bin, but all she finds is an old receipt from the swimming pool. She scrunches it into her pocket.

She picks up the file that she knocked to the floor, apologizing silently to Art. She returns it to his desk and closes the door behind her. Quietly, so as not to further annoy whatever mathematical muses she might have disturbed.

As she heads down in the lift, something gnaws at her mind – a detail overlooked. But she's got nothing.

Just a scrappy stub from the pool. There's a bin as she exits the lift. She unfolds the receipt before tossing it away. *Camberwell Club. 1 x Tea. 6.02 p.m.*

But the date.

It is after she left. The Sunday before the accident.

It is *after* Art told her he'd never go back.

44

CUL-DE-SAC

Back outside, Mimi fastens her cardigan under her coat. Freshly naked autumn trees brace against the breeze. Papery leaves dance at her feet.

Frank's at her elbow. 'Mimi.'

'*Frank!*' He looks sallow, and he's wearing his long grey wool coat. It gives him a baleful air that she finds disconcerting, like armour. She looks in the direction he's come.

His face seems tight. 'I couldn't leave things as they were. Come, let's walk.'

It's so bitter, she'd like to hug into his side. Instead, she clenches her hands in her pockets.

'Where are we going?' she eventually asks.

'Nowhere,' says Frank. He slows to a standstill and touches her shoulder to stop her from walking. 'And that's the whole problem.' The chill slides off the river; it's funnelling right down her neck. 'I don't know what you want from me, Mimi. Even before this whole disaster.' He looks tired, drawn. His voice is flat. 'You know how I feel about you. I'm pretty sure you feel it too, though you won't ever *say* it. I've had to deal with that. I get that it's hard for you to commit to something that disrupts your life with Art, but—' He puts his hand up over his eyes before he carries on. 'Anyway, that's a moot point. Right now, I feel as if there's a gathering cloud around me, around *us*.'

'Frank, I – it's hard.'

'No, it's not that hard.'

'Well, not for you maybe,' she says, and regrets it.

'Really?' His voice crisps. His eyes seem to contract. 'Mimi, he went into *my* car.'

'No, sorry, I know,' she says. He is holding her with both arms now, his thumbs on her clavicles, his fingers on her back. She's imprisoned in the force of his grip, but it feels like a reprieve.

'He's your brother – I get that. God knows, I'm genuinely fond of the guy. But this? It's hell.' His eyes are the iron blue of the river. 'It's *you* that I love.'

'Frank.'

'For some reason you are unable to say that back to me, and yet I know, well, I thought I knew. But your brother has you locked – ah, I don't know.' He takes a big breath. 'Look. We both know Art.' He looks over her shoulder, as if the body of water will deliver the right word. 'He's different,' he says. 'I don't care. I don't care how much time we spend with him, I like being part of your life. I don't care that you've got a weird brother, I don't even care that I have to deal with two different yous – the uptight, careful one at home and what feels like the real one outside. I love them both. But Jesus Christ, Mimi – this accident. It's already wedged itself between us. I don't know how we come back from it.'

She drops her eyes from his gaze and shakes her head.

'Well?'

She looks at his shirt half-tucked in at the front, the rest hanging out like a tongue. 'You've left out a loop,' she says, 'with your belt.' She feels as if she's missed a step, in the way that jolts you awake from a dream. She'd found that same half-tucked shirt so charming, so carefree, before.

'*What*?' He lets go of her, smacks his palm so hard on his buckle it must hurt, and jams his elbows into his sides. 'What the fuck, Mimi? I don't *giveadamn*.' He's regaining the colour in his cheeks. Frank is devastating when he's angry, his eyes flashing. He flings his arm out down the river, his big hand imprints the sky.

'Don't shout, Frank.'

'I'm not. I'm just – this is exactly what he wants – can't you see? When I saw him, he was *so* jealous.' He shakes his head.

She feels the heat rise up to her face. 'You didn't even *tell* me you'd seen him.'

Mimi tries to gather the threads of her thoughts in one place. Frank steps away.

'Frank!'

He wheels round. But he doesn't move. It feels that there's acres between them.

'I don't understand why there's even a shred of suspicion around me, but I sense it whenever I talk to you.' He's shouting over the noise of the traffic, the wind, the river. It feels as if London is bearing down on them, two small people, their lives unravelling on a pavement.

She walks towards him, back into his orbit. 'It's *not* that.' Her voice cracks. 'I really do believe you about that, of course I do.' She wants to believe him. More than anything right now, that's what she wants. 'But I'm scared.'

'I'm scared too – of him coming between us.' Frank looks at her. 'He already has. Here –' he plunges his hand into his coat pocket and brings out a small bag – 'It's a perfect example. You might as well have it.' He hands it to her as

251

though it's as incidental as a takeaway sandwich. But inside is a gift – a hat. 'It's your Christmas beanie,' he says, his voice flat. 'I got it from the market. But I bet Art's told you already.' He sounds sad, but washed in with his sadness, and it makes her insides crinkle to hear how deep it goes, is how angry he is.

And Art *has* told her. It should have alerted her. 'Frank has bought you a beanie,' Art said, straight out, clearly intent on depriving Frank of the pleasure. The malice had been so unlike him; she should have jumped to attention.

'He never was good at surprises,' she says now, trying not to cry. 'For him or for anyone else.'

'Oh, I *know*.' Frank breathes out, it sounds like an accordion squeezing, too tight. 'So – how is he?'

She shakes her head.

'Come here,' he says, 'this is terrifying for you.'

She holds the hat, then pulls it on over her freezing ears. It's taupe, with a cream fluffy button at the top.

'Apparently it's cashmere,' says Frank. 'They said it won't itch.'

'Oh Frank.' The beanie that itched. Her mother, the illness, the all-swallowing pain. She bends at the riverside, in her new fluffy hat, and leans into him. Her sombrero man. When his body curves away from her, just a ripple, she hides her face.

Mimi tugs down on her soft new hat.

'Look, this isn't straightforward.' Frank keeps her folded in his coat. 'I understand you're freaked out.' He smooths her hair into the nape of her neck, keeps his warm hand there. 'Even the police keep questioning me.'

'What did they say?'

Tourists erupt from the Tube station in a burble of foreign languages. 'I have to go back to the station this afternoon,' says Frank. A child in a stroller with its mother drops its toy monkey, and cries. Frank takes a step forwards. 'Look, is there somewhere quiet we can go? Is Ernest at home?'

'Please don't start that.'

'I'm not, it's just, we need to talk, Mimi. Properly.' Frank hesitates. 'We could walk over the bridge, to the National? It's quiet there?'

In tacit agreement, they walk towards Waterloo Bridge. The felt monkey is on the ground, grinning up at them with cheerful embroidered eyes. Frank picks it up. He looks as if he's about to balance it on the railings, but then dashes over to the child's mother, who touches her heart. He returns and takes Mimi's hand.

They cross the river in silence. Big Ben strikes eleven. Frank rubs the wing of flesh between her thumb and index finger but doesn't say a word. A coxless pair of rowers sculls beneath the bridge. The blades slice the water in rhythm, their bodies tip forwards and backwards, in unison.

They walk through the underpass, past graffiti, along the Southbank. The hulking concrete theatre hovers into view, as if rising from the pavement itself.

Earlier that autumn, with Art away at a conference, Frank had brought her to the National, to see a play that narrated the state of Britain through a dysfunctional family. But even the visceral misery inflicted by the characters on each other could not dampen Mimi's mood that night.

She'd worn the necklace Frank had given her for her birthday.

'Hey, Beautiful,' he'd said. 'Your beads go with that top.' He'd smiled and released her hair from her collar. The amber necklace had buttery tones rippled through burned orange beads. It accented the red in her hair.

She isn't sure where the necklace is, now that she thinks about it; she hasn't seen it for a while. Anyway, the point was, Frank cared. What she thought, what she wore. He *noticed* her.

Dear god, she does love him. For himself, and for that. Why can't she just say it?

Because every time she almost does, an image of her pushing Art away, his arms cartwheeling, hijacks her brain.

45

SILVER

Frank ushers her into the entrance near the ticket desk at the National. He buys tea and millionaire's shortbread from the cafe. Sitting on a large green-upholstered disc that looks like a spaceship, she feels safe. She rests her back against a concrete pillar.

'Funnily enough,' says Frank, breaking a chunk of caramel biscuit, 'one of the things the police wanted to know about was this million-dollar reward from the Clay Institute.' He sucks the stickiness from his finger. 'It's this mathematical—'

'I know what it is.' She really doesn't want to talk about Art's work right now. He offers her a piece of the biscuit, but she's queasy. 'What did they want to know?'

'They didn't actually ask a question, if you know what I mean, like they just wanted to see my reaction when they mentioned it. I – I don't know.'

'Did they ask you about Rachel Silver?' she asks before she even knows that she's going to.

'What?' The pulse that flashes across Frank's face isn't what she hoped to see.

'Rachel Silver,' she says again. 'The police asked me about her.'

'Why would they do that?' He looks so shocked it frightens her.

'I don't know, Frank. You tell me.' It feels as though her skin is turning inside out. 'Who is she?'

'She's . . .' Frank says. 'Art has met her. From their American programme. I know her. Art knows her.' He's fumbling for words.

'And?'

'I don't see any earthly reason why the police want to know about her.' But then he crumbles. Tears squeeze out, as if they are running away from the edges of his eyes before they get noticed.

'This is torture,' he says. 'Believe me, she *really* isn't a thing in all of this.'

'I see,' says Mimi. 'And where *is* she a "thing"?'

'She was. Long ago,' he says, shaking his head. 'Uni days. We had a relationship, *short*. It didn't last. Art bumped into her with me the other day. If you are going down the road of thinking there's another woman in my life, it's miles off track. She lives in America. Please, Mimi, please don't add her into what already feels like a cocktail of things we are struggling with here.'

'Okay,' she says. Art might have seen, without knowing what he was seeing, intimacy there, and leaped to the wrong conclusion. It *feels* as if Frank's telling the truth. It would, however, be very unlike Art to believe something without a little more concrete evidence than leftover warmth between exes, but still. 'Okay,' she says. 'Okay.' She puts her trembling hand on his leg.

He holds it for a moment, before letting it drop. His skin stretches at his temples. 'Rachel or not, though, I can see – this is impossible for you.' The words sound thick at the back of his throat. 'Either your brother stepped straight into

256

my car, which is what I'm saying happened – and why the hell would he do that, what with him being so accommodating and all.' The sarcasm rings painfully close to her bones. It's so mean, and so unlike him. 'Or I ran him over on purpose – and I don't know where to even begin with that. Or that you seem to think it's even *possible*.' He takes a deep breath and recovers his composure. He leans his forehead on his hands, looks down at the floor. 'We can't go on with this hanging over us,' he says.

'Frank—'

Frank looks at her dead straight and asks her if she spoke to Art while she was away.

'No,' she says, slowly, 'But you saw him and chose not to tell me. Why?'

He sighs. 'Because it was so odd. He was so wound up, I thought I'd better wait till you got home. Christ.' He rubs his head. 'There's so much to talk about, other stuff, important too, and those things seem to get further and further out of my reach. Art's paranoia is infecting our lives.'

'*Paranoia's* a bit strong, don't you think?'

'Well, he's got some fucked-up ideas and they're getting in the way. That day I came round, when I had something to bring you, both of you? It was important. But he was so peculiar, then our dinner got cancelled, and you had your row, and now . . . I was so looking forward to you coming home. I felt that our life might start, properly, you know? And then I bumped into Art at King's and he had the weirdest reaction to my mention of a mathematician called Mahalanobis – it's pretty esoteric stuff – anyway, it seemed to send him off the deep end.' He laughs, but it's bitter. 'The irony is, I only read up on Mahalanobis after I overheard Art and Ernest talking about it once. I didn't know who Mahalanobis was. I wanted to be able to talk to him about his work on the level. Impress your brother. Who you love so bloody much.' Frank is talking so quickly, Mimi feels the conversation is running away from her. She feels – she knows – that with every syllable, he is stepping away. 'I'm an idiot—' he says.

'Frank, s-stop,' she stammers. 'There's too much coming at us.' She's close to tears.

Frank stands up. 'Look, it's clear that your brother has got into your head about me. I get it, you two have a special bond. It's sweet in many ways. After all you've been through. But it's tough to live with, and now . . . well, I'm not going to hang around and feel accused of – of – Jesus!' He tries to button his coat, but he is shaking so much that his fingers are missing the holes. 'I'll say this. I've said it before, and I won't say it, ever again. But – going back to the accident itself, what was he doing there, Mimi? At *my* corner store?' He turns on his heel in frustration, but circles back, closer in. 'Please. Spend some time really thinking about his actions that day. Do it for me. For us. Before we lose everything.'

Unbidden, an image of him comes at her with force. Frank: older, greyer, his face disturbed by some other crisis – but always, *always*, shadowed with this one. So that's how he will look, she thinks, as she watches him go.

46

BEST ROUTE HOME

Mimi descends the Northern Line lift in a trance. She waits behind the yellow line on the platform as the black hole breathes out its underground air. Her lip is sore and the tissue in her pocket is soggy with snot. She pulls her new beanie over her ears. It's only three stops to Frank's, and the corner store.

Art hates the Northern Line. If he wasn't going to walk his normal way home, he'd have taken the bus. She should've followed his tracks; that would have been her best route to the depths of his mind.

The Best Route Home, he'd written in his notebook.

Every day after school, Mimi and Art had walked home, heads down on Dudley Road in case the Benson boys were loitering at their gate, ready to sneer: *Red hair, brother's queer.*

The best route possible. The logic feels loose and slippery. Her brain hurts.

It seems there is no answer to the best route home. His handwriting squashed at the end of his sentence, and on the list he'd made of his emotions in the back of his notebook. They were so sad: *Anxiety, Worry.* Brief moments of joy.

Her feet smack the pavement; the promised rain has started. You can tell so much about a person from their footsteps. Art's are measured and careful. Frank's are louder and scrape more, as if he's less worried about keeping control.

Her father's steps were solid.

The newsagent across the green from Frank's flat, opposite the playground, is not Frank's regular. The red-and-white awning says *Bhati & Son*. Newspaper trays and stiff bunches of flowers are shielded by plastic. As Mimi steps off the pavement to cross the road to the shop, she's walking in Art's steps. She feels her stomach fall.

Not far down the road is a toppled traffic cone. Striped tape flaps round a lamppost, to which a square yellow sign is attached. Metropolitan Police: Witness appeal. The date and time are filled in with marker pen. Someone has taken the time to write up the case, fill in the sign, hang it up with a double knot of plastic string.

She moves towards the spot itself. Where Mr Bhati talked to her brother as his head bled into the road. Mimi stares at the black tarmac – there's no stain of Art's blood, just the faintest fringe of reddened sand, dissolving in the rain.

The bank of headlines outside the newsagent declares: *The Big Freeze. Storm Chaos*. Art had all those titles about chaos in his office. It reminds her of her father's book, the one in Art's bag. *Chaos*. Ernest didn't know the name of the book Art had found. She must check it out when she gets home.

A man whom she assumes is Mr Bhati steps out of the shop to pick up a fallen Lottery board. Her scarf flaps over her face as she says hello.

'Mimi Brotherton. You helped my brother?' she says, through a mouthful of wool.

'Come in, young lady, come in. Terribly nasty out here.' Back inside, a fan heater paddles out warm air above the till. She pulls off her hat.

From behind the till, Mr Bhati adjusts the packs of chewing gum and asks after Art. 'Stable,' she says.

'I was worried he wouldn't make it.'

Mimi tells Mr Bhati she's trying to find out what her brother was doing in the area. She pulls at her scarf; it's itching. But he just repeats what the police have told her already. That standing in his shop, he heard the screech of tyres, a walloping sound. That he just stood, stuck – then ran. How he held Art's hand. How Mrs Bhati called the ambulance. How Frank leaned over him, shouting, 'Art! Art!'

She breathes out hard through her nose as tears prickle.

Mr Bhati presses a button on the counter and comes round with a stool. 'You've gone a bit pale,' he says.

Mrs Bhati appears through the beaded curtain at the side of the shop, across from the Snapple fridge. 'Ah my,' she says, flapping her hand when she sees Mimi – who must look worse than she'd realized. 'Jaldi Karo! Get some tea. With sugar!' Mrs Bhati touches her shoulder. 'Men,' she says, and shakes her head.

Mimi looks behind her at the CCTV camera trained on the till and the front of the shop. She sees the back of her own head; her hair looks terrible, like raffia.

Mr Bhati brings steaming herbal tea. Mimi seems to be a vehicle for Mrs Bhati to express her displeasure with her spouse, who shrinks back behind the till, under his colourful umbrella of condoms and cigarettes banded with death threats. The tea is sweet and hot. Mrs Bhati, still berating her husband in Urdu invective, disappears.

'Your CCTV is only *into* the store, right? No outside feed?' Mimi supposes the police will have already taken any footage that exists.

'Inside only, young lady,' says Mr Bhati. 'The police have a copy, but it's digital, so I have the full feed here.' He pulls a laptop from beneath his counter. 'But there's nothing to see.' He looks uncertainly back towards the curtain. 'She'll eat my brain if I get involved.'

'I understand,' says Mimi. '*Thank you.*'

He indicates for her to come round to his side. 'I'll email you a zip file, in case . . .'

Behind the till, Mr Bhati fast forwards to the evening of the accident. It's a strange soundless stream of halting images. Ten frames per second, he tells her. There's Mr Bhati, in his shop, at his till. Busy hands. The time registers 18.07 in the top right-hand corner. He scrolls carefully forwards, to a minute before Art's accident. Mr Bhati is pottering behind his counter; a shadow passes in the background – Mrs Bhati. There's no one else in the shop.

Mimi swallows.

They watch Mr Bhati spike a piece of paper onto an upright metal stick. He picks up a pen and scribbles something down on the tab next to his till. It looks as if his pen doesn't work; he scribbles hard, as if to get the ink to flow, then he looks up, alarmed. He was right, he is momentarily frozen. He looks wildly around, as though not sure what to do. You see him shout. Then he runs. He flashes across the camera, head moving as though he is still shouting, but it is hard to see. He's out the door. Mrs Bhati follows.

'A terrible thing.' Mr Bhati shakes his head while Mimi recovers. 'That screech, that sound. I knew straight away, I almost couldn't move, I didn't want to see. Terrible noise. Your poor brother.' He is shaken. 'I think back, on that moment – it tortures me, you know? The milliseconds between the screech of brakes and the hit of his body – if I had only swung round quicker, seen, I could tell you what I think you want to know. But the moment was gone. *Pfff.*' He makes a bursting star with his busy fingers. 'Forever.'

262

'It's okay, Mr Bhati.' Her voice catches. 'Can you show me again?' Mr Bhati slows it down this time. It's horrible to see his face in a slow-motion panic, his mouth moving too slowly as he calls in anguish for his wife. Her sari sails past the lens and out of the shop to the road and to Art. Mr Bhati quietly slides the computer over to her.

She watches again, their silent alarm, sped up this time.

Nothing. Just Mr Bhati. Mrs Bhati. Mr Bhati. Mr Bhati. Mrs Bhati. Gone.

There's a bang outside which makes them both jump and she sees the Lottery sign somersault past the door. The wind is up, much stronger now, and the rain sheets into the plastic covers on the newspapers. 'I knew it would rain harder,' says Mr Bhati. Quickly popping the computer back under the counter, he calls his wife, and dashes out to right the offending board, wedging it up behind his newspaper stand with a shrug. 'We'll call you a taxi,' he says, back inside.

'Before I go,' Mimi says, 'do you sell shortbread?'

While they wait for her taxi in awkward silence, Mimi picks at the plaster on her finger and looks at her phone, which already has Mr Bhati's zip file on it. The recording starts a few days before the accident, so Mimi begins to fast forward to the evening in question. People come and go, at speed. Mr and Mrs Bhati whizz around, looking as if they are battery operated, moving disjointedly on the soundless film. She watches the dates register in the top corner, when something catches her eye. On the day *before* the accident.

She rewinds.

Mr Bhati runs backwards through his shop.

And there's Art.

47

INCREMENTAL

Mimi sits on the bench outside Art's ward and watches her brother, again and again. In Bhati's store. On the evening before the accident. Buying bottled water, or something. Holding a blue plastic bag. She zooms in on the bag and a large, stylized eye – the logo of a surveillance shop on Black Prince Road.

Carrying this bag of amateur spyware, Art is served by Mrs Bhati. Mimi felt twinges of irritation and sadness when both Bhatis said they had no recollection of Art whatsoever – he was that unmemorable.

She's peering at the screen when she hears her name.

It's Rey.

Rey looks shambolic in baggy boots and leggings wrinkled at the knee. Her skin is matt, her hair piled in a knot that's falling out; her fringed scarf coils in a mess round her neck. 'Oh, Sweetie,' she says, as Mimi caves into her arms.

They get coffee and sit, Rey blowing on the top of her thin plastic cup, while Mimi catches her up on the last couple of days. Rey has questions, but mostly just listens, and nods. She asks Mimi to show her the CCTV.

'Be prepared, it's ghoulish.' Mimi fast forwards from the

beginning, to Art's store visit and then the night of the accident. 'And no sound. But we're used to that.'

Rey gasps as Mr Bhati looks up, alarmed. They watch the whole Mr Bhati, Mrs Bhati, gone thing, which Mimi has now seen so many times that she's inured.

'It's awful,' says Rey. 'The poor man's face.'

And Art's face so unmemorable.

'And *spying*! Presumably on Frank?' says Rey.

It's so good to have Rey there, to say words out loud she's been frightened to say; it punctures some of their power. 'I call them Art's Missing Days,' says Mimi, 'while I was in Wales. And we still don't know what happened that evening at the pool.'

'I should have stayed here,' says Rey.

Just then the doors open and Dr Sipos emerges from the ward, talking intently to Art's afternoon nurse about brain function scores. Mimi tucks her phone away.

Rey peers at Art through the half-moon window to the ward. 'He's very flat,' she says, her voice small.

Dr Sipos tells them they'll have Art's fMRI results tomorrow, perhaps even tonight. 'You should go home, it's been a long day,' he says. Meanwhile, Art's progress is 'incremental'. He switches his thumb with his index finger and back again to indicate how modest Art's steps are. 'The critical first two days are over. He has recovered from this morning. Now, we would like to see improvement.'

Rey nods and rubs her arms. 'Is there a medical reason for it being so cold in here?' she says. 'Will he be warm enough?'

'We keep body temperature low to protect the brain,' says Dr Sipos, then turns to Mimi. 'So. Your brother. I've changed his medication a little, we hope he has a peaceful night. We decide tomorrow. If the results suggest it, it might be possible to wean him from the barbiturates. Late morning. You'll be here?'

Mimi nods. Sipos heads off at a clip. 'I try to parse what they're saying,' she says. 'But I still have no idea if he's going to be okay.'

'Can I see him?' asks Rey, looking a little dazed.

'It's good you're here,' says Mimi, and nods. 'They really believe he can hear us.'

In a bed near Art is a woman whose husband massages her curling toes and pigeon pointed feet. He was on the phone to her when a truck hit her car, he's told Mimi. Her arms twist up, clamped against her chest. Her legs shoot out like a starfish.

'Hello Artie,' says Rey, apparently struggling with tears. She tugs at the sheet that's caught under his back. She picks up his hand.

Rey's hands feel different to Mimi's. Like hands of a sculptor, they are squeezing and strong. Her voice has a texture, like felt – she has the consistency of infinity, impossible to grasp but always there in their life.

Art knows both Mimi and Rey are there, although he cannot make out their words. Then they fade in a shower of static and, hard as he tries, he cannot bring them back.

Back at home that evening, Ernest has lit the wood burner and stocked the fridge – there's yoghurt and cheese, fresh lettuce. Rey seems taken aback to find Ernest there. Mimi climbs into the corner of the sofa and explains. 'Ernest promised Art he'd look after me, like you would've done, I guess.'

'Are you staying for supper?' Ernest asks Rey, who tells him yes, and she's cooking. If Mimi wasn't so tired, Rey's

266

proprietorial response would be funny – she's peeling a potato with more zeal than strictly necessary.

Mimi remembers the CCTV recording and the blue plastic bag Art was clutching on camera. 'I wonder if the rubbish has been taken?' she says. Rey looks perplexed at the non sequitur. Without explaining, Mimi levers herself off the sofa. She finds the bin bag squatting down the side of the house, filled with damp, swollen detritus. Stuffed below, is the blue plastic bag in question. It smells and is smeared with an indeterminate sauce. *AXIS SECURITY. Cameras, Surveillance, Protection*, it says. Wincing, she reaches inside and pulls out a receipt: *1 x Voice-activated surveillance adaptor. £39.95.*

She shows Rey, who twiddles one of her earrings round and round. 'Do you think it's for Frank's? Or work?' asks Rey. What on earth did he think he would hear? 'Do me a favour,' she says, 'please send me that footage. The CCTV from the shop.'

48

TRUE OR FALSE

Mimi picks at Rey's potato dish – the cheese is toasted to caramel on top, but she's not hungry. 'I'm sorry,' she says.

'It's been a long day,' says Rey. 'Go. Ernest and I will clean up.' Mimi crawls into bed, her body aching. But she wants to tell Frank that she's taking seriously his exhortation to question her brother's actions. She props herself up, ready to tell him about Art's first trip to the store. His spying, she'll keep to herself for now.

'You in bed?' she asks when Frank answers his phone.

'I'm in front of the TV, watching as though I'm sleep-walking.' He sounds sad, and exhausted. Even so, his voice is like a warm bath.

'I know,' she says, 'I feel a bit broken. I'm not sure which bits of me to listen to any more.'

'I wish you'd listen to yourself. To your own heart.'

'I do, Frank, I do. I just—'

Frank sighs. 'That's the thing. There's always a "just", always a "but".' When she doesn't reply, Frank says, 'Listen. It's not ideal to have this conversation on the phone, or while Art is so critical. I love you enough to share you, Mimi, really I do, I truly understand how important Art is, how

268

much you mean to each other. But I don't think you know yet what it is that you want.' Weariness flattens his voice like an iron. 'From the moment we met at those awards, you've withheld parts of yourself from me. Always.'

Something clicks into place. 'That night—' she says. Art's letter: *in our life for the wrong reasons*. 'Did you already know who I was? Was it me that attracted you?' As she says it, she sees a Google search: her brother, their parents, her. A photo. It wouldn't have taken much. 'Or was it Art?'

Frank is silent.

'Frank?'

'I know that's what Art thinks. That I was trying to meet him. He told me. But it was *not* like that.' Her relief tells her that's what she really wanted to know, that theirs had been a meeting meant by the stars. 'I mean, it *isn't* like that,' he says. 'I promise you, the minute I actually got to know you –' he falters – 'it isn't like that. Now.'

The pain is so intense it slices her throat.

'Mimi?'

She pushes her face into her pillow.

'Mimi, believe me, it might have started like that but it's irrelevant, it's got no bearing on where we are now – I—'

'*Irrelevant?*'

'I know it sounds contrived, deceptive even. But it's so much more complicated than that.'

She squeezes her pillow with her fists, into her mouth.

'Mimi?'

'Oh my god.' She is silent for a moment. 'I've just remembered. You *ordered* the labels, Frank. You knew I'd be there. You'd seen the list. You knew our names all along! You thought you'd give her a whirl to get close to her brother – was that it?' She can't bring herself to say *me, my*.

'Mimi, I promise you—'

'You used me, Frank.' She starts to cry. 'You used me.'

'No, Mimi, I didn't. Stop. That's not at all what happened. Can't you see this whole thing has spiralled out of control since you had that fight with your brother and you went away?'

'It's *our* fault?'

'That's *not* what I said. Look, I'm coming round. There's a lot that I still need to tell you, *give* you. Things you have no idea about. You'll have everything you need to know. I should have done it sooner.'

'Like what?'

'You have to let me explain in person.'

'No. Tell me now.' She tries to find an anchor of patience, but it eludes her. 'Honestly. This, especially the whole Rachel thing. It can't wait.'

Frank sighs. 'This is *not* how I wanted to do this,' he says. She has no idea what's coming, but he suddenly sounds calm. 'Rachel,' he says. 'Yes. Rachel Silver. This is not about how I came to meet you, but I'll start with her.' Relief floods his voice, but it is the deep affection that stuns Mimi into silence. 'We were at Warwick together, as I told you. I cared about her, I did. Then, with hardly a word, she left.' He sounds lighter than he has for days.

'I see.' Frank and Rachel. Rachel and Frank.

'What I didn't know,' he says, still calm, 'was her reason for going back to America.' Frank hesitates. 'She'd fallen pregnant.'

Fallen, like an accident.

'She had the baby there. I never knew. I'm a father.'

Mimi's skin feels hot.

'Rachel and I were never right together. She knew that. And that I wasn't ready for a child. She needed to be at home. I had no idea. I have a daughter, Mimi. A little girl.'

270

Mimi looks at the photograph on her dresser. Her father and her.

'Her name is Kitty.' There is silence. '*Mimi?*'

But Mimi can't talk.

'I'm sorry you've found out like this,' says Frank. 'But it has nothing to do with anything else.'

The thing is, he doesn't sound sorry. He sounds relieved.

'My god,' she says.

Then Frank launches back into trying to convince her that his taking her number, calling her up, that it was all real. 'Of *course* I had heard of your brother. David Charing suggested I meet him—'

He's totally changed the subject. '*David Charing*? My father's old friend? Leave my parents out of this.'

'Look. I did think I'd find it easier to talk to Art if I'd met you first, that you'd be more approachable. And you were. But then you lied about your surname and I was trapped.'

'Trapped? You've just told me you have a daughter! Right now I don't care how we met, or what you do or don't want to do with my brother's work. You have a *daughter*. That changes everything. For you, for us.'

'It doesn't change us, Mimi. That's exactly what I didn't want you to think.'

'You're a *father*! And you didn't tell me.'

'She's being adopted by Rachel's husband. Officially. They live in Massachusetts. It's the saddest thing in my life that I didn't even know she existed until she was nine, four years ago, and that I hardly ever see her. But I don't. I missed her whole childhood, Mimi. And now – Rachel contacted me recently because her husband wants to adopt Kitty as his own.' He sounds raw. 'She and I bumped into Art the other day when I came to collect the adoption papers from her. I

271

wanted to tell you once it was all signed. Kitty is very important, obviously. I've tried to contribute to her education, she's my child –' for a moment Mimi thinks he might cry – 'but she's got nothing whatsoever to do with you and me, or Art for that matter.'

'That's where you're just so very wrong,' says Mimi. 'Don't you see? You didn't tell me, and it's part of the reason my brother is lying in hospital, from what I can make out.'

'That is grossly unfair. *Cruel* actually.' Frank sounds genuinely angry. 'I knew the adoption was nearly finalized and I thought if I presented it to you as a fait accompli it would be easier for *you*! I *know* it's a big thing.'

'You think?'

'Listen, I need to come round. I knew this was a bad idea, on the phone.'

'No, Frank,' says Mimi, and she feels her body separate from her voice. She has the voice of an adult, and it makes the decisions for her, while her child's body crumples on the bed. 'No. I can hear that you are telling the truth about Rachel. And Kitty.' It feels strangely okay to say the girl's name. 'And it's refreshing to hear you tell the truth.'

'Mimi, every last thing I've said is true. But the truth can be messy. When I first saw you, I recognized you from the photographs I'd already seen online, literally a day or two before. I'd been researching Art. But – I mean – how much can you tell really from those little postage stamps on Google Images? You can hardly fall in love with one of those, can you? When I saw the guest list for the awards – Art was attending and so were you. I thought – now *that's* a coincidence, so I went along. I guess if I'm honest—'

'Ah! So now you've decided to be honest, after all these months? I sat there that day we went cycling and poured out my heart about my brother, my parents, and you knew – all along? You didn't let on you already knew my real surname? Meanwhile you'd practically stalked me. The mountain of secrets you kept to yourself. You accuse me of withholding myself! Terrific, Frank. That's a fucking relationship triumph.'

'You're not seeing this straight, *at all*. Which I get, but Mimi – you *lied* about your name. See it from my point of view. Just for a second.'

A small voice somewhere tells her it's possible he might be right, that it may be a good idea to pause, try and see Frank's side. But there's a swarm inside her now, a gathering black that comes up from her belly. It confirms all the voices in her head from over the years. They compress into this single moment – she doesn't deserve it, she's never been enough, she's never been loved unconditionally. There is always, *always*, someone else more important. Her brother, her mother. And now – Frank has a secret daughter. Her thoughts ribbon and spiral in a mad swirling ball. 'No, Frank. No. I've heard everything I need to hear.'

'No, you haven't. I haven't said the most important thing.'

'And what's *that*?'

'I love you, Mimi,' he says, 'really, I do. I loved you from the moment I met you.'

'Well then, that's the difference between us.'

'That's not true. I *know* you love me.'

'That's not what I meant,' she says, and she knows she is lifting a hammer to the wall. She wants to stop, but she can't. She wants to wound him, make him sorry, and then love her anyway, all the more for having hurt her. 'The thing is, you'd already seen me in my photos online, and you didn't love me then. But I loved you the first moment I saw you, across that room. My heart stopped. When you sent me that WhatsApp, I was *already* in love with that stub of a photo. You in that stupid sombrero.' Her voice cracks.

273

Frank doesn't respond. Mimi can't believe she has chosen this moment, this moment now, of all moments, to tell him she loves him.

'But,' she says, trying to hold herself together as she swings the head down, 'I didn't lie.'

'Well actually, quite the opposite,' says Frank. 'You *did*. And I didn't.'

'We are based on a lie. Us – you and me. I cleared up my lie early on. You didn't. Our foundations aren't real. I don't trust you, Frank. Art *told* me not to,' she says, searching for and finding more ammunition to hurt him.

'If you think that,' he says, and his voice goes icily cold, 'there's not much I can do.'

'No,' she says. 'There's not. You've done enough.' *Don't push him,* she thinks. But there's another part of her, a voice that she cannot control, that tells her she doesn't deserve the love he is offering her. She wasn't ever supposed to find the happiness she thought she had found. She feels angry that Frank even tempted her – look where it's got them, look at her brother, lying in a coma. Art might lose everything this time. And it's her fault. *Again.* 'We are built on a lie.'

'Is that what you think? What you really think, Mimi? After these last months?'

'Seems to me, Art was right.'

'Is that so.' It isn't a question.

Silence races down the lines, straight into her veins.

'Well,' says Frank. 'That's pretty clear. I've fought for you, Mimi. You've pushed me and pushed me, but honestly, now – I think that I'm done.'

'Frank—' She's judged it wrong.

'It's better to know. I'd rather know now.'

'No! I'm sorry. I—'

'No, I'm done Mimi. Once trust is gone, there's nothing

left, really.' He sounds flat, and incredibly sad. He's not testing her or bluffing – he's decided – she can hear. He tells her he still has something to give her but she's only half listening, her insides are roiling with the cold fear of losing him. 'For you and your brother. It's a book that belonged to your father, but it's got a complicated story, so I'll bring it myself. I'll call you in a day or two to make a plan. You've got a lot on your plate. I hope Ernest looks after you. God knows, I wanted to.'

'Frank!'

'Go to your brother. I hope he's okay.'

She doesn't say goodbye. She doesn't get the chance.

49

RECURRING

There's a knock on Mimi's door.

'What are you doing?' asks Rey, walking into her room. Mimi is in her nightie, her knees pulled up, a worn piece of folded newspaper in her hands. Soft tears are dripping into her lap.

'He's got a child, Rey.' Mimi is clutching at the piece of paper. 'A daughter. He's a *father*.'

Rey smooths the duvet and sits next to her. 'Oh, Sweetie. Tell me. But first – what have you got there, Mi?'

Mimi hands over the faded article from the local newspaper.

The article was written after the coroner's inquiry into her parents' deaths. There's a photograph of Walter's maroon BMW, cordoned off with striped police tape.

Rey blanches. 'Why are you looking at this now?'

'He's gone, Rey, I've messed it all up.' She doesn't look at her friend, her focus is somewhere else. 'Frank. He says he loves me, *now*, but it was Art he wanted, not me. Art's proof, I guess. But more than that – he's got a *daughter*. She was born when he was twenty-three and he didn't know. He's signing her adoption papers over to her stepfather – at her mother's request – and I could hear it's making him sad, but can I ever be with a man who's failed to tell me he has a child?' She sniffs and points at the newspaper Rey's holding. 'N-n-not when – my feelings are so muddled, I so – I so – my father . . .' She can't finish.

'I know.' Rey puts the newspaper clipping to the side, then holds her friend and rocks her. 'You feel he left you. But they're completely different things, Mi.' She lies down next to Mimi, tucking her head into the crook of her arm and holds her close. 'Listen, you aren't going to fix anything tonight; try to get some sleep.'

After a while, Rey whispers to her. 'I've got to fetch Rizla from Mr Raikes, but I'll stay until you've drifted off.'

'There's shortbread for him in my bag,' says Mimi, muffled in Rey's arms. Later, from a half-sleep state, she feels Rey slip away, hears her footsteps and the click of the door.

She wakes early, in the dark, to find her arm trapped behind her head, curled round the headboard as though she's been clinging to something. It's numb and flops around.

Mimi replays the conversation with Frank in her mind. Perhaps she should give him the benefit of the doubt. Get a bit more information about Kitty and her mum before jumping to conclusions. Frank knows how complicated her feelings about fatherhood are, about the sacrifices she believes fathers ought to make for their children. She would tell him to go and live in America to be near Kitty and her mother. Frank probably knows *all* that.

She turns on her bedside light, and the first thing she sees is the article about her parents on her bedside table.

Couple Decides, says the now-familiar font. *Southwark Park*.

The wide, open park had been a favourite spot of Art and Mimi's parents, filled with acres of enormous trees and wild hedgerows. It was a place they'd gone walking since their first month in England.

This time they'd gone to die.

They'd parked down a quiet track and hidden in the undergrowth until it closed to cars for the night. They'd been found in the back seat of their maroon car, with the garden hose clipped to the front window on the passenger side, the gap stuffed with thick blankets, yellow insulating tape and plastic bin bags. They'd thought it all through. They'd used gloves, as if they were worried that someone might blame one, or the other.

Forensics showed that Christine drove them there. Perhaps they kept the car door open while they ate the wholemeal biscuits that the autopsy detected in both of their systems, and Christine drank her tea laced with Zolpidem from the flask that was found at her feet on the floor. Not talking, music from the radio folding out and over the hedgerows and treescape in front of them. Christine must have turned on the engine, left the driver's seat and got into the back, Walter letting her in first, then sliding in next to her on the back seat. Perhaps he lay her legs across his lap, before she pulled them up into the foetal ball they found her in.

Christine was already so frail. They clearly planned for her to go first.

She was lying in the back, her head on the small, embroidered pillow she'd kept on her bed, her eyes closed. She looked peaceful, they were told. She'd put on eye shadow – Guerlain Slipper Blue that Walter gave her for Christmas. She wore the elasticated trousers that Mimi hated because they'd bagged at her belly as she'd got thinner, and her Aran jumper, as though she might be cold. Her scarf was wrapped over her shoulders; tucked in, the paramedic said. Mimi liked

278

to think her father had done that. She always imagined them agreeing to say one last thing, then no more.

Her father: 'I love you.'

Her mother. Tears. 'They're going to be okay.'

Or, the other way around.

It was harder for Walter. Mimi always supposed that was his sacrifice; he'd made sure she was comfortable first.

Walter's backside was slumped into the footwell behind the driver's seat, his head thrown back. His left hand bunched the hem of Christine's jumper. His right hand was clamped around the headrest in front. His face was cherry red, his jugular swollen, a bluish-grey tinge mottled the base of his nose.

The coroner said that their father had died of cardiac arrest, brought on by severe, asymptomatic hypertrophic cardiomyopathy, the attack exacerbated by the carbon monoxide: 'Death was immediate, and inevitable', said the report.

Through her streams of anger and grief, Mimi had got some consolation from this fact – it was quick. A consolation. Second prize.

Nobody had seen them arriving. But no one could miss them leave. Plastic sheets barricaded the scene for hours at the site and when they finally left it was still side by side, but in an ambulance, with the sirens silent, a police car trailing quietly behind.

It was impossible to believe at first. There were many moments when Mimi was convinced they had the wrong people – like when someone told her the car was red. For months she went back over the details that she and Art had been given, looking for something, anything, to suggest that perhaps they might not have really meant it, that perhaps her father hadn't really meant to abandon them, that he'd intended to tuck her mother in and come home. *Something*.

But there was nothing. It was all so organized, so perfectly planned.

Their radio was playing Classic FM. Even the child locks, which Walter always hated, were on, as if they were worried that they might change their minds. In between the two front seats, secured to the solid centre console, was a photograph from Christine's dressing table.

There were no letters for Mimi and Art. But in the photograph, there the children were. Arm in arm on the beach, their image as eloquent as any letter could ever have been.

Mimi reads the article again.

Couple Decides to Die Using NHS Life and Death Maths Calculations

Lecturer and Wife in Suicide Pact.

A middle-aged mathematics professor and his wife, who had terminal cancer, died in a suicide pact, driven by the idea that the wife's suffering would get 'exponentially' worse, and that the 'marginal benefit of further treatment would decrease', an inquest heard. In a letter to her lawyer, Christine Brotherton, 51, made clear that although her husband might be the expert, she'd done the calculations on her QALYs (Quality of Life Years) – an acronym used extensively by NICE, the department that uses mathematics to decide which medicines should be made available on the NHS.

Mrs Brotherton was diagnosed with terminal cancer after being in remission for years. Her husband Walter, thirteen years her senior, cared for her at home, with their two adult children.

A distinguished mathematician, originally from South Africa, Walter Brotherton worked at Queen Mary University, where he was well liked. 'He kept to himself,' said a colleague. 'A very kind man, devoted to his wife. He clearly didn't want to be without her.'

Forensics suggest that Mrs Brotherton drove the couple to Southwark Park, where they were later discovered in their car. A post-mortem revealed that the couple died just a short time apart. Mrs Brotherton had taken a sleeping tablet and is thought to have died peacefully from monoxide poisoning. Prof. Brotherton died from cardiac arrest, brought on by the carbon monoxide, the coroner confirmed. The inquest ruled joint suicide, and there will be no further investigation.

The couple's planning was evident – they had all the equipment, and the car was carefully hidden – the inquest was told. They were found by two joggers. 'We could see straightaway something was wrong, the window stuffed with tape and padding, the hose out the side,' said Jackie Mayhew, 34, a local estate agent. 'We run there twice a week, but we were too shaken to run home. Luckily a taxi came down Forest Hill for a job that hadn't turned up and the driver took us to call the police. It was a very sad sight, they really weren't that old.'

Mrs Brotherton lodged a letter with her solicitor making it clear that she had in no way been encouraged in this by her husband, ruling out any suggestion of murder-suicide, which can plague the families of the ill who take their lives with their partners. The couple lived in London and are survived by their two children, who, at 18 and 23, are said to have known nothing of their parents' plans and are 'devastated', according to a family friend.

She tucks the newspaper away in her drawer.

50

BREAKING

It's still dark outside when her door opens a fraction. 'Mimi?'

'Ernest?' She twists on her arm, numb from sleep.

Ernest is breathless. 'Mimi, sorry to disturb—'

She's bolt upright. '*Art?*'

'Oh, sorry, sorry, no. Art's okay,' says Ernest. 'But could you come downstairs?'

He closes the door and Mimi grabs her mother's old dressing gown. The velour is stretched, and it gapes at the front. It makes Mimi feel old – old enough to be a parent – like Frank, she thinks, with a jolt. She imagines Frank's daughter, watching her. His *daughter*. She pulls the belt tight and holds it closed at her neck, where her throat is swollen and constricted. She rinses out her mouth, which feels like cloth. Then she hurries downstairs.

The television's on. Ernest is in his San Diego Comic Con sweatshirt, cradling a cup of coffee and staring at the red stripe of Breaking News.

BREAKING NEWS . . . MILLION-DOLLAR MATHS PRIZE SOLVED. *P VS NP*: MAJOR ADVANCE IN MATHEMATICS.

Oh no. No no no no no. **BBC BREAKING . . .** Mimi's insides push up.

'It's happened.' Ernest blinks long and slow, as if he can't look at the screen. 'Art knew it.' The presenter is a dark-haired woman wearing a bright orange dress with a plunging keyhole neckline. At 6.30 a.m. She tells the world how an Estonian recluse living in Cedar Falls, Iowa has proved that *p* does not equal *Np*, after all.

'My poor brother.'

A mathematician YouTuber with a white stripe in his dark hair is waving his arms and scrawling luminous green trails on the TV screen. *p ≠ Np!* he writes.

Mimi collapses on the sofa.

Among the emotions busy emptying her out, as though through a plughole deep in her middle, she feels relief that at least this has nothing to do with Frank. It's as though she breathes *in* pain for Art, then releases it for Frank. Daughter or not.

But for Art, she feels sick.

A conveyor belt of talking heads is proclaiming the astronomically important nature of the discovery.

Ernest puts a cup of coffee down in front of her.

She watches the tendrils of rising steam. 'He's going to be devastated, if he ever wakes up. This is his whole world.'

As for Ernest and Art and their conspiracy theories, and the damage they've done . . . 'My *brother*.' She puts her hands to her face. 'I feel as if between us we've lost everything. And I'm not sure how it happened.'

Next to her, Ernest is blinking tears away.

Back in Mimi's bedroom, light cocoons round the bedside lamp. She climbs back into bed; her sheets have cooled. As she pulls up the blanket, there's a beep on her phone.

Mimi. It's a message from Frank.

284

I know we left things badly last night, but I've just seen the news. You may not want to hear from me, but I wanted to say – I know what this means to your brother. F

She doesn't know how to reply, but it snaps her out of a trance. She gets up and pulls off the dressing gown, grabs a towel from behind her door and flicks on the lights.

Her brother had been right to be worried. It was exactly as Ernest had explained – someone *was* beating Art to it. The ether was pulsing with his ideas because the collective knowledge had reached that tipping point where something was bound to happen.

But her own knowledge has reached a tipping point too. She cleans her face, which looks as puffy and appealing as cauliflower. Frank's never seemed like a man who'd be implicated in some duplicitous maths scheme. He has flaws, they're legion, and they have issues to sort out between them. And yes, her brother had stumbled on one of them – Rachel. The thought of Rachel and Kitty mangles her insides. But their problem isn't, and never has been, maths.

Frank is not scheming and secretive and underhand – that's not who he is. He's careless and sloppy, he doesn't pick his towel up off the floor, she thinks, folding hers. He leaves coffee rings on books and tabletops, he's not security conscious in a way you'd expect someone devious to be – he doesn't even have a password for his phone.

Frank is kind. She chokes at the thought of it. He's kind to her. He will understand, perhaps more than she does, the loss that Art will feel.

Thank you, she texts him. **Please can we talk. x**

For the first time in a long time, in far *too* long, she thinks, she's going to listen to herself.

Frank doesn't reply.

* * *

285

Mimi can't imagine Art coming round and being met with this news, waking to find his work swept away. She pulls back the curtain; light leaks into the sky. She's going to her brother. But first, she's going to find Frank.

She calls Rey. 'Think Occam's Razor,' she says to her perplexed friend.

'Huh?'

'Art always says: look for the simplest answer.' Mimi talks through the jumper that she's pulling over her head. 'I need to get to Art, but before that, I'm going to see Frank.'

'I thought you'd messed it up with Frank?'

'I have, and I'll never forgive myself if I lose him forever, and for the wrong reasons.'

'Give me ten,' say Rey. 'I'll drive you in the van.'

Love, thinks Mimi. You don't know if you will ever fall in love, until you do. And then, it stops your heart. It's like the Halting Problem. You don't know if your heart will stop; it could just keep going forever, untouched by love. And then when it does – well, there's no going back.

51

RULE OF THUMB

While she waits for Rey, Mimi fiddles with the new pepper grinder – different, and lighter than the old one – which still feels like lead in her hand. Even if it's over with Frank, her life with Art can't go back to what it was. Ernest is staring out the window, as though someone has switched him off. Mimi touches his shoulder and briefly, without turning round, he puts his hand on her arm. 'They might lift his coma today,' she reminds him. Light washes the sky outside, a lilac hue filters between the houses. She puts the pepper grinder back in place, as Art might. What would have happened if she'd never picked up that blasted thing that morning? The Butterfly Effect. Chaos.

She remembers *Chaos*, that book in Art's bag. Frank mentioned a book.

The doorbell rings.

She dashes to grab the bag of Art's things the hospital gave her. Her father's book is there, with the old sticker she'd stuck to the front as a child. Mimi shoves it into her own bag, and, with her heart hammering, she hurries out to the van where Rey is waiting.

A car is forced to slow as she crosses the road. The driver hoots and gives her the finger.

Mimi doesn't mention the chaos book to Rey. She needs to talk to Frank.

Meantime, she's aware that the taped Yellow Pages that Rey borrowed is under her feet. 'Art's phone book,' she says. 'He's so attached to it.'

'He's attached to what he knows best,' says Rey.

'He certainly knows how to become attached to an idea.'

'He wasn't totally wrong about Frank. Something *was* up,' says Rey, driving across the intersection. 'There's an irony in Art being right about something being wrong – but getting it so wrong himself. It's kind of tragicomic.'

Mimi picks at the latch for the glove compartment and then looks at Rey. 'He wasn't wrong about our parents. He's never let me forget it.'

Rey goes quiet for a moment, then slows down a bit and asks: 'Is that true – does he really go on about it?' Mimi looks out the window. The sun creeps into view from behind the buildings in a burst of reflecting light that sparkles in all the windows, bright after all the rain. 'Or is that just what you feel?' adds Rey, gently.

Mimi looks at her lap. 'No. You're right, he doesn't really *say* it. But whenever he tells me he's right about something, which he does all the time, I know – I *think*,' she corrects herself, 'he's referring to that.'

'Maybe,' says Rey as they pull up outside Frank's block and she parks the van. 'I don't know.' Mimi walks up the path and rings Frank's doorbell, but there's no answer. She didn't even think to bring her key. She rings again, but she hears the echo, a hollow buzz inside. When Mimi calls him, Frank doesn't pick up.

288

Back in the van, with her head on the dashboard, she tells Rey she's ruined her life. 'I'm like one of those cartoon characters that runs around blowing stuff up,' she says. 'First rule of Hollywood: anything can explode.'

Rey is quiet as they drive towards the hospital, while London wakes.

In Art's ward, there's a constellation of people round one of the beds and the curtain is drawn. They can't see past the fuss to Art.

'Oh no,' whispers Rey.

Dr Sipos looks tired. 'Busy night,' he says quietly.

They've elevated Art, just a fraction. It's slightly less alarming than him lying so flat, and his colour looks different – less blue, less marbled. They've removed some of his bandages; stubble shadows his scalp. She takes in his electroencephalo thingy and his ICP tube. The monitors are the same – beep, beep – as before.

That's it, she realizes. She swings round to look at the curtained shroud of the next bed. There's no noise. The monitors are off. Nurse Kanda shakes her head slowly.

'What happened?' asks Rey.

'VTE. Venous thromboembolism. She's an occupational therapist, so people here know her,' says Nurse Kanda, whose face has lost its shine this morning. 'She was lovely.'

'I'm sorry,' says Mimi. Rey swallows.

Nurse Kanda looks down. 'It happens on this ward.' Then she makes a slow fold along the sheet covering Art. 'See, they raised him up,' she says, and pats the top of his mattress. 'They're happy that his spine is stable now that the swelling's gone down.' She checks his ICP and gives his charts a flick. 'They're bringing him out of the coma?'

'They're going to discuss it,' Mimi tells her. 'But I feel scared.'

289

'They'll be very careful with the decision, look at all his tests. Sometimes, the doctor has to make a judgement. To me, he feels ready,' says Nurse Kanda. 'Can't say why, he just does.'

'It's almost like he's safer in there.'

'I understand,' says Nurse Kanda. 'It can be bumpy. Traumatic even.'

'We'll be here,' says Rey.

'And, for you too,' the nurse adds, nodding towards Mimi.

Dr Sipos is back. 'Now we talk.'

'Nurse Kanda was saying it's a difficult process,' says Mimi. Whatever this man recommends, she decides, is what we will do.

'We go slowly as we can, but it's rough,' says the doctor. 'His ICP sensor is screwed into his skull, so we have to strap him in case he rips it out. The drugs can reduce your blood pressure, so we watch that.'

'What should we expect?' asks Rey.

'Seizures, convulsions, delirium.' He pauses. 'Dizziness, lack of vision, loss of—'

'What's the worst that can happen?' Mimi asks.

Doctor Sipos's eyes slide towards the next bed. 'In this ward, Ms Brotherton, the worst that can happen is always the very worst that can happen. But in life, this is true.' He touches his head. 'It's like withdrawal from addiction. It's unpleasant, and not a straight line. He may blink a little at first, be conscious but confused, he can vomit, feel nauseous, light-headed, then go back to sleep. It is more like a dimmer switch being wiggled than a light being turned on.' Dr Sipos makes a little turning gesture with his fingers.

'Poor Art,' says Rey. She puts her hand on his.

'The coma is reversible. What we don't know yet is the damage underneath. The coma doesn't help that, it's simply protected his brain from further injury in the meantime. I'm sorry, I do not give you more.'

'How long will it take?' asks Mimi.

Sipos tells her it can be a while.

'Like hours?'

'Like hours. Like days. Can take months,' he says.

'*Months!?*'

'Look, we never can tell. But –' says the doctor. He enumerates the facts with his fingers: one, two, three – 'we have careful titration of his medications the last twenty-four hours. We have neurologic assessment, looks okay. I'm comfortable there's no more swelling of brain tissue. His blood is under control. I wouldn't recommend it if I didn't think he is ready.'

'I feel sick,' says Mimi.

'If I had to guess, I feel optimistic, but that's just my gut feeling.'

'Heuristics,' says Mimi. The word pops into her head.

'You're right, that's just what it is. *Heurisztikus*, we say, in Hungarian. This means our very best guess.' He sticks his thumb up in the air. 'Rule of thumb, no? We cannot always make our decision from only the facts. Even in medicine. Sometimes we have to use our gut, our heart. It's our super-power.' He smiles. 'My *ökölszabály* is, your brother will be okay.'

'What about his mathematics, his brain?'

Sipos is holding the green folder. 'Let's go a step at a time, yes? We lucky to be this far. So, good. We start midday.'

Mimi's not sure that 'very best guess' is what she should stake the rest of her life on. Or Art's, she thinks. She looks at her brother breathing through his tubes.

Right now, it's all that they have.

Rey runs her fingers through the stubble on Art's head.

'What's going on in there?' She traces his bandage. 'I wish,' says Rey, 'I just wish I'd paid more attention, you know? I was so chuffed about you and Frank, and that you'd finally taken a pair of scissors to the apron strings you and Art tied so tightly round each other.'

Apron strings?

'Even if they were only with nail scissors,' Rey says, and laughs. 'But still, you were really trying. I guess the job was working well for me too, and Frank seemed so decent.'

'He *is* decent,' says Mimi.

'I should have realized what was going on,' says Rey. 'Art was dying inside. We all know that part of his brilliance is his imagination; he even used to have imaginary friends, remember?'

'God, I *do*. They drove me mad, I felt so excluded.' She remembers Art's friends that 'lived' in a backpack. His magic backpack, he called it. 'I even tried to get rid of them – I threw the bag onto a builder's skip. I remember it flying in an arc and then getting stuck. Boof! Dangling in the air with a rusting pole stabbed through its middle. Art was inconsolable. And the friends *still* didn't die.'

'I remember,' says Rey. 'But his imagination is what makes him a genius. And I saw flashes of that same kind of vision from him about Frank – like the night at that bar when Art wanted to pay, and Frank took control instead, or when Frank bought you those beads for your birthday. His greatest fear, the thing he had always imagined, was materializing in front of his eyes.'

'Art's greatest fear? His work? Someone beating him to the proof?'

'Don't be naive. What's the thing in the world he's most afraid of?'

'Losing his maths. And now it's happened.'

292

'Not quite,' says Rey, touching the side of her friend's face. 'What scares him most in the universe, Mi, is losing *you*.'

The muscle in Art's eyelid twitches with a small spasm. The machine beats out a steady rhythm. She's aware of Rey touching her back, of leaving her alone with her brother.

She puts her cheek flat on his forehead, feels his clammy skin on her face, and whispers. 'They felt immortal,' she says. She means, his imaginary friends. She means, their parents. She means – him. Them. 'Do you remember losing your imaginary friends? Mum encouraged you to give them up because you were being teased at school.' Her breath is on his neck. 'I remember losing you to them,' she says.

She plucks at the bandage on Art's arm, an old injury now. Wales feels like a lifetime ago – the water chasing her ankles on the sand, the cliffs at her back.

'I'm here now,' she says, but there's a current like a tide on soft sand that undermines the conviction in her words. She remembers the briny tang in the air from samphire and laver, spinached seaweed drying at the sea's fringe. She'd felt free. She'd picked at the shell line, found common winkles, razors and dog cockles, tellins like pairs of pale-pink gemstones.

Christine had loved pink tellins best – the tiny bivalves that looked like Mimi's fingernails. 'My two babies,' she'd say, holding a little pink butterfly shell in the middle of her palm. 'This is you –' she'd say, showing Mimi one half of the tellin; then she'd hold the other half – 'and this is you, darling,' to Art. Mimi never understood, because it seemed to her that in nothing at all were the two of them alike. It had struck her in Wales that perhaps it was the two tellins fastened together with invisible glue that appealed to their mother. The tough little ligament holding the hinge.

Perhaps that's what she'd done when she sent the pepper

grinder top crashing into her brother – torn at the ligament, pulling away.

She rubs Vaseline on Art's lips, and on the site where the tube rubs his nose raw. 'See, Mummy?' she says. 'I'm still here. I couldn't break away.' She massages it into the crescents of his nails, which are already longer than Art likes them to be.

She could tell Art how sorry she is. How sorry she *was*. But right now, she thinks, and imagines just a single little shell, pale pink as the nail on her baby finger, sitting in the palm of her hand, by itself. The truth is – she's not sorry to want Frank.

She tells him instead that Ernest has his back. 'You were right about Ernest. He'd do anything for you.' It's true. Ernest's unquestioning devotion to Art is touching. 'He's almost more devoted than me,' she says, and she feels the tugging ligament of love.

'We're waking you up,' she says, holding his hand.

Art is lying on his back, as if in the pool. His head tips up on a cushion of sorts – a Lilo, just under his neck. He's staring at the ceiling, the lights on their strips. It feels different today; he is up at the surface, not swimming in the depths. The tin sky drops its weight on the water and presses down on his chest. Something pulls at his nose. A tug in his skull. He is closer, much closer – he can hear her in here. Waves judder in his ears.

'I remember losing you,' she says. It does not make sense. He has never been away.

He would never ever leave her, never ever go.

52

REMAINDER

Rey is waiting outside the ward. 'I felt as though I was saying goodbye,' Mimi tells her. 'As if I've betrayed him with my thoughts.'

'You don't have to choose between them.' Rey's face is creased with concern. 'What you have to do now is wait.'

'I need to find Frank and tell him what's going on. Apologize. Get him back.'

Rey puts her arm on Mimi's. 'Mi, slow right down. Go and see Frank when things are a bit calmer. By the way, Ernest asked if you'd mind if I sent him that footage from the store too? He's obviously still digging around.'

'Screw Ernest,' Mimi says, feeling a sharp needle-tip of irritation with Rey too. Mimi's defence of Frank bubbles up, unchecked. It feels clean and clear, uncontaminated. It's as if she's found a pure stream that she couldn't tap into before.

'Look, it might be annoying,' says Rey, 'but Ernest told me that Art was absolutely convinced that he'd stumbled on something. When Art went to the pool, he—'

'Hang on,' says Mimi.

Art's missing days. She picks up her coat and checks for the pool receipt. There it is. 'Rey, I've just remembered something.

There's something I've got to do. And then be back for Art. Do you mind staying here, just in case? I know this must seem crazy – me going now, but Sipos said midday, so we've got a few hours. I need to do this.' She pats the pocket of her coat. 'If anything changes – *call me.*'

'Mimi—'

'Straight away. I can't miss it. I need to be here for him the second he comes round.'

'Where are you going?'

'Art went back to the pool while I was in Wales. It might help me find out what happened the night that set all this off. Or about his missing days.'

Mimi calls Frank as she walks, but there's still no reply.

53

UNPREDICTABILITY

t = the Monday before

Art lifted his jacket collar against the squally wind, walked along the Embankment and waited for the bus. His Google route was stored in his mind.

First stop had been the surveillance shop on Black Prince Road. Honestly, you could spy on anyone. No wonder his work felt so vulnerable. Art had phoned ahead; the adaptor was in stock.

Feeling the weight of it now, in its carrier bag, Art walked to the corner of Dante Road. From here he could see Frank's building and his apartment, where the blinds were drawn; he could watch cars and people come and go. A hedge enclosed a small green with a children's playground and beds of leggy shrubs. A child's jumper had been left on the large plastic tunnel. Art looked at his watch – 4.30 p.m. The clock change had thrust the day into twilight.

After a while, he headed across the playground towards Frank's raised ground-floor flat. The front door was approached by a well-planted paved path before the steps, which allowed Art to duck out of sight. As he took Mimi's key from his pocket, he was reminded of denying Frank a key to *their* house. He slid the key into the lock.

It had not occurred to Art that Frank might in fact, be home. It was early on a Monday afternoon; he knew Frank's routine well enough. But as he turned the key and felt the lock give, he heard a clanking sound on the other side. Art's hand froze around the key, immobilized in the Banham lock. How would he explain his presence here, the surveillance bag hanging from his wrist, his opening of Frank's door, *uninvited*? What had he been thinking? He did not dare breathe as he carefully squeezed the key clockwise again, to close the door. But the door was swollen and did not close easily. It needed a heave. The sound of his heart thumping was filling his ears. He pulled the door a millimetre towards him, wincing as the hinges squeaked. One, two, three – *c-lank!* went the noise inside again and suddenly, with a rush of so much adrenalin flooding his body that he thought he might be sick, Art knew what it was. It would make sense that at 4.45, Frank's heating came on. Theirs did the same. Art looked at this watch. That was all that it was.

Holding his breath, Art pushed the door open and next thing, there he was, inside Frank's flat. Alone. He looked around, his body still buzzing. It was all familiar, but also technicolour, as if rendered in high resolution. The lightwell and split rooflines that were designed to maximize space made Art feel off-balance. A window tilted open to the balcony outside.

He needed to be quick.

Checking that his shoes did not leave markings on the parquet – they did not; Frank was not, after all, a stickler for a polished floor – Art stepped around the coffee table and searched for a socket. Bending over the end of the sofa, he found what he needed. He opened the box of his voice-activated surveillance adaptor. He had prepared the batteries and synced it with the receiver while still on the bus. All he needed to do now was plug it in.

Frank would never notice. What a marvel of discretion, thought Art, as he stepped back to inspect what would be his new source of information, streamed live from Frank's life. Rachel Silver – he would find out *all* about her now. It was tempting to search the flat for further evidence, but he did not have time and his heart rate had not yet come down to what Art considered an optimal level since his momentary lapse of reason at the door.

He looked round. The bamboo plant had grown since he was last there, although it could have done with a little water. The rest was much the same; a packet of chocolate digestives was open on the counter, Frank's ridiculous sombrero hung over the upright of the bookshelf. It was time to get out, but for some reason Art picked up the sombrero and put it on his head. It gave him such a powerful sense of having broken all the rules, he felt he was metamorphosing. He could be a different person in this headgear, breaking into people's homes with spyware. The sombrero bobbled, and the straw scratched his forehead.

Alarmed at his own behaviour, Art took it off and tried to balance it back on the bookshelf upright. It would not stay. He considered tying it by its string, but he felt anxious that Frank would know the difference. He was starting to feel anxious about everything actually, especially about hanging around in Frank's apartment, with the minutes ticking by. He picked the sombrero off the floor and with a determined stare, willed it to stay.

As he stood there, a book on Frank's shelf caught his eye. But for his efforts with the hat, he would have missed it altogether. *Chaos Squared*, by Jack Freeman. He recognized the title, not just because it was a book about maths, but because it had been a favourite of his father's. In fact, his father's copy, which had long since lost the dustjacket this one still had, now sat on the shelf in Art's study, looking anaemic without it. Art reached out his hand.

It took Art a moment to realize what he was looking at, and it made no sense. First, it appeared to be his father's *actual* book, complete with dustjacket and a sticker of a strawberry that said *Berry Good*, which a young Mimi had plastered on the front. Mimi's sticker. His father's book. But it was the book *inside* that overwhelmed him with even more questions, and a sense of unease so deep that he almost unplugged his adaptor, with a view to going straight to confront Frank, to drive to Wales to collect his sister, to find Ernest and – he was not sure what Ernest could do but he had popped into his head. The question upon question the book evoked so toppled his balance, Art had to sit down.

Inside was not his father's book about chaos, the one that celebrated Jupiter's Red Spot, oscillation, embryos and Mandelbrot. Instead, it was a book called *Living with Grief*. About coping with death. His mother had written an inscription to his father; her writing was unmistakable.

Walt, Look after them, and yourself, all my love, C

Art flicked frantically through the book, noticing that certain sections were marked up: Children, The Stages of Grief, and Death After a Long Illness. His mother must have given it to their father when she first got her terminal diagnosis.

And that was not all: tucked into the fold of the cover in the back was a half-written letter to Mimi, mostly crossed out. From Christine.

300

Art realized that some time had passed with him sitting in a daze. The lights had come on outside.

Art did not wish to alert Frank to his intrusion. Not yet. But it was impossible to leave this book behind. He needed to find out more, he needed to unearth the lies before he put Frank in a corner, where no doubt, he would be lied to, again. And he certainly could not leave that letter. He put the book in his backpack and rearranged the rest of the shelf so that its absence was not immediately apparent. Frank wouldn't notice straight away. The sombrero remained still, mocking him from a breezy angle.

More than anything, Art needed to get out of there, and fast. By the time Mimi returned from Wales, he would be able to tell her what he had discovered. He did not, however, seem able to break down his thoughts into their usual logical components, they were coming too fast, each was too upsetting. He felt giddy and wondered if he might fall over. He pulled the door closed behind him, walked uncertainly down the few steps, then stabilized himself against a brick pillar. He was relieved to have, at least, avoided an unscheduled audience with Frank inside his own premises.

He walked back down the path, looking left and right, tugging his collar. People walked past in a group. None of them was Frank. He felt the book against his back.

Art returned to the playground. Beyond the hedge, the big bright square of the newsagent's across the road beckoned like a refuge. He looked down at his feet, as if to confirm he was actually there.

Litter gathered at the skirt of the hedge in front of him. As he peered out at the crossing, the shopkeeper emerged from Bhati & Son, which gave Art's solar plexus a twang. Then the slam of a car door made him start. It reminded him of

301

the file of Mimi's Foley recordings he had found when she went to Wales. *Walking in chainmail. Car door slamming. Digital bomb-tick. Body crumples into side of car.*

Art felt as if a bomb was strapped to his back in the form of the book. It made him feel dizzy – *so* dizzy, he wondered if he was about to have a seizure. He had experienced enough fits of a kind in his life to know how they felt from the inside. The spinning sensation, the visions of himself stacking up like a deck of packed cards, the bottomless fall into the dark, the moment he hit the earth – the crunch as it belted through his body, the voices all round and the gasping breath. It always took time to realize – the gasping was him. No, he decided, taking stock of his symptoms, he was perfectly all right: just experiencing shock in a predictable way.

Frank had secrets. This new evidence might have nothing to do with Art's research, but who knew what else he might yet discover? Reminded of the device he had planted, Art checked his receiver was working. He listened to the low hum of noise in Frank's empty home and felt his skin prickle.

It would be best if the shopkeeper did not catch him lurking behind the hedge, his ear pressed to a listening device; Art did not want the police called to turf him from his stakeout. He should check the shop's layout, and the sight-lines of its CCTV.

As an exercise in caution, and to keep his spiralling thoughts in check, Art itemized an exhaustive list of the things that could go wrong. Heavy traffic on the bridge might delay Frank's arrival home in a significant way – he would have to be patient. What if he had to climb into the nasty plastic tunnel to avoid being detected? What about weather? He recognized that his emotions would be somewhat disturbed, but advance planning could keep variables within acceptable parameters – he was counting on his emotions being one of those.

He went into the shop. There was only one camera, trained away from the road. Not a sliver of lens would see him outside. He chose a Snapple from the large fridge. After all the excitement, one sip only or his blood sugar would fly.

Tomorrow, Art knew, Frank did not work late. He would come back tomorrow.

The next day, at two o'clock in the afternoon, and for the second time, Art Brotherton did not do his marking. He did not walk the best route home.

Mimi, he texted his sister, **you are going to have to trust me.** Relieved to have shared at least the spirit of his expedition with her, he set about ensuring everything was in place.

He checked that the file with his work remained encrypted. The work on his proof – does p equal Np? (*no*, was his provisional answer) – was safe. He signed out. A stack of printed papers on the Halting Problem lay on his desk. He wished Ernest was there. He had mentioned the book to him last night, that he had compromising evidence about Frank. Ernest was due back today.

Art was ready.

He freed his cricket backpack from the hook behind his office door. Packed next to the book was his waterproof puffer, tightly rolled, a silver emergency blanket, antibacterial wipes, unsalted almonds in a small Tupperware and flask of hot tea. He hitched the wide straps over his shoulders, then walked to the common room. It was empty today.

He heard his phone buzz. It was Mimi.

What?? she wrote.

Perhaps texting her had been a mistake – he had made her anxious, that much he could tell from the two question marks. He sat down with the bag on his back; he needed to think.

What? texted Mimi again, within minutes.

??? Answer! she wrote.

Such rapid-fire punctuation was alarming. 'I cannot respond. I am sorry,' he whispered, but ignored her call.

His mind was scissoring – he should not have sent her a message. He should have waited. He could see that now.

'Art – are you okay? Art?' asked a colleague.

'Why do you ask?'

'Just that you've been sitting there for a while now, with that backpack on your back. And you're clutching your chest. Are you feeling all right? Can I get you something?'

'I am perfectly fine,' said Art, standing up, feeling light-headed. He adjusted the straps around his tummy in a show of self-sufficiency.

He looked at his watch. 3.00. Where had the time gone? He was going to run late.

His phone buzzed again.

I'm coming home, texted Mimi. **Tonight. OMW.**

Tonight?! OMW? On her way?! That would not work at all. Art sat down.

He had a generous buffer for just this kind of eventuality, he reminded himself, trying to keep calm. In a frenzy of recalibration, he worked backwards. He had left the note that he wrote to his sister yesterday – that was not meant for her *to actually read* – next to the telephone. She could *not* find that. Which meant that he had to go home. He did not want to abort his plan. If anything, he needed more information about Frank than before. If he changed the route to go via home and took the bus, he would make it in time, just. His heart rate quickened further at all the factors he had to reconsider – bus routes, traffic congestion. So many details, so carefully planned, all in disarray.

He looked at his watch; time was hurtling away.

At home, he picked up the letter he had written to Mimi and put it in his bag. He locked his study door and took the key. Now, he was late.

It did not go as planned. Life happened like that. Perhaps his observations of the world happened too close up, too deep in the quotidian layer. It was the big questions, vulnerable to human decision-making, the big events that changed the course of one's life – that he failed to see. There was often no pattern for those. They had the predictability of an unannounced meteorite crashing through the atmosphere, burying itself in your living room. Even that was a lousy metaphor, he thought, as he lay on the road, trying to surface, lights flashing, noise crashing into his head, his whole life and time accelerating away in a siren blur. A meteorite is detectable on a radar, from very far away. Its orbit, trajectory, the force of its impact, could all be determined way in advance. No. Life was more like – he struggled to think what life was like, on the big scale, where things happened that you could not predict.

His parents – he *had* foreseen that, but had not been able to summon enough evidence to convince his sister. Jason Findlay – he still felt the subterranean effects of that shock. There were good surprises too, he supposed. Ernest was one. He had arrived so unexpectedly, Art was not even due to get a post-doc, and then suddenly one day, standing in his office, there was Ernest. Like a parcel, tied up with string, so complete. And then: Mimi – meeting Frank. Art had set her on a path towards seeking a mate; he had *helped*! Then taken her to those awards, insisting they went every year.

Frank, with his pretend interest in cricket, his mediocre maths, his questionable river theory and his devious ways.

Those trousers he wore with fake pockets. Cargo pants, Mimi called them, and epaulettes on his summer shirts – epaulettes! How could he ever have predicted an outcome like Frank?

By the time Art got back to the corner near Frank's flat and took up his position right near the hedge, his pulse was racing – at the rush, at the lateness, at the possibility that he was going to miss the moment of seeing Frank come home. With Miss Silver? He waited at the hedge, testing his listening device, his anxiety spiking in high-jump leaps at the prospect of his plan going awry. High jumps. His heart pounded harder still as he thought of his father.

And then, bang on time – Art's calculation had been perfect. He liked being right.

There it was. Frank's car.

As it came into view, Art peered through the gap in the hedge. The hornbeam leaves were brown and crisp. He pushed into the hedge. The twigs scratched his face. He needed to be certain, so he lifted his head, just a bit, just over the hedge. Oh yes, it was Frank in his pale green Renault coming down the road. Art felt bile rise in his throat. Feeling dizzy, he stepped through the gap in the hedge, out into the open. The man in that car was ruining his life.

Art saw Frank's face at the wheel. Alone. He saw frozen disbelief. In all of his planning, he had not thought of the moment when he would see Frank's face. And now he was standing there, and Frank could see *him*. It was all going wrong. In that critical beat, that fraction of time, he forgot to stay back. The drop of the kerb, such a vertical shelf. The steps he took into the road were like gravity. A vertiginous drop. The hinge of his knee gave way like his mind. The lunge of his breath powered his fall.

Art's hip hit the mirror as he stared at Frank's eyes, his

blown-open expression. His legs twisted under him, ankle caught in the drain. He tried to use his bandaged arm to break his fall. He felt the hard smack at the back of his head – a cricket-bat violence, a smashing sensation, a noise like cracked lightning. There was no pain, just a shimmering nimbus of light and a blurring sensation, the smell of hot rubber, hearing and seeing, dissolving, returning, voices and shouting and flashing and gargling and hands in his mouth and Frank!

54

EVIDENCE

t = 0

In the back of a taxi, after trying Frank again and again, Mimi fishes the pool receipt from her pocket to remind herself what it actually shows. It's for a takeaway cup of tea, and it's dated four days after she went to Wales. Four days after Art had declared he could never go back. She has to know why.

She feels like a particle of foam halfway down a waterfall – 'Who knows where it started, who knows where it will end,' her father used to say.

He hadn't stayed to find out.

The taxi drops her across the road from the pool, right outside the vinyl shop that had opened in time for her father to see it. She remembers him comment on *Dark Side of the Moon*, the Pink Floyd album cover in the window. 'Strictly speaking,' her father had said, 'the light should split *inside* the pyramid too.'

'It's iconic, Dad,' she'd said. 'Don't ruin it.'

He hadn't stayed to discover what other music she'd love in her life.

Most things that happened in the days after their parents' deaths were a blur. But how could they have left, *without knowing*? Her A-level results. Art finishing his PhD. Art had toiled to get there, but when he did, they had gone. All the news, the discoveries. Fossils of the plant-eating Titanosaur, unearthed in Madagascar – what about that? Had they not wanted to know? Even local news – Sally from the Camberwell Subway was mentioned in *The Guardian* for accepting Irish banknotes as legal tender three days after Christine and Walter died.

There are new albums in the window. Her parents hadn't wanted to know enough to stay. Mimi feels surrounded by a moat of loss which, right now, includes Frank.

A pretty girl tends the club reception while scrolling on her phone. Jasmine, says her name tag. Her hair drapes in a long curl over one shoulder, and a bank of earrings studs her right ear.

Jasmine smiles.

'Might you help me, please?' says Mimi. 'My brother—'

'I know who you are, I've seen your brother real regular. I seen you with him, and droppin' him off sometimes.'

'Oh.' Her anonymity whipped away, Mimi feels exposed. 'Art. That's his name.' The girl probably knows. 'He's been in an accident.'

The girl reacts oddly to the news of Art's misfortune. 'Tony left,' she says. She lowers her voice, leans in towards Mimi. 'And I don't mean to be unhelpful, but we're not allowed to say nothing. Is your brother okay?'

'We don't know. But – what? Tony? What are you talking about?'

'We don' need any more trouble.'

'Listen,' says Mimi. 'I don't know who Tony is. My brother

309

was upset the last time I know of that he came here, but then he came back. I just want to know why.' She shows Jasmine the slip.

Jasmine looks back towards her supervisor's door.

'I don't want to go to your supervisor,' says Mimi.

'I was here both days. I remember him leaving wet, and yeah, upset.' Jasmine squints at the ticket, and nods. '*That* one wasn't his usual day. I don't even know if he swam, just got a tea. He'd arrived with nothin'; his stuff must be in his locker, and—'

'His locker?'

'His permanent locker.'

Mimi needs to get into that locker. 'Look Jasmine, I promise not to tell your boss, if that's what you want. But I need your help. Art's life is in danger.' That isn't a lie.

'Oh no. So, like a *serious* accident? Tony's not involved, is he?' asks Jasmine.

'No,' says Mimi carefully, pretty confident that's at least true. She's never heard Tony's name. 'But when Art got upset, maybe Tony – um?' she says, trying to float an open-ended question. 'Look, Art's been hit by a car. Tony may know something?'

'Oh, I don't think it's nothing like *that*.' Jasmine looks genuinely shocked. 'It was, you know, Tony didn't like to feel like, frustrated, you know? And I think he fancied your brother, came on a bit strong and that. That was all, he's not that bad of a guy. When your brother came back, jus' like you said, it was to see if he'd really been fired. He seemed to feel responsible. The boss didn't fire Tony. I think they agreed he could work at one of the other clubs, maybe not at the pool. I'm not s'posed to say. I didn't tell your brother where he's gone.' Jasmine looks over her shoulder.

As a child, Mimi once came across Art folding a towel, over and over, picking up the corners closest to him and pinching them together, twisting it into a tube and bending it into a circle. He was beaming. 'It is called Topology. See?! It has not really changed. As a circle it is the same thing as it was when it was just a towel, it only *looks* different.' She feels like that now – something obvious, which has been right in front of her, has clicked into place.

'*Thank you*, Jasmine.' She touches her hand.

'You don't want to see his locker, then?'

She hadn't even known it existed. 'Yes please, I do. I think he may have left something here,' she says, rubbing the receipt between her finger and thumb.

'As long as you promise . . .' says Jasmine. She points to her supervisor's office. 'Take a pair of those blue plastic shoes and I'll meet you in there.' The turnstile lights green.

The smell of chemicals and plastic assaults her as she walks through the doors to the pool; a fog of humidity escapes as they squeeze closed behind her, a black rubber mat squeaks under her feet. Mimi squishes through the hygiene area in her shoe covers, towards the changing rooms, past the Women's entrance, and into the Men's. She peers into the pool. On top of the lifeguard's chair, a girl with a tight yellow tank top and red shorts dangles a flip-flop from her toes and inspects the underside of her other foot. It's a quiet morning – two men power along inside lanes, and a Splashrobics class of three churns up a corner of the shallow end. Mimi checks her watch.

The pound coin-operated lockers line the left side of the Men's. Long slatted benches separate these from a wall of smaller, key-operated red lockers.

Red squares.

The smell of chemicals makes her feel sick. Her shirt

cleaves to her body, her jeans clingwrap her thighs. Water condenses and slides down the tiles.

The lockers all look the same. She knows it's the red ones, but which one is Art's? And where is his key? She hasn't got time. It's already past ten.

'Miss?' Jasmine appears at the end of the room, a long Allen key aloft in her hand. 'Master key,' she says, 'but the list's in the boss's office, so we gonna have to try them all.'

'I know how he thinks,' says Mimi. 'What's the highest number?'

'Locker number?

'Yes.'

'That's thirty-two. There.'

'Then – it will be thirty-one. The highest prime.'

The door opens easily with the key, clanging against the adjacent locker. 'Art Brotherton' says the handwritten label facing them from the shelf. Looking amazed, Jasmine steps aside.

At the front is a swimming bag, the same as the one Art keeps at home. She can guess what's in there, and she's right. Goggles and nose clips. Beeswax plugs for his ears. Eye drops, an extra pair of Speedos, and a small extra towel.

But it is not the sight of that ordinary bag that catches Mimi's breath. Crouching in the back of the locker is a small, navy, kid's backpack, piped in green.

Mimi doesn't need to hold it to know it has a hole stabbed through its middle. It swings a wrecking ball into her sternum. *Art's magic backpack.* How is it here?

She sees the bag catapult through the air. She can picture it teetering, up on the pole – high as the Empire State, the BT Tower, the diving board in the adults-only pool. Far out of reach, way above her. And so far back in time as to render it impossible that it's here, right in front of her.

312

She touches her hand to the side of her head.

'You okay, miss?'

'Uh.'

'Miss?' She sees – years too late now – an ordinary skip. Her eight-year-old-self had stood below its turtled upside-down legs, staring up. It had seemed so high. Her adult self realizes just how small it must have been, how well within reach of any adult. Of her mother. Christine must have seen it straight away and not told her off. Mimi rocks on her feet.

'Maybe you should sit?'

'Thanks, I'm okay,' says Mimi, steadying herself against the locker wall.

'Can you take what you need? We should be quick.'

'I'll be right out, just leave me in here.'

Jasmine, clearly relieved not to have unearthed actual body parts in the locker, leaves Mimi sweating in the damp, muggy room.

The backpack lies in the locker like an unexploded bomb, ready to detonate backwards through her childhood, through all her memories, which now feel fragile, unreliable.

She stares at all the lockers in a row. *She* needs to compartmentalize.

She reaches for the magic backpack; the strap catches on the hinge of the door as she yanks it out; it swings and clatters to the floor with a heavier thud than she was expecting.

What *did* she expect? The weightless ghosts of Art's imaginary friends?

She sits down on the slatted changing bench and drags the bag towards her. She has a metallic taste in her mouth. She tugs at the zip; it is crusty and stiff. She pulls hard, hoping it doesn't rip apart in her hands. Its familiar whiff jerks her back in time.

313

Inside is a Black 'n' Red exercise book, and a jewellery pouch. The exercise book is full of Art's handwriting, dates and words – like his notebook at home. But the pouch – the velvet drawstring purse had belonged to Christine. Mimi pulls on the cord.

Her amber necklace from Frank tumbles out. It hangs on her fingers like entrails.

She sits down and takes a long look at Art's swimming-pool stub. 'You did not mean for me to find this,' she says, softly, to her brother. 'Any of this. I'm sorry that I did.' She returns the necklace to her mother's soft pouch. It feels too heavy to wear.

55

INFINITY

Art feels as if he's lying at the bottom of a shallow pond. He hears voices, sees faces, reflections, a shimmer. They fracture; a membrane touched by a finger.

'She would want to be here,' Rey says. 'We should wait.'

'Wait,' thinks Art, 'wait.' His mind is in mist.

'We can't wait any more.' The doctor sounds kind. 'We've already reduced his dosage and now I have surgery at twelve. This must happen today.'

'Where's Mimi?' asks Ernest.

'At the pool. And I don't know why.'

'Can you get her a message?' says Ernest. He touches Art's forehead. It feels like a kiss, or the brand of a star. 'I'd like to stay here.'

Their words chink like tin. They break down into bytes. Each syllable splits, with spaces between. Like parts of a puzzle, letters form squares. A Tetris game starts. Kinky tetronimoes descend from above. The blocks keep coming, the spaces unfilled. Endless and endless, forever.

A chair and his backpack, bone hairbrush and comb. Scalextric and vinyl, a suitcase, a phone, fall from the sky.

'Look, Mimi. *Look*. Why can you never see, what *I* can see?'

He is losing his purchase. He *needs* her to see, this time, that his numbers have gone. In their place is an infinite haze. There is no point to it all.

To give up is tempting. The relief, of being free.

There were many things about his parents deciding to die that perplexed Art. It was hard for him to imagine his mother leaving him, not knowing how it all worked out. Not knowing how *anything* turned out. It was no great loss not to know about Blair's time as PM, or Iraq, or 9/11, all that. But she missed so much else, like Art defending his thesis for his PhD, making breakfast for him on the day, being at home to hear how it had gone when he came back. His father had always said he would do a mock oral examination for Art, but he took that ambition to his grave. They deprived themselves of the pleasure they had waited a lifetime for.

Art had not even told Mimi when his big day came. He had gone to the university at the same time as usual, sat down and rehearsed the questions he thought he might get, walked in with his heavily annotated thesis clutched under his arm.

His parents would never know what the external professor, Dundas, had said – how Art had overheard Dundas say, 'Extremely impressive.' *Extremely impressive*: he took the pair of words home like a precious found object, but had only Mimi to give them to.

Devoted. That was the word he would use to describe his parents. And their final act had been one of such devotion that whenever he felt that excruciating pain associated with his parents' deaths, that searing combination of loss and sadness and fury and guilt that pierced the lining of his organs, or weighed on his chest as it did now, he tried to remind himself that theirs had been the ultimate act of love in a lifetime of loving.

It must have taken courage that he was not sure he possessed, to remove yourself from this world. To decide that your journey was at an end – their father especially, who had seemed excited that chaos theory was entering a new golden age – to close the front door and know that what you knew was all you would ever know, that you had come to a finite point in your journey.

Art had never been able to understand. But today – he sees its appeal.

Mimi sits on the slatted bench in the men's changing room. She drops the velvet pouch back into the bag.

The vending machine in front of her stocks goggles and swimming caps, disposable towels. Her life has been reduced to moving between hermetically sealed spaces with *shooshing* glass doors and dispensing machines.

Her head throbs with a deep bass persistence from the recesses of her head. She takes the Black 'n' Red notebook out of the bag. The humid air has softened the paper.

In it is the same list as his notebook at home. *Stable. Excitable.* This time though, it's up to date: *Absent, Involved.*

She flips back through the days: *Worry, Lip, Simmering rage.*

Lip?

She pauses. Simmering rage. Lip.

Lip.

Mimi fans the pages of the book. There it is again. And again. Lip. *Her* chafed lip. Her hand is shaking.

Weeks. Months. Thirteen *years* of observations.

And then – there – tucked into the book, is something she knows as soon as she finds it, she is not meant to see.

A yellowed envelope is taped down, secure on four sides. She peels it off.

Private, it says, in her mother's looped hand. And underneath – the date that they died.

Mimi holds the book like a hand grenade, with the pin half-pulled. She picks up the bag. She has what she came for. And a great deal more.

She imagines the CCTV trained on her back and hopes that there won't be a cost to the girl at the reception desk. She's probably only eighteen.

Art is trapped in a room, there is no door, only sound from the ceiling. No space, and no light.

'This is it,' says a voice, from deep in the wall. 'It's the hardest part. This is the moment that makes all the difference.'

'Did we not say we'd wait for the sister?'

'We can't. This is happening now, we don't have the time.'

Mimi, he thinks. *I am here. Can you come before I go?*

'I'm here, Art,' says Ernest. His hand feels warm.

Mimi was eighteen. She remembers – rattled, she had laughed, but Art didn't lighten up. She could no longer delay the moment when she had to face what Art had told her. Their mother was ill again. She flung her cushion to the side of her bed, and went downstairs to ask her mother – was Art right, was she dying? 'Are you really, Mum? Are you dying?' she'd asked, and a strange look had crossed her mother's face. 'Are you going to be in pain?'

'I'm ready, darling. But I'm not frightened.' Her look had said – *I'm in control.*

Mimi had never understood, with all their planning, why they hadn't written to their children. The one short public note from Christine had been so inadequate as to render it almost more hurtful than nothing at all.

318

She remembers the whispers: *The letter. Don't let Mimi see.*

Of course, she had seen. Even Aunty Pam had to sleep, and once Mimi knew a letter existed, she could hardly think of anything else. It was all she could do to contain herself from screaming: Give it to me! *Now*. They were my mother, my father – that message is for *me*. Me. Me! Mine!

But that letter was to no one.

> This letter confirms that this suicide is voluntary. In the face of my terminal cancer, and Walter's senior years, it is in the best interests of our children; everyone is well provided for, and will take care of one another.
> Christine Brotherton.

Mimi had found it slipped into Aunty Pam's passport, in her bag, on its way back to the States. Once she'd read it, she felt only infinitesimally *consoled* – a word from her new lexicon of grief.

And now here's a letter, after all. Mimi sits on the pavement, peels the tape, and pulls out the paper inside. The letter is long and covers both sides of a page.

> *Darling,* it says.
> *Your sister,* it starts.

So. 'Darling' is Art. Of course it is.

> *Your sister is going to need you.*
> *I know you are not going to be altogether surprised by what has happened, you have*

almost thwarted my plans with all your investigating. At the same time, I think you will understand the logic of what I have done in a way no one else can. That is why I'm being honest with you now. The doctors are convinced there is no hope for me, and I don't want to put you and Mimi through the ugliness of what is coming. Or myself, if I am honest. Your father is convinced that my suffering from here will be 'exponential', as he puts it. He can't bear to watch it, and I can't bear to put any of you through that. I'd rather go quickly, still feeling okay.

Your father and I have made the plan together. I know you will agree it is better like this. And better if you do not share these details. Who would understand? We don't want to burden the pair of you with legal issues. So — it's decided. You, Art darling, will see that we are right.

I know you will care for your sister.

It's a big responsibility, but I have no doubt you are man enough now for the task. I hope that as she grows up, she'll get control of her stutter. She is happiest when life is kept simple.

She will be happy, too, to be your support. She loves you so.

You will have to keep an eye on her. Note her moods; what she eats. When you see it picking up, the frustration coming, just make sure she gets some sleep, not too much sugar. You know the drill. As you know, it never lasts long.

I have confidence that you'll be methodical. Think of it as a problem that constantly needs working out. That's how I approach her, it generally works.

Mimi's a good girl. All that pent-up energy! She just needs love, and care, and a bit of handling, and she'll be all right. Perhaps one day she'll settle into a relationship of her own, I don't know. But while it's just the two of you, I know you'll be fine. I am writing this letter on behalf of us both. Your father loves you both very deeply, he is the rock in all of our lives, but is unlikely to ever articulate these things.

Artie, it is hard to stop writing. My biggest regret is that I will not get to watch you make the impact on the world that I know you are capable of. My greatest joy has been to watch you and Mimi grow and it is hard to leave halfway through, not knowing.

This is my loving goodbye.

Take care of yourself my beloved son. You will have each other and that's the most important thing.

To infinity – and you, better than anyone, know just how far that is.

Your ever-loving

Mum

Your ever-loving mum. *Your ever-loving mum*. Mimi retches into her hand.

* * *

I told you, Art said, his voice choking with pain, the night the police had arrived at their door.

And now she knows why, in all the years since, he's never actually said it again. Sometime between that doorbell, and her staying buried beneath the quilt in her room, Art had found this letter and agreed to protect her.

Protect her from what? From *herself*, it would seem.

She wondered where – for a moment – where would Christine have left it? Under his pillow, like a night-time chocolate? Next to his bed, slipped into the notebook she's been carrying around? Where was *her* letter? She retches again, acid souring her mouth. She sits on the ground, cement cold on the backs of her legs – splayed like a ragdoll.

Mimi's mind revolts.

How dare they? How *could* they? Collude about her? She holds onto her chest, tries to force a breath in but the pieces that she's held so tight inside all fall out. She vomits a thin line of gruel into the road.

She reads Christine's letter again. And Art's book – it's a record of *her* rhythms. Simmering rage. Chafed lip – that is her. Mimi. *Her* moods. Her *life*, annotated by her brother like a fucking accountant. Though to call them moods, or her life her own, seems to somewhat underestimate what has happened, she sees now.

She's not sure what rocks her most. Her mother persuaded her father to die. That's how it seems.

She wipes her mouth. The simmering rage that Art recorded – she feels it swarm.

'Are you okay?' Jasmine touches her shoulder. 'Miss? Are you okay?' She's curled up on the pavement squares, staring at the grout.

'I'm fine,' she lies.

Has she ever been fine? Her life spools backwards,

everything reels through a different lens. Rage, her mother calls it. *Her rages*. Is that what they were? She thinks of the cushions, the flying wheels of the bike, the spinning backpack, the pepper grinder. Suppressed rage, perhaps, but her mother had seen it. Mimi feels it now – the familiar weather of rage.

She feels the girl's hand on her back.

No.

She *can* pull back. She can get back from here.

It's not unstoppable. She slows her breath down.

Perhaps one day she'll settle into a relationship of her own, I don't know.

She'll never know if she doesn't try.

'Miss?'

She wants Frank. She *needs* Frank. She keeps breathing.

'I've got a message for you, there was a call. I couldn't find you,' says Jasmine.

'For me?' The storm inside her stalls.

'From Rey? She called the office. She says come to the hospital. Please.'

Mimi's too frightened to ask. She feels that she knows.

Jasmine picks the plastic shoe covers off Mimi's feet and corrals her into a taxi. 'She's in some kind of shock,' she hears Jasmine say.

She can't talk.

It doesn't matter.

Nothing matters right now except one thing.

While it's just the two of you, I know you'll be fine.

It's the Halting Problem. All outcomes are possible until one outcome actually happens.

Until you know for sure, you don't know anything.

56

RETURN

The traffic slides by until Mimi's taxi turns, and the hospital's there. The grey rhomboid takes up the sky, the sun slides down the windows in a sheen of gold. It's nearly midday.

Ambulance doors open, a trolley rushes out. The blue light spins. A family revolves through the automatic door.

Looking up to the fourth floor, she imagines everyone round Art's bed. Rey, Ernest, Dr Sipos, the nurses.

She steps out of the taxi, carrying two bags: Art's small backpack, and her own. She stands at the entrance and looks at the slabs that are under her feet. She's afraid to go in.

They can't answer their phones, but she could call the ward. She doesn't know what she might find if she turns up, unannounced. She rummages blindly in her bag for her phone.

9 *Messages*, it says. The headlines read backwards. Most recent, from Rey, is first:

Turning my phone off. x.

I've left a message at the pool. From Rey.

They are starting, says Rey.

We can't wait, says Rey.

He's okay, but call me now, says Rey.

Ernest is here, says Rey.

Dr Sipos wants to talk to you, says Rey.

Dr Sipos wants to know what time you will be back, says Rey.

Frank is here, says Ernest. **We owe him an apology. I'm sorry.**

Oh, thank god. But also, *Frank is here. We owe him an apology.* She reads it again. Frank is here. I'm sorry. It's probably too late. But Frank is here. FrankishereFrankishere . . . She is through the doors, pressing the button on the lift. Hurry up! Her brother is up there. He is waiting for her. Whatever else he's done, he needs her. *Right now.* Frank is here. I'm sorry. She wants to shout it in the lift. When the doors open, it's as though they have fallen away. She runs, knowing where to go – the wide arrows and colour-coded patterns on the floor familiar now. She doesn't look up. Left, along the corridor. They've started without her. What if he's dead? What if he's awake? Her mind see-saws. Multiple worlds face her, parallel lives. What if he's awake but can't be himself? Ever again? Can't talk? Can't walk? Can't do his maths. Her legs nearly buckle.

'I'm coming,' she says. Her words are sucked into silence by the deadening walls.

She runs straight into Frank.

'Frank!' He catches her as she brakes.

'It's all over,' he says.

She wrenches away and looks at his face. 'Over?' A strange noise escapes her. 'You've seen him?'

'No. No. Oh god, I'm so sorry. They wouldn't let me in to see Art today. I meant that it's over for *me*.' His face crumples. '*Sorry*. I didn't know if you – but the police called and said something about seeing the reflection of the accident on the newsagent's fridges on CCTV. I'm free of suspicion. Apparently, it was Ernest's idea.' His mouth folds over, he can't stop the tears. 'I don't know—' Mimi tries to pull him in, but Frank looks sad and shakes his head.

'Oh Frank, there's so much to sort out. I don't know how I'm ever going to make all this up to you. Or even explain it. But I can't now. Come with me. I need you. My brother—'

'Honestly, I can't. I'm sorry, but I can't.'

'Please. Please come with me. Whatever it is. I don't know what I'll find. The only thing I do know –' she looks at him – 'I need you with me, whatever happens in there. I always have.'

'I'm sorry,' says Frank. 'It was real, what we had. But we broke it.'

Her mouth dries up; a channel burns down her throat.

'Frank. No, please.'

'I'm sorry,' he says. 'God knows I tried.'

'I haven't got time to explain everything now. You don't know what's been happening, all the things my brother – and you're here now, aren't you?' She's trying not to cry. Her legs want to run and collapse all at the same time.

'Mimi, I hope Art's okay – and I'm sorry, I know the timing for this is terrible, but – I came because – it's what I was trying to tell you about on the phone last night, and the conversation veered towards Kitty and . . .'

'Frank, I—'

'Your father used to work with a mathematician called David Charing. Charing is the man who first suggested I contact Art – and he asked me to give you a book. We both realized how personal it was and then I wasn't sure what to do with it, and I got myself into a knot about it; so I waited.' Frank speaks so quickly his words run into each other. 'Anyway, I waited until it was too late.' He is hoarse.

'Listen—'

'Then, when I wanted to bring it to you this morning, it was gone. I'm sure I'll find it, but honestly, right now, I don't know where it is. I came to say sorry. I feel *sick*—'

'Is there any chance,' says Mimi, as the call to run to Art clamours in another part of her brain, 'it's *Chaos Squared* by Jack Freeman?'

'What?' says Frank. '*Yes*. How on earth do you know?'

'It was in Art's things. I've got it here, in my bag. Look, I don't understand any of it, but I really can't do this now.'

'I know, I know. Look, *thank god*. And you're right, now isn't the time. But I wanted you to at least have it. And, well, now you do. But Mimi,' he says. He puts out an arm to touch her, but then withdraws. 'It's not what it seems.'

'What d'you mean?'

'I don't have an explanation for it, but have a look later. You'll see. I still need to tell you, properly, how I came to have it,' he says. 'I wish I'd given it to you sooner. I sense things might be different if I had. But you must go. Good luck with your brother, I wish him well, really I do. And you too,' he adds.

It feels like she's going to fall.

'Hey. Are you going to be okay?' He puts out a hand to steady her.

'I couldn't be further from okay. I wish I didn't have to go right now, but my brother – he needs me.' She looks to the ward.

'That's just the thing,' says Frank. 'He's *always* going to need you. There isn't space in your life for someone else. And I really understand.'

'Please, Frank, that's not true. It's possible my explanations about what's gone on these last few days could make you even angrier, but I need to tell you everything. Please.'

'I'm not angry, Mimi, I'm sad. Well, no *more* angry than sad. It's such a waste,' he says. 'But anyway, we shouldn't be standing here. You need to go.'

He kisses her temple. His eyes shine with tears. And with that, Frank turns. He walks quickly. Away.

Art's curtain is closed, there's no noise, not a sound.

She remembers the woman in the ward. Deathly silence, it seems, is a thing.

She takes a step closer.

She hears a foot shuffle, a whisper, a question.

An answer, quite loud. 'Is impossible to say.' Dr Sipos. She walks up and whips back the curtain. Art lies there, stone still.

'Oh, *Mimi*.' Rey looks stricken. 'Thank god you're here.'

'Uh—' Mimi tries to talk, but there's no response that makes sense.

'Where were you?' asks Ernest. The sound she produces mangles straight from her stomach, a visceral keening tear.

She lurches towards him. 'My brother!'

'Miss Brotherton,' says the doctor. She stares at the cast standing guard round her brother. Rey and Ernest, the doctor, the nurse.

'Your timing is good,' says Ernest.

'He blinked! Slowly,' says Rey.

The monitor beeps.

'What?'

'Once,' says Ernest.

'Give him time,' says the doctor. 'Is early days. From here, it's up to him.'

Art is bruised and translucent, a tableau of himself. 'Artie?' she says. She traces the line of his jaw to his chin. The hospital gown reveals a parabola of bone – white, concave, splayed. He looks so exposed. She pulls at the fabric, but it snags underneath him. 'Art?' Her tears fall on his skin. 'Answer me. Please.'

'Mimi,' says Ernest. He sounds far away.

Art lets out a moan. Though perhaps it is her. 'Can you hear me?' She's choking. 'Come back,' she says. 'It will all be okay.'

'Mimi,' says Ernest.

'Sweetie,' says Rey.

'Ms Brotherton.' Dr Sipos. From behind tissued layers. She tries to look up.

'I can't,' says Mimi. 'I – what should I do?'

'Listen,' says Ernest, 'to the doctor.' He's holding her up. 'I've got you,' he says.

'His drug load is light,' says the doctor. 'We were able to reduce the barbiturates on quite a steep curve. He tolerates okay.'

Art gasps and lifts, his back arched. Vomit bubbles from his mouth. The nurse moves swiftly – turns him firmly to one side. Mimi can't see his face. She looks up to see Ernest, whose eyes are like moons.

It seems like hours, but really, it's minutes.

Art's body rocks.

'It'll happen like this.' Dr Sipos is calm. 'We will see if he *wants* to come back. It takes time.' Art jolts and shudders, his hips lift off the bed. His arm strains at his side, twists up to his head. Mimi steps forwards but the nurse intervenes.

'He's wanting to pull out his ICP. They all try do that, feels like drills in their heads.' It looks as if she's patting his hand on the bed, but Mimi can see that she's holding him down. Sweat shines her brow.

'Has this happened before?' Mimi asks.

'All morning,' says Rey. 'Well, since eleven.' It's now past twelve.

Rey and Ernest stand, like two wings of an angel laid prone.

And she notices then: Ernest holding Art's hand.

She hadn't seen it. Or realized. *Of course*. It makes sense. Why Ernest believed in him so.

Not evidence. Not the absence of alternatives. Heuristics. The power of love.

She squeezes Rey's hand.

Art blinks again. *Mimi?* He opens his eyes, and the light burns. He catches white corners, a clock, blurred faces, until he can see the shell-pale tips of her fingers, hanging down at her sides, so close.

She looms and recedes. *I'm not going to leave you*, she said. *I promise you that.* He could not be sure that her promise would hold. All he wanted was their old life back.

A hand holds his own. Mimi?

'Artie?' He hears her. But so far. Too far. There is almost a comfort in drifting away. He can slide down the curve of the earth.

And then: '. . . find Frank,' he hears, like a hard-yanking rope. Frank. Art's cells stand to attention. His blood vessels whoosh back to life, as if in response to a primeval thrill. Arteries propel red-hot blood round his body. Steaming and urgent, it gushes unbridled from his heart.

He sees Mimi's back. She walks through the door.

Mimi! The jaw of a drill chucks into his skull. It chisels the bone, boring down to his brain. Words mash in his mouth.

He can hear his own monitor. The beeping. The wailing. The gravel in the road. Blood fills his brain.

His numbers, his maths. His parents, his sister. Everything is gone.

He is being turned over and vomits in his bed.

Mimi goes to the floor below, where there's signal and her phone is allowed.

Please Frank, she texts. She stands with Art's backpack at her feet. **I know sorry's not enough.**

She stares at her phone.

But please, can we try. I need you, she writes. **I don't think I can do life without you.**

Her phone remains still, and mute in her hand.

57

CHAOS

As the days go by, Art drifts away. Time feels stretched taut, each waking minute is painful.

Dr Sipos stops urging her to talk to him. He has periods of lucidity, awake, his eyes open, when he can see and hear, but he doesn't seem to care.

Everything is suspended in hospital-grade, whitewashed limbo. Nothing matters – because it seems that her brother, the gravitational force in her universe, is dying.

And Frank is not taking her calls.

Not ignoring you, he writes, **just think better to give each other space to get through this.** She keeps picking up her phone to call him, to text him, but what can she say? *I don't want space, I want you*. She watches Ernest with her brother. She did not give Frank the unconditional love she sees Ernest give Art.

Can you at least tell me how you came to have that book, she says. She's seen the inside. **I've seen it's a book about grief. It's hard to comprehend.** She's hoping for answers, but hoping too, with a desire that compresses her organs, for an excuse to see him.

Instead, Frank sends her an email.

Dear Mimi

I hope Art is doing okay. Ernest has very kindly kept me in the loop. It sounds as though it's been very difficult, I'm sorry.

She can hardly read on.

Mimi, you (and Art) deserve an answer to your question, but I think it's better we avoid an emotional conversation. I hope you understand.

Before we met, I went to Cambridge to see Professor David Charing about an idea – game theory and chaos combined. Your father had been working along the same lines, and had run it by Charing ahead of a chaos theory conference where your father and Charing had both booked a place. He left his book in Charing's office by mistake.

Charing suggested I get hold of Art, even though the concept was only tangential to Art's specialty. He thought Art would be interested in what your father had been doing all those years ago. He'd heard your brother was very private, and hyper-protective about his work, and suggested I tread with caution. But he also asked me to give Art the book – he felt bad about still having it, he'd only realized about the book inside several months after your father died, and didn't quite know how to approach it. We agreed it wasn't the kind of thing I could hand over at a first meeting.

I *was* intending to meet Art that night, not you. At first, I pretended not to know who you were, but it very quickly didn't matter, because I was bewitched, Mimi. You know that. It was *instant*.

Tears are streaming down Mimi's face, dropping big flat plugs onto her keyboard.

Then you gave me the wrong surname. At first, I thought it might be a professional thing, so I rolled with it. But then I

333

could see it was a shield for something. I knew about your parents and I didn't want to push you – I felt trapped into playing it out until you confessed. I liked you too much to call you on it, I didn't want to frighten you away. But I was stuck – how was I supposed to bring out the book *then*? I already knew, just looking at it, what painful things it would unearth. So, I waited –

And I waited too long.

Frank x

She doesn't respond immediately to Frank's email. She doesn't know what to say other than *I need you I need you*. She stares at the kiss next to his name. The thing about Frank is, careless as he may be, the one thing he's *never* been, is careless with her feelings. He knows she reads subtext into everything; she examines font itself for meaning. Frank won't have put that x there by mistake, unthinking. But perhaps he also knew that the absence of a kiss, of any warmth, would have wounded her too. This whole mess is a combination of *his* thoughtfulness, *her* hesitation, and *her* lies.

You didn't wait too long, she writes eventually. I waited too long.

He doesn't reply.

58

TIME

But in the morning, there are a few short lines from Frank. They are not what she expected or hoped for.

M, I felt nervous to write this yesterday. It was enough that you were dealing with the book and the letter to you. But you should probably know that your father's meeting with Charing was only days before your parents died, and the conference they then booked was for four months *after* that. That seemed important to me. F x

Before? After? She rereads the lines to make sure she's not *mis*reading.

Her emotions are so muddled up. She is reading about her father; she is looking at Frank's kiss. It's impossible to compartmentalize her feelings about the different things. She knows that she doesn't want to navigate a single other step of life without him.

But she doesn't have a choice.

Please can we talk, Frank? Please, she replies in italics. She sends her kiss on a separate line, so he knows that she means it. X.

Mimi stands at the sliding door and stares out. The black

walnut has dropped its yellowed leaves like an unzipped skirt round its trunk. The garden is shutting down for winter. Art loves that tree.

She rereads Frank's email. She understands what Frank is telling her. Her father had plans for *after* they'd died. It doesn't make sense.

But this time, something else catches her eye.

. . . the letter to you . . . It's an odd way for Frank to be describing his email to her, which is how she first read it . . . *the book and the letter to you*, he says. As though the two are attached. *Chaos* is sitting on the coffee table where she'd left it last night after reading her mother's annotations. She picks it up and turns it over in her hands. She's been through all the annotations and there was nothing that seemed meant specifically for her in there. Knowing Art has a letter, the vacuum where *her* letter should be is still like a tunnel through her middle. What did Frank mean?

She picks up the book by its covers and holds it up like a bird, its pages hanging down. As she does, the gap between the dust jacket and the hardcover book about grief yawns open, and there, right there, wedged in between the two, is a letter: *the letter to you*. A lifetime of hope fastens onto it.

It is less than she hoped for, but also infinitely more. Writing with the same pen that she'd used for Art's letter, her mother has started a letter to her. Not even half a letter, really. But it's for her.

My darling Naomi

   Only one day, when you have your own children, will you begin to understand how much I love you.

   From the moment you arrived, your delight

in the world was infectious. You brought us
all untold joy.

   You have always looked after Art, and I
know you always will. And I know it is not
always easy. Now, as ~~different as you and~~
~~your brother are, I need you both to look~~
~~after each other and your~~ .

   ~~Now, the responsibility will be even~~
~~greater.~~

   ~~Now, your father will~~

Her hand is shaking. She sits on the sofa. She's not sure she'll ever be able to get up. 'That's *all*?' she says out loud, to the ghost of her mother who might be standing in her apron at the sink, with her face tipped towards the window to catch the sun. 'Mummy,' she says, and holds the letter to her chest. She can barely breathe.

Her mother trusted her. She loved her. And . . . and! – '*your father will*'. All Mimi can see is *your father will*. You always *will*. The responsibility *will*. Your father *will*. Her father had a future. Just as Frank had so gently implied, he didn't mean to leave her.

She is reading that her father didn't mean to die.

They might never know why Christine didn't finish this letter, what interrupted her, or whether she found it too hard to write that particular day. They might never find the finished one, assuming it exists.

It is hard to believe that a few unfinished lines could make you feel so happy, and so immeasurably sad.

Light shines on Art's face, the world is pink through his lids. Mimi is there but he cannot be bothered to surface. He

337

wishes they would let him float off. He feels her breath skate the top of his lip.

'Art, wake up. *Please*.' She digs her nails into his wrist; the slice of pain feels far away.

She makes a mewling sound when she sees he is awake. 'Well done,' she says, and she comes into focus a little bit more. Her eyes are watery with tears. She holds his hand. 'Stay with me a moment.' She tightens her grip, and it hurts. It might anchor him here for a while. '*Concentrate*. Give me everything you've got. One more time.' The scissoring in his head as he tries to focus on what she is saying is right behind his eyes. 'Art, look at me. I hope you're listening.'

'I am,' he tries to whisper, but the words emerge as a rattle of breath.

'I have some news. It changes everything,' she says. 'I need to show you. Despite his depression, Dad had made plans, Art. For his chaos research. For himself. For *after* they died. He intended to stay. I've got proof.'

'Proof,' Art hears. She holds him by his shoulders. 'Do you see what this means? He didn't mean to leave us. He didn't mean to die.' The cords of her voice are scratchy. He would like to console her. What she says is a fantasy, her dream.

He has had the dream too.

Every time he surfaces that day, a day that feels infinite, there she is, telling him the same thing. Perhaps he has passed over to the other side, to a version of purgatory where your deepest desires are laid bare.

'Come back, Art, *please*. I need you to know. Dad didn't mean to go.'

Art's childhood backpack is still in his bedside cabinet at the hospital, filled with the things that he'd hidden at the pool. Before Mimi leaves that evening, she hooks it onto her shoulder. Then she strokes Art's bristled scalp – his beautiful skull – goodbye for the day.

She hopes she's got through. She's run out of ammunition if she hasn't. She walks down the passage, away from the ward.

She shuffles her feet in the hospital's revolving exit, making sure the backpack doesn't hook on the door. She could just stay in there, go round and round forever. She's heard stories of people's heads getting squashed in revolving doors. Would that be a TBI? An SBI? It could kill a child, she thinks.

She emerges in a funk, trying to remember if she drove here this morning. *I'll hold you up. This is where we're going,* Frank had said, holding her wrist to the stars.

59

TO THE POWER OF

The streetlamps glow orange in Muriel Grove. The orange light is cheaper, but less safe for drivers, Frank had told her. She walks on. Then, as if fashioning a phantom from the constant refrain in her brain, she sees – sitting on the low wall of her house, with his legs out straight in front of him – Frank. Next to the creaking gate of number 19, is Frank. Waiting for her and watching her. He gets up from the wall and brushes off his jeans.

He looks tired. He has dry skin under his eyes, and a day-old stubble. She can only half-smile.

'Hello you,' he says, gently.

When she says hi it sounds like a whisper because her voice won't work. 'Shall I take your bag?' he says, staying where he is. It seems they're not going inside. 'What's this?' he asks, shouldering Art's child-sized backpack.

I hope it's my future holding my past.

She just shakes her head, not trusting herself to say anything other than the one thing she really needs to say. The most important thing.

'I'm here to find out what you meant,' says Frank as though reading her mind. 'When you said that you waited too long. What *did* you mean?'

The wind has stilled, and the road is empty but for them. There's the sound of a car right down the other end – tyres rolling away as though it's trying to be quiet.

'To tell you, Frank Taylor,' she says, but it's not going to work because already her eyes are filling, and her nose is tingling, and she can feel there is no way that she's not going to cry – 'that I love how easily you laugh. I love that you don't ever get your belt through all the loops. I love it when you explain maths to me with cutlery and on the swings. I love it that your eyes change colour with the sky. I waited too long – far, far too long – to tell you that I love you. How *much* I love you. But more important than that – because you know that anyway, even if I haven't said it out loud. I waited too long to tell you that I love you enough to find a new way to live with my brother. It won't be easy. You're right, he'll always need me. And honestly, I need him too. But that can't stand in the way any more. Of us.' She's crying so much it feels that her lungs might tear, but strangely, her heart is lifting. 'There is an *us*, right? There has to be an us.'

It seems impossible that he might forgive her for trusting him so little. When he deserved to be trusted so much.

But already, he's holding her, deep in his arms.

60

PLURAL

Six weeks later

Rey and Mimi climb the stairs to Art's room. When they get to the threshold, Rey leans against the door frame. 'I'll stand here,' she says quietly. 'I'm here if you need me.'

Mimi looks at Art's cupboard and opens the door. His things are all in place, just as he liked it, his T-shirts all folded to the same width, his socks rolled. The hooks of his hangers all face the same way. She picks out his favourite shirt. It's yellow, with a collar.

'What do you think?'

'It's perfect,' says Rey. She pulls out a V-neck jumper, so you'll still see the yellow of the shirt. He'll look like a mathematician in a V-neck. No tie. Ordinary slacks (Art's word). She can't bring herself to put him in his galumphing white trainers, with orthopaedic soles. So – leather shoes.

'He's going to feel he has died when there's no *p versus Np* to work on,' she says.

He's so pleased about being discharged. But then what? She puts the shoes in the bag. Zips it up. Time to go.

Rey and Mimi find Frank making coffee in the kitchen

342

downstairs. Mimi pulls her cardigan on, but the loop for her top button is a little too small. When she looks in the mirror, Frank catches her eye. He reaches round from behind her, and his big fingers navigate the tiny grosgrain hole.

'There you go.' He kisses her hairline. 'It's going to be okay.'

'You look nice.' And he does. 'He's also in yellow.'

'What do you mean?'

It suddenly feels funny. 'Art. I chose a pale yellow shirt. His homecoming shirt.' A giggle rises in her throat. 'I thought it made him look like a mathematician.'

Frank smiles. 'Okaaay.'

'It's all right,' she says. 'I'm glad.' She laughs again. 'Maybe you should wear yellow when you go and see Kitty.' She puts her arms around him again. She's so grateful she can. Forgiveness, such powerful medicine.

'Before we go, I've got something for you,' says Rey with a smile, holding a small cardboard box tied with string.

'Oh?' says Mimi. 'Do I want more surprises?' But she pulls at the bow.

'All that time as a child with headphones clamped to your ears must've heightened your awareness,' says Rey. 'I want us to do this properly. Together.'

Mimi looks at the business cards in the box. '*Sisters in Sound*'. Sisters, this time, with an 's' on the end. *Mimi Brotherton. Sound Artist*. 'Oh Rey.' She throws herself around her friend.

'Don't cry.'

'Well, you did choose today. I'm already right on the edge.' Mimi looks at Frank. He is grinning. 'Where's Ernest?' she asks, through her tears.

'Outside, having a cigarette,' says Rey. 'Last one, he says. *Ever*. His bags are upstairs.'

343

'Leave him for a moment,' says Frank.

Ernest walks in, looking as though someone has replaced his face with a tight mask of skin.

'Are you ready to go?'

Ernest nods. 'I can't believe we're here. That this day has arrived. He's just going to be so sad without his proof—'

'He'll survive. He's lucky to have got this far.'

'I hope *he* thinks that.'

'And,' says Mimi, 'he's lucky – he's got you.' She gives Ernest a peck on the cheek, and they walk down the hall. 'Look,' she says, and shows him her new cards.

'You deserve it,' Ernest says.

'It's true,' says Frank. He turns her and holds her face. 'You are one incredible sister, Naomi Brotherton.'

Mimi catches herself in the mirror as they go. She smooths her forehead and tucks in a wayward hair on her brow. Despite how happy today should be, she still looks so drained. She can imagine what Art might say – 'That cardigan does not suit your complexion.' Do her shoes match her clothes? she asks herself, looking down.

They do not, says Art, in her head.

And she feels okay.

61

EVIDENCE

Before Art had been given the green light to go home, Mimi had brought the book wrapped in *Chaos Squared* to the hospital.

Ernest had left her alone with Art, as agreed. She put her hand on Art's knee and felt him brace. She'd become so used to touching him, rubbing his feet, coaxing his hair back through her fingers. Now he'd receded, back to a place where they didn't touch often. Her hand stayed, and he softened. She looked into her brother's grey eyes.

'So – Frank,' she said, and his knee stiffened under her palm. 'There's been so much to unravel, and it's been painful, but also rather amazing, as if the pain is this deep pool that we've both been in the middle of. We don't want to go back there, but we found out quite a lot about ourselves, and each other. About how we feel about each other.' Art squirmed, so she held his knee a little tighter. *I may be talking about Frank, but I will never not love you* – she sent the message quietly through her hand, the same thing she'd been telling him for weeks as he recovered.

'Mimi, there is only so much I can take in. Ernest says I have to protect my bandwidth.'

345

Mimi loved Ernest, god knows she did, but! Suddenly he was gospel round here.

'Ernest knows all about it,' she said.

'Okay,' said Art, 'but get to the point. I do not need to hear about you and Frank in an imaginary pool.'

Mimi laughed. 'Fair enough.' She took a breath and brought out the book.

'I think you've seen this before,' she said, putting it in Art's hands. 'You might not remember.'

Art looked at the book, took in the strawberry sticker on the front. The colour washed from his face.

It was a moment before he spoke. 'It was at Frank's,' he said, and his voice was hoarse. He closed his eyes, as though needing to block out the present to let the memory in. 'You are right. I *had* forgotten.' He stared at the book, and then at his sister. 'But now. I remember – the sombrero was in the way, and then – oh god.' Art held his head, and coloured. He put his hand to his chest.

'You okay?' He looked punctured. '*Art?*'

'Was there also a letter?'

She nods.

'My memory of that afternoon is patchy. I am sorry. So sorry. How long have you had it?'

'A while,' she said. 'You weren't ready.'

Mimi was convinced that Art had eventually come round because she'd told him their father hadn't meant to die. But once he was awake, Dr Sipos said the best way for him to recover his memories was naturally, organically. 'No shocks.' If he came to them himself, the pathways would heal. She offered Art a sip of water and prayed that she hadn't been hasty.

Art rubbed his wasting muscles as he sat in bed.

Mimi would *not* let things go.

'It has never made sense, Art, if you think about it. The suicide note, just from her. Her fingerprints on the wheel, your letter, only from her. And now mine.' She clutched the yellowing paper of her letter to her chest as though it was her most precious possession.

Art folded and refolded the corner of his blanket. 'I am *not* doing this.'

'Mimi,' warned Ernest, who had reappeared.

'Art, listen. Think of the book. The way Mum wrote in it, and my letter. *Your father will.* The thing we have carried all these years – he *didn't* abandon us. He was even reading up about grief so that he'd know how to help us. And himself. It's the most touching thing I've ever seen.'

Art had looked at the book about grief, turned it over in his hands. The dull brown cover was the colour of the stone that held you down so that you could not breathe, that lived inside you, calcified around your rib cage and stuck to the lining of your lungs. The stone you had to accommodate in your body, for the rest of your life. He did not understand why any of this made Mimi feel better. It haunted him that their father did not die a peaceful death. That when he should have been drifting off with their mother, he was instead, in agony. Art had read all the facts: the coroner's report, the cardiac arrest triggered by congenital heart disease and toxic gases combined, the 30 mmHg of capillary pressure, the interstitial leakage into his alveoli, the pulmonary oedema. He had been left with a vision of his father in pain – his jugular vein distended, his lips ringed with blue. He imagined his last, crackling breath.

The idea that their father had *not wanted* to die, that he might have been in a fighting-for-his-life panic, that he had not chosen his path, was completely unbearable.

347

The coroner said that different degrees of certainty exist. 'Certain, highly probable, uncertain.' *Certain* was their conclusion, and Art had found comfort in that.

'*No*,' said Art, with an intensity that surprised him. 'We know he died of a heart attack and not the actual carbon-monoxide poisoning, but do not let that confuse their intentions. You are forgetting one of the most important details of their deaths. Dad had an absolute *thing* about child locks, remember. Truly, he hated them. But the child locks were on. Mimi, right through our childhood, they were never, *ever* on. Mum and Dad activated them on purpose that day, to stop each other from changing their minds. It is one of the reasons they were sitting in the back, to effectively trap themselves in behind that chunky armrest between the seats. I have thought this all through. So many times. We know Mum took the sleeping pills first, so she will have been sleeping in the back and Dad was probably nervous that somehow he might lose the courage, with her lying there.'

'But Art—'

'I see something different to what you see,' he said to Mimi, trying to sound calm. 'He could not live without her. The child locks—'

'The child locks, the child locks! Why are you so obsessed with them?'

'Because it is the outlier detail,' said Art. 'Dad set the child locks himself. It is not something Mum would have thought about, and it is not as though she would ever have wanted to trap him in there. Not when she had taken the pill first. That is out of the question. We both know how he felt about child locks – how he nearly died in that car, in that river in Natal when he was young. But this *one* time, the child locks were on – even though they frightened him. Also, how would

348

he have got home, stumbling from the car, in the dark, from *Southwark*? These seem like details, but for our father, it was an extreme event. I always tell you, Mimi, look for the outlying data points.'

'I know, Art. And I always tell you, look at the whole picture.'

The next Sunday afternoon, Mimi waited for Frank. He'd gone to Southwark, on a mission to get more information for that very picture. The whole picture had been like a jigsaw puzzle. Mimi could see what it was, but there were always small pieces missing. Now, suddenly, they were filling in. A tipping point, again.

When Frank arrived back at Muriel Grove from hunting down the minicab records, bouncing with yet more news for her, before he could even explain what he'd found, Rey had knocked on the door.

Rey had a key. Rey never knocked.

Art sat in the sunlit activities room and swallowed the array of bullet-sized medication the nurse had given him. He was enjoying time out of bed, perusing traybake recipes in *The Sunday Times*. Ernest had encouraged him to find a new dish each week. He had promised they would try them all when Art came home. Choosing new food was stressful but, surprisingly, energizing too. He felt excited, he had to admit. About *traybake*.

He looked up to see Mimi at the end of the passage with Rey, both looking ashen. Mimi directed him to the Quiet Room, and he hobbled over behind his walking frame. 'Where's Ernest?' he asked, automatically, looking round. He had developed a sense for trouble, and he wanted Ernest there.

Mimi ignored him. '*Tell him*,' she said to Rey. Art had

never, not in twenty-five years, heard Mimi talk to Rey like that. She wasn't angry, but the urgency in her voice told Art to sit down.

And so, Rey confessed to Art.

Mimi sat with Art, Rey and Ernest – who had thankfully arrived – in the windowless Quiet Room, a suffocating metaphor for what their friend had to say.

Years ago, less than a week before their parents died, Rey told Art, she had borrowed Walter's maroon BMW, with his permission. The skin pulled across Art's face. The car had been parked right outside their house, said Rey. Walter had gone up to Cambridge that day. Art was at the university, Mimi was out, Christine was resting. She'd popped in to check on Christine, she said, filled up her water jug, picked up the keys, and gone for a drive with her boyfriend. When he'd had to pick up his sister from pre-school, the little girl had sat in the back. He'd insisted on putting the child locks on.

Mimi couldn't reach Art from where she sat. He had gone so still he looked as if he might fold straight over in his chair.

They'd returned to find their parking space gone, said Rey. She had fretted that Walter wouldn't want the car to be parked so far down the road. The child locks didn't enter her mind.

A few days later, Christine and Walter died.

'When the child locks were made such a fuss of, even at the autopsy hearing,' Rey told the very quiet room, 'I wasn't brave enough to say what had happened.'

When Rey had told Mimi, it gave Mimi the thing she thought she had wanted more than anything in the world. Her father had not left her.

What she had not anticipated, had hardly thought through – and now that it had happened, she could not believe how short-sighted she'd been – was that, spilling into the place that abandonment vacated, flooded horror. Her wish had come true, yes. And *yet*— She had never, not in her whole life, a life not devoid of sadness, mind you, felt pain quite like it.

The image of her dad clutching at the window, trying to get out, heart galloping, mind racing about the children he was leaving behind while his senses fogged over, in excruciating pain – she hadn't seen it coming. She felt sick with guilt, that in failing to imagine it until now, she had somehow made it worse. She'd thought only of herself. Now, after all these years, her old ache might be eased, but a new one – exquisitely, profoundly worse for being *his* pain and not hers – took its place. She knew it would harbour in every cell in her body for the rest of her life.

'It has eaten away at me, all these years, what I did,' said Rey, tears streaming down her face, her bottom lip trembling. She did not even bother to wipe her cheeks. 'I've tried so hard to make it up to you,' she said, 'I never could. There's a chance that – it *feels* like – I murdered your father.'

Art listened without saying a word, obviously in shock. Mimi worried it was too much. She should have asked the doctor. 'What made you tell us now?' he asked.

'When Mimi told me she thought Walter didn't mean to die, first the book and all that, and then that Frank was looking into the taxi driver, and that possibly the only thing in the way of it being true was the child locks, I just couldn't hide it any more. I'm so sorry,' she sobbed. 'I'm so sorry.'

'What thing about the taxi driver?' asked Art.

Mimi took a breath. 'I was going to wait, but since we are here – Frank has been helping me try and piece all this together. He's about to come round, he'll tell you. I hope that's okay.'

Ernest touched Art's shoulder.

'Rey, I do not know what to say to you,' Art said. 'I understand your reluctance to tell us, although of course I wish you had. Perhaps, at the time, the idea of my father dying a traumatic death he did not want would have been too much. We may not have been able to cope. We may have wanted to blame you, *then*. Now, with the benefit of time, and hindsight, and the debt we owe you for caring so much, all these years, we can probably absorb the information, with a bit of perspective. Still, we cannot deal with it all today, just give us time.'

'I know,' said Rey. 'I understand.'

'Was that the longest, most emotionally cogent sentence you've ever said?' asked Mimi, and everyone, out of sheer relief, she supposed, released a shaky laugh.

'The thing is—' said Art.

Art had long ago reread the coroner's report. He had focused especially on time, to assuage his own anxiety. Walter had died quickly. So quickly, in fact, that whether or not he had wanted to die would probably have been immaterial. Most likely, he would have died anyway, despite the accident of the child locks. 'There was hardly time to get out of the car, he was dying *that* fast,' Art said. 'Not *zero* time, but close.' Art had not been convinced by the truth of what Mimi believed, he told them, but just in case she was right – an unusual event in itself, he said with a wry smile – this was a reassuring fact.

Art realized he was speaking to his feet. To get through the difficulty of the words, he had needed to look down.

He looked up now, at his sister's face, and feeling 're-assured' seemed to fade as an appropriate response – both

352

too distant and too benign. She took his head in both her hands and pulled him towards her. She held her forehead to his forehead, just touching. She was crying. She kissed him. Once, on the top of each cheekbone. He tried not to feel startled. 'I know you hate this, my darling brother,' she said. And then she hugged him, hard. He could hardly breathe. He could smell her shampoo.

Frank arrived and appeared a little flustered to find everyone clogged in this little room, and all with expectant looks on their faces – pointed towards *him*. Frank kissed Mimi hello and as Art watched him put a hand on Mimi's shoulder, he realized that it did not lacerate his insides as it once had.

Frank had made a discovery: 'Remember the jogger couple?' said Mimi. 'Who found Mum and Dad and went home in a taxi that had been waiting nearby, booked for someone who hadn't turned up?' Frank had found the police records.

Frank dug in his pocket for his phone and showed them a police photograph of the minicab firm's records of that day. The handwritten name that the taxi was booked for was *Robert Hawton*.

'It was your father, Art,' said Frank. 'Robert Hawton is an anagram of W. A. Brotherton. Walter Arthur. It's your dad.'

Art looked at his sister – her eyes glittered with emotion. It seemed more important to her than to him that their father did not want to die. For him, their *intention* was a fact that did not change much the living with their absence, which was as complete either way. He felt the vacuum of their lives, back through all these years, all the things their father missed, all the things he never knew. And in that moment, Art knew that he would try, he would definitely try, to discover more about what it was his father had been excited about. He owed him that. And more.

Their father had booked the minicab himself, to leave Christine, to leave the gardens – he *really* had not meant to die. He died of natural causes, his congenitally compromised heart, triggered catastrophically by the carbon monoxide.

The conversation swirled about him.

It may not change the fact of their loss, but what it did mean – Mimi was focused on this – was that their parents did not abandon them, to be left alone, responsible for each other.

They would have to come to terms with Rey having kept her secret. It explained her maternal concern for them all this time. But in the meantime, most importantly, it liberated them from the responsibility they believed their parents placed on each of them, for the other. He saw that now.

The truth freed Rey too. She was glad Art had Ernest, she told them. Especially as Mimi had Frank. She could stop worrying about them now.

'I've always understood how you both felt,' said Rey. 'I feel lonely too.'

62

HEURISTICS

And now the day has finally come, Art is going home. He waits in the visitor's chair next to his bed. It has strong woven cloth in a mercurial shade. He spent hours trying to decide as he lay there, these weeks – was it purple or blue? Mimi often says: colour is not the same for everyone, that her purple was everyone else's red. He looks through the semicircle windows on the door, to the strong natural light. He will soon be outside.

His possessions are packed in a hospital bag. His comb and his notebook, his favourite pen. His toothbrush and pants, his pillow from home. He remembers the moment he asked for those things. When he realized – he was *living* in this room, not dying in it.

'Your family's here,' says the nurse.

'What, all of them?' says Art. He pulls at the gown, so it goes past his knees.

'I think so,' she says, smiling. 'Your sister has your clothes. Now remember, still no screens, no mathematics, or tiny writing, for a while.'

Art just nods, so that he does not have to prevaricate.

She straightens the back of his gown, tightens his bow. Her job is done. 'We'll miss you, you know.'

'I doubt that,' says Art. The nurse puts a card on top of his things. He opens it up when she exits the room.

Mathematicians never die, they just lose their functions. Get well soon! Six nurses have signed it – their kind messages all say the same thing. Keep up the hard work. You will get there in the end.

Mimi, Rey and Ernest traipse in. All dressed up.

'Today is the day!' Ernest says with a smile. But his smile is tight. It does not reach his eyes.

'Hey,' says Rey. She lightly ruffles his hair.

He smooths it back down. 'I've just combed it.'

'Yes,' says Rey. 'You know, I think it's grown back thicker.'

'I've got all your clothes,' Mimi says.

'Is Frank here?' he asks. He looks past her, to the door.

'He is parking the car. He'll be up in a minute.'

Art sits with the bag on his lap and takes out his clothes. 'This is all rather smart. I am coming home, not going to the Royal Albert Hall.'

'There's a homecoming theme. Yellow,' says Rey.

Mimi is looking at the clock. Sucking her lip. He sees it is raw.

'What is wrong with you lot? No one has died.'

'Nothing's wrong,' say Mimi and Ernest together. Too quickly.

'Let's get dressed, Art,' says Mimi.

'I'll do it,' says Ernest. 'Might as well.' He shrugs and looks round to Mimi and Rey. 'I've got you,' he says to Art, as he lifts him, frail and skinny, from the bed to the chair.

Rey is swift with the curtain. She leaves them there.

Shift, thinks Art. A transformation in which a graph or a figure – that would be him – is picked up and moved to another location without any change in size or orientation. But the shift is far greater than that. The arms that have moved him are new arms.

They feel fine.

Ten minutes later, Art looks around his ward for the last time. The door is still closed. Through its window, he sees light ahead. The trees are still bare, but it is only just nine and the sunlight is shafting through branches like fingers, right near the top. Perhaps, with the coming light, and Ernest shepherding him through, his brain will continue to sharpen. He feels the wheel of his chair with his palm. The rubber is hard. The rough skin on his hand from his practice presages callouses. It hurts.

'We'll get gloves,' Ernest says.

Ernest wheels Art out. Mimi sees her subconscious was right with the yellow. It diverts your eyes from the fact of the chair. It feels like a smile supporting his chin.

At least Ernest looks better. There's relief on his face. She sees Art's hand bent up behind him, holding Ernest's wrist.

'You have bitten your lip,' says Art. 'What is bothering you now? I am fine with the chair.'

'I know that. It isn't forever.'

'No, thank goodness. You will not have long to push me around.'

Mimi laughs, and Frank arrives. It's a genuine laugh, from her belly – truth belching out. 'You don't know how funny that is.'

Rey takes the moment. It feels as if she scoops up the sound of the laugh, packs it up bravely and gives it to Art. She's squatting in front of his chair.

'Listen, Sweetie,' she says.

'Rey,' says Mimi. 'I think let's get home.'

'No, that's not fair. Let's leave the negative stuff here.' She is looking at Art.

'Spit it out,' says Art, his voice sounding taut.

357

'Rey!' says Ernest.

'Your maths,' begins Rey. 'The p, Np thing. Someone has got there before you.'

'Oh *that*,' says Art. 'I know about that.'

'What?' Mimi says.

'*How do you know?*' The three of them blow back.

'Heuristics,' says Art. He does not want to get Ginny, who had let it slip by mistake when visiting him, into trouble. By way of apology for spilling the beans, Ginny had smuggled in Kampinskey's proof, out of sight of the nurses. Art smiles at his sister.

'I'm so sorry,' says Frank. 'After all your hard work.'

But Art disagrees. 'It's not quite as simple as that,' he says.

Four people stare at him with a mixture of pity and despair – if he is reading their expressions correctly.

'Kampinskey's proof has a fundamental flaw in its assumptions,' he says, still feeling the headache from yet another close read earlier that day, sitting in a corner away from his nurses. 'You will see,' he says, 'like many times before, it will be proved to be a false proof. We have work to do. Me and Ernest.'

'How do you *know*?' they all ask, again.

'I just do,' he says, and he reaches for Ernest's hand. 'Sometimes, you do not need the facts. You just know. Anyway,' he says, 'do you want to find out?'

Acknowledgements

I agree with Art and the Planning Fallacy: everything takes longer than you think. And more people. My thanks to everyone who gave time, patience, love, help and support – without which this would be a file on an overloaded hard drive.

My first attempt at a novel was like a jumper knitted with no pattern; it had several arms. Emma Haynes read it and, astonishingly, she remains a cherished friend. My fellow Faber writers – Shelley Weiner, Nina de Pass (em dashes), Neil Taylor (spliced commas) and Gillian Stern – all advised when things got bumpy, which they did. Sara Sarre, my mentor, is this book's faithful midwife. *Gracias*.

Ace-agent Charlotte Seymour – calm, clever, responsive – mastered the art of answering my email ramblings with concise one-liners early on. With characteristic assurance, she gifted me with a brilliant triumvirate of editors: Sam Humphreys, Jennifer Lambert and Emily Griffin. All judicious, insightful and caring. I loved every minute of our transatlantic collaboration. The hard work and enthusiasm of Alice Gray and everyone at Pan Macmillan's Mantle were convincing from day one; even so, you exceeded my expectations. Likewise, everyone at HarperCollins Canada and USA, and Hélène Butler at J & A. *Thank you all*.

To real mathematicians who make maths accessible, gratitude and respect. Cambridge's Dr Frank Kelly kindly checked the maths, thereby redeeming my ability to sleep. Dr Dilly Murphy took beyond-the-call-of-duty care with the medical details. Pär Carlsson: thanks, foley guru. All mistakes, I claim. Jen White, your counsel was as essential as a tea cosy. Connie Fajardo and Catherine Bolton – thank you for your endless care. Kindness is sustaining, and there are many other acts of kindness not recorded here. I'm grateful for every single one.

Thank you to all my girlfriends – who kept asking how it was going without diminished enthusiasm. Especially Eve Pein, who ran alongside me, literally, for miles, Karen Newman, Betty O'Brien and Kate Edwards, who gave me non-stop advice on titles, covers and life. Mostly life. And told me I had to put them in here.

To the baobab of grandparents and cousins out there – love. And my beloved sisters, Jo and Debs, you both made this book better. '*You're fabulous*,' said the young man in the green suit. Dad loved this book, before he'd even read it. His belief in me is unwavering, his love unconditional, his principles – like his grammar – uncompromising. Mum, Gogo, nurtured us with her energy, intellect and infinite love. Thank you from us all for our crocheted blankets – the one autobiographical note in the book.

Jamie, Tom and Freya – life is always better when you three are around. You kept me semi-sane with your dead-pan comments. Ranging from '*write another book*' to '*you know you always say that, right?*' You advised on words, names, maths, getting published, titles, design. And took jacket photographs. You made me feel this was possible, even when evidence suggested otherwise. I am immeasurably proud to be your mother.

And Richard. My superhero. With many superpowers. It's a tough call, but I think the one I love the most is how much you make me laugh. Thank you. *For (absolutely) everything.*